RETURN TO THE
Big Valley

Center Point
Large Print

Also by Wanda E. Brunstetter, Jean Brunstetter, and Richelle Brunstetter and available from Center Point Large Print:

The Brides of the Big Valley

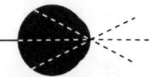

**This Large Print Book carries the
Seal of Approval of N.A.V.H.**

Date: 9/8/21

LP FIC BRUNSTETTER
Brunstetter, Wanda E.,
Return to the Big Valley : 3
romances from a unique ...

3 Romances from a Unique
Pennsylvania Amish Community

RETURN TO THE
Big Valley

Wanda E. Brunstetter
Jean Brunstetter
& Richelle Brunstetter

CENTER POINT LARGE PRINT
THORNDIKE, MAINE

This Center Point Large Print edition
is published in the year 2021 by arrangement with
Barbour Publishing, Inc.

All scripture quotations are taken from the
King James Version of the Bible.

This book is a work of fiction. Names, characters,
places, and incidents are either products of the author's
imagination or used fictitiously. Any similarity to actual
people, organizations, and/or events is purely coincidental.

The text of this Large Print edition is unabridged.
In other aspects, this book may vary
from the original edition.
Printed in the United States of America
on permanent paper.
Set in 16-point Times New Roman type.

ISBN: 978-1-64358-970-1

The Library of Congress has cataloged this record
under Library of Congress Control Number: 2021935084

RETURN TO THE
Big Valley

Wilma's Wish

by Wanda E. Brunstetter

Chapter 1

Reedsville, Pennsylvania

"Whew! I can't believe how warm it is already this morning." Wilma Hostetler fanned her face with one of the quilted pot holders she'd brought to her friend Deanna Yoder's quilt shop, along with several other items she had recently made. For the past year, Wilma had been bringing quilted items here on consignment. Trying to keep up with demand kept her busy at home.

"You're right about the heat," Deanna agreed. "And here it is only the last week of May. Just wait till summer hits and we have days with high humidity to go along with the sweltering heat."

Wilma placed several table runners on a shelf. "I am thankful for all the trees in my parents' yard that shade our home. Without those, as well as the cross-draft we get through our open windows, it would feel much worse."

Deanna nodded. "The hot weather makes us appreciate the cooler months, *jah*?"

"For certain." Wilma smiled. It was good to see her friend's positive outlook. Deanna had been through a lot over the last few years—first, losing her husband, Simon, and then when things seemed to be going well with her relationship

9

with Elmer Yoder, he lost his eyesight and broke their engagement. Disappointed, Deanna had continued to care for her then five-year-old son, Abner, who had been born with Down syndrome. It had taken a lot of persuasion and a good deal of prayer before Elmer came to realize that his life wasn't over and he could support a wife and family. Now, two years later, Deanna had her own quilt shop, which had been built on the same property as their home. Elmer continued to work at Raymond Renno's furniture shop, in addition to making birdhouses on his own, which Deanna sold on the days she set up a table at the flea market in Belleville to sell her quilted items. Despite the hurdles they'd overcome, Wilma's dear friend and her husband had cheerful attitudes and a strong faith in God.

My life has been uncomplicated in comparison to Deanna's, Wilma thought as she took a quilted wall hanging from the oversized plastic tote she'd used to bring her items to the shop that morning.

"Have you picked out the material for your wedding dress yet?" Deanna asked, bringing Wilma's thoughts to a halt.

"Jah, but I haven't started making it," Wilma replied. "The wedding isn't for another six months, so I still have plenty of time to get the dress done."

Deanna moved closer and put her hand on Wilma's shoulder. "You and Israel are both even-tempered and kind, which is why you make a good couple and get along well. I'm sure you'll have a happy marriage."

"I hope so, because I love him very much." Wilma sighed. "I can hardly wait to become Mrs. Israel Zook and raise a family together some day."

"How many *kinner* would you like?" Deanna asked as she put the OPEN sign in her shop window.

"I'd like at least four, but I'll be satisfied with how ever many children the good Lord chooses to give us." Wilma removed another wall hanging from the tote. "I look forward to motherhood sometime in the future, but right now my focus is on getting married and being the best wife I can be to my husband."

Deanna's seven-year-old son, Abner, who had been playing quietly on the floor across the room, came running over to his mother. *"Geb mer en boss!"*

"Of course I will give you a kiss," Deanna replied, "but you must learn to say please when asking for something."

Abner's sandy blond hair swayed as he nodded and then he repeated the question, this time, adding the word *please*.

Deanna bent down to kiss the boy's cheek. He squealed with obvious delight as he hugged her neck.

Although Abner could be a handful at times, Deanna had a special way with him, and could get her son to do most anything she asked. He'd started school last year and seemed to be doing well with the help of the teacher who worked with special-needs children. Now that school was out until the latter part of August, Abner would be with his mother in the quilt shop on the days it was open for business. Although the boy's stepfather could not do some things, Elmer spent time with Abner. The two of them got along well and had developed a strong father-son bond.

When Abner returned to the toys he'd left behind on the floor, Deanna whispered to Wilma, "I think he'll enjoy being a big brother."

Wilma blinked. "Are you in a family way?"

"Jah. The *boppli* is due toward the later part of November."

"That means you must be about three months along?" Wilma's gaze went to her friend's belly.

Deanna bobbed her head.

"I never would have guessed, because you're not showing yet."

"I will be soon, I expect. We didn't know each other when I was pregnant with Abner, but my belly didn't protrude much until I was nearly five months along."

Wilma placed both hands against her own flat stomach. She didn't relish the thought of looking top-heavy, the way her married sister, Judith, had appeared during her first pregnancy. But Wilma looked forward to the day when she and Israel would become parents.

Israel grabbed his lunch pail and headed outside to wait for his ride. He worked for a construction company owned by an Amish man in Belleville. Today they would start building a vacation home for an English couple who'd recently purchased some property up on Back Mountain Road.

Israel enjoyed carpentry and took pride in his work. It paid well, and he should have no problem supporting a wife, as well as a family when the time came that he and Wilma were blessed with children. Israel had been courting Wilma for a year before he asked her to marry him. He loved her so much, and for him, the wedding couldn't come soon enough. He never tired of spending time with her. Just a simple smile or seeing the sparkle in her pretty brown eyes nearly took Israel's breath away. Wilma was a kind, soft-spoken woman, who could make a room light up with just the sound of her laughter. She was everything he'd ever wanted in a wife.

Looking at his pocket watch and realizing he had ten minutes to spare before his driver arrived, Israel headed for the phone shack to see if there were any messages.

When he stepped inside the small wooden building and saw the answering machine blinking, he sat on a stool and pressed the MESSAGE button.

"Israel Zook, this is Simon Smucker, up in Dauphin County. My wife and your sister, Kathryn, were good friends, and . . ." There was a lengthy pause.

Israel reached under his straw hat and scratched his head. *What did Simon mean by saying his wife and Kathryn "were" good friends? Aren't they still good friends? Has some sort of misunderstanding come between them? Perhaps Simon wants me to speak with Kathryn about her relationship to his wife and encourage her to make amends.*

Simon cleared his throat, and his voice lowered as he spoke again. "I regret to inform you that your sister died last evening. Kathryn's oldest son, Mark, found his poor mother inside her horse's stall. It appeared that she'd been kicked in the face by the gelding." Another long pause ensued.

Israel gripped the edge of the wooden stool and leaned forward as Simon's previous words sunk in. *Kathryn was dead. Found in the stall. Kicked by her horse.* He massaged his pulsating forehead. *No, it can't be. There must be some mistake.*

Israel thought about the farrier, Elmer Yoder, and how a few years ago, he'd lost his eyesight after being kicked by a horse when the animal

14

was in the process of being shod. Although Elmer had gone through a stressful time learning to adjust to his blindness, at least he hadn't been killed and was now happily married to Wilma's friend Deanna. Life had been unfair to Elmer and now to Kathryn's boys, who were left without a mother or father.

When Simon spoke again, Israel lifted his head.

"The boys are here with me and my wife right now, but we need you to come as soon as possible. There are many details to be taken care of—Kathryn's funeral, getting her home ready to be sold, going through her personal and household things, and finding a guardian for her sons. Please call me back as soon as possible."

Israel blinked rapidly as he tried to process everything Simon had said. His sister had been a widow, supporting five boys on her own since the unexpected death of her husband a year ago. Kathryn's in-laws were in poor health, so they could not be expected to take the children. Israel's parents and his younger sister, Sybil, were deceased—killed five years ago when the vehicle they had been riding in was hit from behind. They'd been heading to Florida for a vacation and had said they were looking forward to spending some time on some of the beaches near the small community of Pinecraft. What a tragedy that had been for Israel and everyone else who knew or was a part of his family.

Israel had no other siblings, and Kathryn's sister-in-law, Anna, had taken on the responsibility of caring for her ailing parents, so it wouldn't be fair to ask her to take charge of Kathryn's boys as well. Simply put, no one, except Israel, could take the children. It would be a challenge to raise five boys who didn't know him that well, but he would not shy from the responsibility. For his sister's sake, as well as her sons', Israel would do his best by the boys.

As he reached for the phone to return Simon's call, tears spilled from Israel's eyes and dripped onto his shirt. He made an attempt to swallow around the thickening in his throat, but all it did was make the ache seem worse. *Thank the Lord for my dear, sweet Wilma. Once she hears this tragic news, I'm sure she will agree to marry me as soon as possible so we can raise my nephews together.*

When Wilma arrived home shortly before noon, she found her mother in the garden, pulling weeds. "I see you've been busy this morning." Wilma stood just outside of the garden patch. "Would you like some help?"

Mom looked up, shielding her eyes from the glare of the sun. "I won't turn down your offer, but first you'll want to hear the message Israel left on our answering machine." She gestured toward the phone shack, several feet from their unpainted barn.

"If you've listened to his message, can't you just tell me what it said?"

A deep wrinkle formed across the bridge of Mom's nose as her brows furrowed. "It's best that you listen to it yourself. If I try to repeat every word, I might leave something out."

Her mother's serious tone caused Wilma to feel concern. "Is something wrong? Is Israel okay? Should I be concerned?"

Using her hand shovel, Mom knocked some dirt off the weed she'd just pulled and looked in the direction of the phone shack again. "Israel is not hurt, but a tragedy has occurred, and you'd better go listen to his message."

Wilma knew better than to ask more questions. Her mother had never been good about relaying messages and rarely wrote them down. The best thing she could do was run out to the small wooden building and listen to what Israel had to say.

When Wilma entered the phone shack, she sat down and leaned close to the answering machine so that she would hear every word of her beloved's message.

"I am saddened to say that I received word of my sister's accidental death this morning."

Wilma's hand went instinctively to her mouth. "Oh no." She continued to listen as Israel explained the details of how it had happened and said he had hired a driver and would soon be heading for Dauphin County. His final words were that he didn't know how long he would be gone and asked Wilma to be praying for him and his nephews.

Wilma sat as though frozen to her chair. "Those poor children," she murmured. "It's terrible that they no longer have a mother or father. Surely Kathryn's sister-in-law or someone else from her husband's side of the family will take them in."

Chapter 2

Lykens, Pennsylvania

Israel sat on the front porch of his sister's home, waiting for the boys to come out of the house and trying to sort through his disconcerting thoughts. He didn't know how he had survived the ordeal of his sister's funeral or the several days after that, but for the sake of the boys, he'd managed to pull himself together and somehow muddled through.

Israel had been here for three weeks and would be taking the children home with him as soon as his driver arrived to pick them up.

The boys, especially Mark, age twelve, and Ethan, who was ten, had made it clear that they didn't want to go and continued to say they could live in their parents' home and take care of their younger brothers, Josh, Nate, and Micah. They obviously had no concept of how impossible that would be, and Israel had grown tired of trying to reason with them. Last night he'd gathered his sister's sons together and told the older ones to pack their suitcases, while he assisted the younger boys with theirs.

Mark and Ethan had balked, but Israel, in the kindest way he knew, reminded the boys that they were still school age and not old enough to get jobs that would support themselves plus three growing brothers. Once he'd made the announcement that they were now his responsibility and would be going home with him, a battle of the wills began. Apparently Mark thought that if he clammed up and didn't speak to Israel, he would get his way and wouldn't have to move to Reedsville. But Israel remained firm in his decision, since he had no other choice.

Israel had hired a Realtor to sell Kathryn's home and someone else to auction off her furniture, kitchen utensils, and everything in the barn, including Kathryn's horse and buggy. Her clothes would be given to a local thrift store.

His thoughts went to Wilma, and the message he'd left her when he arrived in Lykens. He had given Wilma his sister's phone number, and when she'd returned his call and said she wanted to hire a driver to bring her up to Dauphin County for the funeral, Israel called back, saying it would best if she remained there. He felt bad about shutting her out, but he wasn't ready to tell her about his decision to bring the boys home. Israel needed time to think of the best way to explain his decisions, and he hoped Wilma would be receptive to the idea of helping him raise his sister's children.

Although Israel knew his nephews grieved for their mother, it hadn't taken him long to realize that all five of them had behavioral problems. He believed that Wilma, having been a schoolteacher, would be the best person to help him raise them. If she wasn't willing to take on the task, he had no idea what he would do.

Israel looked up when his driver's seven-passenger van pulled into the yard. He gave a wave and went to get the boys.

Reedsville, Pennsylvania

"You've been awfully quiet all morning, and you didn't eat much for breakfast." Wilma's mother took a seat on the wooden bench inside the room where they did their sewing and quilting. "You're not feeling *grank*, I hope."

Wilma looked up from the quilt she was working on and shook her head. "I'm not sick— just missing Israel and wondering when he will come home."

"When was the last time you heard from him?"

"Not since he told me I shouldn't come to his sister's funeral."

Mom's glasses fell to the end of her nose as she tipped her head. "That seems awfully strange to me. You're going to be his *fraa* soon, so I would think he would have wanted you at his side during the funeral, and even now, as he's dealing with closing up his sister's home and finding a place for her boys to live."

Wilma swallowed hard, determined not to give in to the tears pushing against the back of her eyes. She had wanted to be there for Israel, and the fact that he'd asked her not to come hurt deeply. It didn't help that he hadn't called and left any other messages for her. What was going on? Was Israel shutting her out of his life for some reason, or had he just been too busy to call? She hoped it was the latter, because Israel was her whole world, and it would be ever so hard if something came between them and they ended up going their separate ways.

"Daughter, did you hear what I said?"

Wilma looked at her mother and nodded.

"What do you have to say about it? Don't you think it was wrong that he asked you not to come?"

"I can't say since I don't know his reason."

Mom tapped her foot against the wooden floor. Wilma continued working on her quilt with the Lone Star pattern. She needed to get it done, and she hoped the large bed covering would sell quickly. The money she'd earn would be used to set up housekeeping when she married Israel and moved into his house, which only had the bare minimum, especially in the kitchen.

A short time later, when Wilma heard the *clip-clop* of a horse's hooves, she got up and looked out the front window. Her heart raced with excitement as she watched Israel's horse and white-top buggy come up the dirt driveway and stop at the hitching rail.

She moved toward the door. *He's home. My beloved has returned to me.*

After Israel secured his horse, he saw Wilma come out of the house. He waved at her as she waited for him on the porch. Beads of sweat formed on his forehead. He felt more nervous than he had when he'd asked Wilma if he could court her. Unsure of how she would react to seeing the boys, Israel had left them at his house with his nearest neighbor, Margaret, who happened to be their bishop's wife. Soon after he'd arrived home with the boys, Margaret had come over with a carton of fresh eggs and two dozen chocolate chip cookies. It was during his brief visit with her that Israel asked if she would mind staying at the house with his nephews while he went over to see Wilma. He'd promised not to be gone long and thanked Margaret for her kindness.

Now that he was at the Hostetlers' house, he'd forgotten every single word he'd planned to say to Wilma. Israel longed to take her into his arms and say that nothing between them had changed. But that wouldn't be the truth, because for him, everything had changed. Israel was no longer a bachelor anticipating marriage. He'd become the guardian of five rambunctious boys.

With slow even steps, Israel made his way up

to the porch, his gaze coming to rest on Wilma's pretty face.

"Hello, Israel. I'm glad you're back. How have you been?" She offered him the sweetest of smiles.

Consciously forcing his limbs to relax, he reached out and clasped her hand. "It's good to be home, but I'm not doing so well. The past few weeks have been pretty rough."

She squeezed his fingers gently, causing his pulse to race. "I can only imagine how difficult it must have been to lose your sister and settle her affairs. Were you able to find someone to care for her children?"

Israel let go of her hand and took a step back, avoiding her gaze. "Umm . . . about the boys . . ." He reached up to rub the back of his hot, sweaty neck. "I . . . uh . . . brought them home with me."

"For a visit?" She rubbed her chin.

"No, to live with me."

Wilma's eyes widened. "For good?"

"Jah, I'll be their guardian. There is no one but me to care for my nephews. They have no other place to go." He took a tentative step toward her. "If you're not too busy I'd like you to come with me right now so you can meet them."

Wilma stiffened but nodded. "While you wait for me in the buggy, I'll go in the house and tell my *mamm* where I'm going." She turned and opened the door.

24

Israel watched as she stepped inside, and then he hurried back to his buggy to wait for her. At least that part was over. Now all he had to worry about was Wilma's reaction when she met the boys.

Chapter 3

Wilma sat stiffly on the buggy seat next to Israel as he told her a few things about his sister's boys and how he felt it was his duty to raise them.

"It wouldn't be right to give them up to strangers," he said, glancing over at Wilma.

"No, of course not." It was selfish, but Wilma didn't want to take care of five boys who were not her own. It wasn't fair that she and Israel couldn't start out their marriage like most other young Amish couples.

Of course I don't have to marry him. I could tell Israel that I've changed my mind and don't feel ready for marriage yet. She shifted on the unyielding seat as guilt set in. *You're not being fair to Israel or his nephews. They might be very nice boys, and I'm sure they would feel more comfortable living with their uncle and me than strangers.*

Another thought popped into Wilma's mind. *What's Israel going to do with the boys until we get married? School's out until late August, and someone will need to be with them while Israel's at work.* Wilma drew a deep breath and released it slowly. *Since I'll soon be Israel's wife, I should be the person who watches the children so we*

26

have a chance to get to know each other. But if I'm watching the boys full-time, how will I get any quilting done?

"Well, we're here."

Wilma's thoughts halted as Israel guided his horse and carriage up the lane to the hitching rail near his barn. She had no more than climbed out of the buggy when two young boys—one blond, the other brunette—darted out of the barn. Each held a small black-and-white kitten in his hands. When they approached Israel after he'd secured his horse to the rail, the older of the two boys shouted, *"Die bissel bussli, Onkel Israel."*

Israel nodded. "Jah, the kitten is little—too little to be away from its mother right now. Please take it back to the box where you found it in the barn."

Without so much as a glance in Wilma's direction, the boys turned and hurried into the barn.

Israel looked at Wilma. "That was Nate—he's five, and his younger brother, Micah, who is three. I'm guessing the other three boys must be in the house with the bishop's fraa. Should we go in the barn first and see the kittens before we head into the house?"

Wilma nodded, but she could feel her stomach knot up. Overseeing the two younger boys would keep her busy enough. She couldn't imagine having to supervise three more children as well.

27

Of course she had been in charge of an entire classroom when she'd taught school a few years ago. But she'd had a helper and hadn't had to deal with young children when she went home every evening. Also, over half of her pupils had been girls, whom she had related to better than the boys, so helping raise Israel's nephews would be a challenge.

When she entered the dimly lit barn with Israel and heard the pathetic meows coming from the mama cat's bed, Wilma's thoughts switched gears. As they approached the wooden box where the boys were crouched, Wilma saw the reason for the mother cat's distress. Nate had two of the kittens whose eyes had not yet opened, holding them above their mama's nose.

Wilma was on verge of saying something, but Israel spoke first. "Nathaniel, did I not ask you to put the *busslin* back with their mamm?"

"My name ain't Nathaniel—I wanna be called Nate." The boy spoke in English, which surprised Wilma, since most Amish children didn't have a good grasp of the language until they went to school. And if Nate was only five, he hadn't started school yet. Of course neither had his younger brother, Micah. She assumed the reason for Nate's ability to speak English was because his older brothers, and perhaps his mother, had spoken it to him. This was often the case when children had older siblings.

"I will call you Nate when you do as I say." Israel pointed to the kittens the defiant boy still held in his hands. "Please put the busslin back in the box."

With his forehead creased and lower lip protruding, Nate did as he was told.

Wilma smiled as the meowing stopped and the mother cat began to lick her babies.

"Let's go inside now and see how your *brieder* are doing." Israel placed his hands on top of Nate's and Micah's heads. They hesitated, but with scrunched up faces, both boys finally stood.

Israel led the way, with the brothers following, and Wilma brought up the rear.

When they entered the house, Margaret greeted them with a tray of cookies. "Better help yourselves before the boys eat them all," she said with a grin.

"Maybe later," Israel replied. "I want to introduce Wilma to my older nephews. Are they here in the house?"

Margaret nodded. "They're in the kitchen, waiting for more *kichlin* to come out of the oven."

"Would you please ask them to meet us in the living room?"

"Sure thing." The older woman hurried off with Nate and Micah at her heels. No doubt they didn't want to miss out on those cookies.

Wilma followed Israel into the living room and

29

took a seat on one of the hard-backed wooden chairs. Like most Amish homes from the white-top community, the room was sparsely furnished with just some necessary chairs, a small table, and an overhead gas lamp. Wilma hoped after she and Israel were married, they could buy a rocking chair to put in this room. She would need it when they had their first baby.

Wilma poked her tongue against the inside of her cheek. *How will I ever manage to take care of five active boys and a new boppli?* The mere thought of it overwhelmed her.

I need to stop evaluating all of this and just wait and see how things work out, she told herself. *It may go easier with Israel's nephews than I expect.*

Israel shifted on his chair and glanced toward the kitchen door. "I think maybe I'm gonna have to go get those boys." He got up and ambled out of the room.

A short time later, Israel reappeared with three boys. "Wilma, I'd like you to meet my nephews: Mark—he's twelve; Ethan, who's ten; and Josh. He's seven years old."

"It's nice to meet you." Wilma paused. "I'm very sorry for your loss."

The boys stared at her a few seconds and turned their heads.

"Can we go back to the kitchen now?" Ethan asked.

"In a few minutes." Israel gestured to Wilma. "Wilma and I will be getting married in a few months, and she will become your aunt."

"Will she be livin' here too?" Josh glanced at Wilma then back at his uncle.

Israel nodded. "Jah. That's how it is when a man and a woman get married."

"Unless they both die; then there ain't no *mann* or fraa." Josh's somber expression tugged at Wilma's heart. The child obviously missed his mother and father. How difficult it must have been for the children to be taken from the only home they'd ever known and brought here to live with an uncle they didn't know very well.

And they don't know me at all, Wilma thought. *It will take some effort on my part to win them over so they'll be comfortable with me living here and helping to take care of their needs.* Wilma gnawed on her bottom lip. *I wish I could talk to someone who has been through an experience such as this. It would help me know what to expect and how to cope with situations that may arise.*

"Let's go out to the kitchen now and have some kichlin and *millich*," Israel suggested. "We can talk more there, and it'll give you boys a chance to get acquainted with Wilma."

Mark, Ethan, and Josh shuffled out of the room, and Wilma rose from her chair. More than having cookies and milk, she was eager to be

31

alone with Israel when he drove her home. There were so many questions she wanted to ask—the first being how soon did he expect her to begin watching the boys?

As they all sat at his kitchen table, Israel tried to get a conversation going, but the boys seemed more interested in how many chocolate chip cookies they could devour rather than talking. Every once in a while one of them would grab another cookie from the plate and say something like, "Yum. *Gut* kichlin."

Israel glanced across the table at Wilma, wondering what thoughts might be going through her mind. Had she taken pity on these boys the way he had, or did Wilma dislike the idea of helping him raise his sister's children? He wouldn't know for sure until he drove her back home, which he should probably do soon, since the bishop's wife would need to return to her own home before it was time to fix her husband's supper.

Seeing that there were just two cookies left, Israel was about to offer Wilma one and eat the last cookie himself. But before he could get the words out, Josh and Nate snatched them up in such a hurry that Micah's glass toppled over and what was left of his milk spilled on the table and dripped onto the floor.

Margaret was on her feet and grabbed a dishrag.

While she mopped up the mess on the table, Wilma got out the mop and cleaned the floor.

Nate and Josh, seemingly unaware or not caring about the mess they'd created, chomped on their cookies. Meanwhile, little Micah howled like a newborn calf. Mark shouted at his brother, calling him a crybaby, which made Micah carry on even more. Israel felt like bawling too. He'd been a bachelor on his own for the past five years and had gotten used to the quiet afforded him. It would take some doing and perhaps learning some ways to develop tolerance for unexpected irritating noises before he could feel a sense of peace and contentment in this house. Hopefully, once Wilma took charge of the children, things would go smoother and with less noise and confusion. Israel didn't know how his sister had managed to cope with her sons' outbursts and moods—especially after her husband died, leaving her to deal with everything on her own.

If I'd understood how hard things must have been for Kathryn, I would have invited her and the boys to move in here with me. Between the two of us, we could have parented the boys.

A lump formed in Israel's throat. *And if they'd moved here to Reedsville, my sister might still be alive.* This was not the first time Israel had berated himself since Kathryn's death. He'd told himself almost every day since her death that he should have been more sensitive to her and the boys' needs after her husband passed away. While Israel couldn't go back and change the events of the past, he could, and would, do everything in his power to give his nephews a good, stable home. He wanted each of them to grow up into hardworking men of God.

On the drive back home, Israel was quiet. Wilma wasn't sure if he was concentrating on the road or simply had nothing to say. Was he embarrassed by his nephews' behavior? Did he think Wilma might not want to marry him now?

Of course I want to marry him, Wilma told herself. *I'm just not sure I'll be able to handle those boys. But I won't share my thoughts with Israel. He has enough to deal with right now and doesn't need to know my feelings, which I'm sure would only upset him. Besides, I haven't even spent one day with the boys alone, so there's no way I can know how things will work out between me and them. I just need to do my very best to help all of them adjust. Inheriting five boys and never having been a father can't be easy for Israel either.*

When they pulled into Wilma's yard, Israel reached over and took hold of her hand. "Would it be asking too much for you to take care of the boys while I'm at work every day, or would you prefer that I look for someone else?"

Wilma fought the urge to ask Israel to find

someone else but forced a smile instead and said, "I'll be fine taking care of the boys. If I'm going to be your fraa, then they need to get used to me."

"So you still want to marry me?"

"Of course I do."

Israel squeezed her fingers gently as he released a huge breath. "*Danki*, Wilma. I'm ever so grateful that you're willing. I wasn't sure how you would feel about helping me raise my nephews after meeting them today. It'll be a challenge, for sure, but I'm glad to know you'll be at my side."

He lifted her hand and bent his head to kiss her fingers. "I love you, Wilma, and I feel *seelich* to have someone so special as my *aldi*."

"My heart is filled with love too." Wilma smiled in spite of her doubts about how she would handle the boys. "I feel blessed to have you."

Chapter 4

As Wilma's horse and buggy approached Israel's house the following day, her palms became so sweaty she could barely hold on to the reins. Once Israel left for work, she would be alone with the boys, and she wasn't sure how it would go or what she should ask them to do. Would they cooperate if she assigned them chores? Since she would be expected to fix their meals, she hoped they weren't picky eaters.

Try to relax and deal with one thing at a time, Wilma told herself as she guided her horse, Blossom, up to the rail. She climbed out of the buggy, unhitched the mare, and led her to the barn. Later, after she rubbed down the animal and gave her something to eat and drink, Wilma would let Blossom roam around the corral. Since she would be here most of the day, it would be best to let the horse enjoy the sunshine and fresh air rather than being cooped up in the barn.

Once Blossom had been cared for, Wilma went back to the buggy and removed a plastic tote that contained some of her sewing and quilting supplies. She hoped she would have some free time to get some handwork done on the table runners she'd brought along. Surely the younger boys would take naps sometime after lunch, and she would find something for the older boys to do, which should allow her some time to herself.

As Wilma approached the house, Israel came out the front door. When she stepped onto the porch and set down her tote, he greeted her with a hug.

"Danki for coming. The boys are still in bed, and they haven't had breakfast yet. I was planning to fix it for them, but now I need to leave for work or I'm going to be late."

"It's okay." She managed a smile. "I'll make sure they are fed."

"I appreciate it, Wilma." Israel gave her a second hug. "I'll take your tote inside, grab my lunch pail, and be on my way."

Wilma went in behind him and entered the kitchen. She was surprised to see several bowls in the sink. If the boys hadn't eaten breakfast, then what were these from?

As if he could read Wilma's thoughts, Israel set her tote on the table and gestured to the sink. "I fed the boys ice cream last night and didn't haul in water to wash up their dishes. I figured on doing it this morning but never got around to the chore."

She flapped her hand. "Don't worry about it, Israel. I'll take care of cleaning the bowls after the boys have had their breakfast, because then there'll be more dishes to do."

He pulled Wilma into his arms and kissed

her forehead. "Don't know what I'd do without you in my life. We're not even married yet, and already you've become my helpmate. I can't thank you enough."

A warm flush swept across Wilma's cheeks. "There's no need to thank me, Israel. I'm happy to help." It wasn't a lie. She felt obligated to assist her future husband in caring for his nephews. Besides, she felt compassion for his sister's orphaned sons. The only problem was Wilma wasn't sure she was up to the task. But she would do her best, for Israel's sake, as well as the boys'.

"Well, I'd better get going." Israel bent his head and gave Wilma another kiss. "I'll see you sometime before supper."

After he went out the door, Wilma entered the living room and watched out the window as he got into his buggy, took up the reins, and headed down the lane. She wished he could be here with her today because he knew his nephews better than she did and they would relate more easily to him than her.

Wilma returned to the kitchen to start breakfast. If the boys weren't up by the time it was ready, she would wake them. First she moved her quilting tote from the table to a corner of the room. Next she got out the pitcher of drinking water and the ingredients to make pancakes. Surely this would be something all of the boys would enjoy having for breakfast.

Once she had enough pancakes made, Wilma placed them on a baking sheet, which she put in the oven to keep warm while she set the table.

Wilma glanced at the battery-operated clock on the far wall. It was half past seven—time to get the children up.

She left the kitchen, but when she reached the foot of the stairs, the sound of boys clomping on the floor and shouting carried down the steps. It sounded like a herd of horses had been set free.

The next thing Wilma knew, all five boys bounded down the stairs, still wearing their pajamas. With no acknowledgment of Wilma's presence, they made a dash for the kitchen. Wilma was right behind them. "Slow down, please."

"We're *hungerich*." Mark pulled out a chair and sat down.

"I understand, but being hungry doesn't give you a reason to run in the house. Now, if the rest of you will take your seats at the table, I'll get the pancakes from the oven." Wilma paused. "But first I'd like to say *guder mariye*."

"Mornin'," Josh mumbled, glancing at her before looking away.

The other boys sat staring at their empty plates, even when Wilma repeated her "good morning" welcome. This was not the best way to begin the day, and she hoped it was not an indication of how the rest of the day would go.

39

Wilma removed the pancakes from the warm oven and transferred them to a platter, which she placed in the middle of the table next to the jars of syrup and honey. "Let's bow for silent prayer, and then I'll dish up your pancakes."

"I ain't no boppli. I'm old enough to dish my own." With a sharp lift of his chin, Mark folded his arms and glared at her.

Wilma was on the verge of saying something about his rude behavior but decided to let it pass. "Let us pray." Bowing her head, she closed her eyes. She hoped the boys would do the same. When she opened her eyes a few minutes later, five pairs of eyes stared at her. Without peeking, she had no way of knowing whether they had prayed or not, but she decided not to ask. Israel's nephews needed time to adjust to their mother's death, as well as to their new surroundings. Wilma was a stranger to them, so she would proceed carefully.

Except for a few comments to each other, the boys remained quiet throughout the meal. When everyone finished, Wilma gathered up her plate, as well as those of the two youngest boys. Since Mark, Ethan, and Josh were tall enough to reach the sink, she asked them to clear their dishes from the table.

"Don't see why we have to do it." Mark's jaw and neck visibly tightened. "Thought that's why Uncle Israel asked you to come over here today."

Wilma's gaze flicked upward. *Dear Lord, please give me the wisdom and strength to get through this day. I am quite sure these boys, and this one in particular, do not like me.*

She looked at the children. "I am here to fix your meals and see that you find some things to do to keep yourselves busy, but I expect you all to help out where the chores are concerned."

"I ain't doin' no chores, and you're not our mamm." Ethan got up from the table and stomped out of the room. Soon the rest of the boys followed, even the youngest ones.

Wilma groaned inwardly. *Now what should I do? Would it be best to go after them and demand that they listen to me, or should I let it go for now and have a talk with Israel about how the boys acted?* She grabbed the remaining plates and carried them to the sink. *I should have discussed this with him this morning— found out if he had any chores he wanted the boys to do.*

When Israel arrived home from work that afternoon, he was surprised to see Wilma sitting on the porch, leaning forward as she rubbed her forehead. "Do you have a *koppweh*?" he asked, taking a seat on the chair beside her.

She raised her head and nodded. "The headache came on about an hour ago."

"Sorry to hear. Did you take something for it?"

41

"Jah, but it hasn't done anything to relieve the pain or tension I'm feeling."

"What's wrong?" He touched her arm. "Did you have a difficult time with the boys today?"

Wilma nodded. "They refused to do anything I asked of them. All those children did was fool around and make messes, and I spent most of my day cleaning up after them. I didn't even get any quilting done." Wilma's chin trembled. "They don't like me, Israel. Your nephews kept reminding me that I am not their *mudder*."

Israel's leg muscles tightened as he tapped his foot in frustration. *If the boys don't get along with Wilma and continue doing things to aggravate her, she might not marry me. Then what'll I do?*

"Listen, Wilma . . ." He clasped her hand and gave her fingers what he hoped was a reassuring squeeze. "I'll have a talk with those *schtinkers* and straighten things out. Where are they now?"

"In the barn, fooling with the busslin. I tried to keep them away from there, but no one would listen."

"I'll bet they'll listen to me." He started to rise from the chair, but Wilma shook her head. "I think it would be best to wait until I go home, which will be after I've fed you all some supper and done the dishes."

"No way! You need to go home now and try to get rid of that koppweh. I'll make us some sandwiches or maybe hot dogs for supper. The boys and I will be fine."

"Are you sure?"

"Absolutely. While you gather up your things, I'll get Blossom hitched to your buggy."

"Okay, danki." Wilma stood and went inside.

Israel sent up another prayer before heading to the barn. At the very least he needed to get the boys away from those poor little kittens. With too much handling, it would be a wonder if any of them survived.

Remembering that his first priority ought to be getting Wilma's horse ready to go, Israel went to the corral and got Blossom out. He found her halter and bridle draped over the fence and made quick work out of getting her hitched to Wilma's buggy. He'd just finished up when Wilma came out of the house carrying her plastic tote. Her face was unusually pale, and she squinted against the sun peeking through a few scattered clouds.

"You don't look well, Wilma. Maybe I should take you home, because it might not be good for you to drive the horse by yourself."

"You'd have to come back here on foot," she responded.

He shrugged. "It's only a few miles, and I'm sure the boys will be okay on their own till I get back."

"No, that's all right. I'll be fine going home by myself." She climbed into the buggy and gathered up the reins. "I'll see you tomorrow morning, and please, don't worry about me."

Don't worry about you? How can I not? Israel almost shouted. But he kept his thoughts to himself. He knew his future wife well enough to know that if she felt too bad to make the trip to her parents' house alone, she would have accepted his offer to drive her home.

He stepped back from the buggy and lifted his hand in a wave. "I'll say a prayer for you, Wilma."

"Danki." She gave what he felt sure was a forced smile as she backed the horse from the hitching rail.

After Israel sent up a quick prayer on her behalf, he watched until her rig entered the road and was out of sight, then sprinted off toward the barn.

When he entered the building, Israel caught sight of his nephews sitting on bales of straw, each holding a kitten. His first inclination was to holler at them, but he caught himself in time. The best approach was to keep calm. He could reproach them for playing with the kittens without getting angry.

"How was your day, boys?" Israel asked as he approached the area where they sat.

Mark lifted his shoulders in a shrug. "It was okay, I guess."

"Did you forget what I said about not handling the kittens until they are older?"

All were silent. Not one of the five boys gave him an answer.

"I want you to carefully put them back with their mother, and then I have a few chores for you all to do before we start supper."

"How come we hafta do chores?" The question came from Josh.

"Because there are things to be done, and it's my understanding that you didn't do anything all day except fool around."

"That Wilma lady tried to make us work," Ethan interjected, "but we don't have to do what she says 'cause she's not our mamm."

"Jah, that's right," Nate chimed in. "She ain't the boss of us, right, Brother?" He looked over at Mark.

The older boy gave a nod.

"Whenever Wilma is here taking care of you, she's the boss, and you need to do whatever she says." Israel spoke quietly but in a stern voice.

The youngest boy let loose with a whiny cry, and soon tears began to flow.

Oh great. Israel gritted his teeth. *No wonder Wilma ended up with a koppweh.*

"Now, there's no reason to cry." Israel leaned down so his face was close to Micah's. "I'm not mad. I just want you to put the kittens away and come with me into the house so we can decide what we're going to have for supper."

45

"Isn't that lady gonna fix our meal?" Ethan asked.

"No, Wilma had a koppweh, so she went home. She'll be back tomorrow, though, and I want you all to cooperate with her." Israel looked at each of the boys. "Is that understood?"

All five of them gave a brief nod, and then they got up and headed across the barn to the mama cat's box. Israel watched to make sure they put the kittens away, and then he led them out of the barn. Now that he'd reached an understanding with the boys, things would hopefully go better tomorrow.

Chapter 5

"Are you sure you want to go back there today?" Wilma's mother asked her the following morning.

Releasing a sigh, Wilma set her cup of herbal tea aside. "I don't have much choice. I made an agreement with Israel, and I need to do as I promised."

"If you explain that the boys are too much for you, I'm sure he would find someone else to care for them while he's at work."

Wilma shook her head. "Once Israel and I are married, I'll be responsible for the boys' care anyway, so it makes sense that I should be there to help now."

"But maybe—"

Wilma rose from her chair and pushed away from the table. "I need to go, Mom. If I don't get to Israel's soon, he'll be late for work, and those boys should not be left alone."

"Okay, but do take a homeopathic or herbal remedy with you in case you get another koppweh today."

"Jah, okay." Wilma went to the cupboard where Mom kept all her home remedies and supplements from the health food store. She took out the one that had helped her headaches

47

in the past. Too bad she hadn't had it with her yesterday.

Wilma glanced out the kitchen window. "I see *Daed* has my horse and buggy ready, so I need to go." She gave her mother a hug. "I'll see you sometime this evening."

Mom gave Wilma's back a gentle pat before she moved toward the door. "Have a good day, and remember, I'll be praying that things will go better for you than they did yesterday."

"I'll be praying for that too," Wilma said as she went out the door.

"How do you feel this morning?" Israel asked when he greeted Wilma by her buggy.

She smiled up at him. "My koppweh is gone, and I'm ready to face a new day."

"Good to hear." Israel gave her arm a tender squeeze. "I had a talk with the boys last night, and I believe they will be more cooperative with you today."

"That's good to hear."

"Oh, and I fixed their breakfast this morning. They're at the table eating it now."

"Okay."

"I made plenty of scrambled eggs, so if you didn't eat breakfast before you left home, there should be enough left for you to have some too."

"Danki." Wilma glanced toward the house with a feeling of dread. Would the children really get along better with her today, or had they only told their uncle what he wanted to hear?

Deanna pulled her horse and buggy up to the Hostetlers' hitching rail and got out. After securing the mare, she made her way across the yard and up to the house. Preparing to knock on the blue door, she was surprised when it opened before her knuckles could connect with the wood.

"Guder mariye, Esther." Deanna smiled. "Did you see me pull into the yard?"

Wilma's mother nodded. "I was washing the dishes and saw you out the kitchen window." She looked past Deanna. "I'm surprised Abner isn't with you. Is he at home with your husband?"

"Not today. Abner is with my father this morning. Dad's been wanting his grandson to come for a visit, so I dropped him off on the way here." Deanna chuckled. "By the time I go there to pick my son up, Dad will probably be more than ready to say goodbye to Abner. He's always curious about things and can be quite a handful at times."

"At least you only have one child to deal with—not like my poor Wilma, having to look after five rambunctious boys."

"Yes, I heard she planned to help Israel by watching his nephews while he's at work. Is that where she is now, or is Wilma at home?"

"She's over there—or at least on the way there.

49

She left a little while ago." Esther gestured to the wooden chairs on the porch. "Would you like to have a seat?"

"Guess I could sit a few minutes. I mainly came by to see if Wilma had finished those table runners she's been working on." Deanna lowered herself into one of the chairs.

Esther took a seat in the other chair. "She took her quilting tote to Israel's yesterday but didn't get anything done because she spent most of the day cleaning up the messes the boys made." She clucked her tongue noisily. "Poor thing came home with a terrible koppweh. It was so bad she felt sick to her stomach."

"That's a shame. Really bad headaches are the worst."

Esther sighed. "I guess my *dochder* thinks she won't get any quilting done today either, because she left her quilting tote here."

Deanna was on the verge of commenting, but Esther spoke again. "I don't think it's fair of Israel to expect my daughter to look after the boys when he's not even married to her yet. Under the circumstances, I have to wonder if Wilma might be making a mistake to marry Israel after all."

Deanna opened her mouth to try speaking again, but once more she was cut off.

"Helping to raise five unruly boys, who Wilma says don't like her, might be the biggest mistake of my daughter's life." Esther pursed her lips as she looked at Deanna with wrinkled brows. "Would you be willing to speak to Wilma about this and suggest that she reconsider her marriage plans?"

Deanna's thoughts raced as she tried to come up with the best response to Esther's question. She didn't like being put on the spot like this—especially when it could affect her friendship with Wilma. "Umm . . . I wouldn't feel right about interfering. Whatever happens between Wilma and Israel is their business."

Esther shifted on her chair. "I agree with you in part, but if things don't work out between Wilma and Israel's nephews, it could affect her relationship with Israel too." Esther drew a breath and released it with a huff. "I can't stand the thought of my daughter being unhappy for the rest of her life."

Deanna fought the urge to roll her eyes. Wilma's mother was worrying too much about something Wilma must decide for herself. Deanna was sure that her friend loved Israel very much, but if Wilma should end up calling off the wedding, it needed to be her decision. "I'm sure Israel's nephews will adjust to your daughter soon, and then things will go better."

"I hope so." Esther rubbed the crease on the bridge of her nose. "My three older daughters are all happily married, and I would like to see my youngest daughter living joyfully with her husband too."

"I believe she will be." Deanna rose from her chair. "I should be on my way now. Would you please tell Wilma I came by?"

"Certainly."

"Oh, and I would like her to let me know if she thinks she'll be able to get the table runners done before I go to the flea market in Belleville next week."

"I'll be sure and relay your message."

"Have a good rest of your day, Esther." Deanna gave Wilma's mother's arm a light pat. "Don't worry. I'm sure everything will work out for the best."

After Deanna left, Esther poured a glass of lemonade and went out to the shop where her husband built storage sheds.

"I brought you something cold to drink, John." She placed the glass on the workbench closest to him.

"Danki, it's much appreciated on a warm day like this." He set the tool he'd been using aside, picked up the glass, and took a big drink. "That sure hits the spot."

"It's not too sour, I hope."

He shook his head and drank some more. "As usual, your fresh-squeezed lemonade is just right—not too sour, not too sweet."

Esther smiled. It pleased her whenever John appreciated something she'd done for him. Not that she was seeking a compliment. She enjoyed doing nice things for her husband, but knowing that he appreciated it was like chocolate frosting on her favorite vanilla cake.

Esther leaned against his workbench and folded her arms.

"Is there something else you'd like to say?" John tipped his head.

"Well yes, how did you know?"

"After nearly forty years of marriage, I pretty much know when my fraa has something on her mind." He grinned. "So you may as well come right out and say whatever it is."

Esther rubbed her sweaty palms on the front of her apron. She hoped he would agree with what she was about to say.

"*Raus mit*, Esther. Please say what's on your mind."

"All right then, I'll come out with it. I am deeply concerned about our dochder."

"Which one? We have four daughters, you know." John drank the rest of his lemonade and set down the glass.

"I'm referring to Wilma, the only one who's not yet married."

"But she will be in a few months, so there's nothing to be concerned about."

"Jah, there is."

"How so?"

"You know that koppweh she came home with

yesterday that was so bad she had to go to bed early?"

"Uh-huh."

"It came on because she'd had such a rough day dealing with Israel's mischievous nephews."

"So they gave her a few problems, did they?"

"That's putting it mildly." Esther grimaced. "Wilma told me that the boys don't like her, so under the circumstances, I don't see how she can marry Israel."

His brows arched. "Did Wilma say that?"

"Well no, but . . ."

"But you think it'll be too much for her—is that right?"

Esther bobbed her head. "I was hoping you would speak to her about this—make her realize that if she marries Israel and those boys come between them, their marriage will not be pleasant. Wilma might end up resenting Israel for forcing her to help him raise five boys who are not even related to her. If they were," she rushed on, "it might make a difference, but . . ."

"Whoa now!" John held up his hand. "First of all, I will not interfere, and you ought to mind your own business."

Esther recoiled. "But John, you don't under-stand—"

"You're wrong. I understand that our daughter is twenty-five years old and wise enough to make her own decisions. It is not our place to tell her who she should or shouldn't marry. Israel is a good man, and he will make Wilma a fine husband."

"But what about those young boys? From what Wilma said when she came home yesterday, Israel's nephews are quite a handful."

He shrugged his broad shoulders. "Be that as it may, it's up to Wilma to decide whether she can handle them or not."

"All right, John," she conceded. "I'll keep my mouth shut and say no more on the subject. But I will certainly pray about the matter."

By noon Wilma had begun to wonder if she would make it through the day. It was all she could do to keep from shouting at the children, and her head had begun to feel like it might explode. The two older boys had done their chores when she'd asked them to, but not without complaint. The three youngest boys had snuck into the barn again, and Wilma caught them playing with the kittens. When she'd told the children to put the kittens back in the box, Micah started crying and calling for his mother, while Nate and Josh looked on, calling him a boppli, which only made the little fellow cry more.

After trying to keep a positive attitude and talk calmly to the boys all morning, Wilma had to decide what to fix for lunch. She wasn't all that hungry, but the boys obviously were. She'd surmised that much when she'd caught them eating all the potato chips Israel had purchased from an Amish couple in Belleville who made homemade chips to sell.

After putting what was left of the potato chips away, Wilma got out the broom and asked Mark to sweep the floor, where numerous chip crumbs had landed.

"Why do I hafta do it?" He scowled at her. "I ain't the only one who ate some chips, you know."

"I am well aware," Wilma responded. "But Ethan said it was you who got out the bag of potato chips, so I'm asking you to clean the floor."

Mark grabbed the broom and quickly swept the crumbs out the door.

"There's a dustpan in the closet," Wilma called to him. "You could have swept the crumbs into it and then dumped them into the garbage can."

"I know that already." Circles of red erupted on the boy's cheeks. "I ain't *dumm*, ya know."

"I was not suggesting that you were dumb. I just thought . . . Oh, never mind. If you boys will go outside now and wash your hands at the pump, I'll have sandwiches made by the time you come in."

Josh tipped his head back and blinked rapidly as he looked up at her. "Who says we want sandwiches? Maybe we'd like somethin' else."

"Such as?"

He pointed to the bag of potato chips Wilma had placed on the cupboard.

She shook her head. "Your uncle would not be happy if he came home from work this afternoon and discovered that all his chips were gone. Besides, too many greasy potato chips aren't good for you."

"How do you know what's good for us?" Ethan chimed in. "Our mamm took good care of us, and you'll never take her place." Tears pooled in his blue eyes, and he blinked several times.

"I'm not trying to take her place. I'm merely trying my best to take care of your needs."

"We don't want you to take care of us." Mark's face grew redder as his voice rose. "We can take care of ourselves just fine."

Wilma struggled to keep her emotions under control. She felt hurt by the boys' rejection. Wilma was fully aware that these children would never see her as a mother figure, but she wished she could be their friend, and she told them that too.

Mark shook his head. "That ain't never gonna happen." He jerked open the back door, stepped onto the porch, and then whirled around. "Come on, Brothers. Let's go outside and wash up. Not because she told us to. We'll do it 'cause our hands are dirty."

When they'd filed out the door, Wilma got out a

loaf of bread. She hoped the rest of the day would go by quickly, because it couldn't be over soon enough to suit her. The worst part was, she'd be back here again tomorrow, and then it would start over. Wilma wished she could find someplace to run and hide.

Chapter 6

By the end of June, Wilma was convinced that she'd lost her mind.

I have to be crazy to keep going over to Israel's and attempting to deal with those naughty boys, Wilma told herself as she headed to his place Friday morning. *But I'm doing this for Israel, not his nephews, who have said several times that they wished I wasn't there.*

Wilma was well aware that the children missed their mother and had trouble adjusting, but was that any reason to misbehave?

Yesterday had been another stressful day, when Wilma had served the boys ice cream and they'd poured chocolate syrup all over the table, laughing and acting like it was a big game. Then later, after the mess had been cleaned up, she'd stepped on a piece of gum that one of the boys had chewed and spit on the living room floor. Of course she'd received no confession or apology from the one who had done it.

Wilma shook the reins to get Blossom moving quicker, although she wanted to take her time getting there. Wilma's life, as well as her attitude, had changed since Israel became the guardian of his sister's children. She missed spending time with Deanna, and she needed to finish some quilting projects so she'd have some money coming in. Israel had offered to pay her for watching the boys, but she'd declined. It wouldn't seem right for his future wife to take money for something she would be doing after they got married anyway.

Her jaw clenched. *If only things could go back to the way they used to be. Israel and I don't even have the time for courting now.* She blinked against tears threatening to spill over.

Wilma didn't know how, but she'd managed to finish the quilted table runners she'd promised Deanna. She'd had to stay up late a few nights to do it. If something didn't change soon, Wilma feared she might cave in.

"But what could change?" she murmured out loud. "Israel's nephews aren't going anywhere, and short of a miracle, I doubt they'll ever learn to like me." She was caught in a no-win situation and didn't see any way out unless she broke things off with Israel.

A few tears escaped Wilma's lashes and dribbled down her cheeks. *But I love him, and it would hurt so much if he married someone else.*

Wilma figured if she did break things off with Israel, he would find someone else to marry since he would most certainly need some help raising the boys. She pursed her lips. *I wonder who it would be. Would he choose Emma Byler to wed—or maybe Malinda Troyer? They're both in their twenties and aren't being courted by anyone.*

The longer Wilma pondered this, the more frustrated she became. Would either of the young women make Israel a good wife? Could they handle the boys better than Wilma had been doing? Maybe so, maybe not.

As Israel's place came into view, she clamped her lips together. *I need to quit thinking about this and focus on getting through the day. If I go in with a cheerful attitude, maybe it will rub off on the boys.*

When Wilma stepped onto Israel's front porch, the door opened and he greeted her with a welcoming smile. "Guder mariye."

"Good morning," she replied.

"You look rested. Did you sleep well last night?"

Wilma gave a brief nod.

"I fixed cereal for breakfast this morning, and the boys are at the table eating right now."

"Okay."

"I also left a list of chores for them to do. It's on one end of the kitchen counter."

"All right. Is there anything else I should know?"

"Jah, there is, and it's just three little words." He took a step closer.

"Oh? What words would that be?"

61

"I love you." Israel bent his head and kissed her cheek.

"I love you too," she whispered.

He lifted the lunch box he held. "I'd best be on my way now. I hope you have a good day."

"And you as well."

"See you later, Wilma." He bounded off the porch with a spring in his step.

Feeling a little more optimistic about her day, Wilma went inside. When she entered the kitchen, the first thing she saw was a kitten on the table, lapping milk from Nate's bowl. It was all Wilma could do to keep from shouting, but she managed to keep her tone of voice under control. "What is that bussli doing in the house, much less on the table?"

Nate looked up at her and grinned. "She was hungerich, so I'm givin' her some of my millich."

Nate's brothers, all focused on the kitten, were grinning too.

Wilma's hands went straight to her hips. "Did you get your uncle's permission to bring the kitten into the house, and did he see you with it on the table?"

Nate shook his head. "I hid the bussli till Uncle Israel left the room."

"Please take the kitten back to the barn."

The boy's nose wrinkled as he stared at her defiantly, but Wilma did not back down. She pointed to the back door. "Take the kitten out now."

Nate thrust out his bottom lip and picked up the kitten. In so doing, he bumped Micah's arm with his elbow, causing the little guy to spill the glass of milk he'd been about to drink.

Wilma went to get a dishrag to wipe up the mess. By the time she returned, the kitten was back on the table, lapping up the milk while the boys all laughed and pointed as they sat watching.

Struggling to control her temper, Wilma spoke through tight lips. "I want you to remove that kitten and take her to the barn now."

He looked up at her and blinked. "But she's cleanin' up the mess."

"I will take care of the mess while you do as I said. Is that clear, Nathaniel?"

"My name ain't Nathaniel, so stop callin' me that. I wanna be called 'Nate.' "

"I will call you Nate when you do as I say."

He folded his arms and gave a huff.

Wilma had run out of patience. She pointed to the doorway leading to their bedrooms upstairs. "I want you to go to your room, and don't come out until you are ready to apologize."

Nate looked at his oldest brother, as though seeking his help, but Mark only shrugged and said, "Guess you'd better do what she said. She might get a switch if ya don't."

Wilma had no intention of using a switch on any of the boys, but she did need them to obey her.

63

Wilma looked at Nate with what she hoped was a stern expression. "Do you want me to tell your uncle how you've behaved this morning?"

"Nope." He dropped his gaze.

"Then please leave this table and go to your room."

"Can I take the bussli out to the barn first?"

She shook her head. "I will take the kitten to the barn."

Nate's frown grew more intense, but he finally stepped away from the table and ran out of the room. A few seconds later, Wilma heard him clomping up the stairs.

She reached for the full-bellied kitten and started for the back door. Before opening it, she turned and faced the four boys remaining at the table. "Mark, while I am gone, please wipe up the milk and help your brothers clear all the bowls and glasses from the table."

When Wilma returned to the kitchen a short time later, the boys were gone and everything remained on the table.

Anger simmered in her soul. *How dare those youngsters defy me again? Didn't their mamm teach them how to respect their elders?*

Wilma stepped into the hall and cupped both hands around her mouth. "Mark, Ethan, Josh, Nate, and Micah—I want to see all five of you right now!"

Except for the steady *tick-tock, tick-tock* of the battery-run clock on the kitchen wall, all was quiet.

The boys weren't in the barn—she knew that much. However, they could be some other place outside or hiding from her here in the house.

Clasping the railing, Wilma made her way up the stairs. When she reached the top, she heard a whispered conversation, although she couldn't make out the words. Moving closer to the door from which the voices came, Wilma tipped her head and listened.

"I don't like her; she's mean." Wilma recognized Josh's voice.

"Yeah, and if Uncle Israel marries Wilma, we'll be stuck with her tellin' us what to do till the day we're old enough to move out. I wish he'd break things off with her." It was Mark who had spoken, and his comment hurt Wilma to the core of her being. She had tried to be nice to the boys, but that hadn't worked. Neither had being stern with them, so what else could she do to gain their favor?

She held her hands together, gripping them so tightly, her veins protruded. *Should I talk to Israel about this when he gets home from work? Maybe he has some idea how we can deal with the situation.*

Wilma turned and made her way quietly down the stairs. Right now there were dishes to be washed, dried, and put away. After that, she would sit in the living room and try to get some quilting done. Hopefully the boys would remain upstairs until she called them for lunch.

Or maybe—Wilma bit the inside of her cheek—*they'll stay up there until their uncle gets home. Then those boys will probably lie and say I made them remain in their room without any lunch.*

She released a deep moan. *I know what I must do. Those ornery children have left me no choice.*

Israel entered the kitchen and set his lunch pail on the counter. There was no sign of Wilma, which seemed rather odd. Normally she would be in this room getting their supper ready, but the stove wasn't even lit, and there were no dishes on the table. He scratched behind his ear. *I wonder where she could be.*

Hearing voices coming from the living room, Israel left the kitchen and went across the hall. He found his two youngest nephews sprawled out on the floor with only a blanket beneath them. Their eyes and cheeks were red, causing Israel to wonder if they had been crying.

Mark, Ethan, and Josh sat on the wooden chairs, each with a book in his hands.

"What's going on?" Israel asked. "Where is Wilma?"

"She's in the barn," Mark responded. "Guess she's gettin' her *gaul* ready so she can go home."

"What makes you think that?" Israel asked.

"She said she was gonna get her horse and go as soon as you got home." The answer came from Josh.

Israel's forehead wrinkled. "Why would she leave early and without fixing supper?"

Mark shrugged, and Ethan turned his hands palms up.

"Is Wilma feeling grank?"

"Jah, she is, Uncle Israel," Nate spoke up. "Wilma is sick of us. She's always yellin' at us, and this morning she made me stay in my room."

Israel's pulse rate increased. He needed to talk to Wilma about this. "I'm going out to the barn to see Wilma," he told the boys. "I want all of you to stay right here till I come back in. Is that clear?"

All heads bobbed at the same time.

"Good." Israel hurried from the room and rushed out the back door. When he entered the barn, he found Wilma in one of the stalls, about to lead her horse out.

"What's going on?" he questioned. "The boys said you'd be going home as soon as I got here. Since you weren't in the house and I didn't see any supper started, I figured it must be true."

She gave a slow nod without looking at him.

He went over, stepped inside the stall, and closed the gate. "Are you all right, Wilma? Why are you leaving so early?"

With tears in her eyes, she looked at him briefly and then dropped her gaze. "I'll go back to the house and make sandwiches, if you like, but I need to go home."

"How come? Do you have another koppweh?"

"No. I . . . I just can't do this anymore. The boys don't like me, and nothing I've said or done has gotten through to them." She paused and drew a breath then released it slowly. "I'm sorry, Israel, but you'll need to find someone else to care for them while you're at work."

"Maybe things will get better once we're married," he said.

She shook her head. "It's not going to work out for us the way we'd planned. If you need a wife, it'll have to be someone else, because I can't marry you now." Wilma opened the gate, and leading her mare, she left the barn, leaving Israel standing with his mouth hanging open.

As the reality of the situation sank in, he dropped onto a bale of straw and lowered his head on his hands. Israel wished there was something he could say or do to make the boys warm up to Wilma, but he couldn't think of a thing.

What am I going to do without her in my life? She's my whole world, and I love her so much. Israel couldn't even imagine himself marrying anyone else. If he could not have the woman he loved, then he'd remain a bachelor for the rest of his life. Without Wilma, Israel's life would have so little meaning.

But it has to have meaning, he told himself. *My sister's sons need a father figure, and right now that comes before anything.*

Chapter 7

Wilma clutched her horse's reins, determined not to give in to her tears. Deciding to break up with Israel had been difficult, but she had no other choice. She could never be happily married to him with the way things were between her and the boys. It was an impossible situation.

Wilma dreaded going home and telling her parents the news. Dad might try to persuade her to rethink things, and Mom would probably say that Wilma had made the right decision.

I wonder what Deanna will have to say about this. Maybe I should stop by her house right now and tell her the news before I talk to my folks.

Wilma's mother was a talker, and once she knew about Wilma's breakup with Israel, their entire Amish community would most likely know. Then pretty soon everyone who lived in the Big Valley would hear about the Amish woman who had walked out on her fiancé and refused to take care of his orphaned nephews. Wilma didn't want her friend to find out that way. *It will be better if Deanna hears it directly from me.*

Her decision made, Wilma directed Blossom down the road leading to Deanna and Elmer's house.

• • •

Deanna had set a few items out to start supper when she heard a horse and buggy come up the lane. She went to the back door and opened it. Looking out, Deanna was surprised to see Wilma get out of her carriage and secure her horse to the hitching rail.

Deanna waited on the porch until Wilma joined her. "This is certainly a surprise. Shouldn't you be at Israel's cooking supper about now?"

Wilma shook her head. "I quit, and I won't be going back there anymore." She briefly lowered her gaze, and her chin trembled when she looked up and spoke again. "Israel and I won't be getting married in November."

Deanna's fingers touched her parted lips. "Why? What happened?"

"Can't you guess? It's my relationship with his nephews. Or maybe I should say it's the lack of one. No matter how hard I've tried, they have not accepted me. Besides that, all five of them have continued to misbehave and play tricks on me." Wilma sighed. "Today was worse than ever."

"Let's go inside," Deanna suggested. "You can give me all the details while I finish making supper. In fact, you're welcome to stay and join us for the meal."

"That would be nice—if you're sure you don't mind. I'm really in no hurry to go home and tell my folks."

"That's understandable." Deanna motioned for

71

her friend to enter the house and invited her to take a seat at the kitchen table.

After Wilma sat down, she glanced toward the door leading to the living room and gestured in that direction. "Are Elmer and Abner in there?"

Deanna shook her head. "They're in Elmer's workshop. Before they went out, I said I would clang the dinner bell when the meal was ready."

Wilma's facial features seemed to relax just a bit. "I'd have no problem with Elmer overhearing our conversation, but I would prefer that Abner not hear anything I have to say about those mischievous boys. It might give your sweet child some ideas about bad behavior, which would not be a good thing for him or you."

"True. My son can be impressionable at times."

"I believe that's true with most kinner."

"Jah, but children with Down syndrome, although normally quite sweet and lovable like Abner, often tend to be stubborn. I feel blessed that Elmer has such a special way with my son. Abner does almost anything Elmer asks him to without much fuss."

Wilma's forehead creased. "Wish I had that effect on Israel's nephews."

"So now, tell me what transpired today."

"Okay, I'll start at the beginning."

As Wilma gave the details of her time with the boys, Deanna cut up carrots to go in the tossed green salad she'd already made.

When Wilma stopped talking and sniffed deeply, as though trying to hold back tears, Deanna reached over and placed her hand on Wilma's arm. "I'm sorry you've had to deal with all of this, but you may want to reconsider your decision not to marry Israel."

"How come? Do you think I should continue subjecting myself to the boys' dislike of me, not to mention all the mayhem they seem to enjoy causing?"

Deanna shook her head. "That is not what I believe at all. I just think you ought to pray about the situation, and maybe . . ."

"I have prayed about it—every single night and many times during the day since I began taking care of those kinner. With the way things are now, if I were to marry Israel, all seven of us would be miserable."

Deanna wasn't sure what else she could say. She didn't want her friend, or Israel and the boys, to be unhappy. She gave Wilma's arm a gentle pat. "I'll be praying for you, and if you want to talk about this again, I'm here to listen and offer my support."

"Danki." Wilma slid her chair away from the table and stood. "I'd best get home now and let you finish making supper for your family."

"I thought you were going to join us."

"I was, but I've changed my mind. The sooner I tell my folks that I've called off the w the better it will be for everyone."

73

• • •

Israel stepped out the back door and called the boys in for supper. He'd sent them outside several minutes ago to wash up at the pump, so they would surely be done by now.

One by one they straggled in and took their seats at the kitchen table. Israel noticed a smudge of dirt on Nate's face, but he chose not to say anything. As long as the boy's hands were clean, he had a right to sit at this table.

"Let us pray." Israel bowed his head and hoped the boys would do the same. At least they were all quiet—even Micah who could sometimes be a little chatterbox.

Heavenly Father, Israel prayed, *if it's Your will for Wilma and me to get married, then please cause something to happen that will change her mind. But if it's not Your will, and Wilma sticks with her decision, I ask that You will take away the ache in my heart and help me to move on without the woman I love.*

When Israel finished his prayer, he rustled the napkin beside his plate and opened his eyes. He wasn't the least bit surprised to see five pairs of eyes looking at him with expectant expressions.

"How come we're havin' these for supper?" Ethan pointed to the platter where ham and cheese sandwiches had been piled.

"Because Wilma's not here to cook a hot meal."

74

Israel gripped his glass of water and took a drink. "The truth is, she won't be coming back."

"Good. We're better off without her." Mark lifted his chin and gave a crisp nod.

"Jah, that's right." Josh reached for a sandwich and plunked it on his plate. "She ain't nothin' like our mamm, and I'm real glad she's gone."

Everyone except for Micah bobbed his head. All the youngest brother seemed to care about was chomping on the potato chips he'd grabbed out of the bowl that had been set too close to him.

"I don't need her for nothin'," Nate chimed in. "I'm big enough to take care of myself."

Mark snorted. "Jah, right. You can't even tie your own shoes." He thumped his chest and looked at Israel. "I'm old enough to take care of my brieder."

"You may be able to handle some things on your own, but not when it comes to cooking and washing clothes for yourself or your brothers." Israel took a sandwich, even though his appetite had been diminished by his pain over Wilma's decision.

Ethan grabbed two sandwiches and plopped them on his plate. "If Wilma ain't comin' back, then we'll hafta take care of ourselves."

Israel shook his head. "That's not going to happen."

"You gonna stay home from work to be with us?" The question came from Josh.

"No, I am going to find someone else to be here with you while I'm at work."

"Oh yeah? Who've ya got in mind?" Ethan questioned.

"I don't know yet, but I'm sure there must be someone in our community who'd be willing to watch the five of you."

The four older boys frowned, but Micah kept munching on his chips. The little guy acted like he didn't care about anything except filling his belly.

Israel took a bite of his sandwich and washed it down with a drink of water. *Wish I could be so nonchalant. All I can think about is Wilma and how much it hurts to know that she's not going to be my wife.*

When Wilma arrived home, she found her mother in the kitchen, preparing the meal.

"You're home earlier than usual this evening," Mom said after Wilma set her purse on the counter.

"Jah."

"How come?"

"I quit, and I won't be going back to Israel's anymore." Wilma moved over to the stove, lifted the lid on the kettle, and inhaled the aroma of the simmering potato soup. "Yum—my favorite. Is it okay if I join you and Dad for supper?"

Mom walked briskly across the room and

joined Wilma at the stove. "Of course you can join us, but first I'd like to know why you quit."

Wilma turned to face her mother. "You ought to know the reason. Those boys still don't like me, and today was the worst day of all." She released a hard sigh and closed her eyes. "Would you like to hear about it?"

"Of course." Mom pulled a chair out from the table and sat down.

Wilma took a seat across from her mother and launched right into a description of her terrible day.

"I'm so sorry, Daughter," Mom said after Wilma stopped talking. "I can understand what influenced your decision, but do you think you may have been a bit hasty?"

Wilma's brows shot up. "This was not a hasty decision, Mom. I've done the best I can to take care of Israel's nephews, and they simply will not cooperate with me. Besides, based on some of the things you've said to me previously, I assumed you thought I should call off the wedding." Wilma leaned forward as the muscles in her chest and limbs tightened. "If I were to marry Israel, both he and I would be miserable, and so would those five young boys."

"I understand, and when the news gets out, I'll stand up for your decision, no matter what anyone has to say about it."

Wilma folded her arms and held them tightly

against her chest. For so long she'd wanted to become Israel's wife, but she had to face reality—her wish would never come true. She had to accept that fact, no matter how badly it hurt.

Chapter 8

Wilma bent over to pluck some dead blossoms off the pretty red petunias her mother had planted in the flower bed by the front porch. Noticing a few weeds, she went down on her knees and gave each one a good yank.

It had been three weeks since Wilma had said goodbye to Israel, and it felt nice to have her life back in order and not have to deal with those rambunctious boys. The only thing that didn't feel so good was knowing that she would never become Mrs. Israel Zook. It wasn't right to dislike Israel's nephews, but Wilma couldn't get past her feelings of resentment.

A fingernail on Wilma's right hand broke as she thrust her hand deep into the soil to pull a stubborn weed. *If those boys hadn't come to live with their uncle, Israel and I would still be courting and planning our wedding.*

"What are you doing, Daughter? I thought you were going to get some quilting done today. Isn't that what you said after breakfast?"

Wilma jumped at the sound of her mother's voice. She looked up and saw Mom looking down at her from the front porch. Wilma had been so deep in thought that she hadn't even heard the creaky screen door open.

"I'm still planning to do some quilting." Wilma rose to her feet and brushed the dirt off her hands. "After I checked the phone shack for messages and headed back to the house, I got sidetracked." She gestured to the flower bed. "Some *blieht* needed plucking, and I ended up pulling a few *umgraut.*"

Her mother nodded. "The flowers look so pretty this time of the year, but there are always lots of blossoms to pick and plenty of weeds to pull."

"It's a never-ending job but worth the effort." Wilma went to the pump to wash her hands. After drying them on the towel hanging nearby, she stepped onto the porch. "Guess I'll get busy with my quilting now."

Mom tapped Wilma's arm. "I'm not nearly as good a quilter as you, but if you need any help, let me know. In the meantime, I'll be in the kitchen working on my grocery list."

"Thanks." Wilma followed her mother into the house and headed to the sewing room to work on a wall hanging she hoped to sell in Deanna's quilt shop. Wilma's plastic tote sat in one corner of the simple room, filled with pot holders and table runners she'd already made to sell on consignment.

After spreading a piece of dark green fabric on her cutting board, Wilma picked up the scissors in readiness to cut several squares. The first snip did not cut well, so she tried again, but it didn't go any better.

"What is wrong with these *scheere*?" She scowled at the scissors. "They're so dull they wouldn't cut hot butter."

Wilma spent the next several minutes searching through her sewing supplies for the sharpener. Apparently either she or Mom had misplaced the metal apparatus, because it was nowhere in sight.

With lips pinched together, Wilma set the scissors aside. "Guess I won't be getting much done here till I get these scheere sharpened."

Wilma ambled out of the room and joined her mother in the kitchen. "When you're finished with the grocery list, I'll go shopping for you—unless you'd rather do it yourself," she offered.

Mom's lips parted slightly. "I thought you were going to do some quilting."

"I was, but I can't cut material with dull scheere, and I don't know what happened to our sharpener." Wilma tipped her head. "Have you seen it, Mom?"

"No, I haven't, and it's been some time since I've needed to use the sharpener."

Wilma heaved a sigh. "Guess I'm the one who used it last, but for the life of me, I can't remember what I did with it."

"If you go shopping for me, you could stop by the fabric store and get a new sharpener." Mom gestured to the narrow notepad on the table. "I'm almost done with my list."

"Okay." Wilma held on to the back of a chair. "Would you like to come along with me?"

"Jah, sure, that would be nice. The two of us haven't gone out shopping together in some time."

"All right. I'll get Blossom hitched to the buggy while you finish your list. Would you like to come out when you're ready, or should I come back inside to get you?"

"I'll come out." Mom lifted her notepad. "I'm almost done, so it shouldn't be long."

"Okay." Wilma picked up her purse and headed out the back door. She looked forward to getting out for a while but hoped they wouldn't run into anyone they knew at the fabric store. There had been too much talk around Reedsville concerning her breakup with Israel, and Wilma wasn't in the mood for more questions or comments.

Belleville, Pennsylvania

As Wilma made her way down the fabric aisle in the Country View Dry Goods store, a lump formed in her throat. Three months ago, she'd purchased the material for her wedding dress here, but it still lay on a shelf in the sewing room at home. She could use the material for one of her quilting projects, but the thought of it made her stomach sour. Keeping it on a shelf where she saw it regularly was not good either.

Maybe I'll put the material in a box when I get home. At least then I won't see it all the time and keep on being reminded that I won't be getting married.

Shaking her head, Wilma hurried to the other side of the room, where sewing supplies and the scissor sharpeners were located. She put a sharpener in her basket and was about to look at some spools of thread, when she saw Susanna Hershberger, a woman from their church district.

"Hello, Wilma." Susanna smiled. "How have you been?"

"I'm doing okay. How about you?"

"Just fine, and so is my family."

"Good to hear." Wilma hoped Susanna wouldn't extend their conversation. She was a gossip, and Wilma wasn't in the mood to hear any tales about anyone who lived in or out of their Amish community in Reedsville.

"I saw you at church last Sunday but didn't get a chance to speak to you during the noon meal afterward."

"It's okay, I understand. You were busy talking to some other women."

Susanna's voice lowered. "I was surprised to hear about your breakup with Israel. I heard through the grapevine that you two were planning a November wedding."

"We were, but—"

"But you didn't want to help raise his nephews. Was that the reason you quit watching the boys and broke up with Israel?"

"Well, yes, but—"

"It may not be my place to say this, but aren't you being rather *eegesinnisch*?"

Wilma bristled. "You think I'm selfish?"

"Well, you did walk away from your responsibility, leaving five young boys without a mother figure."

Wilma's face heated. "Things weren't working out between us."

"Between you and Israel?"

"No. The boys and I did not get along." Wilma didn't know why she felt the need to defend herself. What happened between her, Israel, and his nephews, was none of Susanna's business.

"If you'll excuse me," Wilma said, "I need to pay for what I came here to get and be on my way. My mamm's waiting for me in our carriage. I hope you have a nice rest of your day." Without waiting for Susanna's response, Wilma hurried off to the checkout counter. It was hard to be polite to some people—especially a busybody like Susanna. Wilma could hardly wait to get out of the store.

After paying for the sharpener, Wilma rushed out the door, got into her buggy, and took the reins from her mother. "Sorry for making you wait. It took me longer than expected."

"Did you have trouble finding what you needed?"

"No, but Susanna Herschberger came into the fabric shop and had a few words with me."

Mom tipped her head as she stared at Wilma. "Were they negative words? Is that why your cheeks are so red?"

"Jah, I suppose so." Wilma repeated everything that had been said. "Why is it that some people can't seem to mind their own business?"

Mom placed her hand on Wilma's arm. "Don't worry about what other people say, Daughter. You did what you felt was right when you broke up with Israel, and no one should judge you for it."

"I agree, but it hurt when Susanna accused me of being selfish. She has no idea how difficult those boys can be."

Mom gave Wilma's arm a tap. "I know something that might make you feel better."

"What is it?"

"A visit to the Next Generation Bakery. A whoopie pie or sticky bun might cheer you up."

Wilma licked her lips. "I don't know about that, but it sure would taste good. I'll get Blossom going in that direction now."

Reedsville

When Israel's driver dropped him off at his house that afternoon, he noticed Nate and Micah on the porch, each with a kitten in his lap. Israel smiled, in spite of his fatigue. Today he'd worked harder and later than usual and wished he could go inside and take a nap. But that wouldn't be fair to Dorothy Petersheim, the middle-aged Amish woman he'd hired to stay with the boys while he was at work. She had a husband and three teenage sons to cook the evening meal for every evening. Dorothy had made it clear when she first came to work for Israel that she would only be available to watch the boys until he got home from work. That meant Israel would be responsible for fixing supper for himself as well as his nephews. Truthfully his cooking skills weren't that great.

I sure do miss Wilma, Israel thought as he stepped onto the porch. *And not just for the tasty meals she cooked us.*

He paused, reached down, and placed a hand on each of the boys' heads. "Have you been good for Mrs. Petersheim today?"

Grinning, they looked up at him and bobbed their heads.

"Good to hear."

When Israel opened the front door and stepped inside, Dorothy greeted him with wrinkled brows. "You're home a little later than usual, jah?"

He gave a brief nod. "But I'm here now, so you're free to go whenever you want."

"Okay, good. Today's my Henry's birthday, and I promised to bake him a cake." Dorothy grabbed her handbag and rushed out the door. "See you tomorrow," she called over her shoulder.

Israel looked in the living room and then the kitchen, but he saw no sign of Mark, Ethan, or Josh. When he heard voices upstairs, he realized they were in their room.

Heading back to the kitchen, Israel thought about Wilma again and wondered how she'd been getting along. *Does she miss me as much as I miss her?* He rubbed his chin. *My nephews seem to be getting along pretty well with Dorothy. If they'd only cooperated with Wilma, she would still be here. Was she too harsh with the boys? Did she expect too much?*

Israel opened the bread box, relieved to see that Dorothy had made a fresh loaf of bread. He guessed they'd have sandwiches again tonight. Israel was too tired to cook a hot meal.

He fixed himself a cup of coffee and took a chair at the table. As Israel sat staring at the stove across the room, an image of Wilma came to mind.

She's not going to marry me. I need to accept that. Sure wish I could quit thinking about her all the time and keep my concentration only on raising my sister's sons. If for no other reason, I will do it for Kathryn. Maybe after more time has gone by, my feelings for Wilma will fade, just like the setting sun does every night.

87

Chapter 9

Since it was still early and the boys weren't up, Israel decided to walk down to the phone shack. Dorothy hadn't arrived yet, so this was a good time to check for any messages that may have come in.

A blast of hot air hit Israel in the face when he opened the door to the small wooden building. Typically the weather was hot and humid in the middle of July, and today was no exception.

Israel made sure the door would stay open, and then he took a seat on the wooden stool. As expected, the flashing light on the answering machine indicated that there were messages.

Israel clicked the button and swatted at a fly buzzing overhead as he waited to hear the first message. He was surprised to hear Dorothy's voice, and even more so when Dorothy said she wouldn't be coming to watch the boys this morning. She'd be leaving the area for several weeks to take care of her mother, who had fallen and suffered a broken hip. Dorothy ended the message by saying she'd hired a driver to take her to Lancaster County, where her mother lived, and that she would be leaving shortly. She apologized for any inconvenience this may cause Israel.

"It'll be inconvenient all right," he muttered.

The bishop's elderly wife, Margaret, had been down with a mild case of pneumonia, so Israel couldn't ask her. Finding someone else to be with the boys on the days he had to work might prove to be difficult. And unfortunately it could take some time, so he had no choice but to call his boss and let him know that he wouldn't be in for work this morning. Israel also needed to let his driver know that he would not need a ride today.

He sighed. *This is not a good way to begin the day.*

Since there were no other messages, Israel left the building and started back to the house. Once inside, he went to the kitchen to see about fixing breakfast.

Israel had no more than set some cold cereal on the table, when all five of his nephews plodded into the room in their bare feet.

"What's that on your faces?" Israel moved closer and scrutinized the boys. Every one of them had raised red bumps on their cheeks and forehead.

"We don't know, but my face really itches, and I've got a bad koppweh." Mark flopped into a chair, letting his head fall forward.

"What about the rest of you?" Israel questioned. "Do you also have a headache?"

Ethan and Josh nodded, but the three younger boys only stared at Israel with reddened eyes and pained expressions.

At that moment, Israel realized he had to get the boys in to the see the doctor—hopefully today.

Belleville

Since this was a Wednesday, Wilma had gotten up early and gone to the Livestock Auction and Farmers Market to take Deanna the wall hanging she'd finished, as well as some other quilted items. She hoped they would sell today, but if not, Deanna would take everything to her shop. It seemed like there were more tourists in the area this month, and that usually increased sales of Amish-made items.

"Guder mariye." Deanna smiled when Wilma approached her table and set her tote on the ground.

"Good morning." Wilma glanced at her friend's prominent belly. "How are you feeling these days?"

"Other than a bit top-heavy, not too bad. I'll feel better once the boppli is here though."

"I bet too." Wilma looked around the area. "Have you had any customers yet?"

"Just a few, but it's still early." Deanna gestured to the tote. "Did you bring plenty of items for me to sell?"

"Jah, and I got the wall hanging done."

"Oh good. Why don't you take everything out? We'll display the smaller items on the table and drape the wall hanging over the quilt rack I brought along."

"Sure." Wilma knelt down and was about to open the lid on her tote, when she spotted Abner crouched under the table. He looked at her with big eyes and said, *"Hoscht du wasser gholt?"*

"Yes, I brought some water with me," she replied. "Are you thirsty?"

"Jah." Abner crawled out from under the table and stared up at Wilma with a look of expectation.

She removed a bottle of water from her lunch satchel and handed it to him. "Here you go, little man."

Abner dropped to his knees and crawled to the other side of the table; then he stood up next to his mother. "Wasser, mamm?"

"Yes, you may drink the water Wilma gave you." Deanna removed the lid on the bottle for him.

Wilma grinned as she watched the young boy chug the water. "Where's your husband today?" she asked, looking back at Deanna. "I figured he'd be at the table beside you, selling his handmade birdhouses."

"Oh, Elmer's here all right." Deanna pointed to one of the nearby concession stands. "He went to get a few whoopie pies for us to eat. Knowing Elmer, he will probably come back with more than three. So you're welcome to have one if you like."

"Thanks for offering, but I'd better not. I have several errands to run yet today, so I'd best be on my way."

"Okay. Stop by the house sometime soon. We haven't had a good visit in a while."

"I know. I just haven't felt much like visiting with anyone." Wilma drew a couple of slow, even breaths.

"You're still *umgerennt* over your breakup with Israel, right?"

All Wilma could manage was a slow nod. She was still upset over her broken relationship, and it hurt too much to talk about it. After all, there was nothing to be gained from rehashing the topic— with herself, or anyone else for that matter. It was better if she kept busy and tried not to think about it. That was the only way Wilma could deal with the pain of losing the man she still loved. How grateful she was that she'd only seen Israel from a distance one time since they'd parted ways.

Wilma unloaded her plastic tote and placed the quilted items on the table. "Do you need my help setting them out on display?"

"No thanks. I can manage," Deanna replied.

"Should I leave my empty tote for you to put the items in that don't sell today? I can stop by your house and pick it up tomorrow or the following day."

"Jah, that'll be fine."

Wilma was on the verge of telling her friend

goodbye when Elmer showed up at the table. He handed Deanna a small cardboard box, which he'd carried in one hand while using his cane in the other. It amazed Wilma how well Elmer got around in spite of his vision loss.

"Good morning, Elmer," she said, wondering if he would recognize her voice.

Wilma didn't have to wonder long, for Elmer, having given his wife the box of goodies, reached out to shake her hand. "Mornin', Wilma. How's life been treating you these days?"

"I'm doing all right," she replied. "How about you?"

"With a wife who's sweet as cotton candy and a little boy who loves me unconditionally, I can't complain."

Before Wilma could form a response, Deanna chuckled. "Cotton candy, huh? You surely have a sweet tooth, Husband."

Elmer grinned as he used his cane to help maneuver his way around the table and take a seat beside Deanna. "Should we have a whoopie pie now?"

"If you insist." Deanna bumped his arm with her elbow and opened the box. "I see you bought six chocolate whoopie pies, Husband. Why am I not surprised?"

"Because you know me so well." His brows moved up and down.

"Well, there's more than we can eat in one

sitting." Deanna looked at Wilma. "Are you sure you wouldn't like one?"

Wilma shook her head. "No thanks."

"Okay. I'll see you tomorrow or the next day." Deanna took out two whoopie pies. She handed one to Abner and the other to Elmer. "I need to get these quilted items set out, so I'll have a whoopie pie later."

"Why don't you go ahead and eat it, and I'll set out my things?"

"Okay, if you insist." Deanna reached into the box for another whoopie pie, while Wilma began laying out the pot holders and table runners she'd brought in her tote. Once that was done, she draped her wall hanging over the quilt rack. "Guess I'll be on my way now. You all have a good day."

Reedsville

Wilma had made a few stops after leaving the farmers market this morning, including a lunch break at Taste of the Valley restaurant in Belleville. She hadn't seen anyone she knew there, which had been a relief. Tongues were still wagging among some of the Amish women in their community about the way Wilma had left Israel with no thought of his nephews' needs.

"I did think of them." Wilma clenched Blossom's reins and gritted her teeth. "Those

94

boys didn't like me, and they're better off with someone else taking care of them."

Wilma had heard that Israel hired Dorothy, from his church district, to care for the boys. The older woman was probably a good fit since she wasn't engaged to marry their uncle. Wilma had often thought that if she and Israel hadn't planned to get married, perhaps the boys would have accepted her as their daytime caregiver. She'd convinced herself that the reason Israel's nephews rejected her was because they knew that after she and their uncle got married, Wilma would be living with them full-time.

Wilma clung tighter to the reins as she turned onto Kish Road. "Well, it doesn't matter now, because I'm out of their lives forever. They can have their uncle Israel all to themselves."

Wilma's horse and buggy approached the Mount Nittany Physicians Group, where several doctors practiced family medicine. She was surprised to see Israel and the boys come out of the clinic and head for his horse and buggy.

I wonder if one of them is sick. But then why would Israel have brought them all to the clinic this afternoon? She pursed her lips. *Wouldn't he have just brought the sick child and left the others at home with Dorothy?*

Curious to know what was going on, Wilma directed Blossom into the parking lot and guided her up to the hitching rail next to Israel's horse,

Digger. It was a fitting name, since the gelding was prone to paw at the ground and snort, as though eager to go, just as he was doing now.

Wilma waited until the boys climbed into the carriage before she got out of her buggy. "What's going on?" she asked Israel. "Is one of the children grank?"

Frowning, he nodded. "They're all sick with the *wasserpareble*."

"Oh dear. Chicken pox can be quite contagious, not to mention miserable to deal with. Do you know who they got it from?"

"I'm guessing someone's child at church may have had the pox." Israel's shoulders curled forward. "And now I'll have to take time off work to care for them."

"Won't Dorothy continue to watch them, or has she never had chicken pox?"

"I have no idea. This morning she left a message that she'd be going to Lancaster to take care of her mamm, who has a broken hip." He dropped his gaze and lowered his voice. "So I have no choice but to stay home and take care of the boys."

"I had the wasserpareble when I was a girl, so I'm willing to care for them." The words slipped out of Wilma's mouth before she had a chance to think things through.

"Really? You'd do that for us?"

"Jah."

His eyes brightened, and he reached his hand toward her but then quickly pulled it back. "Danki, Wilma. I appreciate your willingness to help out during this temporary situation."

"You're welcome. I'll be over bright and early tomorrow morning. Don't worry about the boys, because I promise I'll take good care of them."

"I know you will. Thanks again."

Wilma got back in her buggy and backed Blossom away from the rail. She bit down on her bottom lip until she tasted blood. *I hope I made the right decision, because I have no idea how the boys will respond to me while they're sick. Will things go better or worse than before?*

Chapter 10

With a jug of water in hand, Israel trudged up the stairs to make sure the boys had everything they needed before going to sleep. Josh, Nate, and Micah shared one room where there were two beds. Ethan and Mark slept across the hall in the second bedroom. The third upstairs room was currently filled with boxes of things Israel had not emptied since he'd bought the house last year. He needed to get them emptied and clear out the room so it could be used as another bedroom, but he hadn't found the time.

Israel hadn't found the time to do a lot of things since the boys came to live with him.

It would be easier if he had a wife to share in the responsibilities. But he couldn't imagine being married to anyone except Wilma.

Israel's thoughts came to a halt when he entered the younger boys' bedroom. Micah and Nate shared one of the beds, and Josh had the other. The poor little guys looked miserable as they lay there staring up at him with the saddest eyes.

Israel poured fresh water into their glasses, which had been sitting on the small table between the beds, and asked them to sit up and take a drink.

"My belly itches somethin' awful." Nate pulled

up his pajama top, exposing several more raised bumps.

Israel shook his head. "Don't scratch them, or you could end up with scars. The rash might even become infected."

"It's kinda hard not to scratch when somethin' itches really bad," Josh interjected.

"I know, but you must do as the doctor said." Israel went to the other side of the room and opened the bottom dresser drawer where some of the boys' winter clothes were kept. He took out three pairs of gloves and helped the boys put them on. "This will help so that you won't be able to scratch at the bumps with your fingernails."

"I don't want these." Tears spilled from Micah's eyes and rolled down his red cheeks.

"Do we hafta wear 'em all the time?" Nate questioned.

"You'll only have to wear them at night, unless you scratch a lot during the day. If that happens, you may need to wear them most of the time." Israel picked up the bottle of Calamine lotion sitting on top of the dresser. Using a cotton ball, he dabbed some of the lotion on Micah's forehead and belly. With fresh cotton balls, he did the same for Nate and Josh. "There, does that feel better?"

The boys bobbed their heads.

"Good. Now I want you to close your eyes and try to sleep. Tomorrow morning Wilma will be here. She will take care of you while I'm at work."

Micah said nothing, but Nate frowned. "We don't like her, Uncle Israel. Why does she hafta come and stay with us?"

"Because Dorothy won't be available and Wilma volunteered to come. She had the wasserpareble when she was a girl, so there's no worry of her being exposed to them."

Josh groaned. "I wish you woulda found someone else."

Israel didn't respond as he shut off the battery-operated light on the dresser and picked up the jug of water. "Good night, boys. I'll see you in the morning."

He left the room and went across the hall to the bedroom Ethan and Mark shared. He found them sitting up in bed wide awake.

"How long till these itchy bumps are gone?" Ethan asked as Israel poured water in the boys' glasses.

"Somewhere between five to ten days, but you'll be contagious until the skin lesions have fully crusted," Israel replied.

Mark frowned. "I hate bein' grank."

"No one enjoys being sick." Israel took a seat on the end of the bed. "When I was a boy and got chicken pox I was cranky as a dog with a sore foot." He reached for the bottle of Calamine lotion and a cotton ball. "If you two will pull up your pajama tops I'll dab some of this on your pox. It'll help them not to itch so much."

Ethan and Mark did as Israel said and then drank some water.

Israel spoke again as he dabbed the lotion over the boys' angry-looking red blisters. "Wilma will be here in the morning to spend the day with you while I'm at work, and I want you to cooperate and do whatever she says. Ya hear?"

Mark's chin jutted out. "Don't see why she has to come back here again."

"Because Dorothy has to go to Lancaster to care for her mother." Israel hoped the boys wouldn't put up a fuss or create problems for Wilma. He needed her help more than ever right now—at least until he could find someone else who'd be willing to care for his nephews. Although it would not change anything between them, he appreciated the fact that Wilma was willing to help out during this difficult time. Israel didn't feel equipped to take on the role of his nephews' father. They needed a woman's hand too, which meant, like it or not, he may have to look for a wife, even if he didn't love her the way he did Wilma. Israel was still hurt by her refusal to marry him. He believed she must not love him enough or she would have been willing to make the sacrifice of helping him raise the boys. Perhaps he should consider one of the other single Amish women in the area, but even if he did find a suitable woman, when would he have the time to court her?

When Wilma went to the kitchen the following morning, she fixed herself a cup of herbal tea, hoping it would calm her nerves. She'd had trouble sleeping the night before, worried about how today would go when she went to Israel's to care for the boys. Since they were sick and would likely stay in bed most of the day, her concerns about them getting into mischief were probably unfounded. Even so, they might not cooperate when she told them what they needed to do because of having chicken pox.

"Are you sure that helping out at Israel's today is the right thing to do?"

Mom's question pushed Wilma's contemplations aside. "Uh, yes . . . and I need to get going soon." Wilma drank the rest of her tea and placed the cup in the sink. "I'll take some quilting along to work on while the boys are sleeping—which I'm sure they'll do plenty of—at least for the next few days."

"If those boys were so naughty when they felt good, just imagine how they might act up now that they're sick. You may want to reconsider your decision, Daughter."

"I have considered it already, and it's the right thing to do. This will only be temporary, and no matter how terrible the boys may act toward me, I'll manage to get through it. So please stop trying to talk me out of going."

"I'm sorry." Mom got up from the table and came over to give Wilma a hug. "I'll be praying that everything goes okay with those rowdy boys. I only want what's best for you."

"I know, Mom, but I'll be fine, so there's no need for you to worry." Wilma grabbed her purse and started for the door.

"Aren't you going to eat some breakfast?"

Wilma snatched a banana from the fruit bowl. "I'll eat this on the way over to Israel's."

"What about your quilting tote? I thought you were going to take it along so you could get some quilting done."

"Oh, that's right." Wilma picked up the plastic tote. "Oh, and don't expect me for supper this evening. I plan to stay and fix something for Israel and the boys, so I'll eat there too."

Mom's lips compressed as she gave a slow nod.

"I'll see you this evening," Wilma said before going out the door.

After Wilma left, Esther added more hot coffee to her cup and fretted about Wilma as she sat at the table.

A short time later, her husband entered the house through the back door and came into the kitchen. "I helped Wilma get Blossom ready to go, and she's on her way," John said. "Think now

103

I'll have a cup of *kaffi* with my breakfast before I head out to work."

Esther got up from the table and poured it for him. After he sat down, she decided to voice her concerns. "I am worried about our daughter."

His brows lifted. "How come?"

"I hope she doesn't change her mind and marry Israel after all."

"Why would she? Wilma's already made it clear that the boys don't care for her, not to mention her difficulty in getting them to mind."

"That may be true, but Israel might put some pressure on her—make our daughter feel obligated to marry him because he knows how much she cares for him."

John blew on his coffee and took a drink. "Would it be such a bad thing if she did end up marrying him? I mean, if she loves Israel and he loves her—"

"Their love for each other has nothing to do with it. If the boys gave Wilma a hard time because they didn't like her, then it would put a strain on her marriage." Esther paused to scoop a few crumbs off the table after pouring their breakfast cereal into a bowl. "Those children may try to turn Israel against Wilma, and when she reprimands them for anything, he might take their side. That could cause a lot of dissension in the home."

He reached over and patted Esther's arm. "Try

not to worry. Just leave it in God's hands and let our daughter make her own decisions."

Esther clamped her mouth shut. Her husband obviously didn't understand the seriousness of this situation. *I can only hope and pray that Wilma doesn't sacrifice her happiness for the good of Israel and those troublesome boys.*

When Wilma arrived at Israel's house, she found him in the kitchen, stirring something in a steaming kettle.

"What are you doing?" she questioned. "I hope you didn't make breakfast."

He looked at her and nodded. "I made some oatmeal, but it's kind of lumpy. Thought I'd save you the trouble of fixing something for the boys."

"It's no trouble." Wilma set down her tote and purse and moved over to the stove. "Here, let me see if I can get some of those lumps out."

"Danki." Israel stepped aside, allowing Wilma to take over. "I surely appreciate you coming over here to help out."

She smiled but didn't look up at him. "How are the boys doing?"

"They're itching pretty bad, but I put gloves on their hands to keep them from scratching at the blisters."

"Chicken pox can be miserable. Even though it's been several years since I had it, I still remember how badly the bumps itched and how

I struggled not to scratch them." Wilma quit stirring the oatmeal long enough to pull up the dress sleeve on her right arm. "As you can see, I was left with a few scars from having scratched so much."

Israel reached out his hand as though he might touch Wilma's arm, but he quickly pulled it back. "I did my fair share of scratching when I had the wasserpareble too." Israel pointed to the top of his head. "Had one get infected up here, and now no hair grows from that spot."

Wilma had never noticed it, but then she'd never really studied the top of Israel's head. "Are the boys still in bed?" she asked instead of commenting on Israel's bald area.

"Jah. I told them I'd bring breakfast up to them if they didn't feel like coming down here to eat."

"Okay." Wilma gestured to the kettle she'd been stirring. "I think this is creamy enough now, so I'll dish it into bowls."

"All right. I'll leave you to it. I need to head out for work now anyways." He grabbed his lunch pail and put on his straw hat. "I hope things go well for you and the kinner today."

"Danki. I'll do my best to make sure they're as comfortable as possible."

He started for the door but paused and looked at her over his shoulder. "There's a bottle of Calamine lotion in each of their rooms. I put some on them last night, and it seemed to help some."

"I will do that too," she replied. "I'll also make sure that they stay hydrated."

"Thank you again for coming to our rescue. Don't know what we'd do without you right now."

Wilma's cheeks warmed. "Have a good day, Israel."

"You too." He gave her a nod and hurried out the door.

Wilma heaved a sigh. It was time to head upstairs and check on the boys.

When she reached the top of the stairs, Wilma heard whimpering. She opened the first door she came to and stepped inside. Josh lay in one of the beds by himself, and the two youngest boys shared the other bed. With gloved hands, all three of them were visibly sweating as they attempted to remove the gloves with their teeth. Tears ran down Micah's face as he struggled with the glove on his left hand.

Wilma understood why Israel had put gloves on the boys, and having had it done to her when she was sick with the pox, she understood the boys' frustration and desire to get them off.

"I'll take your gloves off if you promise not to scratch those itchy bumps." Wilma spoke in a soothing tone.

Micah and Nate held their hands out to her. "We promise," they said in unison.

Wilma removed their gloves, but when she

started toward Josh's bed, he shook his head. "Don't need your help. I can do this myself." With eyes squinted and mouth opened slightly, he grabbed the fingers on one glove in his teeth. When he gave it a tug, the glove came off. "See, what'd I tell ya?"

The boy's smug expression made Wilma bristle, but she chose to ignore it.

"Breakfast is ready," she said. "Would you like me to bring it up, or would you rather go down to the kitchen to eat it?"

"I'm goin' downstairs." Josh pulled his other glove off and clambered out of bed. Nate and Micah followed suit.

Wilma waited until they'd left the room, and then she went across the hall to where the door was partially open. Ethan and Mark lay on the bed with their eyes closed, but Wilma had a hunch that neither of them was sleeping. How could they be with the *thump, thump, thump* of their brothers' feet as they tromped down the stairs?

Wilma stood at the foot of the bed and gave the mattress a few pushes with her hands. "Wake up, sleepyheads. Your breakfast is waiting downstairs."

"I ain't hungerich." Mark rolled onto his side, facing the window.

"Me neither," his brother said.

"I won't force you to eat, but you need to drink plenty of liquids."

No response. The brothers lay there unmoving.

Wilma placed both arms behind her back, gripping one wrist with the other hand. At least the three youngest boys had cooperated fairly well, and she needed to get downstairs so she could feed them.

She moved toward the door then turned back to face the bed. "If you change your mind, come on down, or give me a holler and I'll bring a bowl of oatmeal up to you."

The room was quiet—not a peep from either of the boys. Gritting her teeth, Wilma left the room and started down the stairs. *If these children won't cooperate with me, how in the world am I supposed to take care of them?*

Chapter 11

Y ou look *tired* this evening," Wilma's mother
    said when Wilma got home.

"I am tired," she admitted. "It was a long day."
She poured herself a glass of water from the jug
on the kitchen counter and gulped it down. "Even
Blossom seemed tired on the ride home. I think
she picked up on my fatigue."

"How did it go with Israel's nephews?" Mom
asked.

"As well as can be expected, I guess." Wilma
set her glass on the counter and poured more
water into it. "The boys were pretty miserable
and spent most of the day in bed, which meant I
made a lot of trips up and down the stairs, seeing
to their needs."

Mom wiped a splotch of ketchup from the table
that had apparently been left from her and Dad's
supper. "Are you going back tomorrow?"

"Of course. I promised to help out, and I won't
go back on my word." Wilma glanced through
the doorway leading to the living room. "Where's
Dad? I figured he might be studying for his
sermon, since he will no doubt be preaching this
coming Sunday."

Mom shook her head. "It'll be our off-Sunday,
remember?"

"Oh, that's right. I must be more tired than I realized to forget a thing like that." Wilma glanced out the kitchen window. "Oh, there's Dad. I see him coming out of the barn now."

A few minutes later, Wilma's father entered the house and came into the kitchen. "I put your gaul away for you, Wilma," he said.

"Danki, Dad. I was going to do that right away, but feeling thirsty, I came in here first to get a drink of wasser."

"No problem." He hung his straw hat on a wall peg near the door and stepped between Mom and Wilma. "The hot temperature we had today has dropped some, giving us a nice evening. Why don't the three of us go out and sit on the porch? We can visit and enjoy watching the fireflies put on their nightly summer show of lights."

"Good idea," Mom agreed. "I'll bring out some of the applesauce cake I made today. Would anyone like a cup of tea to go with it?"

Dad shook his head. "I'd rather have kaffi."

Mom shook her finger at him. "You drink too much coffee, John. Besides, it'll keep you awake if you have some this close to us going to bed."

"I'll stay up later than usual then." He looked over at her and winked.

Mom chuckled and poked his arm.

Wilma enjoyed watching this kind of playful banter between her parents. She had no doubt about the love they felt for each other. Despite any ups and downs they may have had in their marriage, her dad always kept a positive attitude and liked to tease. Wilma's mother had always been more serious, but her response to his teasing was never mean.

Wilma envied her folks and their devotion to each other. It was something she'd hoped for when she got married. Her dream of wedded bliss had been shattered when Israel took on the care of his nephews.

"Okay, ladies, I'm going outside. I'll shoo any *katze* off the chairs on the porch."

Dad's comment scattered Wilma's thoughts, and she smiled, reflecting on how some of their friendly cats liked to exchange the bales of straw they slept on in the barn for one of the chairs on the porch.

After Dad went out the door, Wilma got out plates and forks while Mom cut the cake and made fresh coffee and two cups of cinnamon tea.

When they took the refreshments outside, Wilma wasn't surprised to see her father sitting in one of the chairs with a gray-and-white cat in his lap.

He looked up at Wilma and grinned. "I couldn't talk this critter outa my chair, so I decided to share it with her."

Wilma placed the plates of cake on the small table positioned next to Dad. "I hope you're not planning to share your piece of *kuche* with that mangy cat."

He jiggled his thick brows while stroking the feline's head. "Maybe just a little piece."

Mom placed their beverages on the table and took a seat beside him. Wilma thought her mother might say something to Dad about the cat, but Mom just smiled and handed Dad his cake. Of course he promptly pulled off a small piece and fed the cat.

Wilma picked up one of the teacups and took a sip as she stared into the yard to watch the light show put on by fluttering fireflies.

I wonder what Israel is doing tonight, she thought. *Is he managing okay with the boys?* Wilma shifted on her unyielding wooden chair. *I bet if those children weren't grank, they'd be outside right now, catching fireflies in a jar to watch it light up, the way my siblings and I did when we were youngsters.*

Israel had no more than gotten settled in a chair to read the latest issue of *The Budget*, when he heard the patter of footsteps coming down the stairs. A few seconds later, Josh appeared.

"I can't sleep, Uncle Israel."

"How come?"

" 'Cause I itch all over and just wanna *gratz*."

"That's why I put *hensching* on your hands." Israel frowned. "But I see you've taken them off.

You know what'll happen if you scratch. You don't want to end up with scars or an infection, do you?"

The boy shook his head.

"All right then, let's go back upstairs and I'll put those gloves back on." Israel wished there was something more he could do that would help the pox not to itch so much. No doubt when it was all said and done, some or maybe all of his nephews would end up with a few scars, the way he had.

Israel put his hand on Josh's shoulder and gave it a few pats. "After the gloves are on, I'll get you settled into bed. I bet Micah and Nate are sleeping already." *At least I hope they are. The most important thing those boys need right now is sleep.*

Israel followed Josh up the stairs, and when they entered the bedroom, he was pleased to see that the two younger boys had fallen asleep.

After Josh climbed into his bed, Israel put more Calamine lotion on the boy's itchy spots. "Good night," he whispered before turning off the switch on the battery-operated light. "I'll see you in the morning."

"Okay."

Israel went quietly out of the room and took a peek at Mark and Ethan in the room across the hall. Seeing that they were both asleep, he descended the stairs. *Now for a few quiet moments to myself.*

114

Feeling the need for some fresh air, Israel went outside and took a seat at the picnic table. He looked up at the star-studded sky and dropped his gaze to the fireflies rising from the grass.

It was hard not to think about Wilma on a night such as this. He remembered how much he'd enjoyed their buggy rides and long walks during the evening hours last summer when they'd been courting. Oh, how he missed those wonderful days.

"Nothing like this summer's turned out to be," he mumbled. "First our courtship was cut short when the boys came to live with me, and now there'll be no marriage either."

It was difficult not to feel bitter and resentful. Some days Israel's bitterness was toward Wilma for breaking their engagement. Other times Israel caught himself feeling resentment toward his nephews, and even their mother for dying. None of these feelings were good or even legitimate, but they kept coming to the surface. Israel had been in prayer about his private thoughts and negative attitude. As a Christian, he must rely on God to help him do and say the right things, especially toward the boys.

Above all else, Micah, Nate, Josh, Ethan, and Mark are my first priority, Israel reminded himself once again. He bowed his head and prayed, *Lord, help me to feel joy while raising the boys—not to see it as an obligation.*

• • •

Wilma yawned as a feeling of exhaustion overtook her the following day. She'd been running up and down the stairs all morning and had finally asked the boys to come down and rest on the cots she'd set up in the enclosed porch where sunshine streamed through the four windows. Having them all downstairs made things easier, and the porch allowed the boys to see the birds flitting from tree to tree, as well as whatever else went on in the yard.

For the moment, they all slept, which was good, because at least they weren't giving Wilma a hard time. She was tempted to take a nap herself. *That would not be a good idea,* she told herself. *I might sleep too long and wouldn't get the rest of my baking done.*

She turned back to the counter and picked up the wooden rolling pin. Soon two pans had been filled with pie crusts, ready to go in the oven. While they baked, Wilma would make up the chocolate cream filling.

Wilma hadn't gotten any quilting done so far today, but she didn't mind. She'd always enjoyed baking and hoped to make some sourdough rolls before it was time to start supper. If it hadn't been for the five sick boys lying on the sunny porch, Wilma would have almost felt like a newly married woman here in Israel's kitchen. But no newlyweds she knew had a readymade family.

Redirecting her thoughts, Wilma got busy and made the pie filling. After the crusts were evenly browned, she poured the filling in and went out the back door to take the laundry she'd done this morning off the line.

When Wilma came into the house with a basket full of the boys' clean clothes, she went upstairs to fold and put them away.

Upon returning to the kitchen sometime later, her mouth nearly fell open. Most of the filling was gone from one of the pies and a wooden spoon covered in chocolate lay on the counter nearby.

Wilma pressed her lips together and breathed deeply through her nose. Apparently one or more of the boys had done this, and she didn't know whether to laugh or cry.

She marched on out to the porch, prepared to do some scolding, but halted when she saw the children lying on their cots with their eyes closed and big smiles on their chocolate-smeared faces. Although the little stinkers had not asked permission to taste any of the pies, she couldn't fault them for wanting to eat something that would bring a little joy into their lives. In addition to the sadness of losing their mother, Israel's nephews were having a hard time dealing with chicken pox. So for this time, at least, she would let the matter go.

Chapter 12

By Friday of the following week, the boys seemed to be doing better, but Wilma could tell that boredom had set in. She needed to find something for them to do before they created more mischief.

Yesterday Wilma had discovered the lid on her quilting tote had been removed, and she'd found pins, needles, and thread scattered everywhere. She had questioned the boys, but no one admitted to having done it. Wilma was tempted to punish each of the boys, thinking they all may have been involved, but that wouldn't be fair if the mess had been created by only one of them.

Wilma bent to gather the dirty clothes in Mark and Ethan's room, strewn on the floor and even under the bed. Taking care of five children was a full-time job. She wondered how their mother had done it.

She dropped the last article of clothing into the basket, lifted it up, and stood. *All I can say is, Kathryn must have had a lot of patience, or maybe she chose to look the other way and turn a deaf ear to what was going on in her home.* That would not be an easy thing to do. Wilma and her siblings had been obedient when they were children, so to her way of thinking, Mark, Ethan,

Josh, Nate, and Micah should be too. But since they were not, she needed to come up with a way to keep those boys occupied so they'd have less time to think up things to do that would create more problems for her.

Wilma left the bedroom and made her way across the hall, where she was faced with more clothes on the floor. As she knelt to pick them up, her thoughts went to Israel. Ever since the boys had gotten sick and she'd come here to help out, Israel had said very few words to her and rarely even looked at her.

He's either angry with me or hurt because I called off our wedding, she told herself. *And I can't really blame him for that. If it had been the other way around, I'd be upset too, but I wish he could understand and accept my decision without any hard feelings.*

Wilma picked up the clothes and put them in the basket, determined not to dwell on her broken relationship with the man she still loved and wished she could marry.

"Wishes don't make things happen," she muttered. Wilma thought about all the times when she was a girl that she had wished on a star, searched for and found a four-leaf clover, rubbed a rabbit's foot, and crossed her fingers, hoping she would get something she wanted. When Wilma's father found out what she'd been doing, he told her that all those silly things were

119

superstitious, and none would bring good luck or grant anyone's wishes. "One thing I want you to always remember," he'd said, "is that God knows what is best for each of us. If we have wants or needs, we need to pray and seek His will."

My daed gave me good advice, which I have forgotten to take. Wilma closed her eyes and lowered her head. *Heavenly Father, You know the desire I've had to marry Israel and be a good wife. If there's any way possible that it could work out, please reveal Your will to me.*

A few hours later, while Wilma was hanging out the laundry, she overheard the two older boys talking about the pie their little brothers had gotten into the previous week and how they were surprised that Wilma never said anything to them about it. "She must have known that one of us did it," Mark said. "I wonder if she said anything to Uncle Israel about the pie."

"If she did," Ethan commented, "he never said anything to us."

"Maybe she's makin' a list of all the bad things we've done and plans to give it to Uncle Israel when the sheet of paper is full."

Wilma stepped out from behind the sheet she'd just hung. "I will not be giving your uncle a list, but I would appreciate it if you boys tried to behave and would ask me if you wanted to try a piece of pie or any other dessert or snacks I've made."

The boys gave a slow nod and mumbled, "Okay."

"And I'll tell our little brothers too," Mark added.

"Danki." Wilma was surprised by their cooperation. She hoped Mark meant what he'd said. She glanced up at the sky, and an idea popped into her head. "Say, I know something you all might enjoy."

"What's that?" Ethan folded his arms and tipped his head.

"Why don't you get Josh, Nate, and Micah? Then the six of us will spread a big blanket on the grass and lie down for a while."

Mark's brows lowered. "What for?"

"Oh, just to relax and look at the clouds," she replied.

"Whatever." The boy shrugged. "Want me to get the blanket and call the rest of my brothers?"

"Yes, please. While you take care of that, I'll get the remainder of the laundry hung." She turned and watched as Mark went into the house.

By the time he returned with a blanket, Wilma had finished putting the last pair of socks on the line.

"Okay now, if four of you will each grab a corner of the blanket, you can spread it out on the grass."

Mark, Ethan, Josh, and Nate did as she asked, and a short time later, they all lay on the blanket. Wilma asked the boys to look up at the clouds and study their shapes.

Ethan wrinkled his nose. "That seems kinda dumm to me. They're just a bunch of puffy *weiss wolke*."

"Oh no, they're not just white clouds." She pointed to a cluster of clouds directly above them. "Do you know what that looks like to me?"

The boys all shook their heads.

"The big puffy cloud above our heads reminds me of a whale."

"What's a whale?" Micah asked.

"It's a fish, *dummkopp*." Josh snorted. "Don't you know anything?"

Micah's chin trembled. "I ain't dumb."

"That's right," Wilma agreed. "And there will be no name-calling here on this blanket. Do you all understand?"

"Jah," the boys said in unison.

"When I was a girl, I used to enjoy lying on the grass and looking up at the clouds to identify all sorts of animals and objects from their different shapes. You see, boys, not all clouds are the same. They can take on many shapes as they roll across the sky, right before our eyes."

The boys remained quiet until Wilma asked them to tell her what things they saw when they looked at the clouds.

Nate pointed at one. "I see a snake, slithering real slow through the blue sky."

"That's interesting." Wilma looked over at Josh. "What do you see?"

"A prancing horse." He pointed. "It's right up there."

"That cloud over there looks like a kitten curled into a ball," Ethan commented.

"Puh!" Mark flapped his hand. "I don't see no animals—just a bunch of clouds that look like cotton."

"Yes, some of them do resemble balls of cotton," Wilma agreed.

"Look, there's a giant pillow!" Micah's eyes widened as he pointed to the sky.

Wilma smiled. "You might call them *sky pillows*."

They all bobbed their heads, and Wilma went into teaching mode to tell the boys the scientific names of certain types of clouds. "The high-level cloud types are cirrus, cirrostratus, and cirrocumulus. The middle clouds are altostratus and altocumulus. The low clouds are stratus, stratocumulus, and nimbostratus. Then there are clouds with vertical development, and they are called cumulus and cumulonimbus."

Josh pursed his lips, then opened them wide and said, "Wow! Those are some really big words you were usin'. How do you know all that stuff, Wilma?"

"I read about cloud formations in the encyclopedia."

The boys seemed fascinated by all of this information and began to ask questions.

"What are clouds made of?" Nate wanted to know.

"Even though they look like giant cotton balls, clouds are actually made up of water droplets that are so tiny and light, they float through the air. When a lot of these droplets float upward into the sky and hold on to each other, clouds are formed," she explained.

"But how do they get their shapes?" Ethan questioned.

"From the air that surrounds them. You see," Wilma explained, "air temperature is always changing, which affects the shapes of the clouds. Since clouds are made up of millions of tiny pieces of water, when they are high up in the sky where the air is very cold, the water droplets freeze into floating ice crystals. Sometimes, when we see clouds way, way up in the sky, they look like wispy strands."

"Like spaghetti?" This question came from Nate.

"Sort of." Wilma nodded. "When the air is windy, it pushes and pulls clouds, causing them to be squeezed and stretched in different directions. That's when you can see some pretty interesting shapes."

"Wow!" Josh gave a whistle. "I never knew so much about the clouds before."

Wilma smiled. It surprised her that she was actually enjoying herself. The boys seemed to be having fun with this game as well. Maybe there was some hope of them responding more favorably to her. Now she needed to think of some more fun things for all of them to do together.

When Israel stepped into the kitchen late that afternoon, he was surprised to see that the table had been set. His mouth salivated as a pleasant aroma coming from the stove welcomed him.

"Your supper is ready, but I won't be joining you and the boys this evening." Wilma turned from where she stood at the stove.

"Oh?"

"I have plans to have supper with someone else this evening and need to be on my way soon, so I'm glad you got home a little early today."

Israel merely nodded and said, "Okay. I'll go back out and get your horse hitched to the buggy."

"There's no need for that. I'm sure you're tired from working all day, and I can take care of Blossom myself." Wilma stirred whatever was cooking on the stove and placed a lid on top of the kettle. "I made chicken-noodle soup for your supper, and there's also some fresh sourdough bread to go with it." She gestured to the breadbasket on the table.

"Sounds good. Danki." He paused and forced himself to look directly at her. "Guess I'll see you Monday morning then."

"Jah, and I'll make sure to be here on time." She gave a brief nod. "Oh, and I thought you should know that the boys felt a little better today, so maybe they'll have a better weekend than last."

"I hope so." Israel said goodbye and headed for the living room, where he found all five boys sprawled out on sleeping bags, but none of them were asleep.

"How was your day?" he asked, taking a seat on one of the hard-backed chairs. "Have you had less itching?"

Looking more bright-eyed than he had last week, Josh sat up and nodded. "Wilma filled the washtub with warm water and oatmeal, and we all took turns takin' a bath."

"Jah," Ethan interjected. "It took away some of the itching."

Israel smiled. "Glad to hear it."

"We looked at sky pillows today." Grinning, Nate sat up.

"*Himmel kissi.*" Micah pointed upward.

"Is that so?" Israel tipped his head. "And just what is a sky pillow?"

"It's a *wolk*," Josh responded. "We saw all kinds of interesting shapes."

"Jah." Mark bobbed his head. "Wilma told us about many different kinds of clouds."

"That's nice. Sounds like you all had a good day and learned something interesting besides." Israel gestured to the open kitchen door. "Wilma made a pot of soup for our supper. Should we all go in and eat?"

The boys scrambled to their feet. "I'm hungerich!" Nate shouted as he raced out of the room, followed by his brothers.

Rising from his chair, Israel shook his head. *I guess Wilma was right about the boys feeling some better. They seem to be getting their old spunk back.*

His chin dipped slightly. *I wonder if Wilma will be having supper with some available man in our community this evening. Is it possible that she's already being courted by someone and I just haven't heard about it?*

Israel lifted his chin. *Well, it's none of my business. Wilma has a right to do as she pleases now that we're no longer engaged to be married. The only thing that should concern me is taking care of my sister's boys.*

Chapter 13

As Wilma guided her horse toward Deanna and Elmer's place, she reflected on how her day had gone with the boys. What a nice relaxing time they'd all had watching the clouds and naming off the various things they saw.

She smiled, remembering how, later in the day, Micah had fallen asleep in her arms as she told the boys about some of the fun things she and her siblings had done to entertain themselves when they were children. The boys had commented from time to time and asked several questions. Wilma was touched when Ethan talked about some of the fun things they'd done when their mother was alive, like fishing and swimming in the pond near the back of their parents' property. Mark even talked about their father for a bit. Both Josh and Nathan joined in the conversation.

Reminiscing and getting their feelings out was healthy for the boys. As far as Wilma could tell, until now the children had been holding things in, which could have had something to do with their misbehavior. It was bad enough that Israel's nephews had lost their father, but losing their mother too was unthinkable. Wilma couldn't imagine how she would have felt as a child if she'd lost either of her parents. Even as an adult she enjoyed spending time with her folks and felt thankful for everything they had done for her during childhood.

Wilma's musings ended when Elmer and Deanna's place came into view. She guided Blossom up the lane and had her stop at the hitching rail.

Once the horse had been taken care of, Wilma made her way to the house. As she stepped onto the porch, the door opened and Deanna greeted her with a smile. "I'm glad you could make it. You're right on time for supper."

"Danki for inviting me. It's always nice to enjoy a meal with good friends."

"We have a visitor from Indiana with us this evening," Deanna said as she led the way down the hall.

Before Wilma could ask any questions, they'd entered the living room. Elmer sat beside a young, cleanly shaven Amish man with hair the color of straw.

Both men stopped talking and stood. "Good evening, Wilma," Elmer said. "I heard you and Deanna talking in the hall, and now I'd like you to meet my cousin Aaron Bontrager. He and his folks moved to Indiana when I was a boy."

It always amazed Wilma that Elmer could identify her—especially when she and Deanna had spoken only a few words far from where he sat. "It's nice to meet you, Aaron." She smiled.

"Nice to meet you too." Aaron approached her and extended his hand.

Wilma observed the strength and warmth of his hand as she clasped it. "How long will you be in our area?" she asked after he returned to his seat.

"I'm not sure yet, but maybe indefinitely if I find the right job."

"My cousin works in masonry," Elmer put in. "A few years ago he taught school."

"Wilma used to be a schoolteacher," Deanna interjected. "But now she makes quilted items to sell in my shop."

"Teaching has its rewards," Aaron said. "Though with it comes a certain kind of stress."

"You mean dealing with the scholars who won't cooperate?" Wilma asked.

He nodded. "Some stubborn kinner can be difficult at times."

"How well I know." Wilma was tempted to mention the situation she'd faced with Israel and his nephews, but she thought it best not to say anything—especially since she'd just met Aaron. He might think she was a terrible person for refusing to marry a man because he'd become the guardian of five energetic boys. Engaging in a conversation about something so personal with a near stranger was not something Wilma would normally do.

"Supper's ready," Deanna said. "I'll get Abner

now, and we can all meet at the kitchen table." She hurried from the room.

Elmer got up, and using his white cane to navigate, he led the way to the kitchen.

Once again, Wilma marveled at this man's proficiency in dealing with the challenge of his disability. Deanna's determined husband had come a long way since the accident that had taken his sight.

After everyone was seated and silent prayers had been said, Deanna passed the platter of fried chicken around. Next came mashed potatoes and gravy, followed by creamed corn, steamed green beans, and a basket full of fluffy biscuits.

Wilma felt guilty when she thought about the soup she'd left behind for Israel and the boys. It paled in comparison to this tantalizing feast. She wished now that she'd made them something a little more substantial and interesting to eat.

I'll make up for it when I go there on Monday, she told herself. *I might even fix something really nice for dessert.*

"This is good *supp*." Josh smacked his lips.

"Jah, the soup is pretty tasty, all right," Israel agreed. "It would taste even better if Wilma was here eating it with us."

"Wilma takes good care of us," Ethan said. "We like her, Uncle Israel."

The other boys, including Mark, bobbed their heads.

Surprised by Ethan's statement, and his brothers' agreement, Israel blinked several times in succession. "But I thought—"

"Can we keep her?" This unexpected question came from Nate. The boy leaned forward as he grinned at Israel from across the table.

Taken aback, Israel stammered, "Uh, boys, Wilma is not ours to keep. She has her own life to lead."

Micah's chin quivered, and Israel figured if he didn't change the subject right away, the boy might start bawling.

He pushed the basket of crackers in the direction where the two youngest boys sat. "Would you like some of these in your soup?"

They both shook their heads.

Great. Israel pulled the basket back and took a few crackers himself. He crumbled them up and let them drop into his bowl of soup. *Why do these children have to get a fondness for Wilma now? It would have helped if they'd felt that way in the beginning, before she broke our engagement. Of course, just because the boys have changed their minds about Wilma doesn't mean she's changed her mind about them. If she had, surely she would have said something to me. Besides, she may already have another suitor, and I'm not sure I can trust her now.*

• • •

The next day as Wilma sat beside her quilting frame, her thoughts ran in several directions. In some ways she was glad to have the weekend to herself. It gave her the chance to help Mom with some things around the house, as well as catch up on some quilting. On the other hand, Wilma missed seeing Israel's nephews. As strange as it seemed, she'd formed an attachment to them. Although they still did some mischievous things and made messes they didn't clean up without prompting, the boys responded better to her than she'd ever expected.

Since Dorothy hadn't returned from caring for her mother yet, Wilma felt a responsibility to continue staying with the boys while Israel was at work. She found herself looking forward to Monday, when she would see them again. There had been moments, like Friday when she and the boys had studied the clouds together or earlier in the week when she'd enlisted the boys' help in making homemade ice cream, that Wilma almost felt like she was their mother. Next week she planned to make a batch of maple syrup cookies and would call on the boys to help with that too.

Wilma added more pins to the pieces of fabric she was about to stitch by hand. Later today Wilma planned to take the finished crib-size quilt over to Deanna's shop, along with a few other quilted items she'd managed to get done last week.

She reflected on how much she'd enjoyed having supper at Deanna and Elmer's house. Abner had kept her entertained with his unpredictable antics. Wilma had also enjoyed visiting with Elmer's cousin after the meal, when Deanna suggested they all go outside and look at the stars. Aaron seemed like a nice man and easily engaged her in conversation. She was surprised he wasn't married by now. Surely he'd had plenty of women interested in him.

Wilma folded the completed quilt and placed it inside her tote. *Maybe he's not even looking for a wife,* she told herself. *Even if he is, that's none of my concern. If Aaron stays here in the Big Valley, there are plenty of available young women for him to consider courting.*

Wilma reached around to scratch the small of her back. *I wonder if Deanna has some thoughts about me and Elmer's good-looking cousin getting together. Could that be why she invited us both to supper last night and made sure we sat beside each other at the table?*

Wilma felt a prickling along the back of her neck. *I hope that wasn't the case, because I'd never consider marrying anyone but Israel.*

Staring out the front window, Wilma bit her lower lip. *Of course I can hardly go to Israel and say that I've changed my mind and decided to marry him after all. That would be too bold, and I can't stand the thought of his possible rejection. Israel was deeply hurt when I broke our engagement because of the boys, and now he treats me as though I'm nothing more than a casual acquaintance.*

Wilma shook her head. *It's probably too late for me and Israel. I need to accept the fact that unless he comes to me and proposes marriage again, I'll never become Mrs. Israel Zook.*

"What did you think of Aaron?" Deanna asked a few minutes after Wilma entered her quilt shop.

"He seemed nice and was easy to talk to." Wilma set her tote on the counter. "I brought everything I've managed to finish and hope to start more table runners next week," she said, quickly changing the subject.

"What with caring for Israel's nephews, I'm surprised you were able to get any quilting done the past two weeks."

"I worked while the boys were sleeping." Wilma withdrew the crib quilt. "Just finished this up this morning. Do you think it will sell?"

"Oh, I'm sure it will—if not here, then at the Wednesday auction and flea market." Deanna moved closer to Wilma. "Back to the subject of Aaron—Elmer thinks it's good that his cousin wants to make a new start here in our area of Pennsylvania."

"A fresh start can be good for anyone," Wilma said.

"True." Deanna took a stack of pot holders from the tote and placed them on one end of the counter. "What about you, Wilma? Do you feel ready to start over?"

Wilma had a hunch where her friend wanted to take this conversation, but she did not want to play along. In fact, she decided to come right out and tell Deanna the truth.

"The only person I want to start over with is Israel."

Deanna's brows lifted. "Seriously?"

"Jah. I still love him, Deanna, and I believe I always will."

"But what about those rowdy boys? If you married Israel, you'd have to raise them as if they were your own, and since none of them like you . . ."

"I believe they are beginning to warm up to me."

"Oh?" Deanna tipped her head. "What makes you think that?"

Leaning her weight against the counter, Wilma told her friend how the boys had responded to her last week, and especially on Friday.

Deanna stood with her lips pursed. "They've been sick, Wilma. Children are quite vulnerable and unpredictable when they don't feel well."

Wilma felt a tightness in her jaw and facial

muscles. "Are you saying that none of Israel's nephews like me? They've just been nicer because they're grank?"

Deanna shook her head. "That's not what I meant. I just think it's too soon for you to tell. Maybe you should wait and see how they respond to you once they're well. They might go back to their old mischievous ways."

"It's a possibility, but as strange as it may seem, I'm growing attached to them, and—"

"And you want to get back with Israel?"

"Jah." Wilma lowered her gaze. "The thing is, I can't go up to him and say, 'I'm ready to become your wife now.'" She looked up and released a lingering sigh. "Since I rejected him because of the boys, he might not want me back now."

"Would you like my advice?"

"Of course."

"Pray about the matter, and after you've spent more time with the boys, if you still feel that you want to marry their uncle, then be honest with him. Tell Israel what you've told me today."

Wilma's lips pressed together. At the moment, she had difficulty committing fully to any action. Deanna was right—this was something she definitely needed to pray about.

Chapter 14

On Monday Wilma arrived at Israel's and learned that the boys were still in bed.

"They had trouble sleeping last night," Israel explained. "And both Nate and Micah woke up from a bad dream." He stretched his arms over his head and yawned. "They ended up sleeping with me, which meant I didn't get much sleep either."

"I'm sorry to hear that." Wilma wished she could have been here last night to help with the boys, but that wouldn't be proper unless she and Israel were married.

She chanced a quick look at him and noticed his furrowed brows. *I wonder what he is thinking. Does Israel still feel any love for me, or did I kill that love when I broke our engagement?*

A horn tooted outside, and Israel looked out the kitchen window. "My driver is here. I'd best be on my way." He grabbed his lunch pail and headed for the back door but paused and turned to look at her. "I hope the boys won't give you too much trouble today."

"Oh, I'm sure they'll be—"

The door closed behind Israel before Wilma could finish her sentence. She winced. *Was he in that big of a hurry, or did Israel deliberately choose not to tell me goodbye?*

Wilma set aside her painful thoughts and focused on getting breakfast made. Maybe the children would enjoy having pancakes with maple syrup.

She took out all the necessary ingredients and mixed the batter. Since none of the boys had come into the kitchen yet, Wilma decided not to heat the griddle until at least some of them showed up.

Wilma heated some water in the teakettle, and when it was ready, she made herself a cup of peppermint tea. She'd always found that flavor to be comforting. And right now, with Israel acting so cool toward her, Wilma needed all the comforting she could get.

Wilma took her tea outside and sat in a chair on the porch. With the kitchen window wide open, she'd be able to hear the boys if they came downstairs hungry for breakfast.

She looked out into the yard, watching some baby chicks and their mother in the grass. Some ran this way, and others went in another direction, while a few of the babies stayed closer to the hen. Either Israel had let them out of the pen this morning or they'd found a way of escape.

"Whatcha doin'?"

Wilma jumped at the sound of Nate's voice. Caught up in watching the chickens, she hadn't even heard the door open. "I was just having a little quiet time while I waited for you and your brothers to wake up." She smiled at him. "Are you the first one out of bed?"

"Jah, but I think the others will be comin' down soon." Nate moved closer to Wilma and placed his hand on her arm. "You ain't goin' anywhere, are ya?"

"You mean today?"

He shook his head. "After we're over the wasserpareble."

"I'll be with you until Dorothy comes back. Then I'm sure she'll come over to watch you and your brothers again."

Nate's forehead wrinkled and he folded his arms with a huff. "I don't want her to take care of us anymore. Me and my brieder want you to live here with us all of the time." He lifted his hands so that his palms faced upward. "Even Mark says so."

A flood of warmth came over Wilma. This young boy's encouraging words meant more than he would ever know. If only she had the power to make it happen. "Danki, Nate. I wish I could stay too, but it's not possible."

He looked up, with big brown eyes focusing directly on her. "How come?"

"Because your uncle and I would have to be married in order for me to be here all the time."

"Then get married."

"It's not that simple." Wilma gave Nate's arm a tender pat. "Let's go inside now and see if your

140

brothers are awake. I have pancake batter ready to be spooned onto the griddle."

Grinning widely, Nate scurried into the house.

After breakfast was over and the dishes had been done, Wilma called the boys back to the kitchen.

"What do ya want? Did we do somethin' wrong?" With an anxious expression, Josh's gaze flitted around the room.

Wilma shook her head. "Not at all. I called you in here to see if you'd like to help me bake some maple syrup cookies."

"I'm in." Mark was quick to say.

"Me too," Ethan agreed.

The three younger boys bobbed their heads.

"All right then, let's get started." Wilma opened a cupboard door and took out the ingredients, then she gave each boy a job to do. While she lit the oven, Mark greased the cookie sheets. Ethan cracked the egg into a bowl, and Micah and Nate stirred it with a wooden spoon. Josh waited until the egg mixture was nice and fluffy before he poured the right amount of maple syrup into the wet mixture.

The boys watched as Wilma measured the dry ingredients and added them to the beaten egg and maple syrup. When the mixture was ready, Wilma instructed the boys to drop spoonfuls of dough onto the cookie sheets about an inch apart.

"That maple syrup sure smells good." Josh

141

leaned close to the bowl and sniffed. "I can't wait to taste one of them kichlin."

"When they come out of the oven and have cooled sufficiently, we'll each have one," Wilma said.

Nate's lower lip protruded. "Only one?"

"After lunch we can have a few more cookies." She gave the boy's back a few pats. "Are you okay with that?"

"Jah."

Nate and his brothers crowded around as Wilma placed the two sheets of cookies in the oven. "In about twelve minutes, the cookies should be done." She pointed to the bowl. "Since there's still some dough left, we'll bake a second batch, and maybe there will be enough for a third baking as well."

"What are we supposed to do while the kichlin bake?" The question came from Ethan.

"You could sit at the table and draw a picture for me—something I can look at when I'm gone."

"Where ya goin'?" Micah blinked rapidly as he tilted his head in her direction.

"Home to my parents' house."

His forehead creased. "How come? Don't ya like it here?"

"Of course I do," she responded. "But I can't stay forever. Once you are fully recovered from the chicken pox and Dorothy returns, there will be no reason for me to come over here to help out."

Mark folded his arms and turned away from Wilma. "So you're just gonna walk out on us, the way our mamm did." It wasn't a question. It was a statement, with emphasis.

She dropped her gaze to the floor. How could she make these children understand that she wouldn't be leaving by choice?

Wilma drew in a breath and said a quick prayer. *Lord, please help me make them understand.*

"You see," she said, groping for the right words, "I cannot continue to be with you after Dorothy returns. Your uncle hired her, and she will expect to resume her position after she comes back to the Big Valley."

"What's *resume* mean?" Nate questioned.

"It means to start up again."

"Don't we have any say in this?" Ethan wanted to know.

"Probably not," she answered honestly. "It'll be your uncle Israel's decision."

The windup timer on the counter rang, so Wilma grabbed two pot holders and opened the oven door. "The cookies look done, so it's time to set them out to cool."

Seconds after Wilma placed the cookie sheets on the cooling racks she'd put on the table, Micah stretched out his hand.

"Not yet, Micah." Wilma shook her head.

"They're still too hot to remove from the baking sheet, not to mention too warm to eat."

The boy groaned and began pacing the room. *This child needs to learn how to be more patient,* Wilma thought. *All five of the boys need some guidance, in fact.*

"You wouldn't wanna burn your tongue or the roof of your mouth, would ya?" Mark walked up to his little brother and gave him a nudge. "You oughta relax and wait till Wilma says it's safe to eat one of the kichlin."

Wilma pressed her palms against her hot cheeks. "Thank you, Mark, for speaking up so I didn't have to."

Micah stopped pacing and came over to stand beside Wilma. "You smell good. Wish you could be our new mamm."

Micah's brothers, as well as Wilma, said nothing. Everyone just stood there, staring at the cookies.

After a few more minutes, Wilma announced that it was safe to remove the cookies from their pans. "The kichlin might be soft and could easily fall apart, so we need to be careful taking them off. Who wants to go first?"

"I will," said Mark.

She handed him the spatula and watched as he slid it under a cookie, lifted it out, and placed it on an empty cooling rack. "It's your turn now." He handed the kitchen tool to Ethan, who none too slowly removed the second cookie. In the process, it broke into several pieces.

Ethan frowned. "Guess since I messed up I won't get a kichlin before lunch."

Wilma scooped the pieces onto a small plate and set it aside. "It was an accident. Go ahead and try again, just a little slower this time."

The boy did as she suggested and smiled when his cookie came off the spatula in one piece.

He handed the tool to the next brother in line, but Josh shook his head. "I don't wanna mess up." He looked at Wilma. "Can you take off the rest of the kichlin so we don't lose anymore?"

She smiled. "Of course—unless one of you younger boys would like to take a turn."

When Micah and Nate shook their heads, Wilma removed the remainder of the cookies and placed them on the cooling rack. A few minutes later, she told the children they could each take one.

There was no hesitation as the boys got their cookies and gobbled them down.

"Yum. That was *appeditlich*," Mark announced.

"You're right," Ethan agreed. "It's the most delicious cookie I've ever had."

"Jah," the three youngest ones said in unison.

Wilma couldn't believe the change that had come over these boys since she'd come to take care of them during their bout with chicken pox. The more time Wilma spent with Israel's nephews, the more she longed to be a part of their lives. If only she felt free to express that to Israel.

When Israel got off of work that afternoon, he asked his driver to make a quick stop at a local convenience store so he could pick up a package of chewing gum.

Upon entering the building, Israel spotted Wilma's friend Deanna. She stood near the check-out counter, conversing with a young Amish man Israel had never seen before.

Under normal conditions, Israel would have greeted Deanna, but since she was already talking to someone, he chose not to interrupt and moved over to the shelf where candy and gum had been displayed.

"I sure appreciated the tasty meal you provided last Friday night," he heard the newcomer say to Deanna.

"We were glad you came, Aaron," she replied.

"Since I'm new to the area, I don't know many people yet, other than you, your husband, and now your friend Wilma."

"It'll take some time to get acquainted with other people in our community, but I'm sure you'll soon make lots of friends."

"I enjoyed spending time with Wilma. She seems like a very nice young woman, and I hope to get the chance to see her again soon."

Israel's jaw clenched. *So that's where Wilma*

went Friday evening when she said she had plans. He tipped his head to the right a bit, hoping he wouldn't miss anything else that was said. *No wonder Wilma seemed in such a hurry to go that evening. Could this man be courting my ex-girlfriend? If he's new to the area, he sure works fast.*

Israel felt a stab of jealousy as he clenched his teeth, struggling not to mutter anything under his breath. Part of him wanted to walk up to this man and inform him that Wilma was his fiancée, so she was off limits, but he held himself in check. Besides, it was no longer true, and Wilma was free to do whatever she wished.

Israel stared at the peppermint gum he usually bought, thinking it might be best if he just forgot about buying it and left the store. Besides, he didn't want to keep his driver waiting. If he went up to the counter where Deanna and this Aaron person stood, he'd have to offer a greeting. No doubt Deanna would make introductions, and Israel wasn't up for that.

Nope, I can't do it. I have no desire to meet the man that could end up being Wilma's husband.

Israel's shoulders slumped as he walked out of the store. *If it doesn't turn out to be this fellow, Aaron, no doubt some other man will come along and sweep the one I love off her feet. Then I'll have no choice but to look for someone else who'd be willing to be my wife and take care of the boys.*

Chapter 15

The boys were well now, and Dorothy was back from helping her mother. She would be coming to Israel's house tomorrow morning to take over the duties Wilma had done for the past three weeks. After she fixed supper for Israel and the boys this evening, it would be time for Wilma to return to her home and a life of quilting. But would it be enough? Wilma didn't think so. She would miss coming here and spending time with Israel's nephews. She would miss seeing Israel each morning before he left for work and every evening when he returned home. Although he rarely looked at her, they did manage to have a few brief conversations. Any words spoken between them were usually about superficial things, like how well the boys were doing, the current weather conditions, or some event that was going on in their community.

Wilma wished she had the courage to approach Israel and tell him that she'd changed her mind about the boys and wanted to marry him now. Her pride stood in the way, however. And she feared Israel might reject her. Unless he approached her first, Wilma didn't see how it would be possible for them to get back together.

Wilma's pessimistic thinking made it difficult to make any future plans at all.

Releasing a long, slow sigh, Wilma left the kitchen and went outside to call the boys in for lunch. She spotted Mark, Ethan, and Josh playing catch in the yard, but there was no sign of their younger brothers.

"Lunch is ready," Wilma said, walking up to the three playing catch. "Do you know where Micah and Nate are?"

Mark shrugged. "Beats me. Maybe they're playin' in the barn."

"Jah, I think so," Josh put in. "I saw 'em headin' that way awhile ago."

"All right. Why don't you three wash up while I go get your brothers? Once your hands are clean, you can go on in and take seats at the kitchen table."

"Okay." Ethan looked at Wilma with a somber expression. "We're gonna miss ya when you're gone. Sure wish you could stay."

Struggling not to give in to her pent-up emotions, Wilma placed her hand on his shoulder. "I will see all of you sometimes. Maybe if your uncle is okay with it, I can come by and take you and your brothers on a picnic."

"That'd be nice," Josh spoke up. "I bet Uncle Israel would like to go along."

Wilma knew if she responded to that statement, her throat would clog up, so she reminded the boys to wash their hands and went hurriedly to the barn.

Inside she found the two younger boys seated on bales of straw, each with a cat in their lap. When Wilma drew close, Micah looked up at her and began to sob.

She rushed over and sat beside him. "What's wrong, little man? Did the *katz* dig its claws into you?"

Micah shook his head as the tears came faster.

"He's cryin' because he don't want Dorothy to take your place." Nate looked at Wilma and shook his head. "None of us do. We all wish you could stay."

Wilma leaned over so she was eye level with him. "I just told your older brothers that I'm sure I'll see you sometimes. And if it's all right with your onkel, I'll see if I can take you boys on a picnic before summer's over."

Nate's eyes brightened a bit, but Micah kept crying. "Can't ya keep comin' here to stay with us?" Nate asked.

"I wish I could, but since Dorothy is back, your uncle has made plans for her to come here tomorrow, so . . ."

Nate's face reddened. "I don't like Dorothy. She's mean and yelled at us before."

Wilma blinked. This was the first time she'd heard any of the boys say anything negative about their former sitter. Was Nate telling the

150

truth, or had he made it up to make Wilma feel guilty for what he believed was abandonment?

Refocusing, Wilma asked the boys to put the cats down and come with her to get washed up for lunch.

Micah did as she said, but Nate remained in place with a pouty look on his face.

"Come on, Nate." Wilma motioned to the door with her hand. "Lunch is ready, and it's time to eat."

"I ain't hungerich." He dropped his gaze to the cat in his lap.

Wilma wasn't sure if she should force the issue or let him go without eating. Seeing the stubborn tilt of his chin, she opted for the second choice. "Okay, but if you change your mind, please wash your hands before you come to the table."

Wilma clasped Micah's hand and led him out of the barn and into the yard. They stopped at the pump to wash up and then went in the house.

Mark, Josh, and Ethan sat at the kitchen table with such somber faces it nearly caused Wilma to change her mind about speaking the truth to their uncle.

Maybe I should swallow my pride and tell Israel about my change of heart. The worse that could happen is he might reject my offer to marry him. She slid her moist hands down the front of her apron and pursed her lips. *Then, as much as it would hurt, I'd have to accept his decision and try to get on with my life without him and the boys.* Wilma swallowed hard. *And that would not be an easy thing to do.*

As Israel passed the clinic where he'd taken the boys when they came down with chicken pox, he thought of Wilma. Although she'd volunteered to look after the boys, Israel had been convinced that she'd only done it out of obligation. Or perhaps it was guilt because she'd walked out of his life, leaving him to raise his nephews by himself. If he hadn't been so desperate to find someone to take Dorothy's place, he may have turned down Wilma's offer. Seeing her every morning when she arrived and again when he came home from work was difficult. It was a continual reminder that he'd lost the only woman he'd ever loved, and beginning tomorrow, when Dorothy came over to the house, he would be saying goodbye to Wilma all over again. Only this time it would be for good, because there was no way Israel could continue having her in his house and not show his true feelings.

There were times, like last week when Wilma cooked his favorite chicken and dumplings for supper, that he found himself fantasizing and picturing her as his wife. It was a pleasant thought but unrealistic. Israel felt certain that she would never be happy as his wife as long as she had the responsibility of helping him raise the boys.

He shook the reins to get Digger moving at a quicker pace. This evening he would sit at the table with the boys and eat the last supper Wilma would ever cook for him.

"If only things could be different," he muttered. "It just isn't fair."

Israel thought of Psalm 43:5, a verse about disappointment: *"Why art thou cast down, O my soul? and why art thou disquieted within me? hope in God: for I shall yet praise him, who is the health of my countenance, and my God."*

As Israel's horse clip-clopped on down the road, he noticed an Amish woman in her garden, pulling weeds. Further on, he spotted two Amish children running barefoot across their lawn. He saw cows and horses along with some goats as he went by a bed-and-breakfast. With so many positive things to focus on and praise God for, it would be senseless to spend his days dwelling on negative thoughts and wishing for things out of his reach. Even though his sister's boys could be a challenge at times, they were also a blessing. Despite not being married, Israel was beginning to understand what it was like to be a father. He'd come to love and appreciate his sister's sons, and he learned something about their individual personalities almost every day. Mark, Ethan, and Josh liked to play ball and climb into the hayloft to get away from their younger brothers. Micah and Nate enjoyed spending time with the cats. They also

153

liked to play some outside games like tag and hide-and-seek. The older boys would sometimes join them, especially for hide-and-seek.

Israel smiled. Those little stinkers could be a handful at times, but they sure kept life interesting. Although he felt sure all five boys still missed their parents, they seemed to be more accepting of their new life with him.

When Israel entered his house a short time later, he found Wilma in the kitchen, setting the table. Seeing that there were only six place settings, he tipped his head and gestured to the dishes on the table. "Is it you or one of the boys who's not joining us for supper?"

"It's me," she replied. "I have other plans this evening."

"I see." Israel did his best to keep the disappointment he felt out of his tone. Moving across the room to hang his straw hat on a wall peg, he said, "Where are the boys?"

"They're upstairs in their rooms and won't come out."

"How come? Are they being punished for something they've done wrong?"

She shook her head.

"Well, something must have happened between you and the kids, or they wouldn't be up in their rooms, refusing to come downstairs. I'll go get them," he said.

"Please don't. I'm sure they'll come down after I'm gone."

Israel couldn't mistake Wilma's unease as she clutched the breadbasket as though it were a shield.

"There's a ham in the oven, along with baked potatoes." Wilma set the bread on the table and gestured to a plate of cut-up fresh vegetables. "The boys like all these things, so I'm sure they'll enjoy the meal, and hopefully you will too."

Israel gave a quick nod.

Wilma picked up her purse and started toward the door but turned back to face him. "Would you please tell the boys I said goodbye?"

"Of course, but I think they'd appreciate it more if you told them yourself."

"No, it's better this way."

Israel bent his neck forward as he broke eye contact with her. He wanted so badly to say what was on his mind, but the words wouldn't come. She obviously didn't care about him or the boys.

Wilma's chin trembled slightly, and she opened her mouth as if to say something, but then she turned and opened the door.

After Wilma left the house, Israel moved over to the kitchen window and watched as she headed to the barn to get her horse. *I wonder what other plans she has for this evening. Could she be seeing that man I heard Deanna talking to? Should I have asked?* He shook his head.

155

No, I'm sure Wilma wouldn't have appreciated that.

Sighing, Israel left the kitchen and started up the stairs. It was time to bring the boys down for supper.

As Wilma headed toward Deanna and Elmer's house, tears nearly blinded her vision. She had wanted so badly to tell Israel the way she felt about the boys and him as well. But something held her back. Was it the feeling she'd gotten from his bland expression, or could it have been fear of his rejection that kept her from saying anything?

Wilma had told Israel before that she and the boys were getting along better, so he should have realized that she'd changed her mind about helping him raise his nephews. Was he too blind to sense the love she felt for him whenever he looked at her? Could it be possible that Israel was no longer interested in her being his wife?

Wilma felt relieved when she pulled into the Yoders' yard and got Blossom secured to the rail. Although she hadn't been invited to join Deanna and her family for supper, she was fairly sure an invitation would be extended. Even if it was not, Wilma wanted the chance to speak to her friend and ask for advice.

"*Guder owed*," Wilma said when Deanna answered her knock on the door. "I hope I'm not interrupting your supper."

Deanna shook her head. "Not at all. I'm just getting our meal started. If you haven't eaten already, you're more than welcome to join us."

Wilma gave no hesitation. "Danki, I would like that." She set her purse on the far end of the kitchen counter. "What can I do to help?"

"There's not much to do really. I was planning to serve cold, leftover fried chicken from last night's supper, along with a macaroni salad I made earlier today." Deanna gestured to a chair. "From the looks of your red-rimmed eyes, I'm guessing you came by here to talk about your relationship with Israel."

Wilma took a seat and waited until Deanna joined her. "I have no relationship with Israel. I ruined that when I broke our engagement and refused to take care of his nephews."

"But you've been watching them throughout their ordeal with the wasserpareble."

"True, but they're better now, and Dorothy's back from taking care of her mamm. She'll return to Israel's house tomorrow morning to begin caring for the boys again." Wilma groaned. "I've been miserable without Israel, and I wish I'd never walked away from a relationship with him. It was the biggest mistake of my life."

"Have you told him how you feel?"

She shook her head. "I wanted to tell him before I left his house this evening, but I couldn't find the words."

"It's not too late. You could go back there and tell him now."

Wilma sniffed deeply. "It would be too embarrassing, and I'm afraid he might reject me."

"Israel and my husband are friends. Would you like me to ask Elmer to speak to him?"

Wilma's eyes widened. "I would really be upset if Elmer did that, only to find out that Israel doesn't love me anymore. And it would be embarrassing if Israel figured out that you had put your husband up to asking on my behalf. I don't think I could ever face Israel again."

"You're probably right," Deanna agreed. She placed a hand on Wilma's arm and gave it a reassuring squeeze. "I don't like seeing you so unhappy. I wish you'd swallow your pride and be up-front with Israel about your feelings."

Wilma didn't appreciate the reminder that she'd let pride get in the way of telling Israel the truth. But her fear of rejection held her back more than pride, and she saw no way of getting past that.

Wilma's breaths came rapidly as she looked up and closed her eyes. *Dear God, if it's meant for me and Israel to be together, please cause something to happen that will open his eyes.*

Chapter 16

A week had passed since Wilma had seen either Israel or the boys, and she missed them terribly. She kept busy with quilting projects and helping her mother put up produce from their garden, but nothing filled the void in her heart. She wanted to stop by Israel's place and say hello but didn't want to show up unannounced. Even if he was at work when she dropped in, the boys would tell him and he might not appreciate her coming there without his knowledge or permission.

Wilma grimaced as she sat on the porch watching the sun begin to set. *I never needed to let Israel know I'd be dropping by before his sister's boys came to live with him. He came by my folks' place to see me unannounced many times too.*

Things had changed so much in the last few months—and all of it completely unexpected.

The screen door squeaked, and Wilma jumped at the sound of her mother's voice.

"Neither your daed nor I have checked for phone messages today. Would you mind doing that?"

"Sure, no problem." Wilma left for the phone shed and took a seat in the hot, stuffy building. The message light blinked on the answering machine, so she pushed the button to hear the messages.

She straightened when Israel's deep voice sounded from the machine. "I'm sorry to bother you, Wilma, but Dorothy came down with a bad cold and won't be watching the boys tomorrow. If you get this message in time and you're available to be with them until Dorothy feels better, could you please let me know?"

Wilma didn't hesitate to pick up the phone and call Israel's number. She left a message, saying she would be there in the morning and would fill in for Dorothy as long as she was needed.

Wilma hung up the phone and sat, warmth filling her chest. She looked forward to spending time with the boys again, and it would be good to see their uncle as well.

Israel relaxed in relief when he went to the phone shack the following morning and heard Wilma's message. He'd thought about trying to find someone else in Dorothy's absence, but the boys had all insisted that the only person they wanted to be with was Wilma.

Israel still couldn't get over the fact that his nephews had become attached to Wilma during their bout with chicken pox. One or more of the boys had said something positive about Wilma almost every day since Dorothy had taken over their care again. Even the older woman had mentioned it to Israel, saying that she wondered if he should have kept Wilma coming to the house to oversee the boys instead of her helping out.

Bringing his thoughts back into focus, Israel made a quick call to his driver, letting him know that he would definitely need a ride today, since the job he'd be working on was out of the area. If Wilma hadn't responded to Israel's message, or had said she would not be able to come, he would have had no choice but to stay home with the boys today. He appreciated Wilma's willingness to come here on last-minute notice. Israel couldn't help wondering, though, what her motivation was. Had she grown fond of the boys and hadn't told him, or did it make her feel good to do a kind deed? Israel had dealt with these thoughts before, along with wondering if coming to help out was Wilma's way of dealing with any guilt she may felt have for breaking their engagement. Israel had convinced himself that Wilma no longer felt any love for him. If she did, wouldn't she have stayed by his side and made any necessary sacrifices to be with him?

None of that matters right now, he told himself. *She'll be here soon to watch the boys, and I need to get back to the house to ready myself for work.*

"How would you all like to go on a picnic today?" Wilma asked after the boys had finished their breakfast.

161

"Yippee!" Micah and Nate both hollered.

"Where are we going to have the picnic?" Mark asked.

"There are a couple of options," Wilma replied. "We can have the picnic here in the backyard."

Ethan shook his head. "That'd be no fun. We can eat here any old time."

She nodded. "We could also have the picnic at Bender Park."

"What's a bender park?" Josh wanted to know. "Does it have a lot of bent trees?"

Wilma bit back a chuckle. Apparently Israel hadn't taken the boys there since their arrival in the Big Valley. "Bender Park is right here in Reedsville. I'm not sure how it got its name, but it has plenty of picnic tables, restroom facilities, and a nice stream to sit by and listen to the water gurgle."

"Can we go fishin' there?" Ethan asked.

"As a matter of fact, you can. There are some trout in the stream, but I'm not sure if your uncle has any fishing poles."

"Jah, he does," Mark spoke up. "He keeps 'em in the barn."

"That may be, but I wouldn't want to take them out unless we had his permission." Wilma leaned forward with one hand on her knee. "Since it's such a hot summer day, I think it would be fine if any of you boys wanted to splash around in the cold stream."

162

"Guess that'd be okay." Mark grinned. "We can roll up our pant legs and go wading. Maybe a trout will swim by and we can try catchin' it with our bare hands."

"Jah, that'd be fun." Josh bobbed his head.

Wilma smiled. It was good to see the enthusiasm on the boys' faces. She looked forward to the outing as well. It would be a nice change of pace for all of them to spend a portion of their day at the park.

From the first minute they arrived at the park until it was time to head for home, Wilma enjoyed observing the boys. They were so full of life and laughter that they made her feel like a kid again. The boys waded in the stream, squealing with delight as they kicked water at each other, and pitched flat stones into the stream to see if they could make them skip.

Wilma had read a book for a while after she and the boys ate the picnic lunch she'd packed. But as the day grew warmer, she had taken off her shoes and joined her young charges as they frolicked in the stream.

As they headed back to Israel's house with a warm wind blowing into her white-top buggy, Wilma found herself wishing there was a way she could keep the day from coming to an end.

If I were Israel's fraa, I wouldn't have to go home to my parents' house. Wilma felt a small

163

lump form in her throat, and she swallowed a few times, trying to dislodge it.

I can't keep on like this, she told herself. *I need to tell Israel that I love the boys and have changed my mind about my relationship with him. If he rejects me, I'll know it's not God's will for us to be together. I'll tell him how I feel after supper, before I head for home.*

After guiding Blossom up the lane and into Israel's yard, Wilma brought the horse up to the hitching rail. Before she could ask, Mark jumped down and secured Blossom.

"I'll take her to the barn for you too," he offered.

She smiled and nodded. "Danki."

When the rest of the boys got out of the buggy, Wilma asked Ethan to carry the picnic basket up to the house, and Josh took the old blanket she'd brought along so they could sit on the grass near the stream after they'd eaten at one of the tables.

"What can I do to help?" Nate asked as they all began walking toward the house.

"You and Micah can keep me company in the kitchen while I get supper going."

They paused at the pump to wash their hands, and then everyone filed into the house.

After Mark came inside, all of the kids hung out in the kitchen, wanting to help Wilma fix the meal. Although it would no doubt slow the process of fixing supper, she warmly accepted their offer.

Israel arrived home tired and hungry. He, along with the rest of the construction crew, had worked hard today, and the persistent heat hadn't helped. Israel had packed enough water for the day, but he'd made the mistake of making only one sandwich instead of two, as he most often did.

Stepping onto the back porch, he heard excited voices coming through the open kitchen window.

"We sure had a lot of fun today, Wilma." Israel recognized Mark's voice.

"I enjoyed myself as well."

Israel smiled. There was no mistaking Wilma's gentle voice. *If only . . .*

He took a few steps toward the door and halted when he heard Nate speak.

"I love ya, Wilma. Sure wish you could stay here and live with us forever."

"We all love ya," the other boys chimed in, one by one.

"I love all of you very much too, and if I had my way, I would never have to leave you."

Israel spread his fingers out like a fan against his chest. *She loves the boys. Wow, this is sure news to me. Why didn't Wilma tell me that her feelings toward my nephews had changed?*

"What about Uncle Israel?" Ethan asked. "Do ya love him too?"

"Oh jah, very much." There was a pause. Wilma's voice trembled a bit when she spoke again. "I've been in love with your uncle for a very long time—even before he and I began courting."

"Then marry me!" Israel shouted, after he jerked open the door and rushed into the kitchen.

With fingers touching her parted lips, Wilma gave Israel a dazed stare. "You . . . you heard what I said?"

"Sure did." He moved swiftly across the room. "If it's true that you love me and these rambunctious boys, then I see no reason why we shouldn't be married in November like we had originally planned. Unless, of course, you're now being courted by someone else."

"No, there's no one else." Wilma shook her head. "And you know something else, Israel?"

"What's that?"

"I was planning to tell you right after supper that I've come to love and appreciate every single one of your nephews." She looked at him through tear-filled eyes. "I don't have to wish anymore, for God has given me the desires of my heart."

It was all Israel could do to keep from taking Wilma into his arms and giving her a hug and a kiss. But with five pairs of eyes staring at them, he thought better of it. Instead, he moved close to his beloved and placed an arm around her waist. "Wilma Hostetler, will you marry me?"

"Jah, a thousand times yes."

A round of applause went up in the room, and all five boys rushed forward to share in a group hug. The words of 1 John 5:14 came to Israel's mind. *"This is the confidence that we have in [God], that, if we ask any thing according to his will, he heareth us."*

Thank You, Father, he prayed. *Thank You for Wilma and these precious boys.*

Epilogue

Three months later

That turkey roasting in our oven right now sure smells good." Israel stepped behind Wilma, wrapped his arms around her waist, and nuzzled her neck.

"Jah, it sure does." Smiling, she leaned back against his broad chest and closed her eyes. It was hard to believe they'd only been married three weeks. The days had flown by quickly since she and Israel said their wedding vows while facing the bishop.

Today was Thanksgiving, and Wilma had so many things to be thankful for—her wonderful, steadfast husband; the five boys God had given her and Israel to raise; her parents, who would soon be joining them for the afternoon meal; and Wilma's good friend Deanna, who had given birth to a precious baby girl a week ago. Most of all, Wilma felt thankful for an all-caring God, who had showered her with many blessings.

She looked forward to the years ahead and hoped that Micah, Nate, Josh, Ethan, and Mark would grow into upstanding men who would seek God's will in all they said and did. Someday if the Lord allowed, Wilma hoped that she and

Israel would have some children of their own. They might have to add on to the house if more children came. But one thing Wilma knew with certainty: she had enough love in her heart for every child who would grow up in Israel's and her home.

Although Wilma could not look into the future and know what might lie ahead, she had the confidence that her heavenly Father would guide and direct both her and Israel as they walked through life together as one—always seeking, always trusting His will.

Wilma's Maple Syrup Cookies

Ingredients:
1 teaspoon baking soda
1 tablespoon milk
1 egg
½ cup plus 2 tablespoons shortening or butter
1 cup pure maple syrup
3 cups flour
3 teaspoons baking powder
½ teaspoon salt
1 teaspoon vanilla
1 (12 ounce) package semisweet chocolate chips

Preheat oven to 350 degrees. In a small cup, dissolve baking soda in milk and set aside. In large bowl, cream egg, shortening, and syrup. Add flour, baking powder, salt, vanilla, and milk mixture. Blend well. Stir in chocolate chips. Drop by teaspoon onto greased cookie sheet and bake for 12 to 15 minutes.

New York Times bestselling and award-winning author **Wanda E. Brunstetter** is one of the founders of the Amish fiction genre. She has written over 100 books translated into four languages. With nearly 12 million copies sold, Wanda's stories consistently earn spots on the nation's most prestigious bestseller lists and have received numerous awards.

Wanda's ancestors were part of the Anabaptist faith, and her novels are based on personal research intended to accurately portray the Amish way of life. Her books are well read and trusted by many Amish, who credit her for giving readers a deeper understanding of the Amish people and their customs.

When Wanda visits her Amish friends, she finds herself drawn to their peaceful lifestyle, sincerity, and close family ties. Wanda enjoys photography, ventriloquism, gardening, bird-watching, beachcombing, and spending time with her family. She and her husband, Richard, have been blessed with two grown children, six grandchildren, and two great-grandchildren.

Check out more about Wanda, visit her website at www.wandabrunstetter.com.

Martha's Miracle

~

by Jean Brunstetter

Chapter 1

Belleville, Pennsylvania

It was the first week of May, and Martha Yoder's life had become busier than ever. She flung back the sheets to make the bed in one of their guest rooms at the bed-and-breakfast her parents owned. "How long will the Robertsons be staying here?" she asked her mother.

"A few nights. They seem nice, and Mrs. Robertson asked me what other Amish-run businesses are in the area. I told her about some of the places but also let her know that our small town is not like where we came from in Lancaster." Frowning, Mom pushed up her glasses. "Also, I couldn't help noticing that she and her husband had their phones out, taking pictures of things. They seemed especially interested in our black-top buggies."

Most of the people who came to their quaint little B and B were tourists, and Martha had grown accustomed to their ways. Like most tourists, Mr. and Mrs. Robertson were curious about the Amish way of life and full of questions.

She continued to work, straightening the bedding, fluffing up the pillows, and setting them neatly in place. Next Martha grabbed the little waste cans from the room and dumped their contents into a garbage bag. "I have a place in mind where I would like to do some sketching when we're done with the chores."

"Oh, that sounds like a nice idea, and it looks to be a pleasant day for it too. I wonder how your father is doing, being one person short out there today." Mom glanced out the window. "Maybe he needs your help with the sheep and goats."

"Jeanna and Thomas are outside, working with Dad. Christine spent the night at a friend's house, and who knows when she'll be back. I'm sure my younger siblings can manage without my help today."

"As the eldest, Christine does like to get out of the house and spend as much time as she can with her friends." Mom dusted the small table, which held some magazines. "We're about done in here, but we've got some prep work to do for tomorrow's breakfast."

"Okay." Martha paused. "Dad had mentioned we might do some fishing tomorrow. I'm looking forward to that. Sometimes I miss the places we used to go when we lived in Lancaster, but fishing and hunting make up for a lot of that."

"That may be true, but there are other things you can be doing, like attending the work frolic at Diane's place this weekend." Her mother stood with a hand resting on one hip. "I'd like you to come along. You'll never find a husband if you don't spend more time doing feminine things."

Martha groaned softly. Mom wasn't happy about her boyish ways, like going out with her father to hunt or target practice, and this wasn't the first time Mom had brought up the subject. Martha couldn't help longing to be outdoors, like Dad, trying to get the best trophy that would offer them meat. She didn't care for things like quilting, canning, sewing, or baking. Truth was, Martha had never had a serious boyfriend, so maybe her mother was right about what she needed to do to find a husband. *Or maybe,* she thought, *I just won't get married, because it would take a miracle for me to find someone who accepted me for the person I am and not want to change me.*

"I can't wait to attend the benefit barbecue at the fire station this weekend. I'm glad Lori Miller invited me to go with her," Martha commented, trying to distract her mother from more discussion about marriage.

Mom rubbed her chin. "You'd rather do that than attend the frolic with me?"

"Jah." Martha couldn't help being excited about going with Lori to the barbecue. Her good friend was Mennonite, so she could ride along in their minivan. Ever since they'd met two years ago, they had gotten along well. Martha was eighteen at the time, and her friend was nineteen. Lori had other modern conveniences that Martha's family didn't have. Her parents reminded Martha and her siblings at times about letting those worldly things go by the wayside. The nice thing was Martha didn't care about television or many other worldly things. She wanted to remain Amish and join the church one day.

In the kitchen, Martha helped put together a breakfast casserole for the next morning. The Robertsons had eaten earlier and headed out to take a drive to see the area.

Martha cut the bread into small squares and dumped them into a bowl, while Mom stood stirring the sizzling Italian sausage in the skillet.

Martha's younger sister, wearing her work boots, tromped into the kitchen from outside. "I'm tired, but we've got the sheep and goats taken care of." She let out a sigh. "Thomas is still out there with Dad."

"What's he doing?" Mom turned down the burner to the skillet.

Jeanna slipped off her work boots and placed them by the door. "He's helping Dad fix the gate to the pasture."

"I'm glad he's doing that. I had trouble locking it yesterday." Martha began whisking up some eggs and added a little cream, which would be poured over the meat and bread once all the other ingredients were put in.

"I don't like Todd the goat. He kept bumping into me while I helped dad feed them. But to be fair, the silly thing did it to Thomas too." Jeanna took a glass from the cupboard and went to the sink.

"Yep, that male is a funny one. Either your father will want to keep the goofy critter or sell him at auction." Mom drained off the grease into a container to throw away.

"Well, since you guys have taken care of the animals for now, I can finish up here and head out to go do some drawing." Martha waited to add the liquid ingredients to Mom's dish.

Jeanna drank some of her water. "I'm going upstairs to get my laundry to wash. And once I get that going, I've got a book to read."

Martha watched her sister leave the kitchen as she waited for Mom to add the sausage to the dish. "I should bring some bottled water and crackers to snack on while I'm out sketching."

"That would be a good idea. You wouldn't want to be thirsty or hungry away from home." Mom set the skillet aside and added the other ingredients. After she'd finished, Martha poured the egg mixture over the top. "I'll get some foil to cover this, and then I'll put it into the refrigerator to allow it to set overnight."

"I like to do it that way," her mom agreed. "It's easier than trying to rush about in the morning to make the breakfast casserole." She tucked a loose strand of hair back into her *kapp*. "I can take care of the rest of the preparations if you'd like to get going."

"*Danki*. I better get to the barn and get old Dolly out for my little jaunt." Martha grabbed a bottle of water from the refrigerator and filled a ziplock bag with crackers. Then she headed by the desk in the kitchen to pick up her pad and pencil before going out the door.

About two miles from her home, Martha sat in a folding chair near a brook, sheltered from the heat of the day by some trees. Dolly was tied to a tree, enjoying the cooling effect of the dappled shade. Martha got out her sketch pad and pencil to draw the scenery of the brook as it wended through the wooded area. She paused for a moment to sip some water. Off in the distance, Martha saw smoke rising. It darkened as time passed. *Oh boy, I hope that isn't a house.* Martha stood to get a better view.

If someone had called in the fire, she'd soon hear sirens blaring from the fire trucks heading to the scene. She couldn't help watching the smoke continue to rise.

Martha put down her drawing items and picked up her bag of crackers. *I wouldn't have thought something like this would happen.* She kept watch until a hornet came along, buzzing around her food. "Get away from me you crazy bee."

Martha swatted at it but missed the yellow-and-black intruder.

Soon the sound of Belleville's finest was heard. *I don't know how those men do their job, but I'm glad we've got them to help us out in times like these.* Martha set down the food and prayed. *Lord be with the people who live there and with the brave ones who risk their lives every day for this community. Amen.*

She stepped over by the buggy and checked on the horse. Dolly acted as though she didn't have a care in the world despite the sirens going off. Martha patted her mom's horse and looked off in the direction of the smoke again. She wondered how long it would take for the firemen to put out the fire once they arrived. *I don't think I'll be able to get any more sketching done at this point. I probably should put my things away.*

Martha quickly picked up her things, including the crackers. She felt an instant sting on her finger and dropped everything to the ground. "That smarts!" Martha yelled as she eyed a hornet crawling away from the bag of crackers. "I hope this will quit hurting. Next time I'll need to look before I leap."

Martha's finger throbbed, so she stepped over by the brook and knelt, placing her hand in the water. The coolness felt pleasant on the sting, and she allowed herself some time to rest there. Sirens no longer blared, and the area had become peaceful again. Martha looked over her shoulder to see smoke still ascending into the sky. But as she watched, little by little, the thick dark smoke grew more transparent. "It looks like they have the fire under control." She pulled her hand out of the water. The spot where the hornet stung her had a welt but didn't hurt as much.

She stood and wiped her hand on the apron covering her dress. Then she picked up the folding chair and carried it to the back of her parents' buggy. "Well, Dolly, I think it's time for us to head back home."

Martha walked to the spot where she'd dropped her things and picked them up.

She paused again to look toward the smoke and then put her things inside by the front seat. Martha untied the horse and soon was on the road heading back to the house. *I think I'll go see Lori and discuss the plans for our day. But not until I take care of my finger.*

Pulling up to the barn, she saw Dad come out with a few wood scraps. "How was your time out sketching?"

"Okay, but I got stung by a hornet, and it hurt a lot." Martha showed him the spot on her finger.

"Let me see." He was careful as he looked at it. "Yep, it's swollen, Daughter. You oughta put some ice on it. That should help with the swelling."

182

"Don't worry, I'll do that once I get inside. Also, I saw smoke from a fire. It looked to be a house, judging by the black clouds rising into the sky, but I'm not sure."

"It could've been a house or maybe an outbuilding. Either way, hopefully no one was hurt." He set the scraps on the woodpile. "I talked more with Samuel when he stopped by today, and he mentioned another good area to hunt."

"Somewhere new?" Martha tilted her head.

"Jah, it's ten miles farther north of where we went last year. Samuel's brother-in-law recommended the place, and Samuel has a map to it."

She unhitched Dolly from the forks before removing her harness. "I can't wait to go."

"Me either. I hope to shoot another turkey. That tom was the biggest I've bagged yet."

Martha nodded. *If only I could get the biggest one this year. It would really impress Dad, not to mention all the meat it would provide for our table.*

After chatting with her father, she led Dolly back into her stall and gave the animal a good brushing. Then Martha rolled the buggy back into the barn and got out all of her things. The bee sting wasn't fun to work around during her efforts, but soon she'd be putting some ice on it like her dad had said.

Coming into the house, she spotted her brother

in the kitchen eating a whoopie pie. He looked her way and smiled. "There's more of these right here on the plate. Mom made them, so help yourself." Thomas took another bite.

"They look good. What kind are they?"

"Oatmeal and raisin." He drank from his glass of milk.

Martha stepped up to the sink. "After I wash my hands, I'll need to put a piece of ice on my finger."

"What for?"

She filled Thomas in on her outing and the hornet sting. Martha joined him at the table, holding the ice in a paper towel against her finger, and helped herself to one of the treats. "Yum, these are so good."

Her brother nodded.

Jeanna walked in and pointed to the whoopie pies. "Ooo, I'd like one."

"Help yourself. They're real tasty." Thomas got up and threw away his napkin.

She took a seat next to Martha. "Why do you have your finger wrapped?"

Thomas jumped in ahead of Martha as he went to the sink to wash his hands. "Our sister got stung."

"Oh really, what type of bee?" Jeanna grabbed a whoopie.

"A hornet, and boy did it hurt. I stuck my hand into the brook to help cool it off."

"That was a good idea." Jeanna took another bite.

Martha told her sister the story and finished off another pie while they visited. Thomas had gone outside, but Mom came in to get some tea and took a seat with them. Martha looked at the clock in the room. "I'd like to go over to see Lori before we start making supper, if that's okay."

"That would be fine. And Christine should be making an appearance here soon. She shouldn't need to spend the entire day with her friend."

Jeanna swallowed a mouthful of pie. "You know how she is, Mom. I think she'll stay as long as possible."

"Most likely, but she'll get hungry at some point and will want to eat." Mom took the last of the snacks on the plate. "These turned out good, and I'll offer some to our B-and-B guests this evening."

"Your whoopie pies are the best, Mom." Jeanna smacked her lips.

"Danki. I'm glad I listened to my grandmother when she taught me how to make them."

"Me too," the girls said in unison.

Martha rose from her chair. "I'd best get going."

"Have a good visit," Mom replied after she took another bite of her snack.

Once outside, Martha walked down her driveway and along the road to the entrance of

Lori's house. It didn't sit on as much land as the Yoders'. In fact, they didn't use their property for much except having a large yard to mow and a nice-sized garden. Her friend, being Mennonite, had electricity and a couple of vehicles.

Martha walked up the driveway and headed for the door. *I can't wait to attend that benefit barbecue at the fire station on Saturday and enjoy all the grilled chicken and other delicious food.*

Chapter 2

Glen Swarey sat at one of the tables, eating his lunch while looking over at a pretty young lady sitting with his friend Lori. He'd attended the firehouse barbecue benefit today, and his friend Kevin Presley had joined him.

"This event seems to be getting bigger every year." Kevin took another bite of his tasty chicken.

"It has grown, that's for sure, and the volunteers work hard to make it a success." Glen looked again toward the young lady.

"How do you like firefighting?"

"So far it's been good. I've been able to go out on some calls, like yesterday, when we put out a kitchen fire at a residence."

Kevin's brows raised. "How did that turn out?"

"Good."

"I'm sure the owners were relieved about that."

He nodded and looked back over toward the girl. "Yes. The husband and wife thanked us for getting there quickly. They were glad we stopped the fire from spreading further."

Glen had seen the friend of Lori's from his community, but their paths hadn't crossed so far. He'd heard from the other fellas that she was different—not the average girl, but tomboyish in her ways and outspoken. Glen was still drawn to her by her good looks.

Kevin finished his food and wiped away the sauce with a napkin he'd grabbed. "I don't mind donating to this and helping out the fire department. Besides, my wife didn't have to bother making my lunch today." He stood and patted his stomach.

"You've had quite a change in your life during the past two years. Becoming Amish, that wasn't an easy transition. You married Rose Mary, and in addition to that you've become a new father."

"I agree. I've been blessed."

Glen looked up and took in the intense blue sky. "Do you ever miss flying like you used to do?"

"Not so much, I've moved on with my life, my work, and my family. That's my world these days." Kevin stood up. "Anyway, I've got to get going and head back home. I'll be watching my daughter while Rose Mary does some shopping with her mother."

"I bet your little one is growing."

Kevin stood. "That she is. I'm enjoying her and the adorable things she does. One day, my friend, it will be your turn to find someone to be serious about."

"Maybe. You never know." He rose from the table, grabbed their used plates, napkins, and utensils, and threw them away. "I'll see you later. Have fun today." As he watched his friend leave,

Glen thought, *I'm going to go over there and meet this friend of Lori's.* Glen looked down at his clothes, making sure they were presentable, then walked on over to the girls.

Lori looked up at him. "Hello, stranger. How's it going today?"

"Not bad. I've been helping stock the tableware and anything else that needs to be taken care of."

"Sounds good." Lori motioned toward her friend. "Living in our little community, you've probably met Martha by now."

Martha's cheeks reddened. "It's been awhile, but I used to see Glen at church."

Hearing those words, Glen froze. *Great, why did she have to bring up me not being at church? The conviction I'm feeling right now isn't good, and now I'll have to come up with an excuse.* He cleared his throat. "I've been keeping busy with my job and my hobbies."

"He likes to hunt and provide food for his family, don't you Glen?" Lori took a sip of her beverage.

Glen's shoulders relaxed. "I do. And I've been helping my *daed* provide meat for the household."

"I like to hunt and fish," Martha commented.

"You do?" He paused. "What type of hunting do you do?"

"I like to go turkey hunting in the fall with either Dad and his friend or with my uncles. My

189

brother has gone with us, but he isn't as interested in tromping around all day in the wild. He would rather go eat a burger somewhere and hang out near the house."

Glen laughed. "I've gone a couple of times during turkey season, but they aren't the easiest to get."

"I agree. We've had times when it didn't seem like we'd ever find any out there."

Lori spoke up. "Why don't you have a seat with us?"

He smiled, sitting down across from Martha. Glen kept looking at her. "Doesn't your family run that bed-and-breakfast in town?"

She nodded. "My parents got the business up and running not long after we moved here from Lancaster. I don't mind the work, and we seem to have a steady flow of customers this time of year with the tourists around."

"Yeah, I don't notice them as much normally, but today I'm seeing a lot of unfamiliar faces at this benefit." He looked away from her and at the line of people waiting for barbecued chicken.

Lori waved at a couple of Mennonite ladies who had walked in from the road. "I'm going to speak with them for a few moments if you don't mind. I shouldn't be long."

"No problem," Glen was quick to respond.

"Um . . . all right." Martha shifted and watched her friend turn to walk away.

Glen sensed that she wasn't comfortable with the awkward silence between them. *I'll try to keep our conversation going.* "You also have the sheep and goats. How do you like raising them?"

"We enjoy it. The babies of both animals are pretty cute, and they're all healthy."

"We've got chickens to take care of and eggs to collect each day." *I'm enjoying this visit, and I'm glad Lori brought Martha along to this benefit. I hope I can make a good impression on her.*

As the two of them sat together, a little boy laughed and pointed at a buggy horse pawing the ground. His giggles seemed to come from his belly, and Glen tried to hold back a laugh. When he looked over at Martha, she let out a giggle. Then he let out some hearty laughter as well.

Glen tried to think of more to say to Martha as Lori continued to visit with her friends.

"What else do you like to do besides hunt?" he asked.

"I like to sketch scenery, like hills, bodies of water, and sometimes animals." She looked at him with a serious expression.

"Have you done very many sketches?"

"I've got a tablet full of drawings."

"Maybe you could show me some of them sometime."

"Really?"

He nodded.

Martha perked up. "I'd be happy to."

191

He appreciated her enthusiasm and hoped the opportunity would present itself soon.

Later that day, Martha and Lori went back to the Miller home. Lori suggested they sit outside on the patio and enjoy some lemonade and cookies. Lori went indoors to get their drinks and snacks, while Martha found a comfortable chair and relaxed.

It was a nice warm day for the time of year. Martha eyed the scenery from where she sat, contemplating if this spot would be good enough for doing another sketch. It wasn't long before her friend set the glasses down and went back to bring out the cookies.

Martha took a sip from her chilled glass. "That was some good chicken today. I'm glad you invited me."

"Was the food all you liked at the benefit? You seemed to be getting along with Glen all right."

Martha's face warmed. "He seems like a nice person and was easy to visit with."

Lori picked up a soft sugar cookie. "I noticed while he talked to Kevin that he kept looking over at you."

"Really?"

"Jah. I noticed it a few times."

Martha took a cookie and ate a bite. *I shouldn't get too excited about this, because I've been courted before and it hasn't worked out for me.*

"How're things going at the B and B? Are you keepin' busy?"

"Our rooms were full last night. One couple, the Hunts, are from Idaho, and they said they are on vacation for two weeks. The Bakers are from Kentucky, and they're staying with us because their family here has such a small place."

"I see."

Martha let out a sigh.

"Okay, what's up?"

"The same thing as usual. My mom thinks I shouldn't be doing boyish things if I want to get married someday."

Lori remained quiet.

"I can't help that I'm into hunting like my daed. One of these days I hope to get a good-sized turkey to have for the holiday supper." She looked out at the barley field across the way. "And I enjoy fishing even more. Just sitting there, snacking on my favorite goodies, is relaxing. It's the perfect way to spend the day." Martha paused to brush a few cookie crumbs off her dress. "I doubt that I'll ever find a guy who'd want to court a woman like me who prefers to be outdoors doing boyish things over spending time in the kitchen. Jah, that would take a miracle all right."

"I believe you're exaggerating, but since I'm not being courted by anyone at the moment, I really can't say anything."

193

"But you do know I value your opinion."

Lori patted Martha's shoulder. "I think you'll find the right person in the Lord's time."

Martha gave her friend's reassurance some thought. "If only Mom felt that way, it might help how I'm feeling right now."

"Being frustrated or worrying about it won't make things any better. Just pray and wait to see what will happen in the future."

"It's hard, but who knows, maybe someday a special man will come along."

"You've had suitors like I have."

"Yes, but so far no one has been seriously interested in me."

"You're a nice-looking person with lots to offer. I'm sure you won't be waiting long."

A short time later, Martha's older sister, Christine, came up the driveway and onto the porch. "Hello, Lori. How's it going?"

"I'm doing good. Do you have time to sit with us?"

"Nope." She looked over at Martha. "Mom needs us to make up a couple of desserts for the bed-and-breakfast guests."

"Then I suppose we need to head over and get busy. Thank you, Lori, for taking me to the benefit today."

"No problem. It was a nice day to get away for a couple of hours, right?"

Martha stood and drank the last of her beverage.

"Yes, we'll have to do something else together very soon. Oh, before I go, would you like me to help put the things back into the house?"

"No, don't worry about it. You need to go, and I'll see you soon. Have a good rest of your day."

"You too, Lori." Martha turned to her sister. "Let's go."

"Okay." Christine told Lori goodbye, and the girls walked off toward their parents' house. A buggy came up the road, and the driver pulled over by them. He was Christine's friend. "Hey, it's Edward."

He smiled at them and slowed to a stop. "How are you both doing this afternoon?" He spoke in Pennsylvania Dutch.

"I'm doing well." Christine's cheeks turned a light shade of red.

Martha looked over at her sister, who wore a pleasant smile, and then back at Edward. "I'm doing well too." She listened as her sister and Edward chatted. This was nothing new with Christine. Thanks to her friendly manner, she had a good number of friends. She attended any young people's gathering that came along. Martha, on the other hand, wasn't at all interested in the socials. She preferred to plan for the next fishing trip at a local lake—or at the very least to sit in a nice quiet spot and sketch.

I can't believe how different my sister and I are. She always gets so excited about being involved with the young people's gatherings. Martha's thoughts were interrupted when Christine spoke.

"Sister, didn't you hear me?"

"I'm sorry. Please repeat what you said."

"How about you and I going to the singing at Edward's this coming Sunday?"

Martha felt her form go rigid. "Um, I don't know . . . maybe."

"You should come along with Christine. It will be fun, and there'll be plenty of snacks," Edward interjected.

"I'll think about it. Anyway, Mom is waiting for us, Sister, so we need to go. Have a good day, Edward." Martha stepped away and waited for Christine to join her. After a few moments, the young man waved and got his buggy going again.

The sisters walked up the driveway and headed indoors. *My mother and sister are trying to change the way I am,* Martha thought. *It isn't easy conforming to other people's standards, but would I remain myself if I were to change?*

Glen had mulled over whether to attend the young people's gathering Sunday. He couldn't help being intrigued by Martha. He'd like to see her again and have the opportunity to talk in another low-key setting. Maybe he would ask her out on a date. Glen couldn't get Martha off his mind. He recalled her pretty blue eyes and her radiant smile that appeared so genuine. He could hardly believe she liked to fish and hunt. Glen had never met any woman like Martha. She was unique.

He wasn't sure why, but the thought of his father's mercantile business popped into his head. *If I end up not joining the church, how will that change things for me? Becoming a fireman is a definite goal in my book, and nothing will change it.*

Glen took a few swigs of coffee and finished his breakfast so he could get out the door. He didn't have to worry about getting Prince and his open buggy ready, because he'd gotten a driver's license and then bought a car a year and a half ago. His folks weren't happy about it, but Glen was eager to have a modern convenience. They were also unhappy about his disinterest in attending church. Although this was an off-Sunday for their church district, Mom and Dad would be leaving soon to attend a neighboring church in their Amish community. They'd invited Glen to join them, but once again he'd declined.

He enjoyed watching the rays of morning sunlight flow through the dining room window. Closing his eyes, he appreciated the comfort of the warmth on his face.

Dad came into the room and tapped his fingers on the edge of the table. "Just a reminder that the farrier will be by tomorrow. I'll have him take care of the four horses and pay for his work, so don't worry about that."

"Thank you. I know Prince needs to be reshod."

"Your ma's horse is really in need of new shoes. And that's not surprising given how Socks is used more than the other horses to haul us around."

"Yep, Socks is pretty popular." Glen picked up his dirty dishes and went to the kitchen, where he did some quick rinsing. "I'll see you later. I need to get a pack of bottled water and some snacks out to the car for the hike I'm going on with some friends from work."

"We'll see you later then." His father put on his hat and went out the kitchen door to get his horse and buggy ready for the drive to church.

When Glen got out to his car, he tried to start it but nothing happened. "I don't have time for this," he grumbled.

"What's up, Son?" his father called from the barn as he led out one of the buggy horses.

"This thing must have a dead battery." Glen lifted the hood and looked at the device. "I should have known this could happen since the battery is over eight years old."

"Well this horse is over eight years old, and it's far from being dead." Dad chuckled.

Glen rolled his eyes. "Looks like I'll need a ride to meet up with my friends at the firehouse."

"Since we'll be headed your way, I can help

out, but you may be there later than you'd planned."

"I know it, but—" He looked over toward the Thompson's place and saw that their van was still parked in the driveway. *I wonder if he could give me a ride.* He looked at his father as he tossed the long reins into the driver's side of his rig. "I'm going to hurry up to Floyd's and see if he can give me a ride, but if he can't, I'll go with you and Mom."

"All right then." His dad motioned in that direction.

Glen dashed down the driveway and up to the neighbors' house, running all the way to the front door. He rapped on it a few times and waited. The wait seemed to drag on for a while before Floyd opened the door. "Good morning, Glen. What brings you by so early this morning?"

"I was wondering if you were busy this morning and if you could possibly give me a ride to the firehouse. My car won't start, and I'm supposed to meet some of my friends there, so—"

"I've got to be at church early, and I'm running behind," Floyd interrupted. "Sorry, Glen."

"Okay, I'll have my father give me a ride then. Thanks anyway." He turned and made a hasty retreat down the driveway, where his parents now waited for him in the buggy.

Why me? This wasn't the way I wanted my morning to start, yet here I am with a dead

199

battery, and I'll probably be late meeting up with my friends. Glen got into the buggy. "Thanks for giving me a ride, Dad."

"No problem. Oh, and the bag you had setting by the car is now by your feet."

"Thanks, I forgot all about that." Glen watched as the scenery moved by—slowly. His hand matched the frustration he felt as it clutched the end of the upholstered seat. *I hope the guys don't leave for the hike without me*. He tried to refocus his thoughts.

Chapter 3

Martha waited by Mom's buggy for her sister to return from the house. Christine had forgotten to change out of her old worn-out shoes to a nicer pair for the social. Martha didn't want to be late and have all eyes on them as they walked into the singing.

"Come on, Christine, we need to get going." Martha tapped her foot and looked toward the house. "I wouldn't be standing here like this if I'd told you no to begin with. I really don't know how I let you talk me into doing this."

Mom had found out about Martha's decision to go along with Christine to the singing, and for the last couple of days she'd been in an extra good mood. She'd smile when the topic of Martha going to the young people's gathering came up. Mom had also mentioned another work frolic in a couple of days that she'd like her daughters to attend. Martha didn't care to attend any of these activities since she'd have to sit around and listen to all the ladylike things the other women had been doing.

Christine finally came out of the house and ran up to Martha. "Sorry about that, Sister, but I didn't notice I still had on my old shoes."

"It's all right. We're good to go, so let's get to Edward's now."

Soon the girls were headed down the driveway. Christine chatted a mile a minute about what friends would be there and about some of the boys as well. Martha wondered if Glen might show up, but since he wasn't in church earlier, she figured not. At least she would enjoy having a chance to sing with everyone.

The evening was still warm, so Martha grabbed her large water bottle to take a good sip.

Christine jiggled the reins. "Come on, Dolly."

The buggy lurched forward. Water splashed all over the front of Martha's dress. "Oh no, look at my clothes."

"Hurry, and look behind my seat. You should find a towel there. Go ahead and wipe at your dress, and don't worry," Christine added. "It'll dry."

"We've only got about a mile to go, so I don't see how it will dry in that short a time."

"It's only water. Besides, no one will say anything about it."

Martha reached back and retrieved the towel. "I hope you're right."

It wasn't long before they arrived at Edward's home. Christine pulled into the yard next to the other buggies parked near a fence. She set the brake and got out to tie the horse to the post. Martha looked down at her clothes. *I can't help feeling a little self-conscious with a big wet spot on the front of my dress.*

Martha heard a male's voice call out to Christine. It was Edward, standing with someone else. On closer observation, she recognized Glen. Martha's face warmed as she got out of the rig and joined her sister, who was approaching the young men.

"I'm glad you both could make it." Edward smiled at them.

"I wouldn't have missed it," Christine replied.

"Hello." Martha looked at the men.

They stared at her briefly but didn't say anything about the big wet spot.

Glen shifted his stance. "Hi Martha, it's good to see you."

She gave a nod. "Nice to see you too."

Martha couldn't help the excitement she felt seeing this handsome man again. Here was Glen casual but nicely dressed in his English garb. She was dressed in her Amish attire of course. Martha preferred remaining Plain because she was content with that.

Edward motioned to them. "Step this way. I'd like to show you all the new things that have been done. My father added onto this buggy shed several weeks ago. You've gotta see how it looks now."

Martha and her family had been to Edward's home several months ago for church service, held in the buggy shed. The room had seemed cramped, and the only bathroom was in the house, so they'd rented a Honey Bucket for the guests.

Martha was impressed as Edward showed them the new facility. It was large and even had a changing table for the mothers to use for diaper changes during church. He pointed to two new garage doors that had been installed.

The improvements looked nice, and the enlargement of the buggy shed would definitely be useful. The room was divided in half, and benches had been set up in one end for the singing that would take place after their light meal. The end where they stood featured a row of tables holding snacks and desserts.

Edward motioned. "Now that I've given you guys a tour, let's get in line so we can eat."

Martha picked up a paper plate and began to fill it from a selection of cookies, pies, doughnuts, and other items. Christine trailed behind her, visiting with some of her friends and getting her food too.

Martha stepped away and headed to a separate table where the drinks were located. She chose sweet tea from the other choices of water, coffee, and homemade root beer.

"Are you enjoying this so far?" Christine asked Martha as they took seats at one of the tables.

"Jah, the food sure looks good."

"After we're done eating and singing, there's going to be a volleyball game. Edward has everything set up outside. That should be fun too."

Christine's friends came over and sat down. Pretty soon Edward and Glen stepped over with their plates full of food. "Do you mind if we join you ladies?" Edward asked.

"We don't mind at all." Christine smiled up at him. "Please, have a seat."

The men plunked themselves down across from the ladies, said a silent prayer, and began to eat.

Glen looked over at Martha. "How have you been doing?"

"Pretty well."

"Have you done any more drawing?"

"I have been working on a sketch, but it's not finished yet."

"Maybe I could come by and take a look at some of your drawings."

Martha's face flushed with warmth. "That would be fine. How about coming by Saturday? I could make us some lunch and show you what I've done."

"My sister is good at sketching," Christine chimed in. "She's also good at fishing."

Glen's eyebrows rose. "Such praise. How can I say no to that? All right, I'll come by on Saturday."

Martha took a sip of her drink. "How have you been doing?"

"Great. I'm in training at the fire department and working for my folks at their mercantile."

"Which job do you think you'll stick with?" She tilted her head.

"I want to be a fireman, and hopefully in time I'll be able to make a living from it. But for now I'm trying to earn what I can, working part-time at the shop to pay for things."

"That makes sense." Martha nibbled on a chocolate chip cookie.

They continued to visit, sharing some things that were happening around their community. The time seemed to fly by.

It wasn't long before everyone took seats on the backless wooden benches and started singing. The men sat on one side, and the ladies used benches across from them.

Martha settled in next to Christine and one of her friends. *It's too bad Lori had other plans with her folks this evening,* Martha thought. *Although knowing my friend, if she had come with us tonight, she would have made some comment about Glen being here.*

As the singing started, she joined in with the rest of them. *I could easily do this again with my sister, and I hope Lori can come next time.*

Each song they sang contained meaningful references to Jesus. When they'd finished with all the songs, everyone gathered for socializing. Cakes, ice cream, and beverages were available.

Edward stood after a while, cleared his throat, and announced: "It looks like everyone has had

206

their fill of desserts. Now it's time for us to go outside for a fun game of volleyball."

The young people got up and filed out of the building to where the game would be played. Martha wasn't good at the sport, but she'd give it a try.

Once outside, they established teams, with the women against the men. Martha ended up being the first to serve the ball. She gave it a good hit that sent it up and over the net. The ball moved from the men's side back to the women's court a few times before someone missed it. Martha saw Glen grinning throughout the play. She couldn't help catching glimpses of him as they continued to hit the ball back and forth.

When the match was finally over and the girls had won, the men wanted a rematch to see if they could win the second time. Martha went back into the building where the food was and got a cold cup of water. Christine joined her. "Aren't you going to play the second round with us?"

"No. I think I'd like to watch this time."

"Okay, I'm going back to play some more if you don't mind."

"Go ahead." Martha took a good-sized drink and headed back outside where some chairs sat not far from the volleyball area. She spotted Glen heading her way. "Aren't you going to play again?"

"No, I think I'll sit this one out and just watch

the game. Besides, I'm not very good at this sport."

"You served the ball well and seemed to be playing fine." He glanced at the chairs and motioned. "We could both sit and relax. Would you mind some company?"

"That would be nice."

They watched as the game began and the men served the ball to the ladies. It went back and forth until one of the girls missed it.

Glen leaned closer to Martha. "When it's time for us to leave later, would you mind if I took you home in my open buggy?"

"I wouldn't mind. I'll just have to let Christine know what's going on." She smiled.

They continued to visit and watch the game. Martha was glad she'd come. *So far things are going well, but how long will that last?*

Monday morning after the guests had finished up their breakfast at the B and B, they left to go out sightseeing. Mom cleared the dishes while Martha put away the leftover food.

"I visited with your sister after she got home last night, but since you weren't home yet, I didn't get to chat with you. I needed to get to bed so I'd be up early to get things done this morning. How did it go?"

"It went well."

"Your sister mentioned that a certain young

man had asked to bring you home from the singing."

"Jah, that would be Glen Swarey."

Mom didn't respond at first.

"He seems like a nice guy, and we had a good visit. I'll be seeing him on Saturday for lunch here, and I thought I'd show him my sketches."

"I haven't seen that young man in church for a while. And from what I've heard, he is leaning toward not joining the church. Something about him becoming a fireman." Her eyes narrowed.

Martha clutched her apron. "I'm not sure what his definite plans are, and I won't know until I've talked to him more, hopefully on Saturday. When I spoke to him yesterday, he mentioned that he's working at his parents' business part-time and is in training at the fire department."

"That may explain why he hasn't been in church, being busy working at two jobs. Word has it that he's considering the idea of leaving the Amish. If that's so, do you think he's the right person for you to be hanging around with?"

"I'm only starting a friendship with him, nothing more. Besides, you've told me before that my tomboyish ways wouldn't help me win a suitor, so I'm sure Glen has no serious interest in me."

"I was speaking of the Amish men who would be joining the church and looking for a suitable mate."

"You don't need to worry about me. I'll be fine."

"I can't help worrying about you, and I'm not sure what to think about Glen either."

"What are you talking about?" Dad came into the kitchen, carrying his mug.

Martha looked up at her father. "Mom's worried about me making friends with Glen Swarey."

"I see."

Mom's brows drew together. "I'm not sure if it's such a good idea to encourage the young man to come calling here."

"Is Glen making you feel uncomfortable in any way?" Dad looked at Martha.

"No. He's only been nice to me."

"See, Sarah, there's nothing to worry about. And if there were any problems, I'm sure our daughter would tell us."

At that point, Mom kept her peace, but Martha could only imagine what she thought. "Thank you, Dad." Martha went back to cleaning up the kitchen.

Dad filled his cup with coffee and headed out the door.

Mom didn't say much, but it was obvious what she thought of Glen. Martha hoped in time her mother would see things differently. She liked Glen and hoped they could at least be friends.

Martha got the food put away. *I hope my mom*

won't do or say something unkind to Glen while he's here on Saturday. Since none of my other relationships have worked out, Mom has nothing to worry about with this one either.

Chapter 4

On Saturday Glen arrived at the B and B in his open buggy and pulled up to the hitching rail by the barn. The sounds of young sheep and goats could be heard from where he sat. Glen set the brake and climbed out of the rig. His stomach already growled from hunger. He hoped the midday meal would be soon. *I wonder what Martha has made us for our lunch today.* A screen door slapped shut, and Glen turned toward the porch.

With his thoughts focused on Martha so much lately, Glen hoped she would like to be courted by him.

She strolled out to greet him. "Good afternoon."

"Good afternoon to you too." Glen tied Prince to the hitching rail.

"Before we eat lunch, if you don't mind I'd like to show you around. We've got brand-new baby lambs and goats from our ewes." She led him over to where their large corral stood.

Glen stepped up and leaned against a nearby post. "Oh wow, look at all of them. You have a good number. They're sure cute." He pointed at a couple of the young lambs at play, scampering around, while others, like the baby goats, stood under their mothers busily nursing.

"Like I've said before, we have chickens at my folks' place to take care of, but this is much different."

"One of our neighbors has a coop full of poultry, and we often get fresh eggs from them. They let them free range on their place, and the owners also grain feed them."

"That's what we do too." He looked over at Martha and squinted against the sun. "You have a nice place here. It's relaxing."

"I think so too. But the most relaxing time is in the winter when we have few guests and a heavy snow has just fallen, making it tough for folks to get around."

Glen gazed at the sweet baby animals again. *I could listen to her talk all day. Martha has a calming tone to her voice.*

"Have you ever seen the inside of the bed-and-breakfast?"

"Nope. I've only driven by it." Glen didn't mention that he usually drove his car instead of a horse and buggy. A motorized vehicle was his first choice for transportation.

"I can give you a quick tour. After that, if you're ready for lunch, we can eat."

"That sounds fine." He followed her across the yard and past the patio.

"I'll take you through the guest entrance."

Glen followed her onto a porch that had many healthy flowering plants, as well as some comfy

213

looking furniture. It was a good location for enjoying the scenic hills. Next she opened the glass-paned door that took them into a neatly decorated sitting room. Inside were a couple sets of overstuffed chairs, some indoor greenery, and a large cut-glass vase holding fresh flowers. Against one of the walls stood a bookcase crammed with books for their guests to read.

He looked around. "This is nice. Your family did a lot of work."

"Thank you. My favorite thing in this room is the fireplace." She gazed at it longingly. "When the weather gets cold, it's nice to hang out here and roast a marshmallow or read. We have only the two rooms for guests right now. My dad plans to add more rooms later. Let me show you the dining room. It's this way." Martha led him out of the sitting room.

Glen looked around. "There's a lot of wood-work in here. It looks real nice."

"My dad wanted it this way. He put some thought into this area." She smiled.

As he looked at her, Glen couldn't help soaking up that smile. *Martha is so pretty. I can't understand why no one is courting her.*

"Are you hungry? I've made lasagna, buttered french bread, and a tossed salad. I hope that's all right."

His mouth began to salivate. "Sounds great."

"The kitchen is where our house actually starts.

We prepare our own food and meals for the B and B in here. We'll be eating in our dining room out there." Martha pointed at the doorway.

They went through the kitchen and into the dining room. Her siblings joined them soon after. "Glen, this is my other sister, Jeanna, and our only brother, Thomas."

"It's nice to meet you." He took off his hat and set it on a chair.

"Nice to meet you too," they said in unison.

Glen looked at the two place settings across from each other. They featured fancy plates, silverware, and dainty goblets. Setting in the midst of the table was a cut glass vase with fragrant roses resting in water. An embroidered crisp linen cloth adorned the table. *Didn't Martha say we were having lasagna for lunch? I hope I don't get anything on it.*

"If you'd like to wash up, I'll get our food on the table. Thomas can show you to the restroom."

Glen followed Martha's brother through a plain but well-kept living room, then down the hall to a newer washroom. "Thank you, Thomas."

"No problem." He turned and headed off.

After he washed up, Glen went back to the dining room. Martha had set out a nice garden salad, some dressing, and a platter covered with foil. Glen smelled the aroma of butter and garlic in the room. *That must be the flavored french bread.* His mouth watered.

Glen heard someone come into the kitchen and speak with Martha. He figured it must be her mother. Martha brought in the lasagna with pot holders and placed the pan on a trivet. An older woman came in with her.

"Glen, I'd like you to meet my mother, Sarah."

"It's nice to meet you."

Sarah nodded with what appeared to be a forced smile. "Yes, the same to you." Almost immediately she turned to leave.

"Go ahead and have a seat." Martha motioned to the chair closest to him. "Please excuse my mother. She has a lot to do and is hoping Christine will get back from her friend's soon to help her."

Glen dismissed the incident right away and took his seat. He hoped the growling from his stomach wasn't loud enough to be heard by her.

"Let's bow our heads."

After their silent prayer Martha slid the salad closer to him and then the dressing. Everything looked good as he dished himself some food and moved it back to her. With their tossed greens plated, she then rolled back the foil from the platter of bread and held it out for Glen to serve himself. Martha also took a couple of slices then replaced the foil to keep the bread warm.

She started to pick up the lasagna dish but paused. "I'd like to say something."

Glen tilted his head. "What would you like to say?"

"Um . . . this fancy tablecloth wasn't my idea. It was Christine's. I thought it would be just fine having the wooden table showing. I'm a messy eater, using my fair share of napkins, and lasagna on this fabric would be torture to clean."

He let out a chuckle. "Do you want to remove it first? I'm totally okay with that."

"Yes, and thank you. Let's take care of it."

After they situated everything, they took their seats again. Martha slid the main course over to Glen, and he promptly took a serving. She followed suit and placed a steaming piece of lasagna on her plate.

He took his first bite. "Mm . . . this is *gut*."

"Jah, my grandma's lasagna always tastes good."

"Thanks for inviting me over for lunch." He dipped his bread into the sauce and ate it.

"After we're through eating, I thought we'd be more comfortable either sitting outside on the patio or in the living room where I can show you my sketches." She forked some salad into her mouth.

"That sounds fine with me. I'm open to either one."

They continued to eat until Martha's father stepped into the room. "Well, hello there. Who is our guest today?"

Martha stood, as did Glen. "Dad, this is my friend Glen, and Glen this is my father, Abe."

Her father put out his hand. "I've met your folks, and now it's nice to meet you."

"Good to meet you, sir," Glen shook his hand.

"It looks like you're having Grandma's lasagna." He sniffed the air.

"Jah, Dad, and there's more out in the kitchen if you would like some."

"I'll have to do that after I check the mail. You two enjoy your meal." He said goodbye and left the room.

Glen saw the reception from her father was friendly, but he still wasn't sure about her mother's response. He refocused on how tasty the meal was and the pleasant company he was enjoying.

"I've made a chocolate cream pie for dessert."

His eyebrows rose. "That sounds good. I'll have to save some room for it." He grinned at her. "That's my favorite pie."

"Oh good. I hope you'll like my version. I like to add some mini chocolate chips."

"I haven't had one like that, but I'm anxious to try it."

Thomas poked his head into the room. "You'll like it. It's very good." He smacked his lips.

"Thank you, Thomas." Martha took the last bite of her salad.

"I don't like what she's eating right there though." Thomas wrinkled his nose. "That green stuff. I'm not a fan of it."

"You don't like a tossed salad?" Glen took a drink of water.

"Nope, but my family says I should eat green salads because they're good for me."

"I suppose it's not up there with pizza or a hamburger, right?" Martha teased.

"You got it." He played with the hat in his hand. "I'm gonna go outside now to see how my lamb is doing."

Glen took a bite of bread and looked at Martha with raised eyebrows.

"One of the lambs that was born a couple of days ago has spots on it." Martha pushed back her chair.

"Kinda like a Holstein cow." Thomas put his hat on. "See you guys later."

She waited until her brother left, then spoke again. "He'll probably make a pet out of her. He's been wanting to name her."

"That's nice. I'm sure he'll take good care of it." Glen patted his stomach. "That was a good lunch. Thank you."

"You're welcome. I'm glad you liked it."

"I'll go get the pie out now." Martha stood and picked up their plates.

"Would you like some help?"

Her cheeks flushed. "Okay."

Glen helped bring the food to the kitchen, and she put it into sealable containers. Then she put the leftovers in the refrigerator and pulled out the pie. "If you grab the pie, I'll bring out the clean plates and the server."

He set the dessert on the table and took his seat while Martha carved out a couple of good-sized slices for them. "There you go." She passed it to him.

Glen waited until she'd finished serving herself and was ready to eat. Seeing the tiny chips of chocolate floating in the fluffy cream filling, he anticipated the first bite.

As Glen and Martha ate the tasty pie, they chatted about his job and how she liked working at the B and B. By the time they finished eating, they'd decided to sit outside, and Martha led the way to the porch, carrying her sketchbook.

Glen sat beside her. "How long have you been drawing?"

"I've been doing this for roughly four years." She opened the book and showed him her work. "Some of these I did here in the valley, but I'd say most of them are from Lancaster where we lived before."

"Was it hard to move from a larger community?"

"Yes, but I prefer it here because it's quieter and there's more undisturbed land." She turned another page. "I'd like to go fishing soon and hope I can squeeze in a day."

"I like to fish as well." Glen looked at one of

her sketches and pointed. "This is pretty good. Where were you?"

"This is from a vacation we took in Colorado. It sure was pretty country. I could have drawn there for quite a while."

Martha turned over more pages. "It's fun to draw, and when I'm finished I've got a memory of that time. I know it's easy just to take a few pictures, but drawing it for myself is like I'm a little more a part of it."

Glen continued looking at her sketches and agreed with what Christine had said before. *Martha is good at sketching. I think she has talent.*

She looked over at him. "I have a question, and if you don't feel comfortable answering it, don't think you have to."

"What is your question?"

"How do your parents feel about you wanting to become a fireman?"

Glen hesitated. "My folks are not thrilled with my decision. Especially with my dad being a minister. They'd like me to take over their store one day. I like the excitement and the newness of learning how to put out fires." He squirmed in the chair. *I think it's time to change topics.* "Would you be free to go for a ride around the area?"

"You mean in your open buggy?"

"No, I've got a car, and I'd like to take you out for the day."

Martha leaned forward to see him better. "It sounds like fun. When would you like to go?"

"How about next weekend? Saturday again?"

"I should be able to do that."

"Good. I could come by before lunch if that works, and I'll treat us to a meal out."

Martha couldn't believe what a nice time she'd had with Glen. *I wish he would come to church.* She stood at the sink rinsing off the dirty dishes from their lunch.

Christine came in and walked over to her. "How was your time with Glen?"

"I think it went well. It was nice visiting with him."

"That's good. When I helped Mom earlier, she didn't seem too happy about Glen being here."

Martha turned off the water. "Jah, and she wasn't smiling much when I introduced her to him, but we're only friends, so she has nothing to worry about."

"I found the tablecloth I let you use folded off to the side. Didn't you use it?"

"Only at first. I was worried about getting the red sauce on it, and I mentioned my concern to Glen."

Her eyebrows rose. "What did he say?"

"He helped me remove it."

Christine rolled her eyes. "I should tell you that Mom and I came back through when you two were sitting out on the porch visiting. Our *mamm* lingered around the open window."

Martha frowned. "I wonder what she heard."

"Who knows? But I didn't say anything to her at the time. I grabbed an apple and went upstairs to read."

"Thanks for the heads-up. What are your plans for later?"

"I'm trying to talk Mom into letting me go to my friend's house to stay overnight and then go to church with them in the morning. I did help her with the tasks she had lined up, so I'm hoping she'll let me do it."

Jeanna came into the kitchen, interrupting their conversation. "Do what?"

"Go over to my friend's and hang out." Christine picked at a hangnail.

"Maybe I'll ask Mom to do that with one of my friends."

"I'm asking first, since I did a lot of work for her earlier."

"Okay, I'll wait awhile. Then I'm going to ask next."

Martha wondered what her mother had heard her and Glen discussing. *Did she hear us planning for Saturday? I hope she doesn't tell me that I can't go with him.*

Chapter 5

"Thomas, could you please take out the garbage?" Sarah knotted the bag.

"Sure, Mom, I'll get it."

Jeanna finished up her breakfast and brought in her dishes. "I like your french toast."

"Thank you. When you're done, Jeanna, would you mind putting in a new bag for the trash and then put it away?" Sarah washed her hands. "I need to talk with your father."

"I saw him head to your bathroom," Christine said as she came in with her breakfast dishes.

"Okay." Sarah left the kitchen.

Once inside the room, she saw Abe standing at their sink brushing his teeth. Sarah closed the door for privacy. "I need to talk to you."

He rinsed out his mouth and dried his face with a hand towel. "You do? What's going on?"

"It's about our daughter."

"Which one? We have three." He came out of the bathroom and stood near Sarah.

"It's about Martha." She wrung her hands. "I'm concerned about that young man coming around and influencing her."

"In what way? He appears to be a nice enough kid."

"What you've said is probably true, and I'll add that his father is a minister. But you'd think his folks would have better control over that young man." Sarah moved closer to her husband and clasped his arm. "Glen plans to come by here later on to pick up Martha in his car."

"I see. There's a fair number of young people who get cars before joining the church, Sarah. If my memory serves me correctly, didn't we both have one?"

She nodded.

"We didn't turn out so bad now, did we?"

"That was different. We weren't trying to go out in the world and turn away from our upbringing." She tapped her foot while crossing her arms. "I don't want him to undo all of our good work raising our daughter."

"Now come on, Sarah—"

"He's not the right one for Martha. She needs a well-grounded Amish man. If I could, I'd try to talk her out of going with him."

"Talk her out of what? Martha is only friends with Glen." Abe took a deep breath and released it slowly. "Besides, you know our daughter likes to hunt and fish more than sew and cook. Usually the young men she's been with have preferred a more ladylike young woman. My guess is that Glen won't be around long. Just like the others, he'll lose interest." He paused. "Anyways, how

225

did you find out about Martha going out in a car with Glen?"

She froze. *Oh dear. He would ask me that.* "Umm . . . I heard her speaking to him on the porch."

"Where were you when you heard their conversation? Were you outside with them? Were you out of their view?"

She looked down, avoiding his stare. "Okay, I was in the house in the dining room."

"So it sounds to me like you were eavesdropping on their private conversation." Abe frowned.

Sarah sat on the bed. "You're right. I shouldn't have done it."

Abe took a seat on the bed next to her. "It seems to me you are so worried about Glen that you're forgetting some of the things we did in our youth. And I can't say this enough: you've got to let Martha make her own decisions. She's old enough now."

"You're right. It's hard for me to let go."

"You mean it's hard for the both of us to let go." He reached his arm around Sarah's waist and hugged her.

She smiled at him. "Thank you, Abe, for hearing me out. And I'm sorry for carrying on over all of this."

"It's okay. If our own folks got through this when we were young, so can we." Abe hugged her again.

She closed her eyes briefly. *I hope my husband is right. Otherwise my job of keeping watch over Martha and that young man isn't finished.*

Martha had done her chores and showered for her date with Glen. Still wearing her robe, she looked through the closet, trying to make up her mind on which dress to wear. A knock sounded at the door. "Who's there?"

"It's me, Jeanna. Can I come in?"

"Sure."

Her sister came over by the closet. "Whatcha' doing?"

"I'm trying to pick out a dress to wear before I go out with Glen." She slid a couple of blue ones to the side.

"I think one of the boys from school is cute," Jeanna said.

"You do?"

"Well, not enough to go on a date with him." She leaned against the closet door.

"You're only sixteen. You've got plenty of time to find someone."

"I know, and I'm not in any hurry. I'm enjoying doing things that I'd like to do. In fact, I'm getting picked up later. I'll be hanging out with my best friend for a while today."

"That sounds like fun."

"I can't wait to go because her family got a new puppy and a kitten."

"I'm sure you'll enjoy them, just like when you're out with the baby lambs and goats."

"Jah." Jeanna looked in the closet. "That dress is pretty—the bluish-purple one."

"It's a newer one." Martha pulled it out and looked at the garment.

"I'm going to leave you to decide what to wear, because I want to go out and see what Thomas is up to. Maybe he's out with his lamb."

"Okay, I'll see you later. Have fun over at your friend's."

"Don't worry, I will." She closed the door behind her.

Martha held up the dress. "This is one of the three possibilities I would have picked out for myself. Guess I'll go with Jeanna's choice."

She continued to get ready before Glen showed up. Martha couldn't wait to see him again. Today her mother seemed her usual self and wasn't still acting upset. *Could I be imagining things, or is Mom beginning to accept my choices?*

Martha stood primping in front of the mirror. Through the open window, she heard a car pull into the gravel driveway. She heard someone running up the steps and hurrying down the hallway. "Martha," her brother said from outside her door, "Glen is here."

"Thank you, Thomas," she replied. "I'll be down in a minute."

His steps retreated.

228

She grabbed her small handbag, and her stomach fluttered at the anticipation of being with Glen. Martha left her room and headed down the stairs, where her folks waited by the steps. Christine was tidying things by the front door.

"Before you go, Martha, your mother and I want you to know that we hope you have a nice time." Dad patted her shoulder.

Mom offered a weak smile and nodded.

A knock sounded. "It's Glen." Christine opened the door.

"Hello, I'm here to pick up Martha," he said.

"She's right here." Christine stepped back. "I hope you two have a nice time."

"Thank you, Sister." Martha walked up to him.

"Are you ready?"

"I am." She stepped outside with Glen and turned back to wave at her parents and sister.

Martha had seen Glen's vehicle in town but never dreamed she'd one day be riding in it. She did not have a car and didn't care about having one because she enjoyed using a horse and buggy.

Glen led her to the passenger side and opened the door. "Here you go." He waited until she was in and closed it.

Martha and her family had hired drivers and been many places, so she automatically put on the seat belt. When Glen slid in beside her, she noticed how nice he smelled.

"I've made plans to drive up to Boalsburg for lunch. Have you been to Kelly's Steak & Seafood?"

"No, I haven't, but I sure don't mind trying it out." Martha placed her small handbag beside her on the car seat.

"I've been there a couple of times. They do have good steaks."

"That sounds just fine."

He started the car and pulled out of their driveway. The windows were down, and the wind came rushing in. Martha held on to her head covering. "I'll need to roll up this window."

Glen looked over at her. "Here, I can get that." He used his window control button by the door locks. "I apologize for not thinking."

"No harm done. My black outer bonnet did its job."

"It will take us about a half hour to get there. I made reservations for lunch, so we should get there on time." He glanced over at her and smiled.

"How do you like having this car?"

"I'm liking it, but I did have an issue one morning with the battery. It wouldn't start, and I ended up riding in my dad's buggy to the firehouse to meet some of my friends. We were all going on a hike."

Martha laughed. "See, if you traveled by horse and buggy, you wouldn't have had to worry about a dead battery."

"I know, right." He signaled to change lanes. "I've been having trouble lately with my younger brother."

"Oh? What's his name?"

"Leon. He's seventeen. He likes to work at the auctions in town and is training to do taxidermy. Leon wants me back at the store working five days a week with David, like it was before. And because of me being at the fire department learning things, studying for tests, and so on, things are strained with my family. My parents also want me to work full-time at their store."

Unsure of what to say, Martha remained silent.

"Leon's been hard to deal with. At least my other brother, David, who is sixteen, is easy to get along with."

"We both have siblings who are sixteen."

"Yes." Glen slowed to make a turn. "You know, I haven't told you my folks' names yet. They are John and Frieda. I have good parents, and they have gone out of their way to bring me up right. I'm just not sure about staying Amish."

Martha had been wondering when that topic would come up. Strangely enough she wasn't upset over how he felt. Martha hoped she wasn't leaning in that direction herself and just not aware of it. Or was it something else?

"Do you think in time you'll figure out what you want to do with your life? I mean, not all of us can know everything at first, but we don't

231

want to keep making mistakes." She glanced at him, then watched the cars moving down the road.

"I don't want to make many mistakes. Guess I'm wanting to make sure I get to do what I really want in this life."

Martha sat quietly. *I like him. I need to try not to be so opinionated. My daed told me once that was a problem of mine.*

"Can we change topics?" he asked.

"Sure. What would you like to talk about?"

"How about fishing? Have you done any of that lately?"

"Yes, I have. My dad and I squeezed in a few hours last week." Martha fiddled with her purse strap.

"Did you catch any fish?"

"We both did, but his catches were bigger than mine. I still had a good time though. There's just something so fulfilling about being away for a while in the great outdoors."

"I like it too." He looked over at her with his dreamy blue eyes. "Maybe we could go fishing together sometime. You could bring your brother or maybe Jeanna, if she likes to fish."

"Let me put it to you like this: they both could be talked into going. But if my sister went along, she'd be much happier taking a book to read, and Thomas would rather hunt for frogs along the shore."

"That would be fine with me. There's no rule that says you have to fish just because there's a lake or pond in front of you."

"That's a good point."

Soon the restaurant came into view, and she saw that up high next to the building stood a tall statue of a bull. Martha definitely hadn't been here before, and she couldn't wait to go check it out.

Glen pulled into the lot, and they went inside. The dining area was casual but nice. He checked with the host and was told that their table was ready.

Martha followed Glen and the host to one of the tables. It was busy, and she was glad he'd made reservations. It wasn't long before their waitress came with glasses of water. "Would either of you like something else besides water?"

Martha asked for an iced tea with lemon, and Glen went with a soda. She couldn't help gazing at his handsome features. Martha wished he wasn't toying with the idea of going English. That could be a problem if they began courting.

The waitress came by with their drinks and left them menus to peruse.

He leaned across the table, speaking softly to her. "There's something I'd like to ask you."

"You would?" She leaned in too.

"Martha, although we haven't known each other very long, I feel like we have a connection,

233

and I would like to court you. Would you be okay with that?"

"Jah, Glen, I would." Her face warmed, and it took a moment for what had happened to sink in. *Did I just agree to be courted by him? He doesn't even know for sure what his plans are for the future. Yet I'm excited about being with him. I've gotta be nuts. That's all there is to it.*

Glen cleared his throat. "What are you planning to order?"

"I'd like to try one of these steaks." She gestured to the menu. "It's a prime cut. How about you?"

"I'm looking to order the top sirloin. That's one I haven't had here yet."

"There's nothing wrong with trying new things. You never know, it could become a favorite."

"I agree."

She looked out the window and watched a lady walking by with a child. Martha wondered at times if she would make a good mother. Her own mom tried to get her to go to the work frolics or other get-togethers with her sisters now and then. Would she be expected to do the same with her grown children? Lori said she'd come with Martha to help out whenever she asked, but so far she hadn't done it. *Maybe Mom is somewhat controlling, but I'm sure she has my best interests at heart.*

The waitress came up to take their orders. Her

southern drawl made it clear she wasn't from the area. Martha thought it was fun to hear her speak. "Who's ready to order? How about you, ma'am?"

She couldn't help but smile. "I'll have the prime cut."

"How'd y'all like that cooked?"

"I'll try it medium."

"Okay. Would you like a baked potato, garlic mashed, or fries?"

"I'll have a baked potato."

"How about a salad? We have a garden, a Caesar, or the wedge."

"I'll have the Caesar salad."

The waitress looked over at Glen and took his order. Then she left the table.

"Your friend Lori is nice. She's the reason I came up to you that day. She'd told me about you a little beforehand at work and said you might be going to the event at the fire station."

"The same here. Lori told me about you before we met that day. I would have to say my friend is a bit of a matchmaker."

He chuckled and drank some of his soda. "I'd like to bring you by my parents' place soon. It would be nice for you to meet them since I've met your folks."

Martha sipped on her iced tea. "I'm fine with meeting them, so just let me know when."

"I believe you'll be a breath of fresh air to my parents."

"How's that?"

"I used to date an English girl, but she wasn't my kind of person."

"What do you mean?"

He grimaced. "Her personality was not enjoyable. She talked loud and could be very demanding, always wanting things her way. My parents didn't like her, and they told me so."

"Were you glad to let her go?"

"I was ready, and my folks agreed with my decision."

The waitress brought out their salads and said the rest of their food wouldn't be long.

"This looks good," Glen said.

"I agree. I'm looking forward to eating mine."

"Let's bow our heads for prayer."

Martha fiddled with her napkin. She couldn't stop wondering if his parents would like her.

Chapter 6

The next evening Martha rode in Glen's car to meet his parents and brothers. Even though the trip was short, she had plenty of time to worry about how the meeting would go. *Will his parents like me? I hope I don't say or do something wrong.* Martha bit the inside of her cheek.

In no time, Glen pulled his car into the driveway. "Here we are."

Her eyes scanned the yard and house. "It's a nice place."

He turned off the engine. "I like it. Are you ready to go in and meet my family?"

Martha took a deep breath and opened the car door. "I'm ready."

As the couple stepped inside the house, Glen's mother and father greeted them and introductions commenced. When Glen's brothers appeared, they were introduced too.

"Glen has told us about you." John's tone was gentle as he smiled at Martha. "Don't worry, it's all been good."

Frieda's soft eyes fell on Martha. "That's true. Lately our son has been talking about you."

Glen's face flushed.

Martha felt a closeness to his family even though they'd only just met.

John and Frieda seemed genuinely happy to meet her, which made Martha less nervous. They were polite to her and very kind.

Frieda was full of joy as she gave a tour of their place. Her love for her husband was apparent as she spoke about the nice work her husband had done in each room. Her appreciation overflowed, and it made Martha like Glen's mother that much more. All the fear she'd had about not being liked melted away.

After Frieda finished showing her around, they went to the dining room. His folks asked everyone to be seated. Frieda served everyone pie she'd made for the occasion. She also offered coffee and tea.

Glen's family seemed laid back and easygoing. Martha felt relaxed with his folks and especially enjoyed visiting with his mother about several topics. While they chatted, Martha learned that his mother enjoyed fishing and liked to go often.

Martha's mother had been more difficult today, ever since Martha had told her folks that she and Glen were courting. Her dad didn't make any fuss over the matter, but her mom was another story.

I just need to convince my mamm that Glen will not try to sway my decision to join the Amish church and go English. Martha shifted on her chair. *I also need to pray that he'll be willing to give up his car and worldly ideas and decide to join the church too.*

Chapter 7

On a Saturday in the middle of June, Martha had planned a little outing by the water for Glen, Jeanna, Thomas, and herself. Martha and Glen fished and caught some keepers, while Jeanna read a book and Thomas hunted for frogs.

Later they sat together on blankets to eat a nice picnic lunch she and Jeanna had put together at home. Martha paused to soak up the experience. It felt good to relax, staring into the sky with its calming blue tone and dipping into the water to cool her feet in the warmth of the afternoon. The birds sang above in a big maple that shaded most of the area.

As Martha reached into her tote bag for her sketch pad, she glanced over at Glen and was pleased when he offered her a warm smile. Martha couldn't help the attraction she felt toward him. She tried to focus on her sketch pad and began to work, but she heard a little rustling in the grass nearby. "Thomas, can you come check to see what is over there making that strange noise?" She pointed.

"I'll see what it is." Her brother crept slowly, inching toward the area, when something jumped up and away from him. "Oh boy, it's a big frog!"

Jeanna, who sat by the water's edge reading,

came to life, dropping the book and rushing over to him. "Where is it?"

"I see the frog, and it's a real big guy." He inched his way closer, leaning his body in to get a better look.

"Don't scare it," Martha instructed.

Laughing, Thomas grasped hold of the thing.

Jeanna's eyes widened. "You were right. That frog is big."

"Yep." He held it up, grinning from ear to ear.

In the excitement, Martha stopped sketching. Thomas brought the frog over to them. "Look at this guy. I'm sure glad we came here today."

"What will you do with it?" Martha asked.

Just then, Jeanna and Thomas motioned to Glen's pole.

Martha turned and looked. "Hey, you've got something on your line!"

"I sure do." He reeled and kept the tension going. "Whatever is on the line definitely has some weight."

To Martha's amazement, as it came onto the shore, the unusual catch turned out to be a turtle. It was hooked well and was a challenge to remove from the hook, but Glen worked carefully at freeing the poor thing.

Thomas was apparently interested in keeping the frog, and now the turtle could be something he'd want to take home. With some convincing, Martha talked her brother out of keeping the turtle. The frog was another story. He insisted that he was going to bring it home. She couldn't blame him for wanting such a big prize. Martha had a hunch Thomas would show the critter around to his family and friends.

As their outing drew to a close, Martha wished they could hang out longer. Glen had caught more fish after the turtle incident, and once things were packed up, they all rode back to her parents' place in Glen's car.

Sarah waited until Glen had left in his car and Martha was inside. She wished her daughter would give up the silly notion of continuing this courtship. *There can't be any future for them unless my daughter goes English or that young man joins the Amish church. How can my husband just sit back and let this go on?*

Sarah opened the chest-styled refrigerator. "What ingredients do I have to make a fruit salad?"

"Are you talking to yourself, Mom?" Jeanna asked, stepping into the kitchen.

"I guess so. I need to get things ready for tomorrow morning. Did you have a nice time today?"

"I sure did. The fresh air felt great, and the food was sure good." Jeanna took a seat at the table. "It looks like we've got guests in both rooms. I saw two cars out there."

"That's correct, and your sister should be helping me prep breakfast for tomorrow morning." Sarah took the blueberries out and inspected them. "I'm glad Christine didn't try to hang out with her friends today and stayed home to help me with the new guests."

"Who are they?" Jeanna tilted her head.

"The Coles from Montana."

"Wow, that's a long ways from here."

"The other couple, whose last name is Price, will be with us one more night. They're not too far away from home since they live in New York. They're a nice older couple. Mrs. Price said she'd like to come back next year and stay with us."

"That's nice."

Sarah picked out a couple berries to nibble on and put the rest away. "Also, Mrs. Price said that what she's enjoying most is watching the playful sheep and goats out back."

"They're real cute. I think most people like them."

"It's true, but they can be a lot of work."

"I totally agree. And Todd, that funny goat, is still up to his tricks. This morning he bumped into me and stepped on my foot."

"One of these days Dad might sell him."

"I hope not. I'm getting used to having him being around." Jeanna brushed at some lint on her apron.

Thomas bounded into the room. "Look what I caught on our trip."

Mom laughed. "Just look at those bulging eyes."

"Isn't he something?" He held it up to her. "Dad liked him and thinks I should turn him loose to eat the bugs around the yard."

"I think your father is onto something. That big fella could probably eat his weight in insects, and we certainly have plenty for him to consume around here."

"I want to keep him for a while. I just need to come up with something to put him in."

Sarah tapped her chin. "I'm wondering if there's still that big terrarium out in the barn."

Thomas looked at her while continuing to hold the frog. "I'll go see. Jeanna, will you come with me? I could use some help."

"All right, let's go." She got up and followed him out the door.

Sarah was pleased that her younger children weren't having any troubles. She wanted to bring up the subject of Glen with Martha but had decided it was best not to say anything in front of Jeanna and Thomas. There was no reason to involve them.

Sarah went into the living room, looking for her older daughter, but no one was there. She checked upstairs and found Christine trying to take a nap.

Sarah headed back down the steps and looked out the living room window. Martha was leaving the barn, where her father stood. *I wonder if they were discussing today's picnic.* Sarah watched as her daughter came toward the house. She took a seat on the sofa and waited.

Martha came in a minute later. "I'm home."

"How was your day?" Sarah called.

Martha entered the living room and took a seat in the rocker. "We had a good time. Did you see Thomas's frog?"

"Oh yes, and it's a big one. I guess he's out in the barn looking for something to keep him in."

Martha nodded.

"Did you catch any fish?"

"Jah, I caught a few bigmouth bass, but Glen fished longer than me, so he brought six into shore. He also reeled in a turtle."

"He did?" Mom shook her head. "I'm sure that was a surprise."

"It was, and of course Thomas wanted to keep it."

"I'd say the frog is enough for one day." Sarah fluffed the small pillow behind her back. "Where did you end up going in his vehicle to do your fishing?"

"We drove up to Carlisle Run and found a nice spot to rest, eat, and fish."

"I see. Has Glen changed his mind about becoming a fireman?"

"Not so far." Martha seemed to squirm in her spot.

"Hmm . . . are you going to keep allowing that young man to court you?"

"I'd like to. He's a nice person, and I have a good time with him."

"Even so, what will you do if he wants you to go English?"

Martha looked away from her. "He hasn't asked me to do that."

"If he does ask that question, have you thought about what you'll say to him?"

"Not really, but I don't think he will."

"How do you know for sure?"

"Because he's not trying to change me." Martha leaned away in her rocker.

Sarah pushed her glasses to the bridge of her nose. "Things can happen in a subtle way. For instance, you're riding around more in his car."

"Most of the time I'm still using your horse and your buggy or riding my scooter to do my errands." She sighed.

"I hope you continue to do so." Sarah paused as she searched for the right words. "I can't help saying it seems to me that you could still be out looking for other prospects."

"I've already agreed to let Glen court me. We have discussed this before, haven't we?"

"Of course, and I'm still hoping you'll realize that he's not what you need."

Martha stood. "I was having a nice day until this conversation began."

"I'm only trying to give you some sound advice."

"I'm going for a walk." Martha stood and hurried from the room.

Sarah felt guilty for ruining her daughter's day. *Why do I have so much trouble with her? All I want for Martha is for her to be happy. Surely she can't be that blissful with Glen and their strange arrangement.*

Martha went out the front door and saw her siblings carrying a good-sized aquarium. Thomas and Jeanna went to the side of the house, turned on the hose, and washed out the frog's new home. Dad strolled over, and together they watched her siblings' progress.

"I was having a good day until Mom started up with me about Glen and me courting," Martha complained to her father.

"Oh, she did?" Dad ran a thumb up and down his single suspender strap.

"Jah, she seems to think Glen isn't good enough, and that I should be looking for someone else. I don't agree with her."

"You need to do what is best for you. Hopefully in time your mother will ease up and let you make your own decision."

"Do you really think so? Because I'm having a hard time being around her these days."

246

"We need to pray, trust, and believe that the Lord will take care of this in His own way."

"Thank you for the reminder, Dad." Martha hugged him.

"You're welcome." He patted her back. "Just remember to pray and seek God's will for your life."

"I will." Martha smiled. "I was going to go for a walk to work off some of my stress, but now I feel better."

"That's good." He looked back at Jeanna and Thomas. "That frog is a hit with your brother."

"I agree. He seems pretty happy." Martha looked toward the house. *I love my mother, and I'll do what my father suggested. I just hope the Lord will hear my prayers and give me direction for where my relationship with Glen should go.*

Chapter 8

As June turned into July, Martha and her mother became busier than ever at the B and B, getting things in order for the next guests to stay. Mom spent less time trying to sway her into giving up on Glen, which was a relief to Martha.

"We've changed the bedding and gotten the rooms finished. I'll need to prep the strawberries and raspberries to go on the pancakes for tomorrow's breakfast. Would you mind helping me?" Mom asked as she carried the laundry from the rooms to the hallway.

"Sure, I'll help." Martha looked at the clock on the wall.

"You're probably looking forward to going out for lunch today with Glen."

"I am."

"Before I start to prep food in the kitchen, I'll need to run these sheets to the laundry room. Then I will be there to get started on the berries."

"Okay." Martha waited until her mother left before she went to the kitchen and got out a strainer to rinse off the berries. She planned on asking Glen about his spiritual life today. So far he hadn't talked much about his relationship with the Lord, and he didn't seem that interested in attending church. Martha needed to discuss this with someone, but it wouldn't be with her mother. Later today she would go visit Lori and get her take on what she could do.

Martha watched from outside the barn as Glen pulled in nearby with his car. *I have to admit, we've been using Glen's car a lot more often for our transportation. I'll see if we can go to lunch by horse and buggy this time.* She waved and motioned to him. *I hope he says yes.*

"Hi, I thought I could drive us today so we can enjoy the scenery and visit longer, if that's all right with you."

"Um . . . that would be nice if I had the time, but I'll need to get back right after we eat so my brother can go for his training with the taxidermist."

She shrugged and looked toward his vehicle. "I see." *That figures. Wanting to go by horse and buggy is out. I hope Mom isn't right about him trying to sway me into going English.*

He played with his keys and motioned to the car. "This way we'll have more time to eat and visit."

"Okay." Martha followed him.

Glen opened the passenger door for Martha and then got behind the steering wheel. "I hope you're looking forward to having lunch together as much as I am."

Martha looked into his blue eyes and smiled. "I

have been excited about doing this since I awoke this morning." She couldn't wait to be on their way and spend some quality time together.

As they left the yard, she saw her youngest siblings out helping Dad with the animals. They waved to Martha and Glen as they passed.

Martha figured Mom and Christine were inside readying the noontime meal. Mom had mentioned that after lunch she'd be baking something to take to their sick neighbor across the street. Martha liked how her mother was always so willing to help others. She set a good example of showing God's love.

Glen grinned at her and winked. He sure seemed chipper today. "I've got good news to tell you. I'm able to go out on calls for the fire department now."

"Congratulations! That is good news. You told me awhile back that you were getting close to having the required number of hours. Now you've made it."

"Yes, and I can't wait."

Martha was glad for Glen—he'd worked hard for this new role—but she wondered what the days ahead would be like. Until now, Glen's weekly firefighting classes had been held in the evenings. And of course he'd worked at his father's business during the week. But from now on, when the alarm sounded, her boyfriend was obligated to answer the call to serve their community. Martha wasn't sure if she was all that happy about the news, but what could be done? And each time Glen went on a call, he'd face danger.

As they traveled down the road to the restaurant, she hoped the siren wouldn't go off, because once it did, Glen would have to leave her and go quickly to the firehouse. Then she'd worry about his safety. *Would Glen ease my mind and let me know he was okay afterward?*

He bumped her arm. "What are you thinking about?"

"I'm sorry. I was deep in thought about the future."

"What about the future?"

"Just thinking about the days ahead now that you're on duty."

Glen flapped his hand. "Oh that. It shouldn't be hard. I'll be under close supervision with George and Don, the veteran firemen. Besides, they treat me like family. They're a close-knit group."

She nodded. "That's good."

He rubbed his middle. "I'm looking forward to our meal. I can almost taste whatever sandwich I decide to order."

Martha nodded, while her palms grew sweaty. She'd been putting off asking Glen about where he stood with his faith. Martha figured this would be as good a time as any. "I'd like to talk to you on a more personal note."

251

"What do you want to discuss?" Glen glanced at her and then back at the road.

Martha took in a deep breath and let it out slowly. "How do you feel about church and serving the Lord?"

"I don't think that much about either. I've been taking good care of things myself, and it's been working out so far." Glen rolled his shoulders. "Why are you curious about that?"

Maybe he'll open up to me. "I'd like to know if you'd go to church more often if you came with us."

"Sure, I'd go, because I like being with you." His tone softened.

At least he didn't say no. I hope he'll go in the future and not just for me. He needs a relationship with God. Martha shifted on the seat.

"My mother has tried to get me to go, but I've given her excuses to avoid going. I have neglected to attend like I should."

Martha remained silent. *I'm falling for this guy, despite all of his imperfections, but I'm glad he's willing to go to church with me. That's a positive thing.*

Glen applied his brakes, bringing Martha out of her musings. A pickup truck ahead of them was driving quite erratically, swerving and at too fast a speed. The driver was having issues keeping the truck in his lane, and an oncoming car had to turn sharply to avoid hitting it. Then the truck veered off the shoulder and flipped upside down into a ditch.

Martha gasped. "I can't believe what just happened!"

Glen pulled off the road near the accident and turned on his flashers. "I'll go see if that driver is okay."

Martha rolled down her window and watched as her boyfriend looked inside the still-running vehicle.

"He needs assistance!" Glen pointed across the road at a nearby house. "I'm going there to make a call for help!"

Martha's fingers touched her parted lips as she sat in disbelief. She bowed her head. *Lord, please be with this man, whoever he is, and help him to be all right. Amen.*

It wasn't long before Martha heard the familiar sound of the siren blowing for the firemen and volunteers.

Glen came over to her, appearing somewhat shaken. "It won't be long before the injured man gets the help he needs."

The sound of an emergency vehicle grew louder. Glen walked back over and stayed with the gentleman until help arrived. Martha wasn't sure what to do, but she stayed in the car and let him handle things.

The bright red fire truck pulled up to the wrecked truck, and the men got out quickly, getting the items needed to treat the man.

Martha felt useless and fiddled restlessly with her purse strap while she sat watching events unfold. Meanwhile, Glen spoke to the older fireman and then assisted the crew with their work.

One of the men talked into a portable radio, giving the victim's age and other vitals. Martha listened from her open car window and heard that the medic unit would be there shortly. She released a heavy sigh as she watched the men work.

Another siren wailed in the distance, and in no time ambulance lights came into view. The EMTs wasted no time assisting the gentleman and getting him ready for transport to the hospital. Martha watched them put the man on a gurney and secure it before they loaded him into the ambulance. She noticed Glen eyeing his watch as the same older fireman talked with him again.

Afterward he came over to her side of the car, wearing a frown. "It doesn't look like we'll be having our nice lunch date like we'd planned today, and I'm sorry about it." He shook his head, leaning against the vehicle. "We've been here for a while, and I'm going to need to get back to the store. I'll get you home first, and on the way we can plan for another day this week."

"I suppose we should under the circumstances." Martha crossed her arms. This was a bittersweet moment. While disappointed about their canceled plans, her boyfriend seemed pleased to have helped out, and she was happy they had been there when the need presented itself.

Martha waved to Glen as he pulled out of their driveway. She turned and headed to the house, feeling empty inside. "I'm not real hungry, but I could use some food. Guess I'll go make myself something to eat," she murmured.

Thomas greeted her near the entry. "Did you have a nice time?"

Martha set her purse on the floor. "It wasn't what I expected."

"What do you mean?"

Christine came in from the other room. "Hey, you're back. How did it go?"

"I was about to tell Thomas how it went."

Mom, Dad, and Jeanna joined the group.

Soon Martha and her family were sitting in the living room and she was telling them the whole story.

"So now you all know how my time with Glen went today."

"Sounds like you had an exciting day." Dad tugged on his beard. "It's good you and Glen happened on the scene when you did."

Thomas nodded. "I wish I could've been there and watched."

Her sisters sat quietly, shaking their heads.

"You must be hungry." Mom rose from the sofa. "We've got leftover ham and cheese wraps from lunch in the refrigerator."

"They were good," Jeanna spoke up.

Christine licked her lips. "I added some hummus to my wrap to see how it would taste and was surprised that it didn't taste bad at all."

Martha stood. "One of the plain wraps sounds just right to me. I'll go help myself."

Mom followed her into the kitchen. "There's some freshly brewed tea if you'd like."

"That sounds good." Martha went to the sink to wash and dry her hands. Then she got out the food and drink from the refrigerator. "I can see how Glen's kind of work is exciting, but I sure wouldn't want to do it on an everyday basis."

Mom got out a plate and glass for Martha. "Some folks are meant for that sort of work, but not all of us are."

Martha hoped to finish her lunch quickly, avoiding any negative discussion about Glen. *When I'm through here, I'll go next door to Lori's and see if she's available to talk.*

When Martha arrived at Lori's house, she was pleased to find her friend at home and glad they were able to have the living room to themselves so they could visit. She took a seat on the couch and repeated the whole story.

Her friend listened in the sun-filled room,

256

nibbling on one of the homemade brownies she'd brought in on a tray before they'd sat down together. "What a day you've had, Martha."

Martha helped herself to a brownie. "I don't know what to do."

"What do you mean?"

"Glen is excited about working as a volunteer fireman. Can we have a real future together?"

"It depends on how far he wants to go with this." Lori shrugged. "Has he mentioned that he's toying with the notion of taking his position further?"

"No, he hasn't said anything to me about that." Martha took another bite.

When Martha heard the sound of a vehicle outside, Lori rose from the sofa and peered out the window. "It's my friend Sue, her brother, and Ronald's there too. Let's go out, and I'll introduce you to them."

Martha went along with her friend and met the guests. She could see that Lori was interested in Ronald. While the friends didn't stay very long, Ronald said he'd call Lori later. Martha couldn't wait to chat about this new fellow once they were back inside. Besides, she could use a refreshing topic to take her mind off all that had transpired earlier with Glen.

Lori sat back down with a contented smile. "I'm glad you could meet my friends."

"Me too. So tell me about Ronald." Martha grabbed another treat from the tray.

"He's a nice guy who I've been getting to know. Ronald works for his father. They're roofers, and their company is currently replacing the roof on the firehouse."

"Nice. Have you two gone out together officially yet?"

She shook her head. "But I'd like to. In fact, Ronald mentioned that he'd like to take me out sometime."

"How about double dating? You two with Glen and me. What do you think?"

"That would be fun. How about pizza, hiking, or miniature golf?"

"Hang on, you don't sound excited about this, do you?"

"Well, it has been a little while since I've had a date. Can you blame me?"

Martha leaned in. "No, I really can't. I think it would be fun for us to go out together." *Maybe things will be better double dating, and a change of pace might be nice too.*

I hope Mom is happy that I went to one of these again. Martha sat with a headache, waiting in the back of her mom's buggy after a lady's work frolic the next day. She was tired and couldn't wait to get home. Martha, Mom, Christine, Jeanna, and some other Amish women had helped clean a house for a widow friend of one of the women.

Martha would have preferred to be working at

the bed-and-breakfast, but they had no guests, which meant they didn't have much to do. So Mom had insisted they help out. Martha didn't feel that she had much to contribute in the way of socializing and would have liked to skip out, but Lori wasn't available for a visit.

Finally Martha's mom and sisters came out and headed to their buggy. *I'm glad we're done, because my head is hurting, and I can't wait to go lie down. Hopefully this will be gone by tomorrow when my double date with Glen, Lori, and Ronald is scheduled to start.*

The movement of her sister stepping on the foot peg brought Martha out of her thoughts.

"I'm beat." Christine climbed in and sat next to Martha.

Mom sat in the driver's seat. "I'm sorry your head hurts, Martha. I should have something at home for you to take for it."

"That would be nice."

"I think we all did a good job today for the nice widow lady."

"I agree." Jeanna untied Dolly and stepped up into the rig next to Mom. "What are we having for supper?"

"I set out a frozen chicken-and-rice casserole. Your father agreed to put it in the oven at the appropriate time. We've got plenty of macaroni salad from yesterday too, and I can heat up a jar of green beans to have with our meal."

"I can't wait, and the mention of food isn't helping." Jeanna opened her bag and dug through it.

"What are you looking for, Jeanna?" Christine's brows knitted together.

"I'm hoping there's something in here I can eat."

"How can you be that desperate? We did have lunch, you know." Martha massaged her temples.

"Aha, I found some gum. Does anyone else want a piece?"

Mom smiled as she held the reins. "Sure, I'll take one."

"Why not? Please pass it back here." Christine took one and offered it to Martha.

Martha shook her head. Her headache was making her nauseous. She tried listening to her mother and sisters chat, but her mind wandered. *I can't wait for this pain to go away. Also, I can't wait until I get to go out tomorrow with Glen, Lori, and Ronald. I like to be outdoors, and going hiking will be fun. We'll go out for burgers later on. It'll be nice to hang out with my friends.*

During the latter part of the day, Glen was still working in his parents' store. He spent most of his time restocking shelves. Minister Raymond Miller had just come in the door. The gentleman was one of three men who gave the sermons every other Sunday in his church district. "Hello, Glen, how are you doing?" He spoke in Pennsylvania Dutch.

"I'm fine."

Mr. Miller looked around for a moment. "We seem to be alone."

"We are."

"Good. I'd like to chat with you if that's okay."

"Sure. What would you like to know?"

"I'm wondering why you haven't been attending church regularly. Is everything okay?" He pulled his long fingers through the ends of his beard.

Glen hesitated. "Um . . . yeah, it's fine. I attend when I can."

"I see."

"Before I forget, I'd like to tell you I've gotten my hours in as a volunteer fireman."

"So what are your plans for the future? Will you stay here at this establishment and work for your folks?"

"I'm not sure. I mean, I'd like to give firefighting a try and see where it takes me."

"If you plan on following the path of becoming a full-time fireman, it will lead you away from your Amish roots. And that world out there isn't the same as what you are used to."

Glen felt awkward with this conversation, so he remained silent. Minister Miller had a reputation for getting things done and digging deep into the root of the matter with situations going on in his church. He certainly wasn't mincing words now, and it was evident that he cared.

Minister Raymond looked straight at Glen. "I need to tell you that it would be harder out there living in the English world when you've grown up in an Amish home and the Plain ways of our people. I would also like to remind you that living without the Lord by your side, struggling and depending on yourself or even strangers for direction is not the way to go. I can't stress enough how important it is for us to fellowship with other believers. It helps with our faith and keeps us moving down the narrow path to eternity with our God."

Glen listened. What the man spoke went along with what his parents had taught him. But he felt the strong tug of the world pulling at him to be a full-time fireman. Glen admitted, but only to himself, that he wasn't grounded spiritually enough to stay in church on his own.

Glen looked at the minister and spoke courteously. "What you've told me, I'll think about."

"I'll be praying for you, Glen." He looked back when another customer walked in. "I'll grab a couple snacks and be on my way."

Glen was glad when the minister left so he wouldn't have to think about what he'd said. Glen stayed by the counter and waited for the customers to pick out what they wanted. He could hardly wait to go hiking tomorrow, especially because he'd see Martha again. She would be the highlight of his day.

Glen's parents had voiced how much they liked her and even said they hoped he would keep courting her. He couldn't help feeling pleased that they approved of his girl. *Who knows what the future may hold for us? I think I'd like it to be with Martha as my wife someday.*

Chapter 9

The next day, on the return part of their hike, Martha swatted at a pesky bug while she walked the forested trail behind Glen. Ronald and Lori led the way down the hill that ended at the parking lot. It was nice hiking up to the end of the path. Being in nature with the little woodland creatures was Martha's favorite thing. The pungent aroma of the pines and fir trees around them floated on the air with the breeze.

To keep from dehydrating, they each carried an ice cold bottle of water from Ronald's backpack.

"Is anyone else getting hungry? Because I sure am." Ronald slowed down on the trail.

Lori replied, "I'm working up an appetite, that's for sure, and I am looking forward to a juicy cheeseburger."

"I can't wait for the fries too." Glen smiled back at Martha.

"That sounds good to me." She quickened her steps to catch up with him. "I sure like being out here. It's so pleasant, and it makes me think about hunting season."

"You've got a few months yet before that starts."

"That's true. I can always go shoot for some

practice. Dad and I like to do that when he has some spare time."

"Maybe I could go with you sometime for target practice." Glen opened his water bottle and took a drink.

"Okay, I'll talk to my dad." Martha looked down the pathway in front of Ronald. "We don't have much farther to go, do we?"

Glen looked over his shoulder. "Are you getting tired?"

"Nope. I don't mind this at all. This sort of thing is right up my alley." She paused. "It's nice to openly talk about my hunting hobby to you guys without seeming tomboyish."

Ronald and Lori didn't say anything.

"I'm sure in the English world you wouldn't have to worry much about being a lady whose hobby is hunting. I would imagine just about anything goes with them. I mean there aren't any set rules about women caring for their homes and family as there are in the Amish community."

Lori chimed in. "I would have to say in the Mennonite groups it isn't as big of a deal either. If a lady hunts, that's okay. Each of us has different hobbies."

Glen finished his water. "I'd say going English does have its benefits."

"Are you saying, then, that you would consider it?" Martha asked.

"I'm not going to lie to you and say absolutely

not. Yes, I've been giving it some thought, but I haven't made up my mind yet."

"If you did choose to go English, maybe your brothers would be influenced by your actions to do the same."

"I don't think so. My choices shouldn't make any difference to them. Anyway, my brothers haven't shown any interest in what I'm doing as a volunteer. Nor have they voiced any desire to own a car. But I'll admit, I do like having my car, and it would be hard for me to say goodbye to it."

Lori and Ronald both nodded in agreement.

Martha's body stiffened. *Glen is the closest person here to being Amish like me, yet he sure isn't acting it. I'm feeling like the odd person out with these guys.*

Ronald echoed Glen's thoughts. "I know it would be hard for me to give up my vehicle in order to be like you Amish with your horses and buggies."

Lori picked off a flower as she walked and let out a long sigh. "To be honest with you guys, I'm a little uneasy around any horse."

"Why is that?" Ronald questioned.

"Because I've been too close to them on occasions and have been stepped on more than once. And did that ever hurt. My foot was black-and-blue for weeks after the first time it happened to me."

"I'm sorry you had that happen," Martha said

as she brought up the rear. They reached the end of the trail and made their way through the parking lot to Ronald's convertible.

At the car, Ronald opened the trunk and stowed his backpack. Martha noticed Lori was wearing a cute denim skirt with a flowered top. *I think she could almost pass for being English except for her tiny head covering. Just like the guys wearing their blue jeans and T-shirts—they look English.* She bit her tongue. Now wasn't the time to voice her opinions to Glen. She would wait and talk to him in private. *Maybe once we've been dropped off at his parents' place, I'll let him know how I feel.*

Glen paid for his and Martha's burgers before they got ready to leave the restaurant. He'd noticed she didn't eat all her food and hadn't said much to any of them during the meal. Glen wondered what was on her mind.

Ronald got his receipt and put it away in his wallet. "Well, are we ready to head back?"

"I'd like to keep going, but my mother has chores for me to do when I get back." Lori grabbed her purse.

Ronald pulled out his keys. "I'll be helping my dad organize the lawn shed. He wants to get rid of the clutter."

"I hope to take it easy after this nice-sized meal." Glen rubbed his middle.

"If we have any guests staying this evening, I'll be helping with whatever Mom needs or wants done at the B and B when I get home." *At least there I won't feel out of place.*

Once they arrived at the Swarey home, the couples said their goodbyes. Martha slowed her pace as they approached the house. "I need to discuss something with you." Her tone had sharpened.

"I thought something was up, the way you were acting at the restaurant. Okay, but would you like to go inside first?"

"Nope. I would prefer that we stay outside and talk alone."

Glen motioned to a couple of chairs near the side of the house. "How about there?"

"Sure, that's fine."

He took a seat. "So what's on your pretty mind?"

"I'm having a problem with some of the things you said today." Martha plopped down on the padded chair and set her handbag on the ground.

"What do you mean?"

"I'm the only one between the two of us who clearly wants to be Amish."

"I don't have a problem with that."

"Are you sure? Because the way you were talking during the hike, it appeared to me that you'd rather be English."

He nodded. "I'll admit I'm leaning that way."

268

"How is our relationship going to work then?"

"If only you could see things my way. Why can't you consider going English with me? It wouldn't be the worst thing in the world, you know."

"I can't do that." She swallowed hard. "I think you should take me home now, Glen."

He reached for her hand. "Come on, Martha. Don't be like this."

"You are asking me to go English, and I don't want to."

"Okay, I'll take you home." He let go of her hand and rose. "Let's get in my car."

Martha got up, clutching her bag as they walked apart to his vehicle. The drive back was quiet, and it didn't take long until he turned into her driveway. Glen did not pull all the way in like usual. Instead, he parked his car just shy of the house.

Martha sat in her seat, still quiet, and so did he. This wasn't how she pictured their afternoon would end.

Finally Glen spoke. "So what do you want to do about this?"

"I'd hoped you would've made up your mind and wanted to join the church. You and I haven't even talked about that topic." She turned toward him and looked into his eyes. "I didn't want you to feel pressured into joining because of me. I figured it would be best to wait and see what your plans were first, and it looks like I've got my answer."

"I want to keep courting you, Martha."

"I would be fine with that, but it just won't work. Our futures are going in opposite directions." She wiped at her nose with a tissue. "I'm thinking it's best to break up right now."

"I don't want to." His voice sounded strained.

"I don't want to either, but under the circumstances it's for the best." Tears welled in Martha's eyes. "Goodbye, Glen. I hope things go well for your future." She slid out, closed the door, and ran for the house, not looking back. *I won't leave the only life I've ever known and seek a more worldly life. I hate to admit it, but Mom was right about Glen's intentions.* More tears came and fell onto the front of her dress. *What does he know about being English? And what will it take for him to realize he's not?*

Later that day, Glen worked with his brother Leon, cleaning the outside windows of the store. His mother had mentioned several days ago that she couldn't see out of them and wanted them shined up soon.

Glen's youngest brother, David, hadn't come to work today because he was at home recovering from getting a couple of wisdom teeth extracted. Mom had stayed home with him.

Glen was in pain over his breakup with Martha.

He replayed the scene in his mind. *Why can't Martha see things the way I do? And why can't she just follow my lead and give my way a chance?*

Glen picked up a sponge and plunged it into the full bucket. After splashing and sloshing the soapy water onto the ground, he scrubbed at the glass.

"You're not upset about something are you?" Leon's tone carried concern.

"The folks know about my breakup with Martha, but I guess I haven't shared it with you."

"Sorry you two had to call things off. What caused that to happen, if you don't mind me asking?"

Maybe talking about it again would help me in some way to get through it. Glen collected his thoughts and shared with his younger brother what had happened that day. It tore at his heart, but his brother was concerned about him, so why not express his feelings?

When his folks had found out about Glen and Martha breaking up, they were sad. Mom comforted him and suggested he pray about it, and his father agreed. Glen's heart felt bruised, like he'd been hit hard in the chest. Martha could be opinionated at times, but he wanted to keep having a relationship with her. He also wanted to have his way in the English world, and the hard part was, unless Martha changed her mind, he couldn't have both.

"What are you going to do about your situation?" Leon rubbed the sudsy sponge over the window.

"Mom suggested that I should pray about it."

"That sounds like good advice. We should all be doing more of that these days." Leon turned on the nozzle and sprayed off all the soap from the glass.

"Mom can pray—that's what she does. I, on the other hand, have been getting by fine on my own. I'm sure I can handle whatever comes my way."

"Are you sure about that? Life can come at us hard, not just once, but over and over again."

"If it does, I'll manage." Glen's tone was laced with pride.

Leon shook his head, dried the remaining water with a rag, and peeked through the clean window at the clock on the wall. "It won't be long before I leave for my taxidermy class. I'm liking that occupation more and more, even with the challenges of learning the whole process of making the animals look real."

"You'll get it. Besides, you do like to hunt for food, and one of these days you'll probably catch a real prize."

In the distance, the familiar whistle from the firehouse blew and Glen perked up. "I've got to leave you and get to work." Glen looked over to where their father kept his buggy parked. "Dad's not back yet from his errand, but he should return soon, I would imagine."

"But . . . I was going to be leaving here myself for class." Leon's head lowered.

"I'm sorry, Brother, but I've got to go." Glen dropped the sponge and raced to his car.

Chapter 10

The next week on Friday morning, Martha stood watering the plants on the front porch of the B and B. She had heard the whistle sound earlier, and now the siren of one of the fire trucks headed out to help someone.

It pained her to think of Glen. She missed seeing him and couldn't get him out of her thoughts. Despite his flaws, she realized how much she loved him and wanted to one day become Mrs. Glen Swarey.

Martha continued her task of tending the plants, but sometimes she'd be so deep in thought that she would overfill the pot, causing a mess of wet potting soil to splatter onto the porch.

Dad poked his head out of the front door in time to catch her in the act. "Martha, what are you doing?"

"Oops. Don't worry, I'll clean it up." She sprayed the dirt off the porch, leaving it looking nice and clean again.

"Is something on your mind?"

"I've been thinking about Glen," she admitted.

"I'm sorry you had to break things off with him. It was plain to see how much you liked him." Dad joined her on the porch and took a seat in one of the rocking chairs.

"Mom is probably glad we're not together anymore." Martha paused. "She was right about him."

"Your mom was right, but I had hoped she wasn't. The way that young man looked at you, like a lovesick puppy, I bet he won't forget about you too easily."

Martha shut off the nozzle and laid it down. "I've been praying for a miracle where Glen is concerned. I want him to join the Amish Church like I'm planning to do." She took a seat next to her father. "Why would he want to choose the English world over ours?"

"He still has time to make that choice, but no one, not even you, should force him to become Amish."

"I know. That is why—"

He held up his hand. "You broke things off with him, right?"

"Jah. I was the one."

"You, Daughter, have a level head. You state your opinions at times, but that's okay."

"I'm sad, upset, and lonely because of Glen's plans to go English."

"That's understandable, and you have every right to feel that way. Breaking things off with someone you have strong feelings for is hard. It will take awhile for the pain to lessen, but eventually it will."

"What are you two visiting about?" Mom stepped around from the patio.

275

"We're talking about a couple who have broken up." Dad looked at Mom.

"Well, give it some time, Daughter. The pain will diminish, and it should get easier. Breakups aren't easy, but someone new could fill that empty place. Your father did that for me years ago, didn't you, dear?"

He smiled. "Yes, I did. But for Martha it could be different. We'll just have to wait and see how this will all play out."

Mom's nose wrinkled as if there was a funny smell. "If you're about done watering the flowers, Martha, I could use your help inside with some dusting."

"I'm almost finished out here."

Dad rose to his feet. "I'm going to get some coffee first and do a little reading in *The Connection*. Then I'll need to get Christine, Jeanna, and Thomas to help me in the barn, cleaning out the horse stalls."

"That would be good, since Dolly likes her place nice and clean," Mom teased.

Dad winked. "Your horse is spoiled. I've seen you give her extra sweet oats. If you're not careful, she'll put on too much weight. Then she won't be able to pull a buggy."

"Aw, Dolly is in good shape, and she works hard for her oats." Mom chuckled.

"Okay, I'm going in. Enjoy your dusting, ladies."

"We will, and thank you, Dad." Martha got up and hugged him.

"You're welcome."

After helping her mother, Martha went out to the barn to see how things were going. Christine had left already to hang out with a friend. Jeanna and Dad were still inside putting some hay down in a stall. Thomas soon came into the barn with his pet lamb he'd named Cotton. Martha couldn't help walking up to her and kneeling down to stroke her coat. "She's so sweet."

The lamb cried, and Thomas petted her too. "I wanna keep Cotton."

"Your lamb's so friendly and cute."

"Dad says that's because of the bottle feeding we're doing."

Martha nodded.

"Guess the mama couldn't feed both of the girl lambs."

"Sometimes that happens," Martha explained, "and we have to compensate."

"What's *compensate?*"

"You know—balance things out, correct the problem."

"Oh yeah, guess I did know what that meant."

"I thought you did. Anyway, the auction's tomorrow. Do you know which sheep or goats are going?"

"Jah, and I can't wait to go. I like to watch the

animals as they are brought out to sell. And of course I get a hot dog or hamburger while I'm there."

"Me too—when I go along that is. The food is always better when you can eat it outside."

"Hello . . . ?"

Martha looked up and saw Lori smiling as she came into the barn. "Hey there, how's it going?"

"Good." Lori looked at Martha's brother. "Hey, Thomas. What a cute little lamb you've got there."

"Thank you."

She made her way to Martha. "Your mom told me to check out in the barn to see if you were in here."

"It's good to see you." Martha stood up next to her friend. "If you'd like, we can go inside and visit. We made some cinnamon rolls for tomorrow's breakfast, but we have extras to enjoy if you're interested."

"Sure, that would be nice."

Martha and Lori went to the kitchen, where they each took a well-frosted cinnamon roll and headed upstairs to Martha's bedroom. She closed the door, and they sat on the bed.

"Thank you for this yummy treat." Lori forked a gooey piece into her mouth. "Mmm . . . this is so good."

Martha dipped her finger into some thick frosting and tasted it. "Mom likes to keep her guests satisfied with hefty portions. She wouldn't want to have anyone leaving hungry."

They ate their food for a minute or two, before Lori noticed the dress hanging on the door. "Is that a new one?"

"Yes, I'm about done with it. I'd hoped to wear it out with—" Martha stopped talking and lowered her gaze.

"I'm sorry. How are you holding up?"

"Okay."

"I was shocked when you told me the very next day that you two were done."

"I still can't believe we're through. And to make matters worse, today that annoying whistle blew, and right away I thought of Glen."

Lori nodded and took another bite.

"I can't help wondering if he's okay. Since he went out to help with the other firemen, it could be dangerous."

"I can't say for sure about today. But I may be able to fill you in on Glen if you'd like, since I do see him at work sometimes."

Martha managed a weak smile.

"I saw him yesterday, and I've noticed he's not as happy as he used to be."

"What do you mean?"

"He acts like he's kind of bummed out. I can tell you one thing—Ronald wasn't happy about you two splitting up. He looked forward to more double dating."

"I would've liked to have kept doing that too, but you know where I stand on remaining Amish."

"I should've remembered that, but I sure wasn't sticking up for you that day was I?"

"Maybe not, and it did hurt my feelings. I felt like I was the odd person out."

"I'm sorry, Martha, for not supporting your decision. I hope you can forgive me."

"I forgive you, Lori." Martha gave her a hug. "We're best friends, and I always want us to be that way."

"Me too."

"Besides, I'm no saint. I've stated my dumb opinions plenty of times, which I then regretted and needed to apologize for." Martha grimaced.

"None of us is perfect," Lori said.

"That's for sure. All we can hopefully do is learn from our mistakes."

"Yes."

Martha looked at Lori. "You know what we forgot?"

"What?"

"Something to wash down these cinnamon rolls with. How about we go back downstairs and get us both a tall glass of cold milk?"

"That sounds good to me," Lori replied.

They set their unfinished plates aside and headed for the door. "We have chocolate syrup we just bought. You know what that means?"

"Yes I do . . . Chocolate milk to go with our treat." Martha's friend laughed.

Martha led the way down the steps. "That's right, and what could be better than that?"

After they got some chocolate milk and returned upstairs, they visited some more.

"You know what we should do?" Lori rested her fork on the plate.

"What do you have on your mind?"

"Maybe it would be good if you and I took a ride out to a scenic area where you can sketch and I can do some reading."

"That would be nice. I could use that right about now." Martha picked up her glass and took a sip.

"We'll need to figure out when we can go do it."

Martha set down her glass on the nightstand. "I could handle that about anytime."

"Okay then, let's do it soon." Lori stuffed a piece of cinnamon roll into her mouth.

Someone knocked on her door. Martha got up and answered it. "Hi, Dad, did you want to come in?"

"Nope, I just wondered if you and I could go out in a day or two to the firing range for a little target practice." Dad took off his glasses to wipe off the lenses.

"Sure, I'd like that. Thank you." Martha could hardly contain her smile.

"You're welcome. Okay then, that's all I needed to know. I'll let you two get back to visiting." He stepped back and shut the door.

Martha briefly closed her eyes. *Lord, thank You for the special people in my life who care about me. And Jesus, You know how I feel about Glen. Please keep him safe from all harm. Amen.*

Chapter 11

A few more weeks went by, and Glen continued to struggle as he tried to cope without Martha in his life. It wasn't easy. Whenever he drove by the Yoders' place, Glen stared at the bed-and-breakfast, trying to catch a glimpse of his girlfriend outside, but so far he hadn't seen her. He missed their time together and seeing her pretty face. What helped was keeping busy with his work at the store. Volunteering was a good distraction, and he liked it.

Today Glen was at the home of Mr. Phelps. The day before, the older gentleman had fallen and needed assistance. Living alone, he'd been prepared by wearing an alert necklace and had pressed its button to summon their help.

Glen's heart had gone out to Mr. Phelps as he talked about losing his wife over a year ago and how much he missed her. He'd mentioned having problems with his back and said he would have a nerve attack which caused him to lose mobility. Sometimes it led to a fall that added more problems, like sprains or even a break.

Glen remembered how they'd checked the man's vitals and made sure he was all right. Mr. Phelps had visited with the EMT guys as well as the firemen. He seemed desperate to socialize.

Doesn't the poor man have anyone? He should have someone coming by and checking on him every day.

Before the firemen left that day, they'd closed up his place since he'd be at the hospital for a while getting tests run, or possibly be kept overnight. His small dog stayed out of everyone's way, but Glen had known that it would need to be taken care of.

"He's an easygoing dog, only a year old, and his name is Toby," Mr. Phelps had said as he'd lifted his head. "Is there anyone here who'd be able to come by and check on my dog?"

"I'll do it," Glen had offered, as he'd stepped over to the man's gurney.

The man's face had brightened as he told Glen thank you.

Now Glen walked over to Toby and checked on his food and water. When he had taken care of that, he knelt by the dog and gave it some attention. Glen scratched behind the dog's ears, and it leaned into his hand. "You miss your master, don't you? I'll keep coming by until he comes back to take care of you himself."

Martha rode into town with Jeanna to do some shopping. She had hired their driver to take them to the post office to drop off some letters for Mom and then on to the grocery store.

Once inside the market, Martha picked out a

cart, and Jeanna said she wanted to push it along. That was fine with Martha. It freed her hands so she could more easily work off the list and grab the items needed.

"What did Mom say she was making for supper?"

Martha led the way to the produce section. "I thought she said Dad was grilling this evening."

"What kind of meat is he cooking?" Jeanna parked by the fruit, picked up an apple, and set it back down.

"Chicken breasts and hot dogs were the choices."

Martha cleared her throat. "Mom has written on here twenty pounds of potatoes. Would you mind picking out two ten-pound bags?"

"Okay."

Martha looked at the list again and checked off the vegetables and fruit that she and Jeanna were putting in the cart. They were about done, when Martha noticed Glen's mom and his youngest brother, David, coming their way.

Despite her breakup with Frieda's son, she would be as polite as ever. It wasn't hard with a person like his mother who carried so much joy in her heart.

"Hello there." Frieda came right over and hugged Martha. "What a nice surprise. I didn't expect to see you."

"It's good to see you too." Martha hugged her back.

David smiled. "Hi, Martha."

"Hi, David. How have you been?"

"Good, now that my mouth is healing up."

"How's that?" Martha tilted her head.

Frieda patted his shoulder. "David had two of his wisdom teeth removed. He did well through the whole procedure though."

The young man nodded.

Jeanna stepped up to them after setting a couple packets of blueberries in the cart. Martha realized that Frieda hadn't met her sister yet, and Jeanna had not seen David before, so she made the introductions.

"Nice to meet you," they said in unison.

Martha wound the ties of her head covering around one finger. *Should I wait to ask how Glen is doing or not worry about it and jump right in?* This part of the conversation would be awkward for Martha. She cared deeply for Glen and wanted to know how he was, but maybe it was better not to pry.

David spoke up. "Glen's been taking care of a dog named Toby."

Martha smiled at him. "Really?"

Frieda explained about a call Glen had gone on previously and how he'd volunteered to take care of the man's dog.

Martha listened with interest, desiring to hear any tidbit of information about the man she cared about so much. She was glad to find out

286

that Glen was fine and doing a nice deed for a stranger.

"Thank you for sharing that." Martha's shoulders relaxed.

"I should get back to our shopping and let you do the same. It was great seeing you again." Frieda gave a warm smile.

"You both have a good day, and I hope the rest of your week goes well also," Martha replied.

David started to step away but paused. "It was nice meeting you, Jeanna."

"You too, David." Her cheeks reddened a bit.

Martha and Jeanna headed off to continue with their shopping. It was nice to see David and Frieda again. She appreciated hearing Frieda tell the story about Glen's volunteering to care for the poor man's dog.

Martha looked at the list while they were in the baking aisle. She picked out a few different spices and placed them in the cart. She glanced toward her sister, who appeared to be smiling.

"Is everything okay?"

"Yes, I'm fine."

"Is there something on your mind you'd like to talk about?"

Jeanna shook her head and remained quiet as they continued to shop. Martha noticed her sister perking up from time to time, when a certain young man came into view.

Martha held up the list. "Jeanna, I forgot to

grab the condiments. Would you go back and get them for me? I'll meet you by the registers up front."

"No problem."

Martha pushed the cart near the checkout stand and waited for her sister. *Thank You, Lord, for keeping Glen safe. And please continue to keep him from any injuries. Amen.*

The next morning, Glen got up late and rushed to get ready for work. Mom had breakfast setting out and offered him eggs. "Good morning, sleepyhead. You slept a little later than usual, jah?"

"Mornin', Mom. Yes, all of us brothers were up late last night playing a board game, and before bed I forgot to set my alarm clock."

"I see. Your dad has left already, and the boys are in the living room."

"We're out here putting on our shoes," Leon called. "And we'll need a ride to the shop." He came in a few minutes later with David. "We forgot to set our alarms before going to sleep too."

Mom sighed as she set the scrambled eggs and toast on the table. Quickly she went back for the bacon. "Here you go."

"We'd better hurry and eat." Glen took a seat.

His brothers joined him, and they silently prayed.

"We shouldn't have stayed up so late." David slid his plate over to spoon some eggs.

"Yep." Leon picked up a piece of toast and slathered some jam on it.

Glen loaded his plate and wolfed it down, not wanting to waste any more time.

Mom took a seat. "It looks like it's going to be another warm day." She sipped her tea. "Would any of you like to take some coffee with you for work?"

"I'm fine." Leon bit into his toast.

"I don't want any coffee, but could I take a cola with me to drink?"

Mom's brows furrowed. "You'd like to drink that?"

"Maybe. It does have caffeine in it." David bit off some bacon.

"I suppose." She shook her head, as though in disapproval.

Their peaceful breakfast was interrupted by the fire department whistle sounding an alarm. "I've gotta go." Glen rose and put his plate and fork into the sink. "I'm sorry, but you two will have to take the horse and the buggy to work." He turned to head out.

"Please be careful, Glen." Mom's words reflected her concern.

Glen ran to his car, pulling out the keys. He felt his back pocket, making sure he'd put his wallet inside. *I don't want to be driving without my license.*

In no time, he was on his way to the fire department. The sun shone so bright it was sometimes hard to see, but he drove with caution. Up ahead on the road, something didn't look right to him. A truck sat halfway off the road with its hazard lights flashing. Glen slowed down and saw that the driver was outside of his vehicle. The man's form rocked slightly as he held a cell phone to his ear.

Curious, Glen pulled over and saw a huge mess. It looked to be what was left of a buggy, and the horse wasn't moving. The man exclaimed: "I didn't see it because the sun was so bright!" His voice sounded strained. "I've already called 911 and they're on the line with me."

Glen rushed toward the person lying in the weeds, bleeding, and realized it was his father. With heart pounding so hard he felt that it might explode, he knelt down beside him. "Dad, it's Glen, can you hear me?"

No response came from his father.

Glen heard the siren in the distance, and it came quickly. The big red truck pulled in close, and the men wasted no time. Their familiar faces gave him comfort, but Glen couldn't move. "This is my father." He stood as though frozen, watching the men checking on Dad.

George, the veteran fireman, gently squeezed Glen's shoulder. "We'll take good care of your father and get the help he needs."

One of the crew radioed for an ambulance. The responding voice said it was on its way.

Glen watched in fear as they took his father's vitals. He heard the numbers and could tell that his dad was quite weak. The ambulance seemed to be taking forever to arrive on scene. He tapped his foot nervously against the ground. "Where is that medic unit?"

"It shouldn't be long." George assisted with his dad. "What is your father's name?"

"It's John." Glen felt as though he was caught in a nightmare as he continued to watch them work. *I should be helping, but I feel so overwhelmed.*

A police car arrived with its lights flashing, and the officer got out to assess the situation. Glen would have to speak to the officer too. The policeman first asked questions of the owner of the truck.

Sirens in the distance indicated the ambulance was on its way. Glen closed his eyes. *Please, God, help my dad. Don't take him from us, Lord. Help him to get the best treatment he'll need. Amen.*

George came over to him. "Glen, would you like to call home to let your family know what has happened?" He held out his cell phone.

In all the confusion, Glen hadn't thought of that. "Yes, I need to let them know." He took George's phone and punched in his parents' number. The siren became so loud from the medic vehicle that Glen had to plug one of his ears to hear the ringing of the home line.

The driver cut the sound as he pulled up, and the two men moved quickly to get their patient to the hospital.

The phone rang until the answering machine came on, and he waited for the beep. "Mom, this is Glen. Something terrible has happened. It's Dad, he's been hit by a truck, and the medics have just arrived on scene to get him ready for transport to the hospital." He swallowed hard. "He is alive but nonresponsive." Glen hung up. *I hope someone will check the phone messages soon.*

His muscles tensed as he watched the medics working on Dad's motionless body. Glen couldn't believe what had happened to his father. He feared Dad might not make it.

Glen asked one of his crew what time it was. *My brothers may already be at the store. I'll try calling them to leave the same message.*

Glen dialed the number, and soon the greeting came on. Then he left his message. As he finished, someone picked up the phone. It was Leon. "Did I hear you correctly, Glen?"

"Yes. You'll need to leave the shop closed and go home to let Mom know what has happened. I'll come home and take you all to the hospital as soon as I'm done here."

"All right. See you there." The phone clicked off.

The medics had his father on the gurney and

292

were loading him in the back. Glen stepped over to the back doors of the ambulance. "Dad, we're coming behind you to the hospital. I love you." Glen spoke loudly, although his father was still unresponsive.

The policeman came over to Glen. "I'm not going to keep you here." With a look of understanding, the man wrote down his number and asked Glen to call later. Glen thanked him and the people who'd helped his father. Then he got into his car and headed for home. *I hope and pray Dad makes it.* Glen silently repeated the words over and over.

Lewistown, Pennsylvania

At the hospital, Glen paced inside the waiting room, praying for his dad's life. He stopped walking and sat next to his mother, who sat clutching a tissue.

Glen closed his eyes. *Lord, please forgive me for neglecting to pray, and help me to remember to rely on You for my strength. I've tried to take care of myself because I figured I could handle anything that came my way. Lord, I was so terribly wrong.* A tear trickled down his cheek. *I'm a wreck because of my foolishness. I've found out the hard way that this career isn't going to work for me.* He choked back a sob. *I was useless out there today, and the sight of blood made me feel faint.*

Glen felt a warm hand on his. He opened his eyes and looked at Mom.

"We have a loving Father, Son. Let's keep praying for your dad. Our God sees, and He is in control."

Glen nodded in agreement. His mom loved the Lord, and it showed. Although her face showed concern, Glen could tell that she wasn't angry this had happened, nor was his mother asking why.

Dad was in surgery, fighting for his life. It would be touch and go as the surgeons worked on him. Glen clung to the support of his Lord and his family.

Belleville

Martha had gone over with her mother to the B and B to get breakfast for their guests. Mom had already started frying the bacon when Christine came in.

"I'm here to help. What do you need me to do?"

"We need to make up four parfaits." Martha had just started to set out the items on the counter. She pointed to the cartons next to her. "These berries need to be washed off and dried first."

"Those are good-sized berries." Christine slid them next to the sink and grabbed a colander for rinsing. "I wouldn't mind a parfait myself."

Mom looked up from her cooking. "I'm sure

there will be enough for an extra one when you're done putting four together."

Christine licked her lips.

Mom placed the cooked bacon on a paper towel. "Those yogurt parfaits look pretty, but they're also a healthy food."

Christine glanced out the window. "It looks like another vehicle just pulled in. It's Lori from next door."

Martha stepped over to take a look. "Yep, Lori is here. I wonder what brings her by this morning."

Mom answered the door. "Good morning, Lori. Please, come on in."

"Morning. I need to see Martha if she's available."

"I'm here. What's going on?"

Lori hesitated. "There's been a bad accident. I just found out a little while ago."

All eyes were on Lori as she told them what had happened. Martha was beside herself after she'd heard the whole dreadful story.

"Oh, how awful for Mr. Swarey," Mom replied.

Christine looked at Martha. "That poor family."

"I can't believe what I've just heard." Martha's mouth gaped as she stared into nothing.

"The worst part is that there's slim hope he will make it. The next day or two will be crucial." Lori grimaced.

"We'll be praying for their family." Mom spoke

with firmness and went back to check on the food cooking on the stove. Christine nodded in agreement.

"Thank you, Lori, for letting us know right away." Martha gave her friend a hug.

"I couldn't help it, Martha. I really felt that you needed to know as soon as possible."

Martha teared up. "I'll be praying like I've never done before."

"Glen and his family will appreciate all the prayers sent up on their behalf." Lori stepped back. "I should get going and let you all get back to taking care of your guests' breakfast."

"Thank you again for letting us know," Martha repeated.

Mom smiled. "We'll see you later, Lori. I'll have to come by and speak with your mother soon."

"I'll let her know." Lori opened the door and waved as she left.

Martha headed for the doorway to the hall. "I'm going to go freshen up, and then I'll be back."

Mom nodded.

Martha headed to the bathroom and closed the door to have a moment alone. She removed her kapp so it wouldn't get wet and turned on the cold water to splash it onto her face. The bracing cold felt good and helped her nerves relax.

Martha dabbed her face with a soft cloth, then closed her eyes and began to pray. *Lord, I'm asking You for a miracle to help Glen's father through this difficult time. Jesus, let Your love shine on their family with kind, helpful support from others. Thank You, Lord. Amen.*

Chapter 12

The next morning after Martha awoke, she prayed for a while before getting dressed. It was hard to imagine how difficult the Swareys' night must have been. Glen and his family would have to endure another long, tough day ahead. *I wonder if Lori has any updates about Glen's family yet.* Martha's heart felt heavy for them as she headed downstairs to help with breakfast for their guests, as well as for her family.

When Martha entered the kitchen, Mom was looking out the window. "The wind is blowing, and there are some clouds in the sky. Maybe we'll see a little rain today."

Christine stood in front of the sink washing the dishes but glanced over her shoulder. "Hey, Martha."

"Good morning to you both. You know, some rain might keep the heat down today." Martha went over and stood by Mom.

"I'm going to make a batch of scrambled eggs for us and our guests. And I've already put the honey sliced ham in the oven to heat up." Mom pulled a big bowl out of the cupboard.

"I'll get out the eggs," Martha said with none of her usual enthusiasm. She lifted the lid of the refrigerator and pulled out a couple of egg cartons, then returned for the milk. Meanwhile, Mom got out the skillet and turned on the burner. "Martha, could you grab the butter out of there too?"

"Okay."

Jeanna, Thomas, and Dad came into the kitchen.

Dad pushed up his glasses. "We shouldn't be out there long. It's amazing how fast the young lambs and goats are growing—more and more they're eating hay like the adults."

Christine rinsed off a glass. "They're sure cute, and the guests like to sit out on the patio and watch them or come up to the corral fence."

Thomas laughed. "Cotton runs up to me like I'm her mother."

"You've earned it with all the care you've given your lamb." Mom cracked the eggs into the bowl.

Martha brought the butter over to her mom but didn't contribute to the conversation.

"I think Todd wants to stay on our property," Dad announced.

"I'm fine with that, even though he can be so annoying." Jeanna knelt for a moment to fix her shoelace.

"I don't mind him staying." Thomas looked at his dad. "He is kind of cute, in his own way."

Mom cleared her throat. "What do you all prefer—sausage or bacon with the scrambled eggs this morning?"

Sausage won out, so Mom put the bacon back

in the refrigerator and placed the links into the heated frying pan.

Martha watched her dad and two siblings head out of the room. She wished there was something else she could do besides pray for Glen and his family. She'd prayed a lot yesterday and had done the same this morning. *I wish I knew what was happening up at the hospital. I hope the Swarey family stays strong through this.*

"Martha, the oven heated. Could you pull out the container I usually put the muffin batter in? I'll also need you to get the tins out and prep them for the oven."

"Sure, Mom." Martha got out the supplies.

Mom looked her way. "Will you be going over to Lori's this morning?"

"I would like to."

"When you're done prepping the muffins, I'll take over so you can visit her." Mom poured the whisked eggs into a large frying pan. "I'm sure you're eager to find out if she has any news about Glen's father."

Martha nodded and got started on her task. It would be another long day of praying and trying not to worry about Glen's dad.

Lewistown

Glen and his family returned to the hospital in the morning. The surgery to repair a badly broken leg and to relieve pressure on his father's brain had gone well. Dad was still unconscious and lay quietly in the intensive care unit. They were able to take turns going in to see him.

Glen had a hard time seeing such a strong man lying helpless.

The doctor who had performed the surgery yesterday came to the waiting area and explained it would take some time for the swelling to go down on Mr. Swarey's brain. Also, the swelling in his leg needed to go down before the cast could be put on. The physician said that as each day passed, they should hopefully see some changes, and that keeping the patient in a medically induced coma would allow needed healing.

Glen was thankful that his dad was in good hands and receiving fine treatment.

After the doctor left the room, Glen asked if any of them would like something to eat. No one was ready, but Mom suggested he could go to the cafeteria.

He took the elevator to the second floor and found the place. Glen grabbed a yogurt, went to the register and paid. He sat down alone and thought of Martha. He felt the burden of the wrong choices he'd made. *I shouldn't have relied on my own strength. I've found out the hard way that I'm not cut out for a career in firefighting. It's more frightening than exciting—at least for me.* He opened the container and began eating.

Yesterday's accident scene overwhelmed me, especially with what happened to my father. I'm not going to go English, and I'm sorry for trying to push Martha in that direction too. I need to see her. If only she'd be willing to take me back.

Belleville

Martha finished getting the muffin tins ready for the oven, slipped on a pair of sandals, and headed next door. *I hope Lori has some news.* She hurried down the driveway and then up to Lori's parents' home. Their minivan sat running, and Martha saw Lori coming out of the house.

"Good morning, Lori."

"Morning." She stepped off the porch.

"I hoped you might have some word on Glen's dad this morning."

Her head lowered. "I don't, sorry, Martha, but if I hear anything, I'll let you know."

"That would be fine." Martha heard a buzzing.

Lori reached for her phone as it rang. "It's Glen."

Martha froze. *Oh Lord, please let Mr. Swarey be okay.*

"Hi, Glen, how are you doing?"

Martha found it hard to avoid eavesdropping on the conversation, but her antenna was up. His muffled voice sounded concerned.

"I see. So your father is in intensive care, and

302

your family is there? That's good. You need each other right now for support."

Martha heard something about wishing he could've done more.

"Glen, you were in shock seeing your father in that state. We never know how we will deal with a crisis until it happens. No one blames you for not being able to react a certain way." She looked up. "Just keep praying for your dad. That's important."

Lori covered the receiver and looked at Martha. "Would you like to talk to him?"

She shook her head. "No, I can't. I'm not ready for that."

"Okay."

More talking took place, and Martha could make out a little dialogue on his end. Glen sounded less intense, and it probably helped that Lori listened patiently to his concerns.

"Yes, I've seen Martha, and she's doing fine," her friend responded.

He wants to know how I'm doing. Martha looked away. *If he knew I was standing right by the phone, I wonder . . . But Glen still needs to change before I would have anything to do with him.*

"I can let her know how your dad is doing." Lori glanced at Martha again. "You've been doing a lot of praying and won't stop until your dad is better? That's good, Glen."

Martha noticed Lori pacing a little. *She probably needs to hang up with him and get going.*

"Okay, Glen. I'm sorry for what you're dealing with. I'll be praying for you and your family and asking that your dad gets the proper care he needs. Goodbye." Lori put her phone away. "Poor Glen."

Martha nodded.

"I'm sorry for almost putting you on the spot."

"It's okay, but it felt a little awkward even though I didn't speak to him." Martha rolled her tightening shoulders.

Lori moved toward the van. "I should be going to the station to do some work now."

"Okay. We'll talk again soon." Martha turned and headed down their driveway. She was relieved that Glen's dad was still hanging on to life. And it was good to hear that Glen had been praying for his father.

Soon she reached the back door to the kitchen and went in. Mom had taken a batch of blueberry muffins out of the oven. "Oh good, you're back. Did you find out anything about Glen's dad?"

"Jah, he's still in intensive care."

"He made it through the first night. That's a good sign."

"I agree."

Dad stepped in through the back door. "Hello, ladies. Would there be a chance . . ." He paused and sniffed. "Something smells mighty good."

"It must be those." Martha gestured to the muffins.

"Could I get some more coffee?"

Mom looked toward the pot. "I can make more since there's hardly anything left."

"Okay, sounds good." Dad pulled out a chair and took a seat. "Well, what are we talking about?"

Her mother stepped over to the coffee maker and got it ready.

"I told Mom that John Swarey is in the intensive care unit," Martha replied.

"They'll keep a close eye on him, and I hope he'll pull through soon." Dad's tone was upbeat.

"The Swarey family will need our prayers," Mom interjected as she grabbed another tray of unbaked muffins and put them in the oven.

Martha leaned against the counter, watching the coffee brew. "I can't imagine what they're going through."

Mom picked up a plump muffin from the cooling rack and set it in front of Dad on a napkin. "Your coffee is about ready."

He took a bite and practically swooned. "This is the best tasting blueberry muffin I've ever had."

Martha laughed. Dad had a way of lightening the mood in moments like these. Martha couldn't help her concerns for Glen and his family. She hoped for all their sakes that his dad would pull through. *I need to pray but not worry,* she reminded herself once more. *Even though I'm not going to voice my feelings out loud, I still have strong feelings for Glen.*

Chapter 13

A week had passed since his father's accident, and the family had decided to reopen the store. On his way, Glen had dropped off his mother at the hospital. He'd stopped in briefly, and his father had looked a little better. The doctor would come by later to talk with his mother, and Glen kept praying that the news would be encouraging.

He drove to the store and parked in the rear of the building. It was strange not seeing Dad's buggy in its usual spot. Glen got out and went into the back of the building. Once inside he saw Leon working on some bookkeeping.

"Mom's up at the hospital with Dad." Glen put his keys away in a pocket.

Leon looked up. "How did he look this morning?"

"Better. His color seems to be improving."

David set the broom aside and came over. "Did you see the doctor yet?"

"Nope, but the nurse told Mom and me that the doctor would come by later to fill her in. I wish I could be there for that, but I'll be training Isaac when he gets here."

"It'll be good to have another person here to

help out." Leon grunted. "Things are sure tough with Dad gone."

"I know, and I understand that you want to move on with your taxidermy training. I appreciate your willingness to help out with the bookkeeping, and at some point I'll be able to take over for you. I'm committed to making sure you get the opportunity to follow your dreams."

"Bookkeeping isn't that hard, but you do need to keep everything organized."

"I can do that." Glen rubbed his smooth-shaven chin. "Anyway, I'll let you get back to your work, and I'll go do some inventory. That is, until our new employee gets here." He grabbed the clipboard sitting on the file cabinet and took it with him.

As Glen counted the items in the first box of stock, he thought about his conversation with George at the fire station a week ago. Glen had explained that he didn't think firefighting was the right fit for him, and George had understood his concerns and agreed to let him go. It was hard saying goodbye to the friends he'd started to make at the station, but moving on was for the best. *Working at the shop may not be as exciting as firefighting, but that's okay. I've learned my boundaries and what is best for me.*

Voices from the store caught Glen's attention. He wondered if Isaac had arrived, but when he peeked out into the store, he saw that David was tending to a customer.

Leon joined him and looked out. "Is our new guy here?"

"Nope, not yet. He's still got time." Glen pointed out the window. "A horse and buggy just pulled in, so maybe that's him."

Glen set aside what he'd started and walked out into the store. The gentleman his brother was helping offered Glen a wide smile. Then he turned back to David. "Thank you for your help," he said. "I needed to find a gift for my grandchild."

While David rang up the items, the front door opened and Isaac walked in.

"Good morning." Isaac looked toward David and then at Glen.

"*Guder mariye.*" His brother gave the gentleman his change, and he left.

Glen moved over to the register. "Morning, Isaac. You're right on time on your first day, and it looks like you brought your lunch. I'll take you to the break room where the cooler is."

"I'd appreciate that."

"Follow me." Glen motioned.

Isaac followed him to the break room in the back of the store. After Isaac put his lunch away, Glen took him to the storage area and showed him where several items were kept.

"We bring in the deliveries and do inventory

back here. At times we restock out front. The food products and soft drinks usually sell quickly, so we need to keep up on those."

Glen continued to show Isaac around and talked to him about what his job would entail. "I'll take you back up front and show you what you'll be starting with." Glen led the way.

As they passed Leon working on the books, he looked up. "Hello, Isaac. Hope you have a good first day here."

"Thanks." The young man smiled.

"Right up here we have some unopened boxes from the back of the store," Glen explained. "These are glass knickknacks that will need to be set out for display right here." Glen pointed to the spot. "Once you've set them out, I'll have you write down how many items are there."

When David finished at the register, he moved to another part of the shop to do some restocking.

Glen watched as Isaac pulled out and unwrapped the miniature glass animals. He thought about how Mom liked to stay on trend and had seen some new gifts that she'd ordered for a trial run at the store. If they sold well, she would most likely reorder them.

Things were strange around the shop without Dad. He'd always make sure things were getting done. Glen felt that he needed to be certain everything was carried out the way his father preferred.

He walked over to the checkout counter, making sure they had plenty of paper receipts. They did, but the paper bag supply was getting low.

"Hey, David," Glen called.

"Yes?"

"When you get a chance, could you get us some more paper bags for up front?"

"No problem."

The sun shone through the windows, and it looked to be a gorgeous day. Glen decided to take a walk out to the phone shed to check for messages.

He called to his brother again. "I'm going out to check messages and get the mail."

"All right," David replied.

Glen headed out. It had been a couple of days since he'd checked the mailbox or the answering machine. Once he stepped inside the shed, the light on the machine flashed, but there was only one message, an advertisement for storm windows. He shook his head. "At least there wasn't something important."

Glen left the shed and went around to the parking lot in front of the store. Because no one had been there for a week, Glen made sure the hanging baskets and flower beds designed by his mom were well watered. They looked to be doing very well.

Feeling satisfied with his findings, Glen walked

across the parking lot to the mailbox and grabbed the stack of envelopes inside. "I'm glad I checked it today." He closed the door and headed back.

Once inside, Glen saw Isaac motion to him. "I've got this done."

"Okay, give me a minute. I'll be right back." Glen went to where Leon was. "Here's the mail. I'll take it to the house after work."

"Sounds good." His brother smiled. "I can't wait for tomorrow. I'll be at the taxidermy shop for half of the day."

"That's right."

"I'm really liking it. The fellow who's teaching me is good at what he does."

"One of these days when you're up to it and I catch a prize, you can make me a trophy."

"I'd like to." Leon grinned.

"Before I forget, Mom said she had a driver for this evening to pick her up before visiting hours are over."

Leon's brows raised. "Huh? I figured she would've had you come get her as usual."

"Me too, but Mom said she wanted to give me a break this evening."

"That's our mother, always thinking of others and trying to be helpful."

David came back and grabbed some of the paper sacks. "A car pulled in, but the ladies haven't come inside yet, and Isaac is still waiting for you."

"Okay." Glen walked with his brother. "Sorry, Isaac, I took the mail back there and got to talking to Leon. I've got a few boxes over here that you can open for me."

Isaac handed Glen the paper he'd written on. "Here's the amounts of the glass miniatures."

"All right." He took it from Isaac.

"These two boxes have lanterns in them. And this one has the Amish trinkets that'll need to be put out on the shelves." He showed him where. "I'll be near to help you and answer any questions." Glen glanced at the front door.

Isaac opened the closest box next to him and pulled out small, hand-painted glass Amish couples. He had a funny smirk on his face as he set them carefully in place on the shelf for display.

Glen showed him the Amish-styled postcards, key fobs, and magnets. "You can add these to the ones that are already out on display."

The young man nodded and went right to work.

So far the ladies hadn't come in yet, though their car still remained in its spot. *I wonder where they went?* Glen peeked out the window and caught them taking pictures of the buggies. Then they walked over to the buggy horses and took more pictures as they pointed at things.

David came over to where he stood. "What's going on out there?"

"Oh, just a few curious tourists."

"What are they doing?"

"Taking all kinds of pictures."

David shook his head. "Those silly English." He went back to where he stocked shelves.

Glen watched until they started walking toward the store. Then he moved over by Isaac. "I'd also like you to put those calendars out, and the faceless cloth dolls too."

"Okay." Isaac got busy on his next assignment.

About then the ladies came and looked around the shop with their phones in hand. One of them elbowed the other. "Look."

Her friend grabbed a shopping basket and turned. "Yes, I see them."

The ladies took their time checking things out in the aisles, making comments to each other at times and taking pictures of some of the things sold in the store. Glen was interested in how they seemed so intrigued with what he considered his family's normal way of life.

Isaac had finished restocking, and Glen showed him where to put the empty boxes in the storage area. While back there, Glen gave him another job and told him he could take his lunch break at eleven thirty.

Glen walked back to the register in case the ladies had a question. The women continued browsing and gathering items in their baskets. When they saw David working, they got their

314

phones out and snuck a couple of pictures of him from behind.

Glen's brother smiled, looked his way, and winked. Glen could see that David was onto what the ladies were doing.

Leon came out from the back and spoke to Glen in Pennsylvania Dutch. "I need a break. I'm going to stretch my legs and probably check on the horses."

"That's fine." Glen watched him leave out the front door.

One of the women had finished shopping. She came up with her basket and unloaded the items on the counter. "You have some real nice things here."

"Thank you." He began to ring up her items.

She watched him as he worked. "Has this business been here for a while?"

"Yes, for nearly twenty-three years."

"Nice." The woman looked back toward her friend. "Are you about finished?"

"I'm done." The other woman headed over with her basket in tow. "Oh, they have some snacks here."

"Remember, we are going to go grab lunch next."

"I'll just get this candy bar for dessert." She chuckled and put it in with her other items.

"Well, in that case, would you pass me that candy bar right there?" She pointed.

Her friend gave it to her, and Glen rang it up with the first woman's items. He told her the total while putting her purchases into a sack.

While she paid for her purchases, the other woman started unloading her basket. Because she had picked out so many things, Glen figured she must like to shop or was shopping for some family at home. "Where are you both from?" he asked.

"I'm from Georgia, and so is my sister. We flew to Pennsylvania a couple of days ago."

"Your arms must be tired if you flew all the way from there." He grinned.

"Oh, very funny." The woman chuckled.

"You two are a little ways from home."

"Yes, we like to come to what we call Amish country for some downtime."

Glen nodded and continued ringing up her items.

Soon after the women left, Glen's stomach growled. "Can I be hungry already?" He looked at the clock. "Guess it is that time of the day."

Glen had a good feeling about his new employee. And it was an answer to prayer that Isaac had come to work for his father's store.

As he looked out the window, another car pulled into the lot. Being open and serving the public again felt great. Nevertheless, Glen had mixed emotions because he was worried about his father. And he kept wondering how Martha was doing. He wished something could happen to bring them together again, but he needed to focus on his dad. *Lord, You are in control of all things and can hear each of our prayers. Please keep healing Dad so he can come home and be with us again. Amen.*

Chapter 14

That weekend was an off-Sunday, so Glen drove his mother, Leon, and David to the hospital. As they were gathered in the waiting room, the nurse on duty approached and told them that Dad was awake from his deep sedation and doing well. They hugged and celebrated the good news.

"Our prayers have been answered." Mom's eyes teared.

It wasn't long before the same nurse called Mom to go down the hall to see Dad. Filled with joy, Glen and his brothers remained in the waiting room. This was the day they'd been hoping and waiting for. He couldn't wait to go in and see his father. It had only been a little over a week, but it seemed like a lifetime since Dad's accident.

Glen thought about how wonderful it would be to let the rest of the family and his friends know the good news. Immediately his thoughts fixed on Martha. He missed her and couldn't wait to tell her about Dad waking up. He needed to see his girl and speak to her face-to-face.

Glen excused himself from his brothers and went to find a phone. When he found one down the hall, he pulled out his little address book and punched in the Yoders' number. He wished

Martha would pick up so he could talk to her directly. Instead, the answering machine came on. He didn't want to tell her everything over the phone, so he said that he needed to speak with Martha, and that he planned to come by that evening after the visiting hours at the hospital were over.

Glen wasn't sure how he had sounded. *I hope I didn't appear abrupt or pushy. I'm just desperate to see Martha.* He hung up and bowed his head in prayer. *Lord, You know how much I love Martha. I'm hoping there's a chance that she'll be willing to see me this evening and hear what I need to say. Lord, please help this to happen. Amen.*

Later that evening, Martha sat in the living room with her family. Most everyone read in the peace and quiet of the household. Christine had plans with a friend and had been gone most of the day.

Martha looked up from her sketch tablet as she finished some shading on one of her drawings. "I'm going to go outside for a little walk, and I'll stop at the phone shed and see if there are any messages."

"That would be a good idea." Her father barely glanced up from his book.

"Yes, that would be nice." Mom slowed on her mending and looked at Dad. "Remember, we have a few pizzas the girls and I prepped yesterday, waiting in the cooler. I'll heat up the oven when we're feeling ready to eat our late dinner."

He nodded.

"I can't wait for pizza," Jeanna spoke up.

Thomas peeked over his book of amphibians. "Me either."

Martha shifted in her scat. "Mom added extra cheese, so they'll be really good."

"I'm not quite ready for food, but I might be after I've read a few chapters." Dad smiled.

Mom started rocking in her chair. "No problem, I can wait."

Martha rose and carried her tablet upstairs. In her room she took a moment to do some praying. Sundays were a day to rest and reflect on loved ones who needed prayer. Glen and his family popped into her mind. *Lord, I hope John Swarey is getting better. We haven't heard anything for a while, and I hope that it's because he's improving. Loving Father, please be with Glen's dad and their family today. Amen.*

Martha headed back downstairs and went out the kitchen door. The birds on the feeders scattered. "Sorry, guys." She glanced at the swaying feeder and continued her walk. It was nice outdoors in the fresh air, and the warmth of the sun felt relaxing.

She stopped by her family's garden and checked out the plants. The weeding she and Christine had done the other day left the plot looking tidy and well kept. The tomato plants were heavily dotted with little yellow flowers, and the young green beans were growing nicely. So were the squash with their large golden blossoms. She couldn't wait to eat the fresh produce as it ripened.

Martha gave the colorful barn cat some attention after the animal strode over and rubbed against her leg. Calico purred loudly and meowed up at her. She picked up the cat. "You're so cute." Martha stroked her soft fur and then set her down. She moved on, looking at the flowering shrubs and Mom's pretty flower beds around the house.

When she got to the side of her parents' home, Martha could see Lori's place. *I wonder if she's learned anything new about Glen. I'm guessing not since she hasn't visited lately.* Martha walked across the thick, green grass and headed down the driveway to the shed.

Once inside, she saw the flashing light on the answering machine. Martha took a seat on the folding chair and began writing down the information from each call. On the third one, she heard Glen's voice. Martha listened and was surprised that he wanted to come by this evening. *I wonder why he wants to see me.*

When she finished taking notes on the slip of paper, Martha tore it from the notepad and carried it back to the house. Her stomach knotted up when she thought about Glen. The last time she'd seen Glen they had broken up. She didn't know how she would feel when she saw him again.

Martha entered the house and brought the slip of paper to her mother.

"Danki for checking the answering machine."

"No problem. Anyway, the walk was nice."

Mom gestured to the paper. "I see you wrote that Glen called."

"Jah, he is coming by this evening after visiting hours are over at the hospital."

Dad stopped reading his book and gave Martha his attention.

Mom tilted her head. "Did he make any mention as to why he wants to come by?"

"Nope, the only thing he said was that he wanted to talk with me."

"Well, this could be good news. Maybe you'll learn something new about Glen's father." Dad's tone was upbeat.

"Are you ready to talk with Glen?" Mom asked. "It has been awhile since the two of you have spoken to each other."

Before Martha could respond, Dad jumped in. "I'm sure Martha's fine with it. Besides, this way we'll get an update on John's condition, and we will know better how to pray for him and his family."

All Martha could do was nod. *Lord, please give*

me the right words to say when I see Glen later this evening.

Glen walked down the hallway that led to the ICU where his dad was located and took a look through the window in the locked door. No sign of his mother, so he went back to take a seat and patiently waited to hear the latest news.

Leon rose and looked at Glen. "I'm going to get a bottle of water. Would you like one?"

"No, thanks. I'm fine for now."

Thomas stood. "I'll go with you, and maybe I might get something to drink too."

Glen watched them leave and picked up the magazine next to him. Thumbing through the pages, he thought about how his friend Kevin had stopped by the store Friday to check on how Glen's dad was doing. Kevin had mentioned that his wife would be bringing a meal by their place later that day and promised that he and his wife would continue to pray for Glen's dad. It touched Glen's heart to know that his good friend and so many other people in their community were praying for his dad and offering help to the family.

Someone walked into the room, and Glen looked up to see Mom. She was smiling from ear to ear. "Your father is doing pretty well. He's just very tired. But of course that's to be expected."

"How's his leg doing?"

Mom took a seat next to Glen. "The pin and screws they put in during your father's surgery are holding things together well. The doctor said he won't need a cast for his leg."

"Oh, that's good. I didn't expect that. I mean, usually when someone breaks a bone they end up with a cast."

"You're right, but there are always exceptions. Your daed will have to take it easy, but he'll get better with time and by following the doctor's advice."

Glen nodded.

"Your father will have plenty of help from us and the community."

Glen was glad to be a part of such a loving group of people and to know that in time his father would be healed. *Thank You, Lord.*

As the evening dragged on, Martha tried not to be nervous about seeing Glen. They'd had their supper and were reading in the living room. Christine had just come home and wanted some of the pizza. Martha joined her in the kitchen to get some iced tea and visit.

Martha sat at the table and took a sip. "This tea is so refreshing."

Christine got a plate for her pizza. "I'm glad we had leftovers."

"Aren't you going to heat that up in the oven?" Martha questioned.

"Nah, I like eating it cold. I didn't used to though. When one of my friends asked me to try it, I found out that cold pizza tasted pretty good, so now I'm hooked." Christine pulled out a chair and sat across from Martha.

"Did you have a good time today?"

"Yes, and Edward was there too. We went to the park and played some Frisbee."

"I bet that was fun." Martha looked away and sighed.

Christine's brows wrinkled. "What's up?"

"Glen left a message on our answering machine. He'll be coming by soon to talk to me."

"Seems strange. Are you *naerfich* about seeing Glen?"

"Yes, I am kind of nervous." Martha glanced out the kitchen window.

"Do you need to talk about it?"

"No, I'll be fine." Martha figured talking about it would only make her more apprehensive.

Christine finished her snack and got up to wash her hands. "Let's go into the living room and get comfortable."

The girls went out and sat on the sofa. Christine picked up a magazine, and Martha tried unsuccessfully to relax.

Mom came in and sat in her favorite chair. "I was just visiting Lori's parents for about a half hour. Her mother, Miriam, and I made plans to get some meals together for Glen's family."

Martha smiled. "That will be a nice thing to do. I'm sure others in our community will be helping them out."

"Her husband, Sam, offered to take the food we make for them over to the Swarey home." Mom got the rocking chair moving. "I have a couple of ideas for what I'll make for them."

"I'm sure Frieda will appreciate it," Martha said.

They heard a vehicle making its way up the drive, and Jeanna glanced out the window as she came into the living room. "Glen's here."

Martha adjusted her kapp and drew a deep breath.

"Have a good visit." Christine offered Martha a dimpled smile.

Mom looked up from what she was reading. "I hope it goes well."

Martha smoothed her dress and headed toward the front door. *I hope this goes well too.*

Chapter 15

Martha opened the front door with a clammy hand. Glen's car was parked by the barn. Martha stepped onto the porch and took a couple of deep breaths before she strolled across the yard. She came to his vehicle and went around to the driver's side.

Glen rolled down his window and smiled. "Hi, Martha, it's good to see you."

"Hello, Glen." She looked into his blue eyes. She'd missed him, and in her heart wished things could be different.

He glanced around hesitantly before he spoke. "Where can we visit in private?"

"We don't have any guests this evening, so maybe inside the B and B. Or if you'd like, we could go for a walk."

He scratched his chin a moment. "Would you have any objections to us going for a drive?"

"I suppose that would be okay. I'll have to let my dad know before I leave with you. It won't take long—I think he's in the barn."

"Okay."

Martha ran to the barn and found Dad fixing the lawn mower.

Her father looked at her with a question in his

eyes. "I heard a car pull in. I'm assuming it's Glen?"

"Jah. He's waiting for me in his vehicle while I let you know he'll be taking me for a drive so we can talk."

"All right. Thank you for letting me know." Dad went back to working again.

She hurried out of the barn and got into his car. "Okay, I'm ready to go with you."

It felt strange being near Glen again. Martha collected herself before speaking. "How's your father doing?"

"Better. Today he woke up, but he's very tired. They're keeping an eye on the swelling in his brain, but the doctor thinks that with time he will make a full recovery."

"That's such good news. What an answer to prayer. But how are you and your family holding up?" She fastened the seat belt.

Glen started the car. "Mom's been a trouper. She goes in and sees him as much as possible." He backed up his vehicle to turn it around. "Leon and David and I are working hard at the store and praying a lot."

Martha looked over at him and spoke softly. "I've been praying too—for your dad and your family through all of this."

"Thank you, we can sure use it." Glen pulled out of their driveway and headed down the road. "I'd like to tell you some things."

"All right."

"I've made a decision. I'm not going English."

Martha's jaw dropped. "What? Did I hear you correctly?"

He slowed his car and pulled over in front of a big farm with a lot of open land. "Yes, you heard me correctly."

"What brought this on?" she questioned.

"The accident with my dad was a big, big wake-up call."

Martha remained quiet and listened.

"At the scene of the accident that day, I found myself unable to do anything. I froze while the crew worked hard to take care of my father. I never dreamed that would've happened to me, but it did." He stared out the windshield. "Here I thought my life wasn't exciting enough, but I found out that I was wrong." His voice trembled. "There's far better ways for me to have excitement, and volunteering with the fire department isn't right for me. I'd like to apologize to you." His eyes glistened as he looked directly at her.

Martha's heart began to melt. "For what?"

"For asking you to go English. That was wrong and selfish of me."

"I admit it hurt me, but your apology helps a lot."

"Martha, I hope you can find it in your heart to forgive me." He gently picked up her hand.

"I forgive you, Glen." She entwined her fingers with his. "And I'd like for us to get back together."

"I've hoped in my heart that we could find some way back to each other. I would love to court you again, Martha." Glen reached over and pulled her into his arms and gave her a kiss. "I'll want to join the church when my dad is able to come home and things calm down for my family."

"I'll wait with you for that day to come." Martha smiled.

The next few days were much the same for Glen and his family. They took turns going to the hospital to be with his dad during visiting hours. Dad would lie in his bed, getting the rest he needed but saying very little. The swelling in his leg had gone down some, and his head had improved too.

Glen could see the wonderful outpouring of love in his community. People were bringing in meals for them and offering to help out around their place. His mother's joy seemed to be strengthening with each passing day.

Glen went out to the barn to check on things after arriving home from the hospital one evening. The animals looked content and well cared for. A couple of men had come by earlier, made sure the animals had a fresh supply of water, and put down fresh bedding. *Thank You,*

Lord, for the wonderful people who care for us in times like these.

A vehicle pulled in, and when Glen looked out, he saw that it was the Millers' minivan. When Lori and Martha got out, Glen hurried right over. "Good evening, ladies. What brings you by?"

Lori slid open the side door. "We brought you some food."

"I made one of my casseroles for you and your family." Martha picked up the dish, and they headed to the kitchen.

Frieda came in soon after. "Good evening."

Martha stepped over and hugged her. "Hello, Frieda. We brought you some food."

Lori also gave Frieda a hug. "My meal was made earlier today, and it's cold. So you can heat it up anytime."

"Mine came out of the oven not long ago, so it's ready to eat now if you're hungry." Martha set her dish on the stove.

"What did you make?" Glen leaned over it and sniffed.

Martha removed the foil from the glass. "It's a stuffed-pepper casserole."

Frieda looked at her son. "You like green peppers?"

"Sure, Mom." Glen gestured to the casserole dish. "I'm looking forward to trying it." He turned to Martha and grinned. "Can you stay for a while?"

"Well, I came with Lori and would need a ride home."

"I can run you home."

"Okay, if Lori doesn't mind."

Lori glanced at her watch. "That's fine. I should be getting back. I'll leave you all to eat and visit."

Frieda hugged her. "Thank you again for the meal. We appreciate your thoughtfulness."

"I'll see you later, Lori." Martha gave her a hug.

Lori waved and went out the door.

Glen's brothers came into the kitchen and greeted Martha before helping their mom set the table.

"We have a couple of salads we can enjoy with your casserole, Martha." Frieda opened the lid to the refrigerator and lifted them out.

"I'll get the cold water out and five glasses," Glen offered.

Soon the kitchen table was ready, and they bowed their heads for silent prayer.

Glen was pleased to have Martha with them. It somehow made the time without their father easier to bear. He still couldn't believe how his life had improved. Glen was now sitting across from the prettiest, sweetest girl, and being with her eased his worries.

"I'm still grateful that Isaac asked if he could work at the store." Frieda loaded her fork with casserole. "It was an answer to prayer, and it's good to have the store open again. Your daed would want his business running for the community, not to mention that it's our primary source of income."

Martha remained quiet, and Glen figured that since this was a family issue, she'd be more comfortable staying out of it.

He took a bite of the stuffed pepper. "Mmm . . . this is good, Martha."

"I like it too," his mother agreed, as did Leon and David.

"Danki." Martha wiped her mouth with a napkin.

The family talked more about the business, and then Leon mentioned going to the hospital to see Dad in the morning.

After they finished the meal, Martha offered to help clean up the kitchen. Glen and his siblings cleared the dishes while Martha and Mom washed the dishes. It seemed right to have Martha in their kitchen like this, and Glen felt good about the decision he'd made to join the Amish church. He wished that he had listened better to Dad's messages. *But it's better late than never,* he told himself. *I need the Lord in my life, guiding and directing me through every single day.*

On the ride home, Martha thought about what a nice time she'd had with Glen and his family. She felt comfortable and relaxed in their presence.

Glen pulled up by the barn, parked his car, and

shut it off. "Martha. I'm so glad to have you back in my life."

"I'm happy we're together again too. I missed spending time with you."

"It was difficult going to the fire station to let them know about my change of plans, and I'll miss the crew. But not nearly as much as I missed being with you." He leaned over and kissed her cheek. "I'll walk you to the door."

They both got out and walked hand in hand up to the porch. "I hope we'll have another opportunity to be together soon."

"I do too."

Glen leaned in and kissed her lips this time. "*Gut nacht*, Martha."

"Good night, Glen." She stood there a few more seconds then turned and went in.

Martha entered the house and set her sandals by the front door. She then got a glass of water from the kitchen. Hearing her parents talking in the living room, she joined them and sat down on the couch with her water.

"How did it go? Did you deliver the food?" Mom stopped rocking.

"Jah, Lori and I got it taken care of."

"It must have gone well." Dad eyed the clock on the wall. "You've been gone for a spell."

Mom got the rocking chair moving again. "We figured you must have stayed and visited."

Martha nodded.

"I'm going to take a shower and hit the hay. It was a busy day." Dad let out a yawn and rose to his feet.

"I'll be there in a little while," Mom said.

"Gut nacht, Dad," Martha called to his retreating form.

"Good night, Daughter," he responded, looking over his shoulder.

"Where are Thomas and Jeanna?" Martha asked her mother.

"They've already gone to bed, and Christine should be home soon."

A car pulled in, and Martha looked out the window. "It's Christine."

"Good, now everyone's home for the evening." With a satisfied expression, Mom crossed her arms. "Now I can relax and go to bed without worrying."

A few moments later, Christine opened the front door and joined them in the living room. "Mom, should I go ahead and lock the front door?"

"Jah. I'd appreciate it."

Christine left the room and returned shortly. "I'm tired. Think I'll go on up to bed."

"That sounds like a good idea." Mom looked over at Martha. "I'm sure we'll be turning in soon as well."

Christine went over to Mom and gave her a hug. "Good night, Mom. Night, Martha."

"Good night," they said in unison.

As soon as Christine left, Mom looked over at Martha. "I'd like to say something to you that's been weighing on my mind for a while."

"What is it?"

"I want to apologize for the things I said when you and Glen were courting. I'm sorry for interfering and trying to sway your choices. You're an adult now, and you have the right to make your own decisions."

Martha stood up and crossed the room to her mother. With tears flowing, she gave her a hug.

"Danki, Mom, but you don't have to worry about me leaving the Plain life, because Glen plans to join the church soon too."

"That's *wunderbaar*. I'm sure his family must be happy about that."

Martha nodded. "And so am I."

Mom slowly backed up and patted Martha's shoulder. "We'd best get to bed. I'll go ahead and shut off the kerosene lights."

"All right, Mom. I'll see you in the morning." Martha headed upstairs to get ready for bed. She was thankful they had cleared the air. Things looked better all the way around—especially between her and Glen.

Martha sat on her bed and closed her eyes. *Thank You, Lord, for working in my life and helping my relationship with my mother to improve. Also, Jesus, thank You for helping John Swarey get better and for bringing me and Glen back together. His change of heart is the miracle I've been hoping for. Amen.*

Epilogue

One year later

Martha stood on the front porch of the older home she and Glen had found and rented a few weeks before they got married. They had liked what they'd seen as soon as they toured it, and when they moved in after the wedding, they furnished the house with pieces they had purchased and items their parents had given them.

It was fun doing some decorating after painting the rooms. The place had soon become cozy, reflecting their personalities. Two deer heads, his and hers, hung in the living room over the fireplace. They'd gone hunting last fall and both had gotten a deer. They'd had plenty of meat to share with their families, and Glen's brother Leon had done the nice taxidermy work.

Now that Martha was expecting their first baby, she and Glen would be turning one of the spare bedrooms into the baby's nursery. Her life was changing, and she would cut back on her chores at the bed-and-breakfast. In the near future, Christine would take over Martha's position there.

Today they were hosting supper at their place

and had invited both sets of their parents. Glen's brother David and Martha's sister Jeanna were courting, so they were also included. Martha couldn't wait to have a nice meal with everyone.

She thought about their finished dining room, ready for their guests to arrive. *Maybe one day we'll be able to buy this place from the landlord and live here permanently.*

Martha couldn't help the thrill she felt expecting their first child. She looked down at her middle, which barely showed, and gave it a gentle pat. Glen stepped over to Martha and pulled her into his arms. "What are you thinking about, *Fraa*?"

"I'm thinking how happy I am right now, sharing this home with you, dear husband."

"And a baby on the way." Glen gave her a big smile.

She nodded. "We'll have to get busy with the baby's room soon."

"I'll be happy to make it my number one priority." His smile grew wider.

A buggy pulled in, and Martha saw out the window that it was John and Frieda. His new horse was pulling their buggy. She watched her father-in-law coming up the walk with his joyful wife. John walked with a slight limp, but he got along well enough and kept busy at his store.

Martha's life was complete, and she owed it all to the Lord, for He had given her the miracle she'd asked for—a Christian husband who loved and accepted her for the person she was, not what others thought she needed to be.

Martha reflected on Acts 20:24, a verse she and Glen had read during their devotions last night after supper. *"But none of these things move me, neither count I my life dear unto myself, so that I might finish my course with joy, and the ministry, which I have received of the Lord Jesus, to testify the gospel of the grace of God."*

Martha's Stuffed Pepper Casserole

Ingredients:
2 pounds hamburger, browned
1½ cups chopped cabbage
1 large tomato, peeled and chopped
1¼ cups uncooked rice
1 medium onion, chopped
4 peppers, red and green, chopped
2½ cups water
1 tablespoon salt
1 teaspoon pepper
1 cup shredded cheddar cheese

Preheat oven to 375 degrees. Combine all ingredients except cheese. Pour into baking dish. Top with shredded cheese. Cover and bake for 1½ hours or until rice is tender.
   Note: This is a low-fat food.

Jean Brunstetter became fascinated with the Amish when she first went to Pennsylvania to visit her father-in-law's family. Since that time, Jean has become friends with several Amish families and enjoys writing about their way of life. She also likes to put some of the simple practices followed by the Amish into her daily routine. Jean lives in Washington State with her husband, Richard Brunstetter Jr., and their three children, but she takes every opportunity to visit Amish communities in several states. In addition to writing, Jean enjoys boating, gardening, and spending time on the beach. Visit Jean's website at www.jeanbrunstetter.com.

Alma's Acceptance

by Richelle Brunstetter

Prologue

Hopkinsville, Kentucky

Clutching her handkerchief, Alma Wengerd stood among her family and community in the last part of May. The rising sun broke through the dark-clothed mourners like the bright eye of a blackbird.

This isn't real. This cannot be real. Alma rested her fingers at the base of her throat. The soft fabric of her handkerchief could no longer provide comfort. She whispered, "My dear, Michael."

Alma wanted nothing more than to turn away when the casket was lowered into the grave. Her heart descended along with it, and when the casket could no longer be seen, she clenched her eyes shut.

She had been married to Michael for almost a year. Alma anticipated there would be challenges in their marriage, but nothing could have prepared her for his unexpected passing.

A week ago, Michael had been reroofing their home. Alma was tending to the garden plots in the front yard and didn't see him lose his balance. When she went back up to the house, she found him unconscious in the backyard. She'd called

911 from the phone shed, and later doctors at the hospital had confirmed that Michael had experienced severe head trauma. Alma visited him for a few days, hopeful he would recover, but then she received a phone message from the hospital: her husband had died during the night.

Her mother tugged the cuff of Alma's black dress sleeve.

Tears brimmed the corners of Mom's chestnut eyes. "Alma . . ."

Alma embraced her mother, rubbing her back. "I'll be okay, *Mamm.*"

This isn't about me anyhow, Alma thought. *Besides, I cannot ponder the what-ifs. You wouldn't want me to dwell on them, would you, Michael?*

Once the service was over, Alma approached Michael's family, comforting them and offering her condolences.

Whenever Alma was asked how she was feeling, she responded, "I'll be okay." But her body and soul said otherwise. She spent restless nights, wondering if she could have prevented Michael's death if she had found him sooner.

Alma shook her head, clutching her handkerchief. *I cannot keep thinking such thoughts. I have to stay strong. I must do it for Michael.*

Alma needed a clear conscience. Otherwise, moving on would be even more difficult.

Chapter 1

Nearly four weeks had passed since the graveside service, and with the help of her family, Alma had moved her possessions back to her childhood home. Keeping busy helped Alma avoid thinking about her great loss.

While Alma appreciated the help of her parents and younger sister, Makenzie, it made her life more difficult in some ways. *Why would my* schweschder *put the plates from the glass cabinet and the plates from the cupboard in the same box?* Alma asked herself as she dug up tomato plants from her garden to transplant into her parents' vegetable beds. *Those cabinet dishes are meant for special occasions. If I wanted them to be boxed with the cupboard plates, then I'd put them in the cupboard.*

It wasn't just the plates that bothered Alma. She wasn't thrilled with her mother leaving the boxes unlabeled. Alma had to tear off the packing tape, figure out what was in each box, and label them herself. When Makenzie had packed up the clothes, rather than folding the dresses and aprons and placing them in the bins with care, she had tossed everything together willy-nilly, not even keeping the aprons and dresses separate.

Alma got up and brushed off her dress. *I know*

it may upset Mom and Makenzie when I call them out on those things, but they're handling my belongings. I suppose I'll have to accept that I'm more orderly than they are.

She hauled the last of the plants to the buggy, glancing back to the barren garden plots that had once been abundant with fruits and vegetables. First it was the house, and now it was everything. The FOR SALE sign in the front yard caused Alma to tense. She took in a sharp breath, then climbed into the buggy and sat in the front seat, gathering the reins. *I can't think about this. If I allow those thoughts in, they will consume me.*

Alma guided her horse out to the road. The way back to Alma's childhood home was quite a distance, and if she had hired a driver, it would have taken about ten minutes. But Alma figured it would be best to use her buggy, mostly because she wasn't in the mood to converse with the driver and risk the possibility of having to talk about her current situation.

"I've finished moving things out," Alma said to herself. "But now I need to prepare to sell the place. I cannot dillydally. A house with the potential to be a loving home for another family should not be sitting unoccupied." She nodded. "I'm certain whoever ends up living there will be very much happy."

Or they can be destined to the same fate. Alma hitched in a breath, then pressed a hand against her temple. *Come on, Alma. Try to think about something else. Relish the comfortable weather.*

Straightening her spine, Alma rested her hands and the reins in her lap. The morning breeze soothed her for the time being. Thoughts continued to gnaw at her, but she did her best to focus on her plans for the day. Thankfully, her parents' home wasn't very far now, and Alma looked forward to the responsibilities awaiting her. She planned to tend to her mother's garden, as well as the plants she'd rounded up from the other house. Until she found a permanent place to live, she would be keeping the plants at her parents' home.

When she approached the property, her sister was outside with the kittens. Their cat, Missy, who had the fur pattern of a cow, had given birth a month ago. Seeing the tiny fluff balls pouncing in the grass caused Alma's heart to swell. Other kittens attempted to climb the steps leading to the porch where Missy lay licking her paw.

After pulling up to the hitching post, Alma stepped down from the buggy. Makenzie approached, cradling a kitten in her arms.

"Hello, Alma." Makenzie scratched behind the ears of the milky-furred kitten.

Alma returned the greeting, but then her gaze fixed on the kitten and his blue irises. "May I?"

Nodding, Makenzie passed the kitten to Alma.

"Aren't you just the cutest little snowball? Yes, you are."

"That's actually a *gut* name for him, Sis."

"You're right. I am pretty good at coming up with names unintentionally." Alma curled her fingers to rub the kitten's chin. She couldn't help but snicker as he meowed and leaned his head into the touch. The texture of the kitten's fur was like the velvety petals of Mom's hydrangeas.

Makenzie tilted her head. "Everything taken care of over at the house?"

"*Jah*, for the most part. We got all of my stuff out, and Michael's parents took care of his belongings." She paused and sighed. "The garden is barren as well. Thankfully we hadn't gotten a lot of livestock yet, other than horses and sheep. Otherwise it would've been more stressful."

"I have to say, you're handling all of this very well."

Alma did her best to keep a composed demeanor. "Well I prefer to get things straightened out." She met Makenzie's gaze. "Let me tell you. It's best to get everything sorted out right away. It makes it all easier when you have it figured out." Alma's gaze darted over to the garden. "I must take care of the plants. Do you want Snowball back?"

"You can set the kitten down. I have to feed him and his siblings before heading to the store."

"I can feed them. You can go right now."

"You sure?" Makenzie asked.

Alma nodded. "Just be sure to get the list I wrote. It's in the kitchen on the counter below the spice cabinet."

"Okay. Thanks, Alma. See you in a little while."

Alma watched as her sister bolted to the house through the yard in her bare feet. Alma lowered her chin and observed the kitten kneading the sleeve of her dress. She petted his head, and the sight of his eyes fluttering caused a sense of peace to envelop her. Alma smiled, but her vision blurred. "Dear Snowball, don't get me crying." Holding him gently, she went toward the shed where the other kittens waited for their meal.

Belleville

"*Danki.* Here's fifty-two cents back for you." Leila Troyer jangled the change before dropping it into the customer's hand.

"Thank you, miss. Have a good evening."

"You too."

Leila shut the cash register and watched as the customer walked to her vehicle. Leila then squinted at the clock that hung on the back wall above the shelves stocked with stamps.

"That's the last customer of the day. Time to close up." Leila strolled over to the playpen next to the side window. "Isn't that right, little Rachel?" She hoisted the young child in her

351

arms. Rachel gave a wide grin, similar to her father's, but with just a smattering of baby teeth.

Carrying her child, Leila went back to the entrance of the shop, where the front door was propped open, and flipped the OPEN sign over to the CLOSED side. "See how the sun is lowering, dear? That means the day is almost over." Walking back to the window next to the playpen, Leila peered out. "It also means we'll be having supper very soon. You're excited for that, aren't you?"

Rachel giggled as Leila tickled her stomach.

Leila gazed at the trees along the driveway as they bristled in the breeze. Next to them was the white wooden swing set that used to sit on the property of Aden's childhood home. It was the same swing set she had sat on when Aden played his guitar for her. She was grateful his parents had gifted it to them for their wedding, even if they weren't on board with them getting married at first.

Hearing a knock behind her, Leila whirled around and was instantly flooded with tranquility.

"I'd say someone's done workin'," Leila's husband said, his knuckle resting against the wooden frame.

"Aden." Leila hurried over to him then readjusted Rachel to prevent her from slipping. "Wait, were you referring to me or you?"

Leila giggled, giving Aden a peck on his lips. "Welcome home. How were things at work?"

"Same as usual. Sawing logs without sleep." Aden leaned slightly forward to kiss Leila again, though his lingered. Then Aden dropped a kiss on Rachel's forehead. "Did lil' *boppli* Rachel give you a hard time?"

"A little bit." Leila bit her lip, looking down at her child's brown eyes. "I'm thrilled being able to work in the shop finally, but I still need to be attentive to her. She gets hungry, she starts crying, and I have to drop what I'm doing to take care of her."

His smile wavered. "Maybe you should ask Mollie to come by and help."

Leila shook her head. "She's running things in the old card shop with Sally, so I can't do that."

"Sorry I can't help in any way."

"You don't need to apologize, Aden, though I do appreciate your concern." Leila's chest tingled when her friend's situation popped into her head. Leila curled her shoulders forward. "I'm just thankful that things are going smoothly overall, but my heart breaks for—"

"Have you been thinking about how Alma's doing?"

"Jah. When I first heard the news, I couldn't believe it. I still can't."

Leila and Aden had met Michael and Alma when they were on vacation in Pinecraft, shortly before Leila was in a family way. They were perusing the area, wanting to see a mural that was being painted. That exact evening they had come across the newlyweds, and the two couples conversed for a long time. Aden and Michael had plenty in common, since they both were loggers and had witty senses of humor. Leila and Alma bonded over childhood stories, in which Alma said she didn't have many friends due to some being put off by her type A personality. Leila had to admit Alma was a little intense at times, but her friend held her own and wasn't afraid to speak her mind. Leila admired that about her.

The chemistry between Alma and Michael was remarkable. Although they appeared to be polar opposites in behavior, somehow they had fit together. Leila could tell how content they were with one another, so it pained her to have found out about Michael's passing.

"Michael was such a good person." Leila spoke again. "He completed Alma, you know?"

"I do know." Aden gestured to Rachel, and Leila gave him a smirk before passing her off.

"When Alma called me, she sounded so panicked, and I didn't know what I could do for her. But not long after when I called to check up on her, Alma sounded fine."

Aden tapped the tip of Rachel's pudgy little nose, causing her to shake her head. "Well, Leila, people handle grief in many different ways."

"Even so, it doesn't sit right with me. When my mom passed away, I tried my best to seem like I was okay. I hope Alma isn't doing the same thing. You've got to allow yourself time to let it all out." Leila leaned to the side, eyeing the phone shed near the side of the road. "I should get ahold of her tomorrow."

Aden nodded. "I think that's the right thing to do."

They walked out of the card shop, and Leila retrieved her key from her pocket and locked the door. Aden, with Rachel propped under his arm, extended his free hand to Leila, and she laced her fingers around his. Leila was still in disbelief that she had been with Aden for three years. Here they were, with a child of their own and a home they had built together.

"What do you want for supper, Aden?"

With a cheeky grin, he responded, "Whatever Rachel wants."

"So applesauce and broccoli?"

"Sounds good to me."

Hopkinsville, Kentucky

Alma rolled over on her side as daylight peeked through the blinds of her childhood bedroom. "Did I even get any sleep?" she asked aloud, turning onto her stomach and smothering her nose in the pillow.

This had been an every night occurrence since Michael had died. Even when Alma endured weariness on the verge of slumber, she would rest her eyes, but her body refused to shut down. Alma would alternate her sleeping position constantly, though she'd usually give up and read one of the books she had in the lower cabinet of her nightstand. The pattern repeated throughout most of the night.

"I need to water the plants after I pick the berries today," she muttered into her pillow, "or else the sun will shrivel them up."

Scooting to the corner of the bed, she swept away the blond strands of hair that obscured her sight. Alma tugged the sheets off and began getting prepared for the day, slipping into a dress she'd draped on the back of her chair while she'd struggled to fall asleep the night before, and then picked up her brush and worked on untangling her lengthy hair. Once she pinned her hair into a bun, she heaved a big sigh. "Okay, I'm ready."

Alma hastened from her bedroom into the hallway. She turned to the entrance of the kitchen and made a beeline to the lower cabinet. Grabbing one of the colanders stacked on the shelf, she nudged the cabinet door closed and headed for the back door. An assortment of her family's shoes were lined up on a throw rug, evidence of Alma's efforts to organize them the night before.

She slipped on her shoes and stepped outside into the shade from the house.

"I cannot wait to pick some more blackberries." Alma pushed up the sleeves of her dress. "All the pies and jam I can prepare with them makes it worth it."

She strolled to the blackberry bush along the easement, admiring the dark fruits that were ripe for picking. Alma tentatively reached into the bush, avoiding the thorns as best as she could. The berries were easy to squish, so it was a messy process. If she happened to apply too much pressure to one, she'd take a bite out of it, swallowing the tangy juice.

Sometimes she'd stick her hand in the bush too quickly and end up getting scratched. Even her fingertips got nicked. In spite of this, it felt good to be doing something that took all her concentration. That way she kept her thoughts off of Michael and his death—that is, until everyone else went to sleep.

Enjoy picking the berries, she thought, stretching her arm for a berry deep within the bush. *Worry about bedtime when it happens.*

Just a little under an hour later, the colander was filled to the brim with berries and the sun had risen enough so there were fewer shadows surrounding the property. It was time for Alma to carry the blackberries into the house and get everything set up to freeze them. With the colander in hand, she wandered past the phone shed and heard ringing coming from inside. Alma stopped in her tracks, twirled around in the gravel, and went in the shed. Placing the colander on the built-in table, she answered the phone. "Hello?"

"Hello, Alma. It's Leila."

"Oh goodness, Leila. I wasn't expecting a call from you today. Thankfully I happened to be walking by." Alma pulled the folding chair out from under the table and sat down. "What's going on?"

"Don't worry, it's nothing urgent. I wanted to ask how you're doing."

"I got all the plants out of the garden yesterday, we removed the rest of my stuff out of the house earlier this week, and I am making preparations to sell the house as soon as possible."

"That's good," Leila responded.

Silence.

Alma leaned forward to rest her arms on the desk. "Are you sure nothing's wrong?"

Clearing her throat, Leila said, "I need to ask. Are you sure everything is okay?"

"I'm managing, but things could've gone better if little inconveniences didn't get in the way—"

"Alma. What I mean is, are *you* doing okay?"

Alma's throat constricted, and it was her turn to offer silence. Usually she'd tell someone, "Of course I'm doing okay," but she couldn't bring herself to say that to Leila. It troubled Alma not to be fully open with her friend, but she didn't want to pull Leila into her turmoil.

"Alma? You still there?"

She sighed and said, "I'm more concerned for you right now, Leila. You worked in the shop for the first time this week, right? How did that go?"

"It wasn't easy. It wasn't horrible either. More what you'd expect. Rachel is a year old, after all, so she's dependent on me."

"And you don't have any help in the shop?"

"Nope. Only me."

Alma slid her chair closer to the desk, reaching for a blackberry in the colander. "Well, I'd certainly provide you with assistance if I was there."

"Jah, that's true." Leila once again went silent. Then she nearly shouted, "Wait a second."

"What is it, Leila?" Alma plunked the berry on her tongue.

"I've had a thought, although I don't know if I should say it."

She furrowed her eyebrows. "Come on, Leila. You can tell me anything."

Leila paused then took a deep breath. "All right. I was thinking how it would be great if you came to stay with Aden and me here in the Big Valley."

Alma jolted to her feet. "Seriously?"

"I'm aware you have a lot on your plate, but

sometimes it's best to step away from it to clear your head and reflect. So if you're needing to take a break, you're welcome to stay with us for as long as you need."

"I'm not sure." Sitting back down, Alma cupped her chin. A wave of heat washed over her. "I do want to visit you both, but I just don't know if now's the right time."

"I understand. But if you are able to, the offer is always open. I need to open the shop soon. Would you want to talk this weekend?"

"Sure. I'll call you Saturday, Leila. Have a good day."

"You too, my friend."

Alma told her friend goodbye and hung up. She slumped in the chair, eyeing the colander on the table. "I still have to freeze the berries."

She got up and grabbed the container but paused. Alma couldn't shake away Leila's offer to stay with her. *I have to admit, it would be nice to get out of Kentucky. And I have been wondering how much Belleville has changed since my family moved.*

Alma had grown up in the Big Valley in the yellow-top community, but moved with her family to Kentucky when she was sixteen. Alma's parents had wanted to be closer to her paternal grandparents, who were having issues at the time.

I wonder if my old friend Elias is still around.

Then again, it's been six years since we've seen one another. Who knows where he may be?

Elias Kurtz had been a neighbor of hers, and they'd been inseparable back then. They'd visited one another frequently and played together during their school days. Over time, however, Alma had developed feelings for him, but since Elias didn't seem to show any interest in her, she kept her feelings hidden. Alma didn't want to jeopardize their friendship if it turned out he didn't feel the same way.

Leaving the phone shed and heading back up to the house, Alma still wasn't sure what to do. She opened the back door with her free hand, slipping off her shoes and making sure they were parallel with one another. *I could definitely keep myself busy in the card shop. I could help Leila out in exchange for staying with her.* Alma shook her head, then proceeded to the kitchen.

Setting the colander in the sink, she thoroughly rinsed the blackberries. While doing so, she heard the sound of footsteps coming from the hallway. She looked over her shoulder and saw her mom in the entryway of the kitchen.

"*Guder mariye*, Alma. I see you collected the blackberries this morning."

"I sure did. We have so many blackberries in the freezer already, but I had to get more of them." Alma held up the colander. "We can make as much jam as we want!"

Placing it back in the sink, Alma went to grab the quart freezer bags from the drawer where the other storage bags were kept.

"I noticed you were outside longer than usual. Were you out there with the kittens?"

"Not yet. But I'll be doing that in a little bit." Alma put the box of freezer bags on the counter. "Actually, Leila Troyer called me right when I finished picking. She asked me something, and I'm not sure what to do."

Mom gestured for Alma to sit on one of the stools that faced the kitchen island. "That sounds serious."

"No, not exactly. Well, kind of . . ." Alma sat down. "Mamm, Leila offered to have me come live with her in Mifflin County."

"Oh." Mom sat down on the stool next to her. "For how long?"

"She said for as long as I need."

"I see. And how do you feel about it?"

"I suppose it would be nice. I am curious to see how much Belleville has changed. But I have to get the house sold, and who knows how long that's going to take?" Alma strained a smile. "I don't want to run away from my responsibilities."

Mom's eyes narrowed then she wrapped an arm around Alma and pulled her into a hug. "You should go."

She blinked rapidly. "Really, Mamm?"

362

"I think it would be good for you to slow down a bit. You've done enough around here, and I do appreciate it, but you need time to yourself." Mom lightly rubbed Alma's arm. "I'm worried you may be overdoing it a little."

"I'm not overdoing it. Besides, I can't drop everything and leave. Otherwise I'll be stressing over it while I'm gone."

"Your *daed* and I will take care of selling the house."

Alma noticed how sweaty her palms had gotten, so she discreetly kneaded her apron. She swallowed, doing her best to keep her voice calm. "So that's it? I just leave you and Dad with a major issue that I should follow through with? No, I can't ask of that of you."

"You don't need to ask. We'll do it for you because we love you." Mom's tone was tense, yet it did not tremble. "And if you're still uncertain, you should pray for guidance." Mom got up from the stool, patting Alma's back before leaving the kitchen.

"Mamm is right," Alma whispered as tears stung her eyes. "I should pray."

Clasping her hands together, Alma lowered her head. *Lord, I have a request. Please give me guidance in making this decision. If it's in Your will, let there be a purpose for me to go. Allow something good to come out of it.* Her hands quaked, so she squeezed harder to stop them from shaking. *I want to have things under control, but You and I both know I have no control over what You have planned for me. Whatever happens, I will do my best to trust You.*

Chapter 2

Belleville, Pennsylvania

A week had passed since Leila invited Alma to come stay with her, and Alma called back to let her know that she'd be happy to stay for a few weeks. Now with only a couple of hours before Alma arrived, Leila was excited to see her friend. They hadn't seen one another since their Florida trip, and Alma had never before visited Leila at her home.

I don't want to say the wrong thing, Leila thought while feeding Rachel a spoonful of strawberry jam. *If I express too much concern, I may end up upsetting her.*

Rachel squealed and extended her pudgy arms to Leila.

"You want more?" Leila placed the spoon on the counter and grabbed a small bowl of oatmeal, which had been soaking in milk overnight. "You can have more jam after eating something more filling." She scooped the mushy oats and held the spoon in front of Rachel's eyes. "Here you go, lil' Rachel."

Resting her head near the window, Alma sagged against her seat in the back of the vehicle. Her driver, Elaine, was one of the friends she'd made when she first moved to Kentucky. Elaine grew up in an Amish home, but during her *rumspringa* she settled down with someone who wasn't Amish, meaning she never joined the church like Alma did. Alma never understood why some people decided not to join the faith. There was some appeal to the English world, she'd admit, but the unfavorable parts outweighed the good. It was less strenuous to live a simple lifestyle.

She would miss the familiar scenery they were passing, but a new journey was before her, and Alma couldn't wait to return to the Big Valley.

The car ride brought her back to when she'd moved to Hopkinsville. Although it had been disheartening to pack up everything and leave the place where she'd grown up, Alma had been optimistic about the possibilities.

I hope Makenzie won't stay too mad at me for leaving, she thought.

Alma's parents were supportive of her decision, but Makenzie didn't like the idea of Alma traveling alone, as well as staying with a friend in another state for who knew how long. Before leaving, Makenzie had stuck to Alma like sap on a tree trunk. As soon as Alma embraced her parents one final time, Makenzie ran up and hugged her, asking Alma to call home often.

Saying farewell was difficult, but Alma had a feeling this was the right choice. She still had a

sense of guilt looming over her for asking her parents to take care of selling the house, but Alma acknowledged that she needed time away from Hopkinsville.

Her drowsiness reached the point where she could no longer hold off sleep. Her head bobbled along with the motion of the vehicle.

Alma was standing in a dim space, but something waited in the distance.

As she approached it, Alma recognized the out-of-focus image before her. It was the house she'd lived in with her husband. Taken aback, Alma halted. But curiosity beckoned her closer. As Alma moved forward, the house became more vivid: the garden she worked on diligently for months, the gravel driveway where she tripped and scraped her hands and knee when first moving in, and the front porch where she sat with Michael and talked for hours. Then Alma sprinted to the backside of the house and looked up along the roof.

Alma discerned the figure above her— the slender young man who became her entire world.

"Michael!" she shrieked.

He looked at her with a pained stare, but no words escaped his lips.

"Get down from there, Michael! Please!"

It didn't seem like Michael heard her, because he continued to watch Alma as she started to sob. Michael took one step in her direction but then lost his balance and plummeted to the earth.

Alma's eyes shot open. Sweat coated the neckline of her dress. She reached for the bag that lay near her feet and unzipped the outer pocket to pull out her handkerchief. She blotted her clammy skin with a shudder. *Do I have to relive that nightmare almost every time I want to rest?* The pulse in her throat pounded, and if it weren't for Elaine sitting up front, Alma may have lost control of her emotions. *I cannot allow this to affect me. What happened with Michael wasn't my fault.*

Leaning forward, Alma peered past the side of the driver's seat to look at the dashboard clock. "It's a little past seven o'clock. Does that mean we're about two hours away from the Big Valley, Elaine?"

"Yep." Elaine swept her side braid over the shoulder of her light denim jacket. "Though you're gonna need to relay the address to me again."

"Oh, right." Grabbing her bag once more, Alma pulled out a slip of paper. "I have it right here."

Elaine pulled off to the shoulder of the freeway, and Alma stated the address to her as she entered it into the GPS on her phone.

"Thank you." Elaine's soft green eyes focused on Alma through the reflection of the mirror but then shifted to the road as she merged into traffic. "You'll let me know when to come get you, right?"

Alma nodded. "I don't plan on being at Leila's home for too long, but I'll be sure to let you know ahead of time when I need a ride home." Alma's heart drummed. She felt a bit uneasy when thinking about seeing Leila soon. A recent widow living with a loving married couple who had just begun raising a child? She didn't intend to overwhelm her friend's life, but perhaps accepting Leila's invitation was a sense of misjudgment. It wasn't like Alma could ask Elaine to turn back now, so she decided to stick with her decision.

Since Alma couldn't bring herself to try resting again, she lifted her chin to the air vent and adjusted it. Crisp outside air blasted her face, almost causing her *kapp* to slip off entirely. Alma got annoyed when putting her head covering back into place—though the cool air on her skin did alleviate some of her stress. *I really do hope I won't be too much for the Troyer family to handle.*

Alma was astonished when they pulled onto Leila's property. Everything was well kept and presentable. A row of trees led up to the home, and a beautifully crafted swing sat on the right side of the yard. Alma also spotted what she presumed to be the card shop farther to the right on the property. It wasn't immense, but it wasn't dainty either.

Elaine parked at the edge of the front yard. Removing her key from the ignition, she whistled. "I believe this is the place, and a nice place it is." Elaine turned to Alma and cracked a grin. "Ready to get out?"

"Indeed I am." Alma unbuckled her seat belt and got out of the van. She then took the bag that lay on the floor and slipped the strap over her shoulder and closed the door. Alma still had her suitcase waiting in the back, so she walked along the vehicle to open the hatch, only to find it opening on its own.

"Already pressed the button and got it opened for you," Elaine said, appearing from the opposite side of the van.

Automatics take the effort out of everything these days, Alma thought while stepping forward to haul out her suitcase.

"Need any help?"

"Oh sure. Thanks." Alma tugged one end of the suitcase out, and Elaine hoisted the other. They placed it on the concrete with a clunk. Alma chuckled, feeling a smidge winded. "I'm so glad there's no stairs leading up to the porch. Otherwise my arms might give way."

Nodding, Elaine wiped her forehead. "That's a hefty suitcase. Why do you have so much in there?"

"I always want to be prepared. It's best to pack too heavy than too light."

The wheels of the suitcase rolling against the concrete reminded Alma that she was far from home. Although she was on familiar turf, she was about to embark into uncertainty. She strolled to the entrance, where a wooden sign hung by the frame of the door: WELCOME TO OUR HOME. Alma then eyed the door knocker, grabbed the handle, and thumped the door three times.

Not long after, the door opened and Leila appeared. Threads of her scarlet hair glinted in the patches of light peeking through the trees. "Alma!" Leila's eyebrows lifted. "Hello!"

"Good morning, Leila," Alma responded as she rolled her shoulders back. "So, this is the right place after all."

"Yes, it is. And I'm glad you made it here safely." Leila opened the door wide, revealing a small child in her arms, chewing on her own plump hand. "Look, Rachel." Leila beamed. "It's Alma."

Rachel stared at Alma with wide eyes and lowered her saliva covered hand. Then the baby grinned, showing her baby teeth and flushed gums, indicating more teeth were on their way.

Well, that's not very hygienic, Alma thought.

But Rachel doesn't know better, so who am I to scrutinize her? She moved closer and gave a small tap on Rachel's nose. "Hi, cutie."

Leila stepped back. "Please come in. I don't want to keep you outside when it's much cooler in the house. You also have your belongings out here, and I'm sure you'd like to bring them in." Leila looked toward Elaine. "You're welcome to come in too, umm . . . What's your name?"

"Elaine. Nice to meet you." Elaine seemed like she was considering Leila's invitation for a couple of seconds, then sighed. "But that's all right. I'm needing to head out as soon as I can. My husband has been checking up on me every hour since we left Hopkinsville, so I don't want to worry him even more."

"Are you sure?" Leila bit her bottom lip. "Isn't it about an eight-hour drive?"

Elaine gave a half shrug. "Over eight hours. But yeah, I'll be fine. Fatigue doesn't get to me very often."

"Be careful, okay?" Alma slid her bag off her shoulder, settling it next to her suitcase, then gave Elaine a hug.

Elaine returned the hug, patting Alma's back. "I'll try to be. And you be careful too." She released Alma and sprinted to her van. "Goodbye to all of you," she called over her shoulder.

Alma waved as her driver pulled back out onto the road. Her stomach fluttered, but she set aside her uncertainty and grinned.

"I can put Rachel in her playpen and then show you to the guest room." Leila kissed Rachel's forehead, and the little girl's face scrunched in response. "But come on in and have a seat in the living room."

When Leila disappeared from view, Alma picked up her bag and rolled her suitcase into the house, then closed the door behind her.

The living room was the first room to the left, so Alma went in and seated herself on one of the black leather couches. Overall, Alma was impressed with the interior and decor of the room. Two star-shaped candle holders sat on either side of the musical clock that Leila and Aden had purchased while they were all in Florida.

Alma clutched her apron. *I can't focus on that. I need to direct my thoughts somewhere else.*

Noticing the bookcase, Alma's curiosity was piqued. *I wonder what kind of books Leila has.* Alma got up from the couch and headed to the bookshelf. When she pried one of the books out of the middle row, Alma caught sight of the dust that had accumulated along the top. *Leila didn't bother to dust even though she knew she was going to have company?* Alma shook her head.

"Okay, Rachel wanted to fall asleep, so I helped her with that— Oh."

Alma spun around. "I noticed you haven't dusted in a while."

"I did dust not long ago." Leila's eyebrows drew together. "Just not yesterday."

"Leila, no. You have to dust every day. That prevents it from coating layers upon layers. Dust can become a problem if it goes unchecked."

"I see what you mean. I just . . . haven't had time to keep up with everything."

Alma approached Leila and nudged her shoulder. "I understand. You have a child to care for and a shop to run, and I can help you."

"But you have been on the road for hours. Surely you don't want to be cleaning when you could be resting."

"Do you even know me?" Alma asked. "Cleaning soothes me."

Scratching her neck, Leila slowly released a breath. "I'd appreciate it, but you're not obligated to clean anything."

"If I'm staying here, it's the least I can do."

"All right, then I can't say no. But let's get you to your guest room before you go at it. I can provide you with cleaning supplies."

"Actually, I have my own in my suitcase."

"I would be surprised, but I'm not for some reason." Leila chuckled.

Alma followed Leila out of the living room,

then gathered her belongings to continue following Leila until she halted in front of the room at the end of the hallway.

"Here you are, Alma." Leila opened the door. "As I said, you can rest if you need to. I'm not expecting you to do anything else."

Alma pulled her suitcase into the room. It was a pretty good size, almost the same as her room in her family's home, and everything appeared put together properly. There was a queen-sized bed covered with a colorful quilt. "Danki. And this is a beautiful guest room, Leila."

"Thank you." She smiled, but it faded when a whining sound echoed from the hallway. "I've got to check on Rachel. Take some time to get settled in." Leila hurried out of the room.

"Okay." Alma laid her suitcase down and unzipped it. She lifted the flap and found the supplies she had packed.

Alma felt like she had it made staying with Leila. Being here would keep her thoughts distracted, and she could provide aid to a friend. Alma was certain coming back to the Big Valley had been the right decision.

Chapter 3

The day after Alma arrived in Belleville, she woke up feeling rejuvenated for the first time in six weeks. Her slumber had been absent of dreams, and she longed for similar nights ahead. Part of her didn't want to get out of bed, but Alma didn't wish to be lethargic. Every second of a day mattered to her, and she wasn't going to start being wasteful.

Not long after Alma got up on her feet, she donned a subdued purple dress and heart-shaped kapp. *I don't think Leila and Aden are awake yet,* she thought. *I'll have to find something to do that won't disrupt their sleep.*

Alma's motions were rapid yet quiet as she slipped out of the guest room. The only conspicuous noise was the trilling of birds resonating through the open window. She went to the utility room, which was across the hall, and found a broom suspended from a hook. *I did see some dirt and pebbles on the concrete, so I could go out and sweep.* She lifted the dilapidated broom and slid it off the hook. *If my broom could've fit in my suitcase, I wouldn't need to use Leila's. I suppose it'll have to do.*

Carrying the broom in hand, Alma opened the front door and was greeted by a cool morning, typical of early June. She closed the door behind her and paused to bathe in the rays. Shutting her eyes, she tilted her head back. It was unusual for her to be so relaxed.

Well, I'd better get started. Alma positioned the broom in her hands and began sweeping in front of the door. Dirt clouds formed as she glided the broom's bristles across numerous spots along the concrete. The small rocks Alma swept into the driveway gave her a sense of order and peace.

It didn't take long for her to clear up the debris, and once she brushed away the remaining pebbles, Alma went back into the house, wondering what else she could do.

The sound of crying came from the hallway. *Oh no. Rachel.* She set the broom on the floor but then picked it back up. *I can't leave that here. That's hazardous.*

Scurrying to the utility room, Alma hung the broom on its hook, then swerved to where the crying came from. She continued down the hall, and when she reached the end, she saw a room with the door partially open. There was another room adjacent to it that had a closed door, so Alma knew that room had to be Leila and Aden's.

Alma creaked the door open farther and stepped into the room. Rachel was grasping the bars of her crib with tears seeping from her eyes.

"Rachel." Alma shushed the child. "You don't want to disturb your parents, do you?"

The child continued to bawl and used the bars to stand up in the crib. She then stomped the padding at the bottom with her socked feet.

What am I going to do? I don't know how to handle a child. Alma reached into the crib to pick her up, but Rachel screamed louder. With Rachel's expression getting more contorted, Alma felt as if her intestines were looped into knots. "Please, Rachel," she pleaded. "Please stop crying." Alma knelt down on the floor and covered her face with both hands while Rachel carried on with more wailing. *Why did I even think I could calm her down? I could never do this. I was not meant to have a child.*

"What's going on?"

Alma's head shot up. Leila stood in the doorway, her hair tousled and her eyes bleary. "Leila, I'm so sorry. I didn't want Rachel to wake you, but I didn't know what I should do."

Leila wandered over and patted Alma's shoulder. "It's all right. I'm not upset." Leila scooped up Rachel, who, still crying, clung onto the sleeve of Leila's cream-colored nightgown. "You grumpy, Rachel? Are you missing me and Papa?"

Alma observed Leila as she gently swayed with her child, and Rachel's expression relaxed. The baby's cries shifted to faint cooing sounds.

"Aden and I recently decided it was time to have Rachel in the nursery rather than with us

378

in our room. She does fine by herself most of the time, but has moments of loneliness. And hunger." Leila chuckled.

Alma got up from the floor and dipped her head slightly. "I really am sorry."

"There's no need to apologize. I know you were trying to help."

"Still, if I had a hard time with Rachel, then I probably wouldn't have done well if she was my child."

"What do you mean by that?" Leila asked.

"Michael and I were planning to have a baby." Alma's throat thickened. "It was probably for the best that it didn't happen."

"Alma, a person never knows if they're going to be a good parent. I still worry about what'll occur years from now." Leila smiled down at her daughter. "But having Rachel, even through the tough times, got rid of the doubts I had before. And I know if you were to have children of your own someday, you would figure things out and get the hang of comforting them. But you'll never know for sure until it happens." Leila looked at Alma with a thoughtful expression. "I know you'll be diligent raising a child. You'll just have to ease into it first."

Momentarily closing her eyes, Alma felt a sense of giddiness from Leila's words. "Maybe I would get the hang of it."

Leila nodded. "And when the time comes,

if you have any questions, you can ask me whenever."

Alma turned her attention to Rachel, who returned the stare with intense focus. Her little mouth opened a sliver. "May I hold her, Leila?"

"Of course."

Leila passed Rachel to her, and carefully Alma wrapped her arms around the child.

Wow, this kid is so adorable. Alma used her fingers to comb Rachel's light brown hair.

Rachel's mouth stretched, and she burst into giggles.

"See? She likes you, Alma."

A swirling sense of weightlessness filled Alma's being. Rachel's genuine joy reminded her of how much she desired to have a baby of her own. *Perhaps I will have a boppli someday. When that happens, I'll love that child more than anything.*

"What are you up to?"

"I'm taking a breather to work on this." Elias Kurtz swiped away some sawdust that had piled up on his worktable. "Do you think Mamm will like it for her birthday?" He held up a miniature shelf, admiring the vines he'd etched on the sides.

"That looks nice, Son. She'll like anything you give her. Though I don't think it will be much of a surprise. You always gift her with the wooden items you make."

"I guess I should include something else with

her gift." Elias put down the shelf, pivoting to face his father, Amos, and shrugged. "Not sure what that'd be."

"Most folks would give someone a card, Elias."

"You know how I feel about store-bought cards, Daed. They're mass-produced flimsy notes with generic messages. There's no devotion or craft in them."

"I can't argue with you there." Elias's father tugged the end of his peppered beard. "Your mother told me about a card shop in our community where the owners create some well-made cards. Could be an idea."

"Jah. I could include that with what I'm carving for her."

"But for now, we have a few orders we got to finish before the day is out."

His father was right. They only had a couple of hours until they closed.

At the end of the workday, Elias got the address for the card shop from his dad, prepared his horse for the trek, and headed out. When he arrived, he noticed a home next to the shop, which was set up similar to his father's shop.

He secured his horse to the hitching post, and curving a finger around his single suspender, Elias entered the shop. The first thing he noticed was the clothesline of cards hanging in the back. Then he saw a young Amish woman at the register. Elias approached the counter, but she seemed preoccupied with something else, because it wasn't until he cleared his throat that she glanced at him.

"G–good evening," she stuttered. "Can I help you with anything?"

"Word on the street is you have some homemade cards for sale, and I was wondering if you have any birthday ones for me to look at."

She leaned toward the shelves and raised her trembling voice. "Sally, do we still have birthday cards?"

"I'm sorry, Mollie. But we ran out of them earlier today." A much older woman, who had silver hair peeking from her head covering, emerged from behind one of the shelves with a box in her arms. "There are a lot of birthdays in June it seems."

"Okay then. Thanks anyways." He turned to the door to leave.

"Wait!"

Elias rotated back and waited to see what the young woman had stopped him for.

"M–my friend Leila still has cards, I believe. She . . ." She trailed off, averting her gaze.

The older woman interjected. "The previous owner of this shop has another one in the black-top community, and it is still open for another half hour. You can get a card there if you hurry."

"Could you give me the address for the shop?"

"I can get it for you!" The young woman's hazel eyes shone, and she was quick to grab a pencil and paper to jot down the information. Once she finished, she provided the slip of paper to him. "Here you go."

"Danki. I appreciate it." Elias took the paper and folded it. He offered a smile before leaving. "Nice evening to the both of you."

Although Elias had a ways to go before he made it to the shop located in the black-top community, he wasn't too worried about whether he would make it on time. *Even if the shop closes today, I still have until the end of this week before Mom's birthday, so I can always try again.*

"You're really good at making cards, Leila," Alma said as she admired the result of the card Leila had finished.

"Thanks. And you are too. You weren't kidding when you've said you had prior practice."

"My mamm used to make them all the time when I was little. Glad it can help out now."

Leila clipped the cards they made on the clothesline and put the rest of them in a container. "I take these cards to the old shop where Mollie works. She gives me her cards in exchange, but she doesn't think her card-making skills are any good, which isn't true. I adore her cards, and so do the customers who've purchased them."

Alma was about to respond, but then she caught

sight of something outside. "Someone has their horse and buggy at the hitching post, but I don't see anyone with it out there. It's a buggy with a yellow top."

"Strange." Leila leaned toward the window.

"Maybe it's someone your husband knows."

"Could be. He does know a lot of people." Pursing her lips, Leila went over to the window.

"Oh, there he is!" Alma exclaimed. "That person just came from your house."

"I'll step out and see who it is."

"Leila, that's not a good idea. Who knows what he could do?"

"We'll be fine. Besides, if something goes wrong, there's two of us and only one of him."

Alma eyed Rachel in the playpen. "I'll stay here with her."

Shaking her head, Leila propped the door open before leaving. "Excuse me, sir. Were you needing something?"

Wanting to hear the conversation, Alma tiptoed to the counter.

"Yes, I was," he said. "I'm sorry if it appeared like I was doing something suspicious. I noticed the CLOSED sign, so I went to knock on the front door of that house. Do you have any homemade birthday cards?"

"We do," Leila responded. "We closed the shop ten minutes ago, so you'll have to come back tomorrow."

Alma inched to the door and peered out. Leila blocked Alma's view of the customer, so she had no choice but to come out if she wanted to see who it was. When Alma did so, a familiar face came into view. She recognized it instantly.

"That's all right. I won't be needing it right away, so . . ." His speech dwindled when he looked at Alma, and his mouth opened. "Alma?"

"Eli!" Alma bolted to him. "Oh my goodness. I can't believe it." Embracing Elias brought back so many memories with him, and her eyes prickled with tears.

He returned the hug. "Good to see you too. I can't believe I'm seeing you either. You moved to Kentucky years back, didn't you?"

"I did, but now I'm back—at least for a while." Detaching from Elias, she turned to see Leila with a blank look on her face. "Leila, this is Eli. I mean Elias. We grew up together when I lived here in the yellow-top community."

"I figured you two knew each other from the hug and all." Approaching them, Leila extended her hand to him. "I'm Leila. Good to meet you, Elias."

"You too." Elias shook Leila's hand. "Were you from the yellow-top community as well?"

"I was. How did you guess?"

"Your friends from the other shop mentioned you, saying you were the previous owner. Put two and two together. And I think I may know your husband. Aden Troyer, right?"

"That's him."

"He told me you have a daughter who was born last year. Congratulations."

"Danki. We're very fortunate to have her." Leila smiled.

Alma clasped her hands together. "How have you been, Eli? Or Elias? Whichever you're okay with. I know it's been so long, so—"

He held up a hand. "Eli is fine, as long as I get to call you Alm. And I've been good. My dad has me working under his wing with furniture crafting."

"Just like you always wanted," Alma commented. "Anything else? You have no beard, so are you married?"

Elias rubbed his bare chin. "Not at the moment. Guess I haven't found a reason to settle down yet." Taking off his straw hat, Elias carved his hand through his thick, light brown hair. "You must have gotten married. I know that you always wanted a family of your own."

Alma's mouth dried up, but she couldn't allow that to prevent her from speaking. *Get it out, Alma. It's okay to be upfront.* Finally she said, "I'm widowed."

"Oh, I'm so sorry." He grimaced then shuffled his feet. "For how long?"

"About a month."

Folding his arms, Elias shook his head. "I'm really sorry for your loss, Alma."

Alma didn't want to linger in those thoughts, so she recalled what Elias had said about needing a birthday card. Turning to Leila, Alma forced herself to grin. "We have birthday cards, don't we, Leila?"

Leila nodded, looking at Elias. "We do, but we're actually restocking cards right now."

"That's all right. I can come back tomorrow before you close."

Alma clasped her hand on Elias's upper arm. "Why don't you make a card with us tomorrow?"

"Me? Make a card?" Elias chuckled. "I don't know."

"It would make the card more personal, and with your experience in crafting wood, I know you'd create something unique. What do you think, Leila? Would it be okay if we taught Elias how to make a card?"

Leila's gaze jumped from Alma to Elias and back again. It appeared she was at a loss for words. Rachel chose that moment to start crying. "Oh, Rachel," Leila mumbled. Before heading back into the shop, she turned to Alma. "If Elias wants to stop by to make a card tomorrow, I'd be okay with it." She disappeared into the shop.

"Well okay." Elias exhaled, tugging his hat back on. "I'll see you tomorrow, Alm. Have a good evening."

"You too." She waved. "See you tomorrow."

Alma watched Elias as he headed to his buggy. For some reason, her pulse hammered in her chest. The feeling was all too familiar from years ago. *Maybe getting to know Elias again by inviting him to make a card wasn't a good idea.*

Chapter 4

The next morning was the second time Alma awoke with a sense of rejuvenation. As she cleared her mind, her brain stitched together snippets of the dream she'd had during the night.

First, she'd encountered Elias. A sense of caring emanated from his bronze, upturned lips and gentle blue eyes. This evoked strong feelings within her. Then Michael stood far off from her, and Alma ran to him. No matter how fast Alma's feet sped toward him, she drifted farther from Michael. Finally she sank into the floor, struggling to pull herself out. She gave in eventually and allowed the floor to swallow her up. For what felt like hours, Alma kept sinking until she finally slipped out of the space and landed in another area. It was the card shop. Leila was there with Rachel in her arms and Aden beside her. They didn't seem to notice her, and Alma remembered feeling crestfallen.

It wasn't the most pleasant dream, yet she was inexplicably comfortable after waking up. That in itself concerned her.

Alma pressed her face into a pillow. *It's only a dream. It doesn't mean anything.* She didn't want to think about the dream anymore and instead latched onto what had bothered her when having dinner yesterday.

Alma helped prepare dinner both nights since arriving in Belleville, but she found the placement of the items in the cabinets to be inconvenient. The cabinets above the counter had two shelves, and the glasses and plates were stacked on the top shelf while the bowls and mugs had been placed on the shelf beneath it. Alma hadn't understood Leila's decision to have plates and glasses on top when they were more likely to be used. It could be because it wasn't much effort for Leila to reach up and grab a plate, considering she was very tall. Alma was only a couple of inches shorter than her, yet she had to stand on tippy-toes to get the dishes down.

It may not be my kitchen, but it's proper to organize a kitchen so it's easier to maneuver in. She rolled out of bed, got dressed, then went downstairs. The house was quiet, so Alma was the first person awake once again. Alma entered the kitchen, which adjoined the living room, and the cabinet door creaked as she opened it. She stared at the disorganized shelves. *This is not good. Items that are used more frequently need to be accessible.*

She pulled out the mugs first, one by one, including a mug covered with tortoises and the words SARASOTA, FLORIDA. Alma grimaced. *I'm placing you behind all of the mugs when I get around to putting them on the top shelf.* She set it with the rest of the mugs accumulating on the counter. Once they were cleared from the shelf, she went for the bowls. Some of the bowls were used for cereal and soups, so Alma decided those could stay on the lower shelf, but the miniature bowls had to be moved to the top.

When the shelf was empty, Alma placed a finger on her chin. *I can get the plates near the edge but not the ones toward the back.*

She turned to the entryway of the dining room and lifted up the end chair that hadn't been pushed back under the table. *Why didn't you scoot your chair back under the table, Aden? That is a hazard,* Alma thought as she brought the chair into the kitchen and placed it next to the counter. *Speaking of hazard, I'd better make sure I'm careful.*

Alma steadied herself, then got up on the chair and peered into the top section. She took a few plates at a time, and soon both shelves had been cleared.

Alma placed all the mugs and smaller bowls in the upper section and then stacked the plates, glasses, and regular bowls and aligned them precisely where they needed to be. She admired the finished appearance of the dishes then shut the cabinets. *Okay, there we go. Now I need to get down from this chair and—*

Alma lost her balance as she bent forward,

and her calf leaned against the back of the chair, causing it to topple over and crash onto the floor. She landed face first on the chair, and her vision went dark. All she could feel was the chair back pushing against her torso.

"Are you okay?"

She heard the disembodied voice, which she recognized to be Aden's. "I–I'm not sure." As she regained her sight, Alma made out Aden towering above her arms. She forced her legs to stand her up away from where the chair fell. "I can move my limbs, and my face doesn't feel broken, so it seems I may be fine."

"Not a moment worth cherishing."

"I'll say. That wasn't the most graceful thing I've ever— Wait." Alma turned to him, and he snorted after she gave him the stink eye. "Chair-ishing? You did not do a witty wordplay just now."

"Wasn't gonna say it if you had seriously hurt yourself."

"The joke hurt more than the fall." Tending to the chair, Alma placed it back on its four feet. "I'm surprised you're up before Leila. Don't you usually sleep in as long as you can before heading to work?"

"Usually. But some mornings I want extra time to myself. Good opportunity to reflect on my own life. That, and it's good to get chores done earlier. It's the best kind of leisure."

"I can agree with you there." Alma snickered. "You're a lot like Michael, Aden."

Aden's smirk slacked, and Alma instantly regretted letting those words slip past her lips. Rather than explaining herself, she gave Aden a big smile and laughed. "Thanks for helping me up. I need to lie down for a bit. Got to recover from falling."

"All right. I'll put the chair back in the dining room for you."

Aden walked by her to lift the chair, but Alma could almost feel his eyes on her as she left the kitchen. *No doubt he feels sorry for me.* She headed back into the guest room, closed the door, then went straight for the bed to flop belly first onto the mattress. She allowed the tears to fall as she muffled her sobs in the pillow. Breathing became difficult, so she leaned away from the pillow and inhaled as she dried her face with her sleeve.

I want to move on, but I'm worried that I can't do it. Alma rolled over on her side and closed her eyes. *I miss you so much, Michael. I don't know if I can keep up this brave face.*

Elias's workday was ending, and part of him looked forward to heading to the card shop. He knew his mother was going to adore a homemade card, especially since purchased cards were one of her pet peeves whenever they celebrated birthdays. Elias hoped he'd be capable of creating a beautifully crafted card.

Of course he was thrilled to see Alma again. He'd certainly been caught off guard when he saw her yesterday, which was why he was relieved their reunion had been brief. He still couldn't wrap his head around the fact that she'd lost her husband recently, and here she was in the Big Valley.

Elias crouched down by a rocking chair, smoothing the surface while his dad finished carving another cutting board to include on the display hanging on the wall. The only sounds came from their work, and it was like that for a good chunk of the hour. But then his father surveyed the room, probably to make sure they were alone.

"Did you find a card for your mamm yesterday?"

"No, but I'm going to make a card for her after work." Elias blew away some dust from the arm of the chair.

"Even better. Good for you."

With a lot on his mind, Elias figured it would be best to get his thoughts out in the open. He got up, brushed off his knees, and asked, "Do you remember Alma Wengerd?"

"Haven't heard that name in a long time. Why? Have you gotten in touch with her recently?"

"Sorta. She's staying with the owner of the card shop. Do you know Leila Troyer?"

"I know of her father, William Fisher. The card shop I told you about is on the Fishers' property." Dad's forehead crinkled. "Wonder why your friend moved back. And if she's staying with William's daughter, I guess the rest of the Wengerd family are still in Kentucky."

"Alma was married."

"*Was* married?" His father's mouth gaped open, and his eyes widened. Then he nodded as though understanding. "So she's a widow?"

"Jah. That's what she told me."

"How did it happen?"

"She didn't say. I wouldn't want to pressure her to open up if she isn't ready to."

"I suppose all you can do is support your friend during this time." His dad reached up and slipped out a pencil through the little black bow of his straw hat. Then he got out a notepad from his pants pocket, flipped through a few pages, and wrote down something. "We have a newly wedded English couple who are coming to haul their order out of here, so we need to be prepared to help them put it on the bed of the truck."

"Yes, sir." Elias pinched the brim of his hat and tipped it.

"Gut. Keep up the good work. I'm going to get another jug of water from the house." Flipping the notepad closed, Dad slipped it back into his pocket.

Once his father went out, Elias thought about

Alma some more as he continued to smooth the rocking chair. *I still can't believe she lost her husband. She's only twenty-one.* He jerked, remembering that Alma's birthday was at the end of the month. *The twenty-second, and she'll be turning twenty-two on that day. It's amazing how many years it's been since I last saw her.* Elias thought about Alma's upturned nose, her light complexion that mirrored the hair peeking from her covering, and her welcoming and confident presence.

She did a good job growing up, he thought. But a dullness filled his chest. *If I'd known that things were going to pan out this way, I would have been open with her about my feelings back then.* Elias pressed his hand over his heart. *Now I don't know how to feel. But it would be wrong for me to admit these feelings to her when she just lost her husband.*

"Mornin', dear," Aden said as soon as Leila saw him.

Leila, with Rachel in her arms, approached the dining room table where he sat with a mug. She leaned over to kiss the top of Aden's head; giggling as his dark strands tickled her nose. "Same to you. Good job waking up before me." Leila seated Rachel in her high chair.

"Your friend had both of us beat. Don't know how she does it."

"She woke up at four again? I thought she was still asleep."

Aden picked up his mug and took a sip before continuing to speak. "Alma was in the kitchen earlier, near the cabinet. Think she may have been rearranging dishes."

Leila gripped the ties of her kapp. "Was she now?"

Nodding, Aden raised his mug. "You know how much effort it took to get this mug down?"

She shook her head. "You're taller than me, Aden."

"By one inch, and you've got lanky arms."

Pinching the bridge of her nose, Leila went right into the kitchen. She yanked the cabinet door ajar, scanning the shelves and confirming that the dishes were no longer in the same spot. *Did Alma have to go this far to mess with my kitchen? There was nothing wrong with it before.*

But when Leila got plates from the lower shelf, she acknowledged how much easier it was with things being at eye level. Same thing with the glasses and bowls. *The rearrangement isn't too bad. Though it would've been better if she'd kept the mugs on the lower shelf.* Leila reached for the top shelf and removed a mug. *Not that it's any problem for me and my "lanky arms."*

Once she set out dishes on the counter, Leila walked to the side door located in the living room and went into the pantry, where they stored perishables of all sorts. She perused the tea collection on the pantry wall and chose peppermint. Behind her was the chest fridge, and she tugged the door and got out a carton of eggs she'd collected from the chickens. She also got out Rachel's breakfast of presoaked oatmeal before shutting the fridge.

She came back inside, carrying everything to the kitchen counter. Then she carried Rachel's oatmeal into the dining room. She looked at Aden. "How would you like your eggs today, short arms?"

He chuckled. "I'm sorry for calling your arms lanky."

"I'm sorry too." Leila hummed. Then she jerked her head back. "Oh no. I forgot about Alma. I'd better go check to see what she wants for breakfast."

"It would be good to check on her. She did have quite a tumble from the chair earlier."

"She fell off the—" Leila covered her mouth. "Why didn't you tell me that sooner?"

"She said she was okay." Aden took another sip from his mug before speaking. "Besides, I don't think the fall is what's bothering her."

Leila's stomach tensed up. Biting the inside of her cheek, she wondered what she might do to help Alma grieve properly. Leila knew how terrible it was to lose someone in an unexpected way, but she wasn't sure if there was anything she could do to get Alma through it. A person never fully recovers from such a loss. Leila, to this day, had times when she would break down and vent to Aden about how much she missed her mother.

I hope having Alma stay here wasn't a mistake. I don't want her to go through any more hardships, especially while she's still dealing with her grief.

Chapter 5

Later that day, Alma worked with Leila in the shop. A steady stream of customers had kept them busy but not overwhelmed, so there was plenty of time to restock the shelves and display more cards on the clothesline. During another break, Leila got more boxes out from behind the counter. They were filled with finished cards to hang up on an empty clothesline.

"Whose cards are these, Leila?" Alma pointed to the box in front of her.

"Those are Mollie's cards."

Alma plucked one from the peak of the pile and was about to hang it up, but she stopped, eyeing the outside of the card.

"Something wrong?" Leila slanted toward her.

"It's a well-made card. Though it would look more appealing with a white ribbon instead of this blue one." Alma handed the card to Leila so she could see for herself. "The card is already blue, so a white ribbon would contrast with the card instead of blending in."

"I see . . ." Leila glanced away, plucking out a card from another box and fastening it on the clothesline.

"I'll let Mollie know when I meet her. But other than that issue, this card is beautiful." Alma took Mollie's card and wedged it underneath the pile. She picked up the next card and studied it. "This is nice, but it lacks dimension. Mollie only decorated it with stamps." To demonstrate, she went to the worktable where the supplies were set out and stuck her hand in a container, digging out a couple of buttons. She went back to Leila, then thumbed the buttons on the card's cover. "See how it adds more to the card? It makes it more captivating to the eyes. Do you think she would mind me gluing these buttons on?"

Leila's lips curled. "Just find another card from her box, okay?"

"All right. I'll find something." She dug her hand back into the box and pulled out what she considered to be a sellable card. When Alma hung it, she got to thinking about Leila's friend. Leila had mentioned that Mollie had grown up in the white-top community. Alma had talked with Amish from the white-top community years ago, but since she'd moved away when she was sixteen, she was eager to know more about them.

"Leila, Mollie's from the white-top community, right?"

"She is." Leila attached another card to a clothespin. "Why do you ask?"

"I know our communities are distinctive, but in comparison to the black-toppers and yellow-toppers, white-toppers have noticeable differences—like them having no suspenders.

Why don't the men in the white-top community wear a suspender?"

Shrugging her shoulders, Leila kept hanging cards without faltering. "Let's continue focusing on our work."

From the way Leila shut down the conversation, Alma realized she may have unknowingly crossed a line. She figured it was best to drop the subject.

As the end of the day grew closer, Alma felt increasingly tense. Elias would be showing up in a matter of hours, and although she was delighted to reconnect with him, she couldn't deny that her old feelings lingered.

Alma reflected on the day five years ago when she had been informed of her parents' decision to move to Kentucky. Devastated, she'd hurried to Elias's home to tell him she'd be leaving. Over the years, they had often gone to the school field to play baseball with other kids, so Elias had offered to play one last game with her. The bittersweet game had kept her mind off moving, and afterward Alma had refused to admit how much of a struggle it had been for her to leave her childhood world.

She'd always felt selfish for not wanting to move out of the Big Valley. Even though she'd thought of staying behind if Elias returned her feelings, she decided not to risk telling him. Given that her family was leaving to help her grandparents in Kentucky, Alma would have felt guilty if she'd stayed behind.

As their workday wound down, fewer customers stopped by. Alma worked the register as Leila left the shop with Rachel, and as Leila went into the house, a buggy with a yellow roof pulled up.

There's Elias, she thought, looking out the window. A wave of heat washed through Alma as she watched him get out of the buggy. To distract herself, Alma focused on the horse chomping at the bit, bobbing its head up and down. *I'm glad the horse is relaxed, especially during this humid weather.*

But the horse didn't keep Alma distracted for very long. Elias, with a thumb looped around his single suspender, advanced toward the shop. Alma whirled back to the register to appear preoccupied. *He's just a friend, Alma. You should not be feeling nervous.*

"Hello?" Elias's voice echoed in the shop as his head poked past the doorframe.

Alma gestured him to come in. "*Willkumm,* Eli!" She stepped around the counter and approached, offering a smile.

"Danki for the welcome, Alm." Tipping his hat, Elias stepped into the store, giving her a knowing grin.

"Leila will be back shortly. Her daughter was getting hungry, so they're in the house for the

403

moment." Alma pushed her shoulders back. "But we can get set up for card making at least."

She grasped Elias's wrist and led him to the table, which had the supplies lined up and decorations categorized.

"I think you already have it set up." Elias scratched the side of his nose.

Letting go of him, Alma pressed both hands to her face. "Huh? I suppose I did."

He gazed at her and snickered. "This reminds me of when we were young and making crafts in the schoolhouse. You always went behind the rest of the kids after they made a mess of things, and you talked about the importance of keeping everything in order." Elias propped his hand on the surface of the table and leaned. "I'm glad to see you haven't changed."

"Eli, trust me. My organizational tendencies have gotten stronger." Alma looked toward the entrance when she heard shuffles on the gravel outside. "Either there's a last-minute customer or Leila's coming back in."

Sure enough, Leila walked through the doorway with Rachel. "Hello, Elias. Nice to see you again." Leila smiled then carried Rachel over to her playpen and lowered her in. "I think it's about time we closed up shop for today and made some cards. Don't you both agree?"

Alma clasped her hands together. "I'm super excited to begin."

After Leila flipped the sign to indicate that the shop was officially closed for the day, she joined Alma and Elias at the table and began to concentrate on card making. Alma provided input as well, and then both got a sheet of construction paper from the pile and demonstrated for Elias.

Alma made sure to thoroughly explain the process while creating the card. The sheet she folded was beige, so to spruce it up, she went for a red sheet to glue on the front. Alma looped a pair of paper edger scissors around her thumb and index finger and cut out a rectangle that was a smidge smaller than the cover of the card. After gluing the piece on, she reached for the spool of white mesh ribbon. She cut off a length, tying it into a bow.

After Alma added the ribbon to the brim of the card's cover, as well as lining the bottom with pearlescent buttons, she contemplated which stamps to use for the outside and inside of the card. She eyed one of the stamps then placed it next to her project.

"That is coming along quite nicely," Elias commented.

Darting a glance at him, Alma almost got tongue-tied from his compliment. "It's almost finished. I only need to pick out a couple more stamps and an ink pad—then it'll be ready to be displayed on the clothesline sometime soon." Alma leaned toward Leila. Her card was made with light blue plaid and white construction paper with a cutout heart adhered to the top that jutted out from the card's surface. "Looks like Leila's card is almost finished too. I love the added dimension with the heart cutout. What did you use for that?"

Leila smiled. "I glued a rubber stopper to the card and glued the heart on top of it."

"I agree with Alma. You certainly have a passion for your work. I can see why you attract lots of people into your shop."

Lifting her chin, Leila directed her cocoa-brown eyes toward Elias. "I appreciate your kind words. If it wasn't for my mother, I wouldn't be doing this right now." Leila's hands stilled, but her shoulders quivered. "I don't know what I'd be doing right now if it weren't for her."

Alma went over to Leila and squeezed her shoulders. "Leila, your mother would be pleased with you."

Turning to her, Leila grasped Alma's hand. "I sure hope she would be."

Alma and Leila pressed on to get their cards done. When they'd added the finishing touches, they placed the cards at the end of the table to allow the glue to dry. With the demonstration concluded, it was now Elias's turn to create a card.

"All right. Do you have a better understanding of how to go about crafting a homemade card?" Alma asked him.

"I think I got it. Though, I'm not sure where to start—"

Elias was cut off by Rachel's screeching from the other side of the shop. It was astonishing how such tiny lungs could produce so much sound.

"I'm sorry," Leila stepped from the table. "I need to take care of her. Will you guys be okay by yourselves for a while?"

Although she was uncertain about being alone with Elias, Alma nodded her head to let Leila know it was okay for her to leave. So Leila hurried to carry Rachel out of the shop.

Rubbing moist palms against her apron, Alma prepped herself. *You've got this, Alma. There's no need to be nervous.* She pointed to the piles of construction paper. "Since this card is for your mom, it would be good to personalize it with decorations that would resonate with her. For instance, what is her favorite color?"

"It's yellow, I believe." Elias reached for the construction sheet, then laid it in front of him.

"Now, you can use the yellow paper as the main part of the card, so you would fold it in half, or you can use it for the rectangle piece to apply on the cover."

It went on like this for a few minutes. Elias followed through with what Alma advised him to do, and when it was time to include stamps, he asked her which ones to use.

"You can use a stamp for decoration, like one of your mom's favorite flower perhaps?"

"I want to do that for sure. She loves lilies, so if you have a lily stamp, I'd like to use it." He tugged on his burgundy sleeve. "Isn't your favorite flower a red carnation?"

Clasping her hands, Alma was taken aback. "I–I'm surprised you remembered that. I know I mentioned it to you in conversation years back, but I figured you would have forgotten a lot of what I said."

Elias moved closer to her. "What reason would I have to forget about my best friend?" His eyes narrowed, then he continued. "You wouldn't believe the number of times I thought about you after you left."

Adrenaline cascaded throughout her frame like a thunderous waterfall. *He means as a friend. Elias never had feelings for you, so he doesn't mean it in the way you're taking it.* Biting the tip of her tongue, Alma stepped to the side away from him. "I'm glad you didn't forget about me. But even if you had, I would have reminded you when we bumped into each other."

Elias sighed, removing his straw hat. "I know."

"Now, come on." Alma slapped the end of the table. "Let's get this card ready for your mom."

They finished composing the card, but Alma couldn't stop thinking about what Elias had said. He'd even referred to her as his best friend.

Conflicting thoughts swirled through her mind, and her old feelings for Elias made it worse. Was it acceptable for Alma to feel those emotions when she'd grieved her husband's passing just that morning?

Chapter 6

As the moonlight streamed through the windows, Alma lay reading one of Leila's books by the light from her gas lamp on the nightstand. But she wasn't taking in the words on the page.

It was a little after three in the morning, and Alma wasn't able to sleep. All she could think about was her mixed feelings over the conversation with Elias at the shop a couple of days ago.

Just as they had finished making a card for Elias's mom, Aden had returned from work. Because he knew Elias, they'd chatted for a while outside the shop. It went well until Elias decided to head home. He asked Alma if he could talk to her, and when she walked along with him to the hitching post, Elias invited her to his mom's birthday dinner. She'd agreed, and that dinner was this evening.

Alma was unsure about seeing Elias's family again. Although she had been close to Elias, he had siblings who were much older. Elias briefly mentioned his sister, Lauren, having three young children while his brother, Daniel, had four preteens, so Alma already knew it was going to be a rowdy group. It didn't help that the birthday celebration would be held in public view at a restaurant.

Not only that, but Elias hadn't said where they would be eating. Alma had asked him, but he'd only told her to be prepared to leave around seven o'clock. All this uncertainty left Alma feeling jittery.

Then there was the issue of the gift. Alma had made a card for Elias's mom the day before and figured the card by itself would suffice. Now she wondered if she should have gone out to get something to include with the card.

I could try some last-minute shopping today. Alma clasped the book and set it next to her on the sheets. *But I don't know what to buy for her. I don't want to waste time going out and end up not finding anything.*

Alma turned from the amber glow of the gas lamp, tugging the sheets up to just below her eyes, and stared at the corner that lined up with the bed board. *I want to go above and beyond, but I feel as if my motivation is dwindling. It's weird. All of this is weird.* She curled her fingers and pulled the sheet over her head.

As Alma rested her eyes for a moment, she remembered something her friend Elaine had once said to her. When she was searching for jams to make, Elaine came across a recipe that piqued Alma's interest. Over the years, Alma had prepared a variety of jams—strawberry, blueberry, grape, and blackberry. But she never would have guessed there was a recipe for a jam that didn't involve fruit. However, it might be worth trying.

Leila has the ingredients I need—I know from when I was organizing her pantry shelves and chest fridge yesterday. Alma sat up. *And she does have what I'd need for the main ingredient by the side of her house. If I made a jar of it for Elias's mom, it would be the perfect gift. Homemade, full of effort, and unique.*

Alma sprung from the mattress, straightened out the jumbled sheets, and fluffed the pillows. After that, she got dressed and went to the kitchen, where she got out measuring cups, a large pot, a medium-sized bowl, and a wooden spoon. With how much Alma had rearranged Leila's kitchen, it felt like her domain, and she navigated it with ease.

Alma went to the pantry connected to the living room and got out lemons, cane sugar, and pectin. There was also a collection of mason jars on the lower shelf in a cardboard box, and she grabbed one jar from it. Alma planned on making a serving large enough for one jar, but she'd make more if it turned out to be delectable.

She had everything she needed except for the one ingredient that made the jam special. Alma grabbed another bowl and went out the front door. Walking to the left side of the home,

Alma stumbled upon what she needed for the jam.

Her fingertips grazed the flushed petals, and she knelt to get a whiff of the floral fragrance. *I can't believe I'll be making jam with rose petals,* she mused. *Then again, rose petals are edible. I've heard they have some health benefits too. But will the jam actually taste wonderful?* Alma plucked a rose from one of the bushes. *There's only one way to find out.*

When Alma had gathered a sufficient number of roses, she went back in the house, got out a colander, and began picking the petals from the stems. The bed of rose petals in the colander looked beautiful.

Alma heated the saucepan to allow the petals to simmer in water. They became less color saturated as they cooked, but once she stirred in the sugar and lemon juice, the petals turned vibrant again. Not only that, but the steam from the saucepan was enchantingly sweet and quickly permeated the kitchen.

Whenever she went about cooking blackberry jam, Alma would simmer it for around twenty minutes and it would be ready to transfer into jars. But after twenty minutes of simmering, the consistency of the rose petal jam concerned her. *Why is it still liquid? Shouldn't it be thick?*

Alma wondered if she needed to let the jam cook much longer, so she allowed it to simmer for another ten minutes. But as time passed, the candy-like fragrance that once delighted her smelled more of something burning. *Oh no. No no.* Alma floundered while removing the saucepan from the heat. But as she hastily moved it, Alma's index finger touched the caramelized sugar.

"Goodness gracious!" she yelped. She let go of the handle, and the saucepan clanked against the wooden floor. Alma squawked multiple times as she caught sight of the blob of piping-hot sugar on the pad of her left-hand index finger.

When her body finally caught up to her brain, Alma ran her finger under a stream of cold water, which soothed it. But she hadn't yet picked up the saucepan, and when she removed her hand from under the faucet to do so, the initial pain returned. It felt like her flesh had melted to the bone. Alma grimaced, running her finger in the cold water again. *That is not a first-degree burn.*

"Alma? What happened in here?"

"I burned my finger."

"Oh dear." Leila went over to Alma. "How burned is it?"

She brought her finger up to eye level. Alma's skin throbbed, and a bulbous blister had formed. "Now that's a second-degree burn."

"Looks like it." Leila got the saucepan off the floor and set it on the counter. "Be right back with a bandage."

When Leila left the kitchen, Alma began to question where she'd gone wrong in preparing the jam. She had all of the measurements figured out, so what mistake had she made?

Leila came back in with a bandage as well as an ointment to heal the burn. Alma dried her hand with a small towel that hung on the wall. "I'm sorry for causing a ruckus."

"It's fine. I'm just thankful it wasn't worse than what I thought. First the chair, now this. Anything's possible." Leila took Alma's hand and tended to the wound. "What were you trying to make?"

"Rose petal jam for Elias's mom."

"Rose petal jam? Never heard of that before." Leila finished applying the ointment, then she unwrapped the bandage to wind around Alma's finger.

Even though her finger felt better, Alma continued to feel the burning sensation. "Elaine brought it up one time, and I wanted to see if I could make it to include with the card. I didn't have to go through the trouble, but I couldn't help myself."

"Are you gonna have another go at it?"

"I don't know." Alma crossed her arms and glanced at the saucepan. "It caramelized so quickly. That's never occurred when I've made jam before. Maybe Elaine was pulling my leg with this being an actual jam."

"How long did you simmer it?"

"Forty minutes. It wasn't thickening, so I kept it heated until I smelled it burning."

Leila fidgeted with the collar of her nightgown. "If you were to do it again, maybe try not to simmer it for quite as long. You were working with petals rather than fruit, and that could be why you were having a hard time knowing if it was ready."

Alma was stunned that Leila would encourage her to try again, especially after the fiasco of dropping the saucepan and making loud noises.

Scrubbing the saucepan clean of the hardened sugar, Alma calculated what she'd do for her second attempt, confident enough to try again. "Danki, Leila. I'll have another go."

With that, Alma prepared the ingredients to attempt the recipe once more.

That evening Elias picked up Alma at the Troyers' home. She wore a turquoise dress and black apron, the ensemble accented her flaxen hair. The sight of her made Elias's heart flutter.

They had ridden to Angelo's Italian Restaurant in Lewistown, where Elias's family went quite often for birthdays. The menu was massive, the atmosphere mellow, and Elias certainly enjoyed the Italian cuisine. When Elias sat across from Alma, he was so focused on their conversation that he almost forgot his family was seated at the same table. When Elias looked at them momentarily, he noticed his mom's questioning stare.

Elias told himself to put on the brakes. He was attracted to Alma, but it was not appropriate to pursue a relationship with her.

The dinner sped by, and Alma was close to finishing the rest of her garlic butter pasta, slurping the last few noodles on her plate.

"Seems like you enjoyed your meal." Elias crossed his legs underneath the table.

"I never have leftovers. Even when the portions are large, I power through and savor every bite." When she ate up the last morsels on her plate, Alma picked up her napkin and dabbed her lips. "How was your ravioli?"

"Pretty good. Though I think there's room for dessert."

Alma groaned. "We can't do that and still have room for your mamm's cake at your place."

"We can share dessert. That way we'll still have room for birthday cake. Besides, we're the first ones done with our supper, so it'll give us something to do."

Tapping her chin, Alma's eyes trailed to the tinted light hanging over the table. "Well, when you put it that way, I suppose there's no harm."

The waiter serving their table came over to provide refills of soda, mostly for Elias's nieces and nephews, and Alma got the server's attention to request a list of desserts. They browsed the menu and went for the ice cream.

Soon enough, the meal was over, and they headed back to the Kurtzes' home for cake, as well as a couple of pies Lauren had brought over for anyone who didn't want to eat cake. Elias still had room for a slice of everything.

Finally it was time for his mom to open her gifts, and that was when Elias gave her the shelf he'd crafted.

"It's beautiful, Elias," Mom's eyes glistened as she admired the vine etching along the sides. "Danki for making this for me."

"I have this for you as well." Elias handed her an envelope.

Her mouth gaped open. "Is that a card? You never buy cards."

"Actually, I didn't buy it."

His mom's jaw dropped farther when she pulled out the homemade card, and seeing her so enamored with it gave him a sense of giddiness. *Finally gave her a gift she wasn't expecting.*

"This is wonderful. The color, the lilies." Mom adjusted her glasses. "I am impressed with how much care you put into this."

"I had a good teacher." Elias turned his attention to Alma, who had the widest grin he'd seen from her in a long time.

Alma presented a finely concealed present

418

in a gift bag, the handles of which were looped together with ribbon.

Mom untied the bow and took papers out of the bag, then pulled from it another envelope. She nodded when she looked at Alma's card. "I see who your teacher was, Elias. This is very nice, Alma."

"There's also a jar of jam that I made."

Reaching into the bag, Mom lifted out a mason jar filled with a pinkish-red substance that glistened like a jewel. "What's in there? Is it strawberry jam?"

"Those are rose petals, fresh from my friend's rosebushes."

Mom twisted off the lid of the jar. "Did you come up with this on your own?"

"My friend from Kentucky told me about it, but I did play the recipe by ear since I had nothing to go from—other than my experience making jam from fruit, that is."

Mom tried the jam with a spoon she grabbed from the kitchen. She gave Alma a radiant smile. "This is really good, Alma. It kind of reminds me of something, but I can't put my finger on what it is."

Elias got a spoon for himself, and when he tried it, the consistency didn't remind him of jam. It was syrupy. Then it dawned on him. "Tastes like honey."

Alma nodded. "That's exactly what I thought

419

when I tried it. I don't know if that's how it's supposed to be, but consider my batch as honey or jam."

Other members of the family came over, asking to try the jam for themselves. Lauren even asked Alma if she would make some for her. Elias was happy with how well the evening played out, though he still felt his mom's stare piercing his back at times. *Mom made it clear to me that she doesn't want me to be with Alma. Even after telling her we're only friends, I don't think she trusts me.*

Elias watched as Alma gave a spoonful of jam to his youngest niece, and her pigtails bounced as she ran away with the spoon. With her head turned toward Elias, Alma looked at him with glowing eyes and a soft smile.

Maybe Mom has good reason not to trust me, he thought as his heart radiated warmth.

Chapter 7

A week had gone by since the birthday dinner for Elias's mother, and Alma was cleaning Leila's home before dawn yet again. She was in Leila's sewing room, pruning the pins from the cushion as the dust particles floated up to her nose.

Either Leila hasn't sewn in a long time or she's slipping in taking care of stuff like this. Alma pounded her palm against the cushion.

She went after the walls next. Dust bunnies in bunches drifted onto her sleeve. The cloth Alma used was coated with huge clumps of them.

Alma's thoughts drifted to Elias. Once church services were over on Sunday, he had approached her. He'd asked if Alma wanted to play baseball at the schoolhouse yard today. She had responded eagerly with a yes, but part of her felt uneasy—though it wasn't as if he'd asked her to have dinner, and they weren't going to be alone. A few people they knew from their childhood still lived in the area, and when Elias reintroduced Alma after the service, they'd seemed thrilled to see her again.

This isn't okay. Alma scrubbed the beige walls aggressively. *The more I'm with him, the more these feelings arise. Even if he feels the same way . . .* She rung the cloth. *I feel like a horrible person. Even if he should have feelings for me, would I be able to admit mine?*

Finishing up in the sewing room, Alma pondered what to do next. She had been diligent with keeping up the kitchen, the bathrooms, and the living room. But Alma hadn't gone into one particular room since she arrived. The room right across from the nursery.

Leila jolted awake, eyes opening wide. "Did you hear something, Aden?" she asked in a hushed voice while rolling over on the bed.

Aden lay facing away from her, and responding with a mumble, he burrowed his head into the bedspread.

He's too precious. Leila gave his shoulder a light squeeze, but then she heard the sound of rummaging coming from the entry of the adjoining bathroom, located at the foot of their bed. *So I guess I wasn't dreaming those noises.*

Shifting on the mattress, Leila got out from under the covers, then stopped near the doorframe of the bathroom. Sure enough, Leila's suspicions were on the mark. She had an intruder, but it wasn't a rodent or stranger. "Alma."

Her hands rearranging the contents of the medicine cabinet, Alma glanced over. The dim light from outside shone on the side of her face and shoulder. "Guder mariye."

Leila's stomach clenched. "How long have you been in here?"

"Not long. I snuck in through the crack of your door, trying not to disturb you both."

Pushing a knuckle to her temple, Leila felt her veins pulsating. "We need to talk." She gestured to the door leading out of the bedroom.

Leila waited for Alma to step into the hallway, then shut the door as delicately as she could so as not to wake up Aden. She stared straight at Alma. "What makes you think it's okay to sneak into our room like that?" she hissed.

"I hadn't cleaned in there yet." Alma blinked a few times as she rolled the sleeve of her burgundy dress.

"That is Aden's and my room. It's put together the way we want it to be. Goodness, Alma. It's already enough with other rooms. This doesn't even feel like my own home anymore."

"I was only trying to make it easier on you guys."

"By sneaking into our room while we're sleeping?" Leila bit her inner cheek. "Alma, this is excessive. You have no right to come into my room and poke around, especially without permission."

"That isn't fair of you to say. I've organized for you, helped you make dinner, watched Rachel for you, and you get angry with me?"

"That's not what I—"

"What do you expect me to do?" Alma's nostrils flared. "Nothing at all?"

"I was hoping you'd be more understanding. How would you feel if you had your home changed around?"

"I did. When I had to move out. And you still have a home and your spouse!" Alma's anguished expression faded and her eyes widened. Covering her mouth, she bolted away from Leila and disappeared from sight.

Leila stumbled against the wall. Her throat felt as if a scarf was too snug around her neck. *I was too harsh, wasn't I? I tried not to be abrasive, but I hurt her.* She rested the back of her head on the wall, closing her eyes. *Aden was right— people do handle grief differently, and I feel like I've failed my friend for not approaching her grief properly.*

A little before the afternoon, Elias picked up Alma from the Troyers' home. They were on the road together in his buggy, and Alma was looking toward a field with a massive silo. Two medium-sized hounds sat on the front of the property and barked plenty loud until the buggy was farther down the road.

"So, Alm, are you nervous to play a game again?" Elias asked as he swiveled to the right.

"Are you kidding?" Alma bounced up in her seat when she turned to him. "I have been playing ball with friends in Kentucky. If you're on my team, you're going to win. If not, you're going down."

"We'll see about that. Out of curiosity, what is it like in Kentucky?"

Elias watched as Alma's lips opened a sliver. She leaned her back against the seat, bending her neck forward.

That isn't good, Elias thought. *Say something to her. Let her know she doesn't need to answer.* Beads of sweat formed under his hat, so he took it off and slid it over his shoulder to have it land in the back of the buggy. "You don't have to talk about it, but know I'll lend an ear if you're willing to share."

Alma's posture straightened, and she cleared her throat before speaking. "The day I settled in Hopkinsville was when it dawned on me that my plan of having a future in the Big Valley wasn't going to happen. I came to terms with it and had to begin my life at my new home as soon as possible."

"Must have been a tough adjustment."

"Honestly, it terrified me. But I needed to make it work. I got jobs at stores and restaurants to help provide for my grandparents." She grinned. "It did wonders for them in the end. From that work, I made connections with other Amish young people around my age, as well as non-Amish from my short-lived rumspringa." Alma's smile faded. "I met Michael not long after."

Instinctively Elias rested a hand on hers, which was placed between them on the seat of the buggy. "I'm really sorry for what you've been going through, Alma."

His face warmed. But before he could lift his hand, Alma clasped it. That made him feel both relaxed and anxious.

Her smile reappeared. "Well, I've made the most of it, and I'll make do with what I have now. Even if it's only for a little bit longer." Alma squeezed his fingers tenderly before placing her hands in her lap.

"Were you planning to go home soon?" Elias grasped the reins, steering the horse to get closer to the shoulder of the road.

"I've been calling home most evenings since I've been here, and Makenzie has asked me that question whenever she's returned my call and left a message. I do want to spend my birthday here at least, so I'll get ahold of Elaine to figure out when she can come and get me."

"That's about two weeks away. You don't want to stay longer?"

"I may have overstayed my welcome at Leila and Aden's place." Her gaze dropped to her black stockings and footwear. "Besides, as nice as it is to be back here, I have to be prepared to continue my life when I return home."

"Then we'll make your last two weeks worthwhile." When Elias saw the building with the bell on the point of the roof, he pointed to it. "There's the schoolhouse over there."

A line of buggies sat by the side of the quaint building. Most of the buggies were topped with yellow, but there were also both black and white tops in the row. Some young people sprinted around in the field with no shoes covering their feet. Seeing them taking in the beautiful mid-June day was quite a sight.

Once Elias parked his buggy next to the other ones, he and Alma headed over to where everyone else was. A few of their old classmates recognized Alma right away, and they ran over to greet her. She met them halfway and embraced each one with enthusiasm.

Elias caught up with them, and it wasn't long until they were getting ready to play a game. He and his friend Robert were chosen to pick who they wanted on their team. They decided who would pick first, based on majority vote, and from that result, Elias got to choose who he wanted first.

I could pick Alma to be on my team. Elias rubbed under his chin, gazing at Alma. *Or I could make things interesting and have her on the opposing team.* Smirking, he made up his mind. Elias called out people in the group, and when he required one more person, he looked to her, and when he saw a glint in Alma's eye, Elias called for the last teammate without hesitation. He did not call Alma's name.

Elias was aware of his pitching skills. He threw curveballs that would disorient whoever was up to bat, and his fastball would cause some to swing too quickly. Elias had developed his technique over the years, and it had sure aided in his victories.

He got out the first two players who went up to bat, but the next batter was Alma. She retrieved the bat from the ground and nested it on her shoulder. From what Elias recalled, Alma was an exceptional batter, though she hadn't started out that way when they were younger.

Elias had explained to her that there was a method to hitting the ball. He had told her, *"People have a habit of either swinging far back or far front. Swing too far back, the bat will fly from your hands. Swing too far forward, you're likely to miss the ball. Or if you did hit it, an outfielder may catch it. But if you keep the bat steady enough, you'll bunt the ball. Then you'll run to first base."*

"Show me what you got, Eli." She positioned the bat and gave a curt nod.

Elias watched the hand of the catcher and nodded when she had signaled three fingers. He bent his knee up, then threw the curveball.

The ball cracked when it came in contact with the bat, and it went over the heads of everyone on the field.

Alma wasn't exaggerating. She really had been

practicing, Elias thought as Alma celebrated her home run. Seeing her run around fluidly with cheers for her made him feel weightless. *I'm glad to see you when you're truly happy.*

They continued to play until daylight no longer blanketed the area. Elias had had a wonderful day with Alma, and he desired more opportunities like these before she had to return to Kentucky.

"I had a lot of fun tonight, Eli. And I'm happy I was on your team at least twice." Alma looked up at him.

They were standing by the row of trees in the Troyers' property. It was fairly dark, but the light from the moon let her distinguish Elias's features.

"Jah, I'm sorry for not picking you the first go-round."

"Because you needed me on your team to win, right?" Alma nudged his arm.

Chuckling, he prodded her arm in return. "Exactly."

They laughed together as they strolled to the front door. Their pace was slow, but Alma didn't mind one bit.

"Do you want to hang out again? Maybe after church tomorrow?" He wrapped his thumb around his suspender.

She hummed. "I would love to."

Once they told one another goodnight and Elias headed back to his buggy, Alma twisted the doorknob and went into the house. She knew Leila and Aden had already eaten supper, since they usually planned to have it around six and it was already past eight.

Her stomach rumbled. *I knew I should have brought a jar of jam and some bread to the game with me. I better have it now to combat my hunger.*

Alma went into the kitchen and planned to gather something to eat from the pantry. But when she entered the living room, Leila sat on the couch with a notebook and pencil.

When I had that outburst earlier, I don't know what came over me. Alma hesitated to step forward. *I hope Leila can forgive me for going off on her.*

"Oh. Hi, Alma." Leila tapped her pencil against the notebook. "Have a good time with Elias?"

"It was tons of fun." Alma swallowed. "Leila, about earlier—"

"You don't need to apologize." Closing the notebook, she fixed her gaze on Alma. "You've been through a lot, and I'm sorry for the way I responded. I should have handled it better."

"No, I should be apologizing. You were right. It was wrong of me to go into your room and mess with your stuff. I know I wouldn't like it if that happened to me."

Leila's eyes widened, but then she placed the notebook beside the lamp and rose from the couch. "I forgive you, Alma. Thank you for the apology."

Alma was on the brink of tears, and she didn't know why. But she hurried to Leila, and her arms trembled as she hugged her friend tightly. Alma whispered, "Thank you," repeatedly, trying to suppress the emotions she felt inside.

Praying, she also thanked God for them getting through their argument. Alma hoped it would be the last time they had to go through something like this, because she did not want to lose Leila.

Chapter 8

Alma had woken in a panic from another nightmare. Her eyes were agape, yet she struggled to differentiate dream from reality. Sweat coated her skin like condensation on a chilled glass of water.

She continued to see blurbs of Michael then Elias, and of her hands cradling teeth like a collection of seashells. Alma grazed her teeth, aware she still had them in her mouth, but it felt as if they were absent from her gums.

Her upper body jittered. Alma was in dire need of fresh air. Rather than unlocking and sliding the sash of the window, she left the guest room and went out the front door. Alma quickened her pace to the side of the house and seated herself in front of the line of rosebushes. She raised her head to the starry sky, bringing her knees to her chest and wrapping her nightgown-covered sleeves around them.

Breathe, Alma. Just breathe. Alma took in the humid air, exposing her neck by sweeping up the hair behind her shoulders.

The days had flown by since she and Elias had played baseball by the schoolhouse. Alma had been seeing Elias often because he'd drop by the card shop right at closing time. Some evenings they would chat with the Troyers in the house. Other times Alma wandered the property alone with Elias, conversing with him until the evening light faded.

Alma leaned forward to rest her cheek against her knee. *Should this be taking its toll on me? I'm trying to move forward, but those thoughts creep in, and then the dreams. . . . How can I make them go away?*

Fiddling with a blade of grass, she listened to the rosebushes gently rustling. Alma's eyelids shut on their own, but she opened them right away. *I should go back in and see if reading will put me to sleep.* She stretched her arms then used them as leverage to scramble to her feet. *I need all of the energy I can muster for later today. It is my birthday after all, so I'd better be ready to celebrate.*

State College, Pennsylvania

Alma, Leila, Aden, and Elias had planned to go to State College for Alma's birthday to shop and eat at a restaurant. Leila had dropped Rachel off with her stepmother on their way out of town. Aden's friend Randy chauffeured them, and it took just over thirty minutes to arrive in State College by vehicle.

Upon arrival, they drove to downtown State College, noticing a number of people wandering

433

along the partly bricked sidewalks. The sight from the backseat window exhilarated Alma. She couldn't wait to commemorate her twenty-second birthday in the company of her close friends.

One of the shops they visited was Kitchen Kaboodle. The Troyers went off in a separate direction, while Elias stayed beside Alma as she browsed the products on display.

"Look at all of these culinary utensils." Alma picked up a tool used for zesting. "If I still had a kitchen of my own, I'd definitely be buying some of these."

Elias peered over her shoulder. "You could always save it for the future."

Her stomach quivered. "Jah, I'm sure."

"Would you get married again?" he questioned while shuffling his feet.

"Hard to say. I mean, I would want to get married someday, but who knows what'll happen before then?" Fidgeting with the item, Alma grabbed another tool, which was used for peeling vegetables. "Though I suppose buying for the future wouldn't hurt."

As Alma approached the counter to pay for her items, Leila was already there. Aden stood with her, chatting with the worker behind the counter during the transaction. Alma pulled out her wallet as soon as Leila was finished.

When they left the shop, Alma asked, "What did you find, Leila?"

Leila brushed a strand of hair behind her ear and pointed over to a bench. "Let's sit there for a bit so we can show what we bought."

They perused more stores while strolling through the area. However, after a couple of hours, each person in the group started commenting about being hungry. So they began looking for a sit-down restaurant.

Fortunately they found a restaurant above the Hotel State College called Allen Street Grill. The interior was simple yet refined—just the way Alma preferred. She adored the massive windows for viewing the bustling streets. The four friends were seated in a booth with coal-colored cushions, and the light fixtures resembled hourglasses.

Alma was not at all surprised when Elias ordered the gnocchi, a pasta dish. Alma decided to order pasta as well but went with the mezzelune. On the other side of the table, Leila and Aden each ordered rib eye steak. That started them on a tangent about how they usually ordered the same meal.

The way those two interact is as if they've recently been married. Alma's arms tensed as she stared at the Troyers' nonstop affection. *I am happy for them being so close, but it all feels too familiar, and them getting to have that when I'm left with nothing is unfair.*

Caught off guard, Alma eyed her hand, which

rested on the seat of the booth. Elias's hand brushed hers. She glimpsed his narrowed blue eyes, nodding with what Alma assumed to be sympathy.

Heat tickled her nose. *He's only comforting you. Calm yourself.* Alma attempted to sway her focus from Elias to the windows on her right.

Later on the four finished their meals, and it was time for Alma to pick which dessert to share with her friends. She spotted the french apple cake, and her decision was made.

"Anyone here detest us having the apple cake?" Alma thumbed the side of the menu.

Aden shook his head. "I'm in favor of it. Leila?"

"It's your birthday, Alma. Anything you want, I'm okay with."

"I agree with Leila." Elias patted Alma's arm. "We trust your decision."

When the cake was brought to their table, they all got a spoon ready and scooped in. The dessert vanished in moments. The waiter came by afterward, asking who would be billed for their meal.

"I'll pay for my own, and I'll treat the one who was born on this day," Elias said to the waiter, bumping Alma's shoulder.

Alma chuckled. "In that case, I want a bunch more of the apple cakes to go."

"I know you're joking, but if you do want

one more cake, I wouldn't mind sharing." Elias winked.

The hairs raised on the back of Alma's neck. But she brushed off her feelings yet again. "Danki, Elias. I'll take you up on that offer."

By the time they left the restaurant, it was past five o'clock, so they all agreed to leave State College and head back to Belleville. Alma was content, especially because she had arranged to call her family when she returned to her friend's home.

Belleville

The sun had begun to set on the Big Valley, and Elias was standing by while Alma enjoyed the white swing outside the Troyers' home. The gold flecks in her eyes reflected the fading light.

"How is your finger doing? You burned it while making the jam for my mom, didn't you?" Elias pressed a hand on the painted wood of the swing.

Alma brought her finger to eye level. "There's a mark for sure, but it's almost completely healed." She rubbed the reddened patch with her thumb. "The downside is that I cannot feel anything in that spot."

"Damaged nerves, huh? Who knew heated sugar could be so dangerous?"

"I did, but sticking my finger in the failed jam was a slipup. Certainly not voluntary." She grasped the sides of the seat. "By the way, I'm glad you were able to join us for the ride to State College. It made my birthday much more special."

Elias tipped his hat and smirked. "Are you only saying that because of the cake?"

"I'd be lying if I said the cake had nothing to do with it." A smile crept over her face. But then it dissipated and her gaze lowered. "You comforted me at the restaurant, and it helped take my mind off what I was feeling. That means a lot to me."

Elias sank onto the lawn and rested his back against the swing's side support. *Now's your moment. Tell her what's really in your heart.* "I do care about you, Alm. Even after you moved and we grew apart, I still prayed for things to work out for you in Kentucky. I wanted to check up on you, but I didn't want to intrude on your life, and since you hadn't gotten ahold of me, I let it be."

Sighing, she stretched a hand to his shoulder. "I'm sorry for allowing our friendship to falter. I thought that by distancing myself, it would make adjusting to my new life much easier. But I know now how selfish that was of me, and I hope you can forgive me for that."

"Course I do." His pulse quickened. "And I hope you can forgive me for not being honest with you back then."

"What do you mean?" Alma asked with a raised brow.

"I know I treated you for the meal, but that wasn't your only gift." Elias rose from the ground, then offered her a hand up. "Come with me to my buggy. I'll give it to you before I leave."

Alma's heart thudded. "When did you make this?" She studied the envelope, wrapped with a brown string tied in a bow.

"I bought supplies from the shop last week when you went into the house, and I made the card as soon as I got home." Elias stood on the foot lift of the yellow buggy, with the waning sunlight glimmering against the top of his hat, making the rest of his form appear as a silhouette.

She lifted the tab of the envelope, tugging out Elias's homemade card. The card folded across the top and had a cutout construction sheet glued to it. A pink ribbon decorated the upper left-hand corner. The overall card was baby blue, and the white sheet on the cover had been stamped with black ink reading HAPPY BIRTHDAY!

"It's beautiful, Eli." Her fingers grazed the ends of the ribbon. "You've got a knack for this. Have you considered working with us instead of your father?"

Elias chuckled. "I don't think he'd be thrilled with me quitting on him."

Alma lifted the bottom of the card, revealing a handwritten note on another glued-on sheet. It also had stamps of balloons on both sides. She went on and read Elias's message:

Happy 22nd Birthday, Alm,

Your devotion to be on top of things is inspiring, and I hope you understand how much I value you as a friend. You got me through thick and thin, and even when you left, memories of the times we shared always remained with me. Even through past hardships, you always did your best to be optimistic. But know that anything you're struggling with now or later, I will do whatever I can to make those hard times more bearable.

Thank you for the memories I cherish to this day, and I hope to make more with you before you leave.

Elias
Romans 12:2

Alma wished she was still sitting on the swing set, because she had the urge to crumple to the ground. She attempted to fight the feebleness in her limbs, yet it didn't stop her from stumbling to where she almost didn't catch herself.

"Are you okay?" Elias jumped down from the buggy.

440

"I'm fine." Alma held up her hand. "I must've been locking my knees." Brushing a hand on her apron, she looked directly at him. "Anyways, that was well written, Eli. Thank you."

"You're welcome." Elias got back up in the buggy and took off his hat and laid it on the front seat. He reached for something in the backseat. "I have this for you as well."

He unfurled it before Alma and hopped down to give it to her. Alma was smitten by what was in his grasp.

The words escaped her lips. "Red carnations." She curved her fingers around the stems. The vibrant petals lightly prodded her nose as she took in the spicy fragrance.

"What I didn't tell you back then was from fear of ruining the friendship we shared. Now there's a chance of that happening again, but I am not going to make the same mistake twice, regardless of the risk." He fidgeted with the collar of his shirt but then moved his hand to cup her elbow. "Alm, my care for you goes beyond friendship. The truth is I had feelings for you then and I have feelings for you now."

It was as if an electrical current flowed through her as she processed his words. *Did he just say that he has feelings for me? Even back then?* She looked up at him. "D–do you really mean that?"

Elias didn't blink. "I do, Alm. Even if you don't feel the same, I needed you to know."

441

"I feel the same. But . . ." She trailed off, trying to gather her thoughts. Her sight flittered to the carnations then back to Elias. "We can't pursue this. I don't even know how we would without scrutiny. I wasn't married that long ago, and courting shortly after losing Michael . . . Everyone would . . . They would believe I didn't love him."

Elias removed his hands from her arms, draping them at his sides. "I'm sorry. I really should have told you back then."

They stood still, turned away from one another. If Alma went with her feelings, what would come of their relationship? Was it worth giving it a chance? It would probably cause more issues than anything.

"What if we didn't make it official?" Elias asked. "We could keep our relationship private for a while, and in the meantime, we can still hang out like we usually do."

Alma shook her head. "That wouldn't bode well either. I have to return home at some point, and I already told my family I would be coming back soon."

"Try to stay for a little longer. Please, Alma." He grasped her hands, adding urgency to his plea. "Aren't you even slightly curious to know if we could make this work?"

The sight of her hands surrounded by his with the carnations caused her yearnings for Elias to convulse. The uncertainty of where this would go if she agreed concerned her, but Alma wondered if this was why she had come back to Belleville. For weeks she'd been at odds with herself, but after being with Elias again, Alma was no longer pretending to be okay. Without a doubt, Elias had made her happy again. What if Elias was Alma's answer? What if he was the key to moving on from her grief?

On a whim, placing the carnations at their feet, Alma embraced Elias. "Okay, we'll give it a shot. I'll let my family know that I'll be staying here for a bit longer."

Elias gently patted Alma's back. "You won't be sorry, Alm. I promise."

Chapter 9

State College, Pennsylvania

In early July, Elias suggested they go to State College on a date. They had been there for dates before, and one of their favorite places was Auntie Annie's. The pretzel establishment was at the shopping center, and Elias had admitted going there plenty of times while on rumspringa.

They had browsed the assortment of stores in the mall area, but none of the fashion trends piqued Alma's interest. It was too overwhelming for her to fathom, and some of the clothes were too immodest for her comfort. In one of the stores, English students had been goofing off in the middle of the walkway, acting as if they weren't surrounded by other people. Their actions reminded her of when she was expected to follow suit with her friends in Hopkinsville. It was one of the reasons Alma wasn't always enthusiastic about going to State College. Still, having Elias to divert her concerns made it worth the trip. Not to mention visiting the appealing gardens at the arboretum.

Alma and Elias went to Annie's Pretzels and ordered two salted pretzels with cheese dip. Soon after, she stood by the counter while he went to

444

look for a table. After being served their orders, Alma gripped the tray and transferred it over to the eating area, scooting out the chair facing him. She rolled up her sleeves while smiling at Elias. "Got us our pretzels."

Elias gave a wide grin. "Thanks for getting them, Alm."

"And thank you for saving my seat." She nodded as her face warmed. "Now let's silent pray before we eat."

As she sat across from him, Alma watched Elias bow his head, and she followed suit. *Lord, while I doubt it at times, I have a feeling that You brought me to Elias. Although I'm afraid of what could happen, please give me the strength and the opportunity to be straightforward with my feelings. In Your wonderful name, amen.*

When Alma opened her eyes, Elias still had his head lowered. He sighed, which caused her mind to race through the possibilities of what he was praying about.

Tugging her sleeve down, she lowered her head once more. *I hope You can help with what Elias may be going through as well. He has a strong will, Lord. But having a strong will leads to more trials along the way.*

Once they finished praying, they enjoyed their lunch, discussing what had gone on during the week. Alma discussed her week at work and talked about how Leila had introduced her to

Mollie. The three women went shopping for supplies for the two shops, then crafted some summer-themed cards for the stores. Business had increased some, and Leila had told her that was common during the summer months.

Elias had mentioned that he and his father were getting along with one another in their shop, but his father hadn't asked anything about her and Elias's relationship. He was aware that they were hanging out, but it was unclear if he had been catching on or if he assumed Elias and Alma's relationship was platonic as it had been years back. Elias had also talked about his other friends, such as Robert, and their shenanigans. Apparently Robert had recently tried to set up Elias with someone, which made sense considering no one was aware of his and Alma's relationship. Alma knew Elias hadn't been interested in anyone before she came back, which kept her mind at ease.

Elias did admit, however, that his mother disapproved of him possibly courting Alma, but Alma had known that already. When she had been invited to the Kurtzes' home for supper after church, Alma had overheard a conversation between Elias and his mom as she strolled past the kitchen after being in the restroom. Alma figured that even if being seen as only friends, their relationship was still going to cause tension within Elias's family.

Alma shifted in her seat. *All of that could've been prevented if . . . No, I can't think about that. Elias wants to be with me, and I want to be with him.* Moving away from such thoughts, she broke off a piece of pretzel.

Elias took his pretzel and shoved it in his mouth. He attempted to say something, but his voice was muffled by the bread in his mouth.

"Hmm? What did you say? It'd be easier for you to speak if your mouth wasn't stuffed with pretzel." Alma bit into the crispy bread.

"Sorry. I forgot about my table manners. I was trying to say, 'It's so yummy.' " Elias picked up his napkin in an exaggerated fashion and patted at the salt lining the bottom of his lip.

Snickering, she bumped Elias's leg underneath the table. Alma shook her head, then took a sip of her iced tea. "That's one of the things I appreciate about you."

There were plenty of reasons why Alma appreciated him, but she was still too uncertain to admit them to herself.

They continued talking, but at times Alma faded out of the conversation. It was so easy to lose awareness when just the two of them were together. Her body always felt warm with fulfillment.

Regardless of the possible consequences, Alma was doing her best to be optimistic. Everything could work out, and if it was meant to be, then it would happen. Alma wanted nothing more than to focus on the now and not overthink the future.

Once they'd finished eating their lunch, Alma went to the trash bin and dumped the scraps. Facing Elias, she asked, "Ready?"

"Jah. Let's get going."

Belleville

After another baseball game by the schoolhouse, Alma and Elias's day together was almost over. Watching the others departing in their buggies, Alma realized that only Elias and she were left on the field with daylight fading.

Elias settled on the blanket he and Alma had spread out on the grass. She had brought a basket with her, and Elias already knew what Alma had cradled in there.

Alma revealed a glistening jar of the jam made with rose petals, as well as a bread loaf in plastic wrap. She also pulled from the basket two bottles of water.

"You went all out. Did you also make the bread yourself?"

Nodding, Alma lined it up on the plaid blanket. "I aim to please. It's a compromise for not being able to go out to have supper."

"Right. All thanks to my parents' growing suspicious. You're fortunate in this case. Your

448

parents have no way of knowing what we're doing."

"I don't know if I'd call it fortunate." Alma's smile quivered as she peeled back the plastic from the loaf. "I'd want nothing more than to have no secrets."

Then why do you keep on telling me you're okay when I can tell you're not? he wondered, clenching his suspender.

She spread a moderate amount of jam onto a slice with a butter knife then handed it to him. Alma twisted the lid back on once she got a slice for herself.

"Danki." Elias pinched the crust and sunk his teeth in, enjoying the honeyed, sugary sweetness. Elias still had a question lurking in his mind, so he swallowed, then parted his lips. "You say you don't want secrets, so why not try to be more honest?"

Alma dipped her head toward the jar resting on her knee. She took a bite from her bread, then another and another. She continued to chew while tapping the lid of the jar. Over time she ate up her slice and finally responded to his question. "Being too expressive can negatively impact others. It may cause whoever is listening to dislike you for expressing your personal issues in the first place. It just isn't worth the tension that comes from it. There are times when being silent is necessary to keep the peace."

The muscles in his neck stiffened. "But if you suppress your feelings about your circumstances, that can do some damage inwardly. Keeping things bottled up does more harm than good, especially when you don't convey what you're going through properly. In the end, even if your intent was to prevent tension, you can end up causing more from not saying anything, especially when you had chances to do so."

Her gaze tore up to him. Alma laid down the jar and got up from the blanket. "What are you saying then? Are you suggesting we should tell your parents the truth about us?" She spoke with sweeping gestures.

Elias hoisted himself to his feet, feeling a tad light-headed from standing too quickly. "Aren't you getting tired of sneaking around? Alm, while we're with family and friends, I have to resist the urge to hold your hand." He touched Alma's forearm, and she lowered it. He unhurriedly encircled his fingers around hers. "Don't you want to do that all the time without worrying about being seen?"

"I do. But if we're not careful, not being able to hold hands will be the least of our worries." Alma's mouth curved like a bow of ribbon. "We've only been keeping our relationship hidden for a couple of weeks. Leila and Aden also know about us, so we don't have to pretend at their home. Aren't you content with that?

450

Aren't you worried about jeopardizing what we have?"

"If we get caught, we'll be jeopardizing it regardless. It could be a softer blow to admit it before that happens." Exhaling, Elias loosened his fingers. "But I'm not going to say anything unless you're up for it."

Alma grasped his hand and inched closer to him. "All right, Eli. I don't want our secrecy to affect us anymore, so if you believe it's the right choice, then we may as well try." Sighing, she let go of his hand and plopped back onto the blanket, gesturing to the snacks. "Can we at least finish our evening here before we ruin everything?"

He joined her on the blanket. Though their interactions were normal, a heaviness enveloped them. Alma seemed to be having a hard time keeping her optimistic attitude.

I hope from doing this she doesn't end up losing trust in me. The hairs on the back of Elias's neck rose as he pondered the consequences of telling his parents the truth.

"I already know they're going to want us to end it." Alma's temples pulsated as she stood with Elias on the staircase up to the porch. She was on the verge of slipping off her cardigan, given how unbearably warm her upper body had become.

Elias took ahold of her hand and gave it a

gentle squeeze. "We'll get through it. Just trust me on this."

Even though Alma valued Elias's comfort, it wasn't enough to ease her dread of what was behind the door at the end of the porch. She felt as if she had lumps of cotton lodged in her throat.

When they got to the front door, Elias grasped the knob, thrusting the creaky door open.

Lord, when I asked for Elias to get through his trials, this isn't exactly what I had in mind. She tugged at the hem of her sweater before they stepped into the house.

The entry of the house was the kitchen, and there stood Elias's mom in the middle of cleaning dishes under the spigot.

"Willkumm home." His mom turned and peered at Elias from above her frames. Then her gaze shifted to Alma, narrowing without a blink. "And good evening to you, Alma."

Alma clutched her own arm. "Evening, Mrs. Kurtz."

"Oh Elias, you're sure back late. You missed supper," Elias's dad declared as he roamed from the living room and into the kitchen. Noticing Alma, the man slowly nodded. "Evening."

"Evening, Mr. Kurtz."

Elias stepped forward and said, "We were wondering if we could talk with you guys about something."

His parents obliged, and they all headed into

the living room to talk. Amos and Grace sat in the rocking chairs facing the couch, where Elias and Alma had already taken seats.

"So how do we say this, Alm?" Elias asked, shifting on the cushion.

She pressed a hand to her neck. "Shouldn't we have discussed that before coming in?"

"Well probably." Elias fiddled with his hands.

His dad raised an eyebrow. "What is it you have to say?"

Alma glanced away from Mr. Kurtz, noting how Elias's mom was motionless in the rocker. With crossed arms, her gaze was fixed on her son.

Elias severed the silence. "Alma and I want to have a courtship."

Shaking her head, his mom settled her elbows on the arms of the chair. "Elias, I told you this wasn't *schmaert*, yet you went behind our backs and outright did it anyway."

"Mrs. Kurtz, if you aren't okay with this, then—"

Elias cut her off. "What is so wrong when we both want to be together? We don't plan to rush into anything. Isn't that enough to where we can make this work?"

Grimacing, she turned to Alma. "You're so generous, and if you hadn't lost your husband recently, then I'd be more than happy for you to be with my son."

"What difference does it make?" Elias rose from the couch. "The only thing that matters is that we care for each other and we both want this."

"Because it's not appropriate. If it was a year or two from now, then it would be fine."

"Your mamm's right, Elias. Alma should at least wait for a year."

"What do you think, Alm?" He leaned close to her and gazed deeply into her eyes.

Alma raised her chin. His tender facial features made her heart ache. *See, Elias? This is why I told you we should have kept it hidden for a while longer.* Tension stiffened her shoulders. *But I know you have good intent, and I agreed to this, so I'll follow through as I said I would.* Grasping his hand, Alma nodded, "I want to be with Elias now."

That response wasn't well received from his mom. "We'll see what the church leaders say about it."

"That isn't fair, Mamm."

"Unfortunately, Elias, life isn't fair. Even if you both want to pursue your courtship, you're going to have to gain their approval."

Elias continued to go back and forth with his mom, and then his dad jumped in as well. While this was happening, Alma didn't say a word. She would have if her stomach hadn't been roiling.

"I feel nauseous—" Alma bounded from the couch and hurried out of the room.

Thankfully the restroom wasn't far, and she fastened the door as soon as she went in. Alma pulled her covering off and chucked it to the sidewall, then leaned her head above the sink and began vomiting.

After a few minutes, nothing came up, and the nausea grew faint. Trying to breathe, Alma knelt on the tiled flooring. *I must be more stressed than I thought.* She reached for her covering and brushed it off and pinned it back on her head.

A knock sounded on the door. "Alm, are you okay? Alm?" Elias asked with the pitch of his voice higher than usual.

"I'm okay. I'll be out soon." She clambered to her feet. *What are we going to do, Elias? Is it worth approaching the church leaders about this when your parents disapprove of us courting too early?*

Chapter 10

Alma was settled on the couch in the Troyers' living room, holding Rachel in her arms. She peered to her left toward the window.

Today she and Elias were going to the bishop's home. Elias had gotten ahold of the bishop the day after admitting their relationship to his parents. Although Elias had conveyed his dismay with the situation, he had attempted to soothe Alma, letting her know that he wanted to strive for their courtship.

Before the meeting, Alma had to inform her family of their situation as well. They hadn't expected it, and like Elias's parents, her family agreed that going to the church leaders for their approval was a good idea.

Now Alma sat waiting for Elias to show up so they could ride over in his buggy. Concerns plagued her as she waited. With the responses from their families, Alma couldn't begin to bear to think how Michael's parents would feel when they found out.

Rachel yanked the shoulder of her dress. The little girl's gaze met hers, and she gave Alma the cheekiest of smiles.

"Imagine. The only trouble you have is wondering when you'll get love and affection."

She gently stroked the side of Rachel's face, and the child shut her eyes and giggled.

Leila had gone out to take care of the chores in the chicken run. Alma would usually be doing chores herself, but Leila insisted that she take a break. Alma still wanted to do something, so she had been tending to Rachel's needs most of the morning. Not only did it distract her, but Rachel had sparked delight in Alma ever since she'd gotten used to taking care of her.

"Hey."

Alma lifted her chin to lay eyes on the figure standing in the entryway. "Hello, Aden."

He strode into the living room with his hands in the pockets of his black trousers. "Got a lot on your mind?" he asked.

"How can you tell?"

"Well, you're keepin' yourself preoccupied with my daughter for one thing. Besides, I have a sense of these things." Taking a seat on the other couch, Aden stretched his left arm across the back cushions. His eyes shifted to her before speaking. "Look, I know you're stressed over today and probably have questioned if you and Elias should've revealed your relationship." He paused, sinking into the back of the couch, then proceeded. "The thing is, the choices we make will usually meet with someone's disapproval even if we believe it's the right thing to do. You gotta think of what's best for you." His brows lowered. "Sometimes you cannot go down the path of least resistance. So whatever the bishop advises you to do, try to do what's best for you and Elias."

Alma understood what Aden was saying, but it didn't sit well with her. As much as she desired to be with Elias, Alma didn't want to continue to cause problems among his family any more than she already had. Perhaps pursuing the courtship wasn't worth upsetting those around them.

But Alma nodded to show Aden that she at least considered his words. "You and Leila have been so supportive of us, and I'm grateful for that." Shuffling her bare feet on the throw rug, Alma questioned him. "You two seem to have it figured out. How do you guys do it?"

Aden shook his head. " 'Cause we've been there, and we still face those issues." He blinked, and then his gaze toward her intensified. "We've learned to acknowledge them."

She got up from the couch, bouncing Rachel on her arm. "Elias should be here any minute, so I suppose I should wait for him outside."

"Let me take Rachel from you." Aden extended his arms like the branches of a tree.

After he'd safely nestled Rachel in his arms, Aden said he'd be praying for them. Alma rushed to the guest room. She had her stockings and footwear set out, so she sat on the edge of the mattress to slip them on.

She rocked on her heels as she stood. *I'm not looking forward to what may come of this, but I do need to consider what I should do if it doesn't go well. And I'll need to tell Elias when I have it figured out.* She let out a deep, weighted sigh. *I remember the days when I had a better grasp of how to prevent my life from falling into pieces.*

When Alma and Elias entered the residence of Thomas Lapp, the bishop of the yellow-top community, he asked them to meet with him in the dining room. The pleasant space included on one wall a small quilt in the Mariner's Compass pattern, using a variety of blue fabrics.

Six chairs surrounded the table, and besides the bishop, Alma, and Elias, two other church leaders were present.

The bishop's wife, Carolyn, entered and placed a platter containing an assortment of whoopie pies on the center of the white table runner.

"Enjoy. And if you two want something to drink, I have a pitcher of strawberry lemonade for you that I freshly squeezed this morning." Carolyn adjusted the white covering atop her salt-and-pepper hair.

Elias agreed to the lemonade, and when Carolyn left, he went for the platter straightaway.

Typically Alma would be eager to savor the spongy texture of the cream-filled treat, but the sight of the pies perturbed her. Not wanting to come off ill-mannered, she removed one of the whoopies from the platter and sunk her teeth into the chocolate exterior. For some reason, the texture seemed all wrong to her.

When Carolyn brought out the pitcher, Alma thanked her for the whoopie pies. Carolyn also set a couple of glasses on quilted coasters and filled them with lemonade. To her surprise, Alma wasn't troubled by the sight of the strawberry bits floating to the surface. The bishop and two ministers had mugs of coffee that Carolyn had already poured for them.

At that point, Thomas commenced the conversation. "So, Mrs. Wengerd, you grew up here in the Big Valley in the yellow-top community, correct?"

"Yes, sir." Alma's throat felt parched, so she took a small sip from her glass.

"Currently you live in another state. Which state do you live in?"

"Kentucky."

"Are your parents aware that you want to have a courtship with Elias?"

Alma nodded, resting the glass back on the coaster to dry her hands with a napkin from a stack on the table. She wondered if the moisture was from sweat rather than from condensation on the glass.

The bishop gestured to Elias. "This young man

told me that you became widowed not long ago. When did your husband pass away?"

"In May."

The exchange went on with her being asked questions and giving brief answers. During that time, Alma glanced at the platter, which was now barren of any whoopie pies. Elias's jaw was moving up and down.

"The concern I share with Elias's parents is, why do you want to be with Elias right away, even though you lost your husband recently?"

Alma rolled her shoulders back. "Elias and I grew up here, and I moved out of the area when I was sixteen. When I came back to stay at the Troyers' home in the black-top community, I saw Elias again, and we began hanging out frequently. Then he admitted to liking me as more than a friend, and it turned out those old feelings we once had were still within us." Alma traced the rim of her glass. "Putting it simply, it felt right to act on them."

Thomas directed his attention to Elias, and Alma observed that, while Elias was doing his best to stay composed, his frustration could be heard as he spoke. It made Alma feel guilty for putting him in this position.

"Mr. Kurtz, have you considered courting anyone other than Alma?"

Elias crossed his arms and fixed his stare on the bishop. "With all due respect, there is no one else

461

I want to be with. If there was any reason Alma couldn't be with me, I'd fight for it. That's why we're here now." He glanced at her and brought his attention back to Thomas. "Unless she says otherwise."

One of the ministers squinted at him. The loose skin around his eyes crinkled. "Do you understand what a courtship will entail? Are you expecting to marry her right away?"

"I assure you, we won't make a permanent commitment for at least a year."

Alma glanced at the wall clock hanging by the quilt. *Has it really been over an hour since we've been here?*

Not long after, Thomas seemed to have made his assessment, because he looked to the other church leaders and nodded at them. He clasped his hands in front of him on the table.

"We have to discuss this privately, so if you would seat yourselves outside, we'll call you both back in." The bishop motioned to the entrance of the dining room.

Elias walked out of the house with Alma. A swinging bench by the home faced the property easement. They seated themselves, and Elias pushed his feet against the ground to get the bench to sway.

"I'm sorry, Alm. I thought this was the way to go, but we're in this because I was too impatient."

"Hey, we both agreed to this, didn't we?"

"I know, but I initiated it. Maybe we could have kept it going in secret." His jaw trembled. "It just felt wrong to do that."

"No, I get it. I told myself it was fine, but it was driving me crazy too." Alma folded her hands in her lap. "Eli, if they say that we shouldn't be together, then—" She fastened her lips and clenched her eyes shut.

"We'll figure out a way to make this work."

She opened her brown eyes and gaped at him. "How? We most certainly can't have a courtship where I live. And could you imagine if we both moved to another area? How much trouble that would cause? News travels, Eli. There's nowhere we could run to." She bent her neck forward, no longer looking at him. "Which is why I think it's best for me to move back home if they tell us we can't have a courtship."

The bench sat nearly motionless. Elias felt like his body wanted to crumple in on itself from Alma's words. But she was right. There was no point in denying the repercussions of their relationship. He understood where Alma was coming from, and as much as Elias wanted to go with his heart, he had to consider the logical option and compromise. Because one thing was certain: Elias did not want to lose Alma if he could help it.

Eventually Elias placed his hand atop hers.

"Even if you moved back to Kentucky, we could still wait a year. Then it will be okay for us to be together."

Alma lifted her gaze to him with widened eyes. "You're willing to be patient for that long?"

"Trust me, I was already doing well with not dating anyone before you came here." He smiled, but his heart sank a little. "As for not being with you during that time, it'll be difficult. But it'd be worth the wait."

Alma pressed a kiss near his ear. Right away she slapped a hand to her cheek. "Whoops. Sorry about that."

"What are you sorry for?" He beamed.

They kept talking until one of the church leaders came out of the house to invite them back in. Though Elias was anxious to know what Thomas had decided about their future, he centered his thoughts on the positive outcomes.

Entering the dining room, Thomas rose from his seat and circled the table to be face-to-face with them.

"So since the two of you are willing to take this at a slow pace, we have agreed that you are allowed to have a courtship."

Alma pressed a hand to her throat. "Am I hearing that correctly?"

"Jah you did. Just don't give us any reason not to allow this to continue." Thomas adjusted his frames. "I'll be letting your families know right away. So rejoice." He held his hand out to Alma. "It was a pleasure talking with you, Mrs. Wengerd."

"D–danki, sir." Alma almost yelled, but she managed to contain her excitement and shake the bishop's proffered hand.

Thomas then gave Elias a handshake. A smile crept on Elias's face as he thanked him. Carolyn came into the room and wished them the best, giving them a container of whoopie pies to take home. Alma had no interest in the whoopie pies, but she accepted them nonetheless.

Holding hands, they left the premises and went to Elias's buggy at the hitching post.

"Can you believe this? They actually said yes!" Elias shouted as Alma climbed up to put the container of whoopie pies into the yellow buggy.

"I know!" Alma exclaimed. The bottoms of her shoes scuffed the pavement as she jumped down. She then ran to Elias and practically collided with him.

He enveloped her with his embrace. "I could kiss you right now."

Chuckling, she blinked back her tears and bestowed him a smile. "You could. We are officially courting, aren't we?"

The heat in her face rose as they drew closer. She brought her hands to the sides of his face, grazing his clean-shaven face as she leaned into

465

him. Alma was still in disbelief that she was about to be kissed by her childhood friend.

Moments before their lips met, she tugged from his hold and covered her mouth. She staggered, wrapping her arms under her rib cage as a sense of wooziness overtook her.

"Alm? You all right?" Elias squeezed her shoulders, which prevented her from falling over.

"I'm fine, I think . . ." Gulping down some air, Alma fought against her body, which felt like it wanted to thrust out the whoopie pie she'd eaten. "I need to lie down."

"Let's get you back to Leila's, okay?"

Elias assisted her with steady strides. As he helped her into the back of the buggy, his words gradually became difficult to understand. *I haven't felt like this since I got the flu bug last year.* She scrunched close up to the backseat. She barely noticed Elias hurrying to get his horse unhitched from the post, and then her eyes closed.

Chapter 11

The month of July was winding up, and Leila felt bewildered with how the weeks had sped by. It seemed not long ago that her friend had arrived.

Thinking of her friend, Leila was thankful that Alma had been feeling better this past week. She had been under the weather two weeks back and had kept to the guest room most of the time as she regained her health. Without Alma in the card shop, all the stress of working alone with Rachel returned. Leila had managed to get through it without any major hang-ups, but one thing was certain: it had affirmed Leila's appreciation for her friend's assistance. Leila also appreciated that Alma had quit trying to clean things to the point of rearranging her home.

The first half of the day in the card shop was over, and as Leila managed the register, Alma restocked the shelves.

"Where did you two run off to yesterday?" Leila asked Alma as she moved to Rachel's playpen.

"We went to the one place you took me and Mollie to."

"Taste of the Valley." Humming, she heaved Rachel into her arms and kissed her forehead.

Leila tilted her head toward Alma. "All right, but I don't think it takes five hours to eat a sandwich."

Alma's cheeks flushed. "Elias and I wandered into the markets afterward." She stretched to place one more stamp on the shelf, aligning it neatly with the other stamps.

Putting Rachel back into the playpen, Leila came near Alma, lacing her fingers behind her back. "It's nice to see you doing much better."

"I am. That week was horrible for multiple reasons." Alma's gaze lifted to the ceiling. "Not being able to do anything except *kotz* wasn't very productive."

"You were productive in bouncing back."

"Well, you helped with that. You were frequently checking up on me."

"Elias also did his fair share." Leila giggled.

Alma's mouth drew into a straight line. "While I am glad he did, I was flustered with him seeing me so unkempt."

Their interaction was cut short when both of them noticed a vehicle pulling into the property. Leila recognized the car right away as Randy's, which meant Aden was with him. But Aden always took his buggy to work, so if he had Randy take him back to the house, something was urgent.

Aden wrenched the door open, gasping for air as he looked to Leila. His face was as pale as fresh snow, in stark contrast to his jet-black beard. "We gotta go. Now!"

"What's the matter?" Leila's heart pounded as she saw how panicked her husband was.

"I got a call from my mamm at work. They took him to the hospital. Leila, my father had a heart attack."

Leila had known something was awry, but she hadn't expected it to be this bad. "Goodness . . ." Leila shook her head to get back on track. "I'll get Rachel ready."

"Leila?"

Turning to her friend, Leila hadn't considered what Alma should do. She needed to act quickly. She placed a hand on Alma's shoulder and asked, "Could you close up early for me today?"

"For how long?"

"A couple of hours, I guess. Would you mind?"

Shaking her head, Alma placed her hand on her chest. "Not one bit. I've got this."

"All right." Leila hurried to the counter to grab the shop's key fob, which she handed to Alma. "Then I appoint you with that responsibility. Thank you, Alma."

Once she'd gathered everything, Leila carried Rachel to the car, and Aden followed with a car seat. Rachel was placed on the left side of the vehicle, and Leila climbed into the right with Aden sliding in after her.

This is too similar to— Leila curled her hands

in her lap. *Aden, I really hope your dad gets through this.*

"Thanks for coming in. Have a *guder owed*." Alma waved to the older Amish couple leaving the shop with their purchase. She propped her elbow on the counter, supporting her chin with her hand. *It's been over an hour since they've left. I really hope Aden's father is doing all right.*

It was gradually growing dim outside. Since the shop was presently without customers, Alma considered taking a break from standing behind the counter to craft some cards at the worktable. She got out the supplies and began to fold a sheet of construction paper.

She was on her fourth card when a sudden onset of nausea overtook her, and on impulse, Alma applied pressure on her gut with her palm. Her gaze trailed to the windowpane, seeing an orange pickup truck rolling onto the property. Alma tried to stamp out her need to spew by shutting her eyes and taking deep breaths. But as she tried to overcome it, the nausea sharpened as if she'd ingested sewing needles rather than pancakes for breakfast. *I can make it quick. I've just got to get to the house.*

Alma hastily fastened the door. She yelled out to the truck, saying she'd be right back, then bolted past the row of trees and into the house. When Alma crossed the threshold, she heard

470

the muffled ringing of the clock from the living room. Alma didn't have enough time to reach the restroom, so she beelined to the kitchen. Ripping off her head covering, she slanted toward the sink and retched repeatedly

Coughing, she collapsed to the floor and sagged against the lower cabinets. The nausea was easing up a bit, although her stomach quivered feebly and the inside of her throat stung. Alma got up and grabbed a napkin, moistened it at the sink, and used it to wipe her face clean. Discarding the napkin in the garbage bin, Alma dusted off her covering and slipped it back into place over her bun. *I need to hurry over to the shop to help out the people who pulled in. If they haven't left, that is.*

When she went back out, the truck was gone. Alma walked over to the building, then stood in the shadows from what was left of the daylight. The door of the shop was ajar. "No." Her jaw dropped.

The flooring by the shelves was cluttered with stamps and ink pads, and some of the ink pads' lids were flipped open, exposing the colors. The clothesline for the cards was draped over the table like a disconnected cobweb. As for the boxes containing the card decorations, those were toppled over with ribbons unraveled and buttons scattered about.

She turned to the counter, and the register's

drawer caught her eye. When Alma approached it, she saw right away that the register had been cleared out except for a nickel and four pennies in the main column of the drawer.

Her heart sunk. *It had to have been the people in the truck.*

Alma's shoulder bumped the doorframe as she ran out of the shop to the phone shed. The gravel beneath her feet nearly caused her to stumble when she reached it. Alma slammed the door open, grabbed the phone, and dialed 911. Her arm shook as she brought the receiver to her ear and waited for a response.

"Hello? It's an emergency! My friend's shop has been vandalized!"

Leila was situated between Aden and Rachel in the backseat on their way home from the hospital. The drive from Lewistown to Belleville had been dismal, and without Randy engaging with Aden a few times, it would have been spent in silence.

Leila stroked Rachel's feathery curls. Their daughter was asleep in the car seat with a dribble of drool escaping from her mouth. Leila brought her hands to her lap and fixed her gaze on Aden. Her spouse had his arm up by the window as his reflection stared vacantly back.

"How are you feeling?" Leila questioned.

"I'm more worried about him than ever. I'm glad they revived Daed, but the problem is he keeps stressing himself out." Aden's voice rumbled like an avalanche as he slowly turned to her. "It may not be the last time he has a heart attack. And next time could be fatal."

Leila's throat ached as she observed Aden's pain. His eyes were like ocean waves cascading the shoreline as tears threatened to spill over.

"I'm very sorry this had to happen, Aden," Leila said softly as she clasped his hand. "You don't have to disregard your feelings. I know this is affecting you emotionally, just as it is your mamm and schweschder."

His shoulders drooped, but he clutched her hand in return. "Appreciate the assurance." Aden offered her a smile. "At least he'll be looked after for a couple of days."

Nodding, Leila placed her other hand on top of his. "We can visit him again tomorrow if you want."

"That'd be good."

"Pretty sure we'll see your sister there tomorrow." Leila leaned against his shoulder.

Aden exhaled. "Still can't believe Sue's almost married. She was only sixteen when you first met her."

"Without Sue, we may have never gotten married ourselves."

"Hey, what's going on at your place?" Randy asked abruptly.

Leila peered along the right front seat, where

shades of blue and red beamed through the windshield. "Huh?!"

When they drove onto the property, two police cars were by the card shop, and Leila noticed Alma standing with one of the officers. Randy parked nearby, and Leila hopped out of the vehicle and hurried over.

"There they are." Alma darted across the gravel, meeting Leila halfway. "I'm so sorry."

Attempting to catch her breath, Leila panted before she responded. "What happened?"

"Someone vandalized the card shop."

"How? You were here watching the shop." Leila's body trembled.

"I left it unattended for a few minutes, but—"

"You what?!" Leila brought her hands up in resignation. "I can't deal with this right now. It's been enough for one day."

"Hear me out, please?"

The feverish heat Leila felt in her face combated the brisk cool of the evening. Leila wanted time to allow her frustrations to diminish. Nonetheless, she choked out, "I should've closed up before I left. Suppose I have myself to blame for that."

Alma unpinned her bun and brushed out any tangles as she prepared for bed. After everything that had taken place, this day couldn't end too soon.

As soon as she slipped into her nightgown, Alma sank into the mattress. There was no doubt she was drained, yet there was still plenty on her mind that she couldn't dismiss. As upset as Leila was, Alma had decided not to make the situation worse by pestering her, so she kept her distance.

It is sort of Leila's fault. She didn't have to ask me to keep working in the shop. But Leila had a family emergency, and I agreed to help when I could have declined. I also didn't take the time to lock the door of the shop when I left. Alma swiveled about on the bed. *Am I really trying to rationalize letting my friend down and allowing the card shop to get ruined?*

Rising from the mattress, Alma heard tapping on the bedroom door, so she got up to open the door.

"Leila?" A breath hitched in Alma's throat.

"Hey, Alma." Leila almost replicated Alma with the nightgown and her loose locks tousled about. "Could we talk?"

"I mean, it is technically your room, so sure." She moved out of Leila's way and gestured. "Come in."

Leila went in, seating herself by the front of the bed on the floor. Alma joined her. Light from the gas lamp flickered throughout the guest room.

Alma cleared her throat. "Leila, I just wanted to say that I'm sorry for not locking the shop when I went out. You blamed yourself for not closing up, but you trusted me to take care of it while you were gone, and I failed you. So I'll do whatever I can tomorrow to get the shop back in order."

Sighing, Leila formed her hands into a steeple. "We're both being ridiculous for blaming ourselves. The one who made the decision to take advantage is at fault. Even if we go through the effort to keep ourselves out of harm's way, some may see a moment of vulnerability and seize it." Leila broke the steeple and rubbed her earlobe. "You did leave the shop, but you didn't plan for it to get vandalized. Careful or not, we're not to blame for someone's malicious actions. I couldn't imagine what may have happened if you hadn't left. Honestly, locked or attended, the shop probably would've been broken into today. I'm just thankful nothing worse went down." Squeezing Alma's hand, Leila's eyes pooled over. "And you did all you could do, Alma. I can't thank you enough for that. I'm sorry for not stating that before."

Alma's vision blurred from her own tears as she wrapped her arms around her friend. Leila returned the hug, and they proceeded to comfort one another for the next several minutes.

After they collected themselves, Leila chuckled as she wiped her eyes with her sleeves. "Fortunately the money taken from the register was only from today, so it wasn't a big loss. I only hope the cops will find whoever did this so it won't happen again. It could be someone else next time, but still . . ." Leila sat up. "Wait, why did you go back into the house?"

Shifting in her spot, Alma curled her lip. "I got sick again and threw up."

Leila's eyes widened. "You positive?"

"Either that, or I have a serious life-threatening condition. Or food poisoning." Twisting her blond strands, Alma gazed at the open door of the guest room. "I thought it was stress when it first started, but now I'm not so sure."

Leila tapped her finger against her freckled chin, "It could be . . ."

"Could be what?"

"I've had symptoms like yours before, and it was from a sickness, but not from the flu." Leila rested a hand on Alma's shoulder. "Alma, is it possible that you're in a family way?"

Alma was flabbergasted by Leila's assumption. Stammering, she replied, "You're not assuming that Elias and I—"

"No, no. I'm not." Leila's cheeks flushed. "But didn't you mention that you and Michael wanted to have a child?"

That's impossible. I tested myself a few days before he passed away, and the results were negative.

"Even if you aren't, something isn't right. It may be good to get it checked out. I have my doctor's number if you need it."

She couldn't respond to Leila. The notion of being in a family way increased Alma's worries. If she was expecting a baby, how could she continue with her current circumstances? What about her relationship with Elias?

Regardless, she needed an answer, and Alma hoped there wasn't anything seriously wrong with her. If something was amiss, Alma prayed for anything other than a pregnancy.

Chapter 12

Alma sat tight in the clinic's waiting area, keeping herself preoccupied by watching a cooking program on the television.

She had her assessments done a few days ago and was in today for the results of her blood work. Unfortunately, after being asked several questions, the doctor had said that fertility was a possibility. But Alma had also been told that her symptoms could be from emotional stress, and if they were, her nausea would ease up over time. She'd also been made aware of her symptoms possibly indicating a more serious issue, such as inflammation of her stomach lining. Her tests were designed to give an accurate diagnosis.

Leila had offered to go with Alma today, as she did when Alma went in the first time. But Alma felt she should go in by herself. Depending on what the blood work revealed, Alma needed to make a choice without anyone else's influence.

"Alma Wengerd?"

Casting her thoughts aside, Alma got up, heaved her bag strap over her shoulder, and strolled over to the nurse, forcing a smile. "That would be me."

"Follow me then." Tapping his pen on the

clipboard, the nurse spun from Alma and ushered her through the doorway.

As they went down the hallways of the clinic, the nurse engaged in small talk. Alma went through the motions as if she wasn't nervous about her results. But she felt droplets of sweat forming on her numbed skin. The nurse halted in front of one of the rooms, opening the door for her.

"You can have a seat there." He motioned to the chair adjacent to the examination table. "Dr. Taylor will be with you in a moment."

Nodding, Alma thanked him and sat down as he exited the room. She turned in her chair to unzip her bag, rifling through her belongings until her hands felt what she'd been yearning for. Pulling out her container of water, Alma got the lid off and took a swig. The cool liquid soothed the back of her throat.

"Welcome back, Mrs. Wengerd." Dr. Taylor's dark curly hair bounced as she strode into the room and greeted Alma. The doctor lifted up a stack of papers stapled together. "So I have the results of your blood work. I understand you have some concerns about the nausea you've been having as of late."

Alma crossed her ankles underneath her seat. "Very much."

"I can assure you that what you're experiencing at the moment isn't fatal. In fact, your symptoms are quite regular in correspondence to what people like yourself are going through."

"And what would that be exactly?" Alma asked, slipping the water bottle back into her bag.

"From what I've gathered from your blood work, your cortisol levels are fairly high, which is understandable since you said you lost your husband recently." Dr. Taylor's thick eyebrows drew together. "You're going through grief, and stress comes along with it. How you may be handling the situation can harm your health. If you choose to ignore your stress, it can be disastrous to your adrenal glands, and your stress could lead to heart disease due to high blood pressure. So you must find ways to help reduce your stress. Otherwise your health may be on the line."

"Okay, less stressfulness. Got it." Alma let a faint breath flee from her lungs. *This is good. I could have a future here with Elias after all.*

"Which brings me to the next thing that was discovered from your results." Flipping through the papers, the doctor stopped at one page and shook her head. "I'm not sure you're gonna want to hear this, but as a doctor, it is my obligation to tell you." She pressed her finger onto the page. "Your HCG levels provided the answer to whether your nausea is caused by pregnancy." Clicking her heeled foot on the floor, Dr. Taylor made direct eye contact with

Alma. "Mrs. Wengerd, you're going to be a mother."

Alma's insides felt like a tangled ball of thread. Here she had presumed everything was fine. But now all the strain that had slipped away moments before rushed back in, severer than ever. *That can't be. There's no way I'm hearing that right.*

Dr. Taylor squeezed Alma's upper arm. "You all right, Mrs. Wengerd?"

"I'm fine. Just . . ." Alma hesitated. She almost verbalized her uncertainty toward the news, but she refrained. "Thank you, Doctor."

"I know that you don't live here, but if you are planning to stay longer, then I'm willing to assist you. We can set up another appointment for you to come in."

"I appreciate it. But I'm not sure if I'll be staying here yet."

That at least was an honest response. She had hoped for a better outcome, but now Alma was left with devastation. It wasn't that she didn't want to have a child—she always had. The problem was Alma was with Elias now—the person who had already endured scrutiny from his parents. What if they found out Alma was in a family way? What if the church leaders found out? Would their courtship still be allowed?

She leaned forward and massaged her forehead. *How will Elias respond when he hears my unexpected news?*

• • •

Later in the evening, after having supper with Leila and Aden, Alma reflected on how she had spent most of the day after the appointment rationalizing where to go from here. After hours of fighting with herself, Alma came to terms with what she had to do.

She now sat in the phone shed near the Troyers' home, delaying a call home by using her fingers to trace the curves of the desk. Even though her heart was set on stepping out of the shed without making any calls, Alma had to do what was ethical. She needed to let her mother be aware of her next move.

Dialing, Alma lifted the receiver to her ear and listened as it rang repeatedly. *I guess no one's around the shed right now.* When the automated voice said to leave a message, Alma swallowed and spoke after the tone.

"Hey, Mamm. It's me. I was hoping to speak with you, but I suppose a message will do." Alma paused, gulping a portion of air in an attempt to curb her emotions. "Something has happened, and I know that I've caused a lot of worry for you and the rest of the family. I am in a tough spot, and from what I found out today, I had to figure out what to do." Almost in a whisper, she uttered, "I can't stay here any longer. I'll be calling Elaine and having her come get me soon. I will explain everything when I return home. I'm sorry for worrying you and Daed, and thank you for being supportive of me coming out here in the first place. But it just isn't going to work." Alma gripped a fistful of her apron. "Talk to you soon. And Makenzie, if you hear this message before Mom does, please let her know I called. Goodbye, and I love you guys."

Placing the phone on the receiver, Alma's entire body wilted like the carnations she'd gotten from Elias. Alma couldn't fathom all that had taken place, and when she thought back to certain moments, part of her was perplexed by how she second-guessed herself. The right choice was blatantly there. Alma should've stayed in Hopkinsville, and if she had, she wouldn't have caused so much pain for those around her. Now she was going to negatively impact the life of the person she'd grown to care for more than anyone.

I have to tell Elias tomorrow. Alma's gaze flitted to the unlit gas lamp, and though the shed was entirely absent of light, she didn't bother to ignite it. *I can't tell him why I'm leaving or why we can't be together. There's no telling how he'll respond. I don't want to hurt him or his family anymore. I don't want to hurt my family.* Alma gave in and wept. *I will not burden him with a child that isn't his.*

Alma and Elias had just finished their lunch at Taste of the Valley. As usual, Alma had gathered their trash and dumped it into the bin.

Although their meal together had been pleasant, Elias noticed Alma's mannerisms seemed less natural. Her smiles were smaller than usual, and her eyes didn't have their normal sparkle. Elias had done his best to disregard these issues after he'd asked Alma how she was doing and she'd said she was just feeling out of it today.

They climbed into his yellow-topped buggy and rode out to Peachy's Greenhouse, which was about four miles from the restaurant.

Elias turned his head toward the fields to his left when they reached Greenwood Road. It was a brilliant summer afternoon, with small clouds skidding across the deep blue sky.

"Isn't it a *brechdich* day, Alm?" He turned his gaze to her.

Alma didn't respond. She had her head lowered and kept fiddling with the end of her black apron.

"Alm?" Elias poked her arm with his knuckle.

"Oh jah." Alma straightened her posture and gave Elias a grin that quivered like strummed guitar strings. "Very beautiful day."

"You sure nothing's bothering you?" His chest stiffened.

She offered a laugh that sounded tight and nervous. "Of course I'm sure. Don't worry about me."

Elias's hands grew clammy as he curved his fingers around the reins. *Something is bothering*

Alma, and whatever it is, she doesn't want to discuss it.

The afternoon had transitioned to evening, and after they had finished spending their day in Belleville, Elias brought Alma back to the Troyers' home. They sat together on the lawn along the side of the house, basking in the blaze of the sunset.

But Elias was unsettled by Alma's behavior. She had a habit of keeping things to herself, but it was painfully obvious that something serious was troubling her.

"Alm, I can tell you've got something on your mind that you need to tell me, so go ahead and say it."

Her mouth contorted as if she had eaten something bitter. Alma stood up, wrapping her arms around her lower torso. "There isn't any easy way to say this." Alma spoke into the breeze rather than to him. "These past couple of months have been a whirlwind, and being with you has been wonderful. But . . ."

Elias tilted his head. "What is it?"

Swiveling to face him, Alma's eyes fluttered shut. Her lips, resembling rose petals, quivered as soon as she answered. "I need to move back to Kentucky."

He sucked in a breath. *I knew it.* Elias rested both his hands on her shoulders. "Did your parents say you had to?"

Opening her eyes, Alma shook her head. "I made the choice. This situation has gotten out of hand already. I'm far from home, staying at my friend's place, and having a courtship that's caused no end of trouble. Aren't you afraid of something else being thrown at us?"

"There's nothing too difficult for us to go through." Elias gave her shoulders a tender squeeze. "That's why I've stuck by you this far."

"But it isn't fair to you, Eli. I didn't want to dwell on Michael's passing because life moves forward." Alma lifted a hand to her mouth momentarily before bringing it back down. "It's just happening so quick. Your mother was right. If things were different . . ." She hitched a breath. "I don't want to hurt you."

Clenching his jaw, Elias withstood the sensations he felt from hearing her words. But when he spoke, he couldn't hide the pleading in his tone. "Then stay. Please reconsider, Alm. We can make this work. We already have so far. You being here won't harm me at all."

"It will. That's why I need to leave." A tear trickled from her eye. "I cannot allow myself to pull you into my struggles anymore. I shouldn't have to begin with. I'm so sorry, Eli."

Elias couldn't shrug off the feeling that there was still something Alma wasn't telling him. But he cherished her with all his being, so he had to respect Alma's decision. Letting go of her shoulders, Elias folded his arms around her. "I told you I'd fight for us as long as you want me to. I can't stop you from leaving." His eyelids grew damp. "But I am sad you are choosing to go."

Embracing him, Alma relaxed her chin on his shoulder. Elias could feel her tears seeping through the fabric of his shirt. She continued to whisper "I'm sorry" into his ear as he swayed with her for a long while.

Chapter 13

At the foot of the bed, Alma had been folding the dresses she'd brought. She would have packed the night before, but the unrelenting drive that normally motivated her had been lacking. Alma hadn't packed her cleaning supplies either, because she wanted to do last-minute scrubbing, swabbing, and disinfecting in her guest room. She deemed it a proper way to repay Leila for providing her a place to stay for two months.

In the midst of wiping down the window, Alma eyed the birthday card Elias had made for her, which stood upright on the sill, sheathed in the morning's sunlight. Positioning the cloth and spray on the nightstand, she tweezed the card between her fingers, Alma brought it up to where she had a proper view. She smoothed out the pastel ribbon pasted to the upper corner.

Three days had passed since Alma had ended her relationship with Elias. It was grueling for her to accept, but she had to drum it into her soul, especially since she was leaving in a matter of hours. Elaine would be arriving around three o'clock, and Alma had called her family and told them she would be back in Hopkinsville in the late evening.

Alma wondered whether she should have

told Elias that she was in a family way. But she immediately drove the idea away. *I don't want to know what Elias would've done. Besides, it isn't his problem. It should never be his problem.*

Smearing the grit from her eyes, she flipped the cover of the card. Engraved on the inside was the paragraph Elias had written for her, and underneath his signature was written "Romans 12:2."

Alma recited the scripture by memory: " 'And be not conformed to this world: but be ye transformed by the renewing of your mind, that ye may prove what is that good, and acceptable, and perfect, will of God.' "

Folding the flap of the card, Alma crossed over to her suitcase on a chair. *I know why you included that scripture. You had hoped for me to be open with my struggles and to base my choices on what God had planned for me.* Alma stowed the card in the inner pouch of the suitcase between the kitchen utensils she'd purchased weeks ago. *I don't know for sure what I long for anymore. I want to live a carefree life with you, but I'm afraid of your reaction to this. Even if you were willing to raise a child that isn't yours, I'm worried of what others may think. They might believe the child is yours, and how would we overcome that? I keep fighting myself on this, but I know what the right decision is. It's best not to tell you. And to avoid any more scrutiny, it's best for me to raise this child on my own.*

● ● ●

Elias etched the leg of a table he was assembling piece by piece. When he gave himself a break from his project, he stroked the sawdust away from the chisel and set it down on the worktable. While he worked, Elias reflected on how things had gone when he'd swung by the card shop yesterday to pay a visit to Alma one final time. Alma had informed him that she had one more day in the Big Valley, which happened to be today. Elias had scarcely a few hours to see Alma off. Pleading with his father the night before, Elias asked to leave work early. Thankfully, Dad had given him the go-ahead.

Elias yearned to be at Alma's side—hands intertwined, putting down their roots, and spending the rest of their lives in one another's company—that was his deepest yearning. He was driven by the need to be with her. Her decision to break things off with little explanation had hurt him deeply. He'd had feelings for her when they were young teenagers, and after five years of separation, those emotions were part of his soul. Yes, it was insane to start a relationship so soon after Alma became widowed, but it was worse to deny how he felt about her.

We're not together now, but Alma is still my friend. Elias took off his hat, raking his hair with his fingers. But with their courtship concluded, Elias wasn't left with many options. Alma was set on going back to Kentucky, so all he could do was be supportive and accept her decision.

He twanged his singular suspender then turned to the entrance of the shop as his father bounded in.

"Heading out soon, Son?"

"I will be." Elias flung on his hat.

"With all of the effort you've put into your relationship, I am shocked you're not going to do more to convince her to stay."

Jutting his chin, Elias advanced toward his father. He shook his head. "As much as I want Alma to stay, I can't decide that for her."

Dad patted Elias's back. "Well, if it's any reassurance, you're doing what's right."

But is it right? Elias wondered. *Like you said, all of the effort we put into being together seems like a waste now.* Weaving past his father, Elias opened the door. "I'll be back in a while."

Shutting the door behind him, Elias leaned against the support beam of Dad's shop, taking a good look out to the silo next to the red barn. As much as he tried not to, Elias continued to wonder what made Alma decide to move back home. Too many scenarios wriggled in, but most of the ideas involved something Alma probably couldn't conceal. She was a very verbal person who spoke her mind about most things. Except to herself. So whatever Alma was refusing to tell him had to be something personal. She had been ill in bed for a week, so what if Alma was terminally ill?

The prickling sensation traversing his neck caused him to shudder. *There's no use fretting over it until I know for sure. I've got to give my concerns to God and hopefully end on good terms with Alma.* Elias roamed over to where his horse and buggy awaited him.

After having their lunch break in the house, as well as going out to the barn to give feed to the chickens and cattle, Alma and Leila went back into the card shop, propping the door open to allow the outside weather to circulate inside the building.

Alma had her bag and suitcase packed for her departure in a couple of hours. It hadn't kept her from helping Leila throughout most of the day. Besides, as the months pushed on, Alma knew she would be advised to do less physical labor, so it was a good thing to get the need to be productive out of her system. Or at the very least, try to cut back.

"Do you need any help with your side? I'm done here," Alma said as she stretched like a cat to situate the last ink pad from her box onto the top shelf.

"I'd appreciate it," Leila replied.

Alma moved over to her friend and began transferring the stamps from the box on the floor onto the shelves needing to be restocked.

"Hard to imagine this place was once in shambles. Right, Leila?"

"Jah. It cleaned up nicely." A smile gradually developed on Leila's speckled features. "Couldn't have done it without you."

"Danki." Alma knelt down to scoop up as many stamps as the hollow of her hands could accommodate. "Will you be okay here on your own?"

"Having you made it abundantly easier, but I do have to learn to manage the shop on my own." Leila looked at Rachel, who was giggling up a storm in the playpen while teething on one of the squeaker toys. "Maybe not fully on my own— though it would be great if Rachel was a tad bit older."

"Let's hope my organizing tendencies rubbed off on her during my time here."

Leila shrugged. "Anything's possible." She put a stamp on the highest shelf with ease and tipped her head toward Alma. "Out of curiosity, how are you gonna go about telling your parents?"

Sighing, Alma trailed a hand to her stomach. "I'm not sure. I'll have to tell them soon after I return home, but I don't know how to approach the subject." She peered at the slight protrusion of her apron. "I have to say something. Otherwise my body will give it away."

"What about Elias?" Leila asked.

Her throat constricting, Alma rolled her

shoulders back to defuse the strain in her muscles. "There's no need to. We've broken up, haven't we? Elias doesn't need to know about me being in a family way with Michael's child."

"What?!"

Alma's entire figure froze. She didn't need to look to know that it was Elias who had burst into the shop. Yet Alma moved her head toward him, meeting his gaze.

"Is that why you ended our relationship?" Elias scowled. "I can't believe this." He turned from her and went out of the shop in hurried strides, drifting to the front side of the home past the trees.

"Eli, wait!" Alma bellowed, praying it would derail him. Fortunately Elias came to a standstill in the driveway, and he focused on her. Alma ran to him, gasping for breath. "I get it, you're upset, but that's why I didn't tell you. I knew you'd be angry about it."

Staring Alma down, Elias's glare impaled her. "Don't you get it? I'm not angry because you're in a family way but because you didn't tell me the entire truth." He pounded a hand to the core of his chest. "Did you really believe I would end things with you if I knew?" Elias's blue eyes flashed. "Or was it because you knew I'd choose to stay with you?"

"Would you have been happy raising a child that isn't yours, Eli? You may say you don't care, but who wouldn't?" she sputtered, motioning to her lower torso. "You didn't choose this. I didn't want you to be stuck with me because I have to raise a child on my own!"

"I want to be with you because I love you! What about you, Alm? If I'm okay with it, then what's preventing you from feeling the same?"

She stiffened at his words. Alma couldn't offer an explanation, not because she didn't have an answer but because she was in a perpetual state of being overwhelmed whenever it crossed her mind. Temptation arose, and Alma wanted nothing more than to tell Elias how much she loved him. Instead, she ducked her chin, refusing to answer.

"You know what? Maybe you're right. If you're unsure of being honest with me, maybe us not being together is the right choice." He wiped his eyes with the sleeve of his burgundy shirt. "I guess this is goodbye, Alma. Have a good ride home."

Her vision blurred as she watched Elias storm to his buggy. A surge of heat rushed through her body, and dark blotches overtook her sight. She closed her arms around herself as she tried to steady her stance.

Not wanting to worsen the situation, Alma didn't intercept him. She collapsed to the gravel; pebbles pressing against her knees. *I chose this. I chose not to tell Elias, and now I have to accept*

496

the repercussions of my actions. She gripped a handful of gravel as her sight speckled back. The dark spots were now replaced with haziness.

It's better this way, isn't it? Because now Elias won't have to be brought into my problems anymore. Whimpering, tears trailed down her heated cheeks like rain. *I don't deserve to be happy with him. Not when I've been nothing but selfish to those around me. Especially you, my dear Michael. I was selfish for moving on too quickly.*

Chapter 14

Into the first week of August, Elias had been having a hard time moving past Alma and their relationship. He struggled to find motivation while crafting in his father's shop but had expedited his work despite his lack of ambition.

Today was Sunday, and Elias lingered in his bedroom after church. He would normally play baseball on a day such as this, but he wasn't in the right frame of mind to get any gratification from it. He had felt this way ever since Alma left.

Dusk had been his blissful retreat. He hated getting out from under the comforter on his bed in the morning. Whenever he got some shut-eye, he'd dream of his moments with her. Some memories were from childhood, like the day they first met, and others were from their dates. The instant he awoke, Elias wanted nothing more than to descend back into sleep and relive those days again.

That's why he plonked onto his mattress as soon as he returned home. Elias hadn't even bothered swapping out of his formal attire for church to his casual clothes—except for his hat, which he'd sent sailing toward his desk, and the black shoes he had kicked to the corner of his bedroom.

I've got to put myself together. He cinched his eyes as he wound up in the comforter to block out the light that skimmed the simple moldings along the ceiling. *But I just want to lie here and hope to dream about her.*

Abruptly Elias heard thumping. He unraveled from his cocoon and gaped at the door on the farthest side of the room.

"Elias!" his mother called. "A couple of your friends dropped by and are downstairs asking for you!"

He clenched his jaw. *I told Robert I wasn't up for playing later, so it better not be him.* Getting up on his feet, Elias shuffled over. "Be there in a minute!"

Elias lumbered down the staircase that led to the lower section of the house. Midway down the steps, he saw who stood by the entrance at the end of the kitchen.

"Leila? Aden?" Elias stepped down from the last tread. "What's with the unexpected visit?"

"I called you earlier and left you a message." Leila glimpsed at him. "I suppose it's not likely that you've been in the phone shed."

Rachel, who was swathed in her mother's arms, nuzzled Leila's shoulder.

"I'll say," Aden remarked. "Still got his fancy garb on from church."

Nudging Aden's arm, Leila looked directly at Elias. "We wanted to talk with you."

Elias's stomach roiled. "If it's about Alma, I'd rather leave it be."

"Please, hear us out for a sec," Aden pleaded. "I promise it won't take long."

Sighing, Elias invited them to sit in the dining room that adjoined the kitchen. He scooted out one of the chairs and sat down, then waited to proceed after the Troyers followed suit. "All right. What is it you have to say?"

Nodding to Leila, Aden stroked his beard, then spoke. "We think you should go after Alma."

"I want to, but she made it clear that she doesn't trust in me. Alma would've told me the truth if she did."

"Elias, she didn't tell you about being in a family way because she was afraid to." Leila pressed her free hand to the center of her chest. "I know, due to living through similar circumstances."

"What?" Elias flinched. "I thought Rachel was both of yours."

"Not what Leila meant." A firm line appeared by Aden's broad brow. "Before we were married, while we were courting, Leila broke up with me."

Leila affirmed his statement with a nod. "When I lost my mother, there was no one else to take care of my sister Elsie. Daed and my youngest brother, Henry, needed me as well. By breaking up with Aden, I assumed I was saving him from living through the pain I was experiencing."

Tapping her nail against the cedar table's surface, Leila leaned forward. "I have regretted doing that to him, even if I thought it was the right thing to do at the time."

"I cannot force Alma to be with me." Elias clung to the ivory sleeve of his shirt. "If she wants to raise Michael's kid on her own, I have to respect that."

"Trust me on this, Elias. Alma didn't end your courtship because she wanted to. She wanted to protect you from her burdens. You gotta let her know that what she's going through isn't enough to separate you two." Leila kissed the top of Rachel's head. "From what we saw from you both during the couple of months you were together, I don't think what you guys have should've ended."

A shiver coursed through his body. Elias wondered if Aden and Leila were called upon to urge him to go to Alma. If that was the case, then it could be his opportunity to rekindle his friendship with her. Or at the very least, bring it to a proper conclusion. Elias felt contrite for leaving on terrible terms with his best friend, and if he could at least let her know how sorry he was, then he would be able to make peace with that.

"I don't know if we'll end up together if I go see her, but I should not have left Alma like I did." Elias propped his elbows on the table. "Despite how hurt I was, I shouldn't have stormed off, and I should have been more straightforward about how much she means to me."

A smile crossed Leila's face. "I do have her parents' home address."

"And I can get my pal to drive you over." Aden tilted his head. "So what are you gonna do?"

Elias stood up. "All right. I'm going to Kentucky."

Hopkinsville

Alma stood along the picket fence of the cemetery. The gusts that blew through the community in the afternoon had died down, leaving light breezes and gray clouds in the gloaming. The loose strands of her hair caressed the tip of her nose when the breeze momentarily bustled about the area.

She hadn't been to the cemetery since the graveside service back in May. But it didn't seem that long since she stood here with her community, having to come to terms with the reality of her husband's permanent absence from earth.

Roaming the string of gravestones, Alma approached Michael's at the other end of the fence. When she came face-to-face with his plot, Alma got down on her knees. The stone was surrounded by yellow field flowers in the grass.

During her first week of being home, Alma had been spending most of her days getting reacquainted with her routine. She had told her parents about the results of the blood work that was done at the clinic in Belleville. Although they were surprised by the news, they had both been sympathetic and welcomed her home.

She had been appreciative of the support from her family, especially Makenzie. They had found homes for Missy's kittens, but her sister had kept Snowball, so he would be waiting for Alma when she came home.

The memory of Elias leaving the Troyer property kept resurfacing in Alma's thoughts. She had stayed with Leila for two months, anticipating a miraculous improvement. But given how her visit ended, she questioned if she'd received any benefit from going back to the Big Valley.

Eyes turned to the silvery clouds, Alma began speaking her thoughts aloud.

"The morning I heard that message from the hospital, I couldn't accept what they told me. I wandered back into our home and laid motionless on the floor of our bedroom. I couldn't even blink. I was immersed in darkness, staring at nothing, and I was all alone." She intertwined her index finger around a field flower. "I feel so guilty because I'm still here, yet you had your life taken from you in a matter of moments. I could've done more to prevent you from going up on the roof." Alma shuddered. "I could've done more to keep you here, Michael!"

"Alma."

She recognized that voice. "Eli?" Shooting up from the ground, Alma turned to meet his gaze. "How did you know I was here?"

"I was at your home, and your mom told me you were here." Elias took off his straw hat and brought it to his chest. "My condolences on your loss of Michael."

"You heard what I said just now?" Alma covered her mouth.

"Sorry for that. I didn't mean to eavesdrop." Placing his hat on the grass, he rushed over to her. "There's nothing wrong with being uncertain about what you've endured in all of this. Plenty has changed in your life. It's okay to mourn, and you need to." Elias cupped both of her elbows. "You have a good heart, Alm. But if you're not honest about what you're going through, the goodness you have may be drowned by your struggles. It could be gone forever." His lips quivered as he offered her a smile. "Forgiveness will release the guilt that's been weighing on you."

Alma grasped the front of his shirt and let loose the tears she'd been holding back for so long. "I'm so sorry for ending our courtship, Eli. And I'm sorry for not telling you the truth before."

"I understand why, and I don't hold it against you. I'm sorry for leaving you when I could've kept fighting for us."

"I probably would have pushed you away if you'd tried." Alma lifted her chin, observing the droplets on his cheeks. "But I don't want to now. Not ever again."

Elias urgently tugged her into his embrace, and she encased him in her arms—tighter than she ever had before. Droplets landed on her scalp, and at first Alma assumed they were his tears. But then the droplets landed more often. The next thing she knew, her hair was entirely drenched. She realized they were in the midst of a downpour.

Laughing shakily, Alma looked up at him, offering the biggest grin she could give.

His eyes widened, but then he beamed. "There's that authentic smile."

In one another's arms, Alma and Elias were drenched like a garden being watered. But neither of them budged. Alma let her head fall back, and all the tension she had felt for months fell away.

"I love you, Alm. As I said before, I'll stay by your side as long as you want me to."

She bent her head down. "What about me being in a family way?"

"We will approach the church leaders again and explain this new situation. If they don't approve, we will find another way."

"Sounds like a good plan." Alma extended her hands to the sides of Elias's damp face, falling into the depths of his blue eyes. "And I want you to stay with me as long as you want."

Lowering his voice, he answered, "Always."

She drew him in so tightly there was barely distance between them. "I love you, Eli."

With that, Elias closed the smidge of space that was left and placed his lips on hers. She closed her eyes and deepened the kiss.

Now I know why I returned to the Big Valley. Elias is the one I was destined to be with. I no longer need to dwell on your passing, Michael. I will always love you, and you will forever be in my heart. But I will no longer distract myself with projects and pretend I'm fine. I will mourn for you in a way that's sincere. I'll move on, not because I have to, but because I've genuinely accepted your passing. Thank You, Lord, for reminding me to put my trust not in my own hands but in Yours.

Epilogue

Belleville, Pennsylvania
Three years later

One evening in early April, Alma sat on the living room rocker that had been crafted by Elias's hands. She cradled her bundle of joy, swaying as the child's fleshy eyelids concealed her blue eyes.

"How did I become so blessed to have a boppli as precious as you in my arms, Natalia?" Alma spoke with a hushed tone. "You and your brother have both been such a blessing to us."

Leaning forward, she savored the moments observing her toddler seated on the wooden floor. Mikey entertained himself with the stuffed animals lined up along the rug. His blond cowlick curved upward, replicating a crescent moon.

I'll continue to raise and protect our son, Michael. Elias and I will do whatever we can to let him know how loved he is.

Elias chose that moment to amble into the room, a spindly feline in tow, and sat down on the couch beside the rocker.

"Snowball here has been a little terror today." Elias flattened his lips, raising the cat up almost to the ceiling with his milky paws dangling. "He tried to squabble with the horses again."

Alma stilled the rocking chair. "Do you think Snowball sees them as gigantic *katze*?"

"Whatever he sees them as, he needs to cut it out." He lowered the feline, and Snowball cried out in a pathetic *mmrrow* and proceeded to lick Elias's wrist. He snickered. "Snowball's fortunate that he's a pretty kitty."

Chuckling, Alma reached over and began scratching Snowball's chin, which he cuddled against her hand. She glanced at her husband. "Your birthday is the fourteenth of this month."

"Oh jah. That slipped my mind."

"Thankfully I already scheduled reservations at Angelo's, and I got ahold of everyone to meet at the restaurant at six o'clock next Saturday." Alma bopped Snowball's strawberry nose with her pinkie.

"You're always one step ahead, Alm."

"At least with the things I have control over." Leaning back against the chair, Alma turned her head to the pot on the windowsill. The fringed, scarlet pads of the carnations looked exceptionally vibrant in what was left of the daylight.

Though Alma was a meticulous person, she had improved in handling her stress over situations where she had no control. After all, anytime she got frustrated about her circumstances, she could revert back to a few years ago. Back to when she stood with Elias in the rain. Having married Elias and now living with him in their own home in the yellow-top community, nothing would hold Alma back from what the Lord desired for her life. She acknowledged to God that she would accept whatever happened in the future as His will.

Smiling, she remembered the words of Romans 12:2, the verse that Elias had written in her birthday card for her twenty-second birthday. *"And be not conformed to this world: but be ye transformed by the renewing of your mind, that ye may prove what is that good, and acceptable, and perfect, will of God."*

Alma's Rose Petal Jam

Ingredients:
2 cups rose petals
2 cups sugar
3 tablespoons lemon juice
1½ cups filtered water
1 teaspoon pectin

Place rose petals in bowl. Add ⅔ cup sugar to petals. Massage petals and sugar with fingers until juice is released from petals. Pour petal mixture into pan.

Add remaining sugar (1⅓ cup), lemon juice, and water to pan. Stir to allow sugar to dissolve. Simmer mixture 20 minutes. Add pectin and stir to dissolve. Simmer for 5 more minutes.

Test jam's consistency by spooning out small amount onto plate. Press spoon against plate. If jam wrinkles, it's ready. If not, simmer remaining jam until it wrinkles when tested. Pour into empty, sterilized jar. Cool before placing in refrigerator.

Note: Must be refrigerated.

Richelle Brunstetter lives in the Pacific Northwest and developed a desire to write when she took creative writing in high school. After enrolling in college classes, her overall experience enticed her to become a writer, and she wants to implement in her stories what she has learned. Just starting her writing career, her first published story appeared in *The Beloved Christmas Quilt* beside stories by her grandmother, Wanda E. Brunstetter, and by her mother, Jean Brunstetter. Richelle enjoys traveling to different places, her favorite being Kauai, Hawaii.

Books are produced in the United States using U.S.-based materials

Books are printed using a revolutionary new process called THINKtech™ that lowers energy usage by 70% and increases overall quality

Books are durable and flexible because of Smyth-sewing

Paper is sourced using environmentally responsible foresting methods and the paper is acid-free

Center Point Large Print
600 Brooks Road / PO Box 1
Thorndike, ME 04986-0001 USA

(207) 568-3717

US & Canada:
1 800 929-9108
www.centerpointlargeprint.com